Also by Allan Smith

□

Consequences
The Sherlock He Knew
The Road Less Travelled
Cometh Evil

Allan's Excellent Adventure 1945-2015
(private distribution only)

Berlin Midnight

Allan Smith

Printed by Lulu Press, Inc
627 Davis Drive, Suite 300
Morrisville NC 27560
United States of America

First Edition 2020
ISBN 978-0-646-82698-1

Published by Grambo Ink
154 Sixth Avenue, Inglewood
Western Australia 6052
wahra37@gmail.com

For my wife, Sharon.

Berlin Midnight

Allan Smith

Grambo Ink
Western Australia
2020

Acknowledgements

Once again, two people who have done similar things several times before applied their critical faculties to the first rough draft of this book. The result was a great many helpful observations and suggestions. I am yet again indebted to both Marilyn West in Australia and John Scotford in the UK for their willingness to suffer my repeated attempts to construct an interesting story. Thank you, both for your continuing help and friendship.

A newcomer to the world of unpaid editorial assistance is my sister-in-law, Gabriele Smith. She is no fan of the mayhem and violence which permeates my books, but she brings to the editing process a German born-and-raised level of understanding streets ahead of mine. She has generously donated her time and knowledge to ensure my gaffes about matters German are far less frequent than they would otherwise be. I am grateful for your help, Gabriele.

Dan Bonner, as readers of previous books will know, is my in-house technical expert, and he has once more waved his digital wand over my ham-fisted indications of what I think the dustjacket should look like. If he'd known the extent to which I'd be leaning on him in later years, he might have had second thoughts about marrying my youngest daughter. I'm very grateful, Dan. (For the help as well as the marrying.)

Acts of black night, abominable deeds,
Complots of mischief, treason, villainies.

William Shakespeare
Titus Andronicus, Act 5, Sc.1

1

"Heil Hitler!"

Standartenführer Stefan Schmidt snaps his right arm up, fingers extended, palm down, holds the position for three seconds precisely, then brings the arm back to his side and waits. The young secretary who has ushered him into the room retreats soundlessly, pulls the steel-reinforced door shut as she goes.

Five metres away sits a smallish bespectacled man teetering on the cusp of middle age. His dark hair is cut very short at the sides, less so on his crown, all of it complemented by a neatly trimmed toothbrush moustache. He is seated behind a large and plain mahogany desk. The desk mirrors the rest of the room, an office in fact, spacious but unostentatious, the minimal amount of furniture in it both sturdy and practical. This is a working office, its only concession to luxury the enormous burgundy carpet nearly filling the floor. The bespectacled man puts down the pen in his right hand and briefly raises his arm in response before leaning back in his swivel chair.

"Heil Hitler," he says softly, almost tiredly. He gestures towards the two armless chairs in front of his desk.

“Sit, please.”

Standartenführer Schmidt strides forward, eases into one of the chairs, and laces his long fingers together in his lap as he waits for the other man to speak. Despite his senior rank, the British or American equivalent of Colonel, Schmidt is not in his SS uniform. Few people in the building have ever seen him in anything but civilian clothes. Even fewer understand what are his duties. It’s of little consequence. He knows what they are, as does the man sitting in front of him – the only one to whom he is answerable.

Reichsführer Heinrich Himmler commands not only Standartenführer Schmidt, but every other member of the SS. He’s come a long way since 1929 when Hitler appointed him to head the Führer’s 250-man protection squad, the Schutzstaffel. In the intervening twelve years he has relentlessly expanded his authority, and his SS now totals nearly half a million men. Under the same umbrella now resides, among other organisations, the Kriminalpolizei, the Security Service and the Gestapo. Himmler has gathered unto himself every police or security force in Germany. He might look and sound like an insurance salesman or hotel clerk, but his incomparable administrative skills and ruthless ambition have combined to hand him a vast empire of authority, the power over life and death on an industrial scale. Heinrich Himmler is the second most powerful man in Adolf Hitler’s Third Reich.

He is in his usual field-grey uniform with its smattering of Party insignia, the large ‘old Party fighter’ chevron prominent on his right sleeve. He chooses to steer a middle course between the studied man-of-the-people austerity of Hitler’s uniform and the flamboyant excesses of Hermann Göring with his perfumes and self-designed comic opera uniforms. As Schmidt watches, his boss takes a key from his breast pocket, leans to the left and unlocks a desk drawer. Himmler brings out a large brown envelope and lays it on the desk before pulling out of it two other envelopes, each smaller than the last. Finally, from the smallest of the envelopes, he removes a folded sheet of paper and a photograph.

"This," he says, as he holds up the largest envelope so Schmidt can see, "was delivered today. Despite what it says, it was opened by one of the clerks." As always, Himmler speaks quietly, unemotionally, reveals little in the tone or volume of his voice. He could be explaining how to assemble the ingredients for an omelette.

Schmidt can clearly see the address in cursive writing on the front of the big envelope.

Reichsführer Himmler
Reich Central Security Office
Prinz Albrecht Strasse 8, Mitte

Above the address, in large block letters, an instruction.

HIGHLY PERSONAL. TO BE SEEN
ONLY BY THE REICHSFÜHRER.

Schmidt lifts one eyebrow slightly. Himmler waves a dismissive hand.

"These things arrive every day. Usually they're nothing." He holds up the second envelope. "When the clerk saw this he took it to the mail room superintendent."

The middle-sized envelope has no address, just more large block letters.

REICHSFÜHRER HIMMLER WILL WANT NOBODY
ELSE TO SEE THE CONTENTS. THEY MUST
BE PUT BEFORE HIM PERSONALLY.

Schmidt is expressionless, says nothing, continues to await Himmler's exposition. He's been down similar paths before, knows when to speak and when to wait. It's one of his many strengths.

"The superintendent is an experienced and sensible man. He made the decision not to open the second envelope. Instead, he immediately brought it to the attention of Hauptsturmführer Knoechlein."

Schmidt inclines his head, signifies his agreement with the wisdom of the superintendent's decision – if the envelopes spell danger, best that the Reichsführer's adjutant is the one in the firing line. Himmler continues.

"The Hauptsturmführer has my authority to act on his own initiative in these matters. He opened the second envelope. Then he brought the third one to me unopened." Himmler pauses before he adds, "You can see why," as he passes the smallest envelope across the desk for Schmidt to inspect. This time the writing is much smaller, cursive again. The Standartenführer's pale grey eyes swivel back and forth as he examines the document.

If anyone other than Reichsführer Himmler
sees the contents of this envelope they will
incur his extreme displeasure and will suffer
for their actions. It is for his eyes alone.

Schmidt's face gives nothing away as he returns the envelope to his superior officer. Himmler takes the envelope, lays it on the desk, then picks up and unfolds the sheet of paper it enclosed.

"The envelope was x-rayed and tested for poisons. Then Hauptsturmführer Knoechlein brought it to me. Here."

Schmidt takes the proffered paper, reads its typed contents.

The oppression of the Roman Catholic church must cease. Priests held in concentration camps must be released. It is within your power to bring this about. If positive and public steps are not taken within one month of this note, the document will be made public.

There is no name, no signature, no address.

Schmidt and Himmler both know exactly what the letter refers to. They both know the Concordat reached with the Pope in 1933 effectively ended papal criticism of the Nazi regime in return for Hitler's undertaking to restore Church authority in religious affairs. But the Party's unabated nazification of the Catholic Church in Germany led Pope Pius XI in March 1937 to issue an encyclical, *Mit brennender Sorge*, 'With Deep Sorrow', reminding the regime of the Concordat's provisions, at the same time criticising the State for its actions. The following wave of arrests and detention of Catholic clergy throughout Germany demonstrated both the Pope's impotence and the Nazis' unwavering intentions. Nothing has changed in the intervening four and a half years – the regime continues to demonise the Catholic Church and its priests continue to suffer.

Schmidt finishes reading, hands the note back to Himmler, who wordlessly passes him the accompanying photograph and a large magnifying glass from the desk. The photograph is small, amateurish in its lighting and focus, but there's enough detail for Schmidt to see the document depicted and to read the crucial words. And to see why the sender wanted it to be seen by nobody other than the Reichsführer. He goes to hand the photograph and magnifying glass back. Himmler takes the glass, waves the photograph aside.

"No, keep it until this is over."

Schmidt puts the photograph in his inside coat pocket.

"What do you require, sir?"

They're the first words Schmidt has spoken since delivering the compulsory Hitler salute as he entered the room. His accent is light Frankfurt, his pronunciation cultured and precise. He might be a poet, a radio newsreader, a professor of literature.

"I believed the original document no longer existed," says Himmler quietly, almost musing to himself, staring at the papers on his desk. "It is the only record left now. I made sure all the others were destroyed years ago. But this one . . . The man was questioned at the time . . ." His voice trails off before he abruptly sits erect and turns his gaze on Schmidt. "Clearly, my belief was mistaken. Whoever sent the photograph obviously has access to the original document. He was once the custodian of it, and we have to assume still is. You will find him and you will bring the document to me. You can have whatever resources you need – men, money, whatever is required. And you can take whatever action you think necessary. Without limitation or concerns about the consequences. Without limitation. Do you understand me, Stefan?"

This is another path Schmidt has been down before.

"I do, Reichsführer. It shall be done."

2

The big man extends his tongue, rolls it around the ice-cream cone in his left hand and, lizard-like, flicks the creamy white mixture into his mouth. He half-grunts, half-moans his unabashed pleasure.

"You'd never believe there was a war on, eh?" he says, waves his free hand to encompass the surroundings.

Kurt Schneider towers over his companion. He's nearly 188 centimetres tall, built like a bear and almost as hairy, but there's more muscle than fat beneath the imposing bulk. He's about thirty, but looks five years younger, a baby face suffused with innocence and goodwill. Children warm to him, old ladies want to cuddle him, other men discount him thinking he's slow-witted and naïve. He's happy with that. More than one man has learned the hard way that Schneider's not all he seems.

His partner looks sideways at him before replying.

"Never believe there's a war on? No, I suppose not. As long as you kept your eyes closed when you walked through what the RAF left of Schöneberg. And kept your ears blocked during the air raids. And didn't take any notice of the yellow stars on the

Jews. And didn't mind going without proper coffee." He pauses, thinks it best to leaven his remarks. "But this is as near to perfect as it's going to get for a while." Max Neumann gestures ahead with a lift of his chin, indicating the riotous autumnal scenery. He's enjoying his confection, a deliciously decadent treat in these times of deprivation, and a stimulus to his intermittent lack of appetite.

The pair have bought their ice-creams from a striped-canvas stall on wheels they passed outside the former British Embassy in Hermann Göring Strasse before continuing down the street and turning into the Tiergarten. That the vendor has managed to obtain enough sugar and cream for his confections is prima facie evidence of black market connections, but the two policemen have chosen to set aside any misgivings about his criminality. They stroll towards the paved roundabout circling the gilded Victory Column in the centre of the park. Erected to celebrate a series of Prussian victories in the late nineteenth century, the 70-meter tower and statue originally stood less than a kilometre away, outside the Reichstag. Someone in the Party thought it would look better somewhere else, and so it was taken down and re-erected in the middle of the Tiergarten. Now it throws a long shadow across the park, briefly shading Schneider and Neumann as they approach its polished red granite base.

The park is full of other Berliners enjoying the greenery and the autumn sunshine, everybody aware that another miserable hard winter is just around the corner. There are young women in long pencil skirts and close-fitting jackets strolling in short steps on high heels. Couples holding hands walk past, nannies push babies in prams, elderly men sit grumbling on the abundant benches with their 'Only for Aryans' signs. On the grass nearby, a dozen or so children kick a ball back and forth in a cacophony of inarticulate shrieks and exclamations. A group of women sit to one side on blankets in the shade of a clump of maples, lindens and oaks, animatedly chatting while keeping an eye on their raucous offspring.

"You are just an old cynic, boss. I think you were probably born cynical."

"A cynic? Isn't that what an optimist calls a realist?"

Schneider shakes his head sorrowfully. "You must have missed school on the day the milk of human kindness was handed out. You can't help it, I suppose. It's Irmgard I feel sorry for. She has to put up with you more than . . ." He stops mid-flow as Neumann interrupts.

"Don't look. He's up ahead. About a hundred metres. Standing next to the stone lion. Green jacket."

"Exactly where your canary said he'd be. You'll go left?"

"I'll pass him and double back in the traffic."

"Right. I'll get as close as I can. The klatch on the path can help me."

"Remember, nothing until the buyer turns up. And let's try to keep our guns in their holsters."

Neumann can see the group of women Schneider's talking about – half a dozen of them, in their mid-to-late thirties, standing talking about ten metres from the man near the stone lion. He's got no idea how Schneider's going to get the women to help, but there's no time to press him for details. The handover isn't due until three, nearly another ten minutes away, but anything could happen in the meantime. He keeps his eyes away from their quarry.

It's unlikely the man in the green jacket, a career safebreaker named Heinz Kadow, is expecting to be grabbed, even more unlikely that he's expecting to be grabbed by two casually-dressed men eating ice-cream. His eyes restlessly scan the surroundings as he searches for someone already known to him, someone carrying a fat bundle of Reichsmarks. So he pays little attention to the two ice-cream eaters as they split up about twenty metres away from him with cries of 'See you tomorrow' and 'Give my regards to your lady'. One continues on past him. The other one, a great lump of a man, changes direction to approach a nearby group of gossiping women. Kadow hears the big man say "Good afternoon ladies" as he lifts his straw hat and smiles broadly before adding, "I would be obliged if you could help a stranger with some local knowledge."

Schneider positions himself among the women so he can still see Kadow out the corner of his left eye. As he presses the ladies for information about the Victory Column's history, he spots a thin rat-faced man in a brown suit walking directly towards Kadow.

Neumann is standing behind a thick wolfberry shrub, heavy with bright red berries, no more than five metres from the target. He can't see his partner but has no doubt Schneider's also spotted the approaching buyer, ten minutes early for his meeting. Neumann waits, watches, can't help thinking that they could have missed the rendezvous, belatedly questions the wisdom of them stopping for ice-creams.

The rat-faced man reaches Kadow, and the two shake hands. The newcomer reaches into his coat pocket and pulls out something in a paper bag, hands it to Kadow, who opens the top, peers inside, then reaches into his own jacket pocket and brings out a small package wrapped in cloth. He gives it to the other man, who starts to unwrap it.

Neumann is already moving. He launches himself towards the two men, covering the intervening ground in seconds. At the last moment, the brown suit spots him and bolts, displays astonishing speed and agility as he sprints away down the path. Kadow is slower to react, has barely started to move before Neumann barrels into him, sending him sprawling onto the grass, winded, shocked. Before he can recover his wits Neumann is kneeling on his back, wrenching his arms, snapping handcuffs on. Neumann looks up in time to see Schneider hurtle diagonally at full speed into the fleeing brown suit. The smaller man is flung heavily onto the path, seems to bounce once, then flops down again and doesn't move. Schneider adjusts his clothes, unhurriedly pulls out his handcuffs and clicks one loop onto the prostrate man's right wrist before putting the other onto his own left wrist. Then he bends down and hauls the other man upright before semi-dragging him, now half-conscious and groaning, back towards Neumann.

Neumann has Heinz Kadow on his feet, pushed against the granite plinth of the Victory Column. The man is speechless, overwhelmed by the suddenness and violence of his downfall. Straight-armed, Neumann thrusts his Kripo warrant disc towards the knot of spectators who have gathered and now stand gawping from a safe distance.

"Kriminalpolizei!" he barks. "These men are under arrest. The show's over. Move on, please. Move on."

The spectators don't need further encouragement. Gestapo, SS, Kripo, it hardly matters – you don't want any of them telling you something twice. By the time Kurt Schneider and his semi-conscious captive reach Neumann, the crowd has dispersed.

"Nice tackle, Kurt," says Neumann to a grinning Schneider. "Have you thought about a rugby career?"

"Not until now. Would I have to tackle full-sized men? Or could I specialise in squashing runts like this one? And could I still carry a gun?"

"I'm fairly certain the rules prohibit guns or knives."

"Well, that's my rugby career over. No fun at all if . . ."

Both men turn their heads towards Kadow, who has suddenly found his voice.

"Are you fuckers going to play music hall all day? If you're taking us to the Alex, let's get it over with."

Neumann and Schneider exchange a look. Not many people

actually ask to be taken to the Alex. Neumann shrugs, affects a theatrical sweep of his arm towards their two captives as he speaks.

"Then let's make haste away, and look unto the main!"

The cuffed men just stare at him. Schneider resignedly rolls weary eyes – he's suffered Neumann's Shakespeare before.

✠

Neumann can't begin to count the number of times he's passed through the foreboding façade of the Imperial Police Praesidium on Alexanderplatz. The ugly great gothic-styled fortress, surmounted by towers at each corner like a medieval keep, seizes the heart of everybody who enters it unwillingly. Even the Kripo detectives and administrative staff who attend the Alex every day feel the oppression oozing from the structure, feel bone-deep its thick dull menacing presence. It's not known as the 'Grey Misery' for nothing. The Praesidium might grace the central government and business district of Berlin, Mitte, but once you're inside you could as easily be back in the dark ages, a time of torture chambers and dungeons. Neumann sees all this in the faces of the two handcuffed men accompanying him and Kurt Schneider down the passageway leading from Entrance Five to the Serious Crime squad's rooms.

Neumann's own face falls suddenly as from a doorway near the end of the passage ahead a familiar figure appears and turns towards them. The man is short, cadaverously thin, completely bald, with a face constructed around distaste and disapproval. Kriminaldirektor Karl Becker heads Serious Crime, is superior to both Neumann and Schneider, harbours an implacable dislike for both men. It's understandable, given his subordinates' flexible approach to their duties. To everyone who works under him, and even among those who don't, Becker is 'The Little

Accountant'. It's not a sobriquet of admiration for thoroughness and attention to detail, but one of ridicule. For Becker, the rules are everything, the written word is God. If it isn't in the book as allowable, then it's prohibited. If the rules say three steps are required, then no Kripo investigator under his authority dares take only two. As Becker turns towards the small group in the passage he recognises Neumann and Schneider and his nose wrinkles a response.

Neumann's dismay has barely registered before it's stopped in its tracks by the sight of a second man following Becker through the doorway. With palpable relief, Neumann sees the new Reichskriminaldirektor, Gottfried Tanzinger, less than two months in the job since 'Onkel' Artur Nebe was promoted and taken off to command Einsatzgrüp D somewhere in Russia. Tanzinger is a policeman's policeman, a veteran of law enforcement and investigation since the days of the Weimar Republic, days when Berlin's debauchery and crime rate skyrocketed. The Nazi ascendancy has changed that, brought with it a new and puritanical approach to entertainment, sexuality and public order. At least on the surface, on the public face of the regime. Beneath, little has changed.

Tanzinger's seen it all for decades, he's done it all, and he looks the part – a weathered worldly blue-eyed face sitting on a streetfighter's thickset frame. Thanks to Onkel Artur's parting advice, he's well aware of Max Neumann's investigation record.

Tanzinger and Becker slow to a halt as they draw closer to the four men filling the passage, wait for them to approach. Tanzinger is the first to speak, a half-smile on his face. He seems amused by the situation.

"And what have we here, Kriminalkommissar?"

Neumann and Schneider stand at attention, hold fast to their two captives.

"Burglary, sir, and receiving. This man," says Neumann, as

he jerks his head sideways at Kadow, "blew a safe in Dahlem and got away with a diamond necklace worth more than ten thousand Reichsmarks. We grabbed him when he tried to sell it to the other one, the brown suit."

Tanzinger briefly examines the two handcuffed men with only casual interest before turning his attention back to Neumann. He rubs his jowls thoughtfully.

"Burglary? Isn't that a bit routine for you?"

"The murder business is a little slow at the moment, sir. We help out wherever we can."

"I see. And now?"

"We thought we might sit down and have a cup of coffee with these gentlemen, sir. Introduce them to the klieg lights, see if we can't persuade them to tell us a bit more about themselves."

Neumann sees Becker's face blanch at the casual exchange between himself and Tanzinger. He knows Becker's views on how subordinates should address superiors, especially superiors as lofty as Reichskriminaldirektor Tanzinger, knows that Becker thinks he's bordering on insubordination. Which is mainly why he behaves as he does. Tanzinger gives no indication he's noticed, resurrects his amused look as he speaks again.

"Very well," he says, as he moves aside and motions for the silent, impotently seething Becker to do the same. "Don't let us detain you in your pursuit of the truth."

"Thank you, sir." Neumann and Schneider echo one another as they move forward, dragging their prisoners with them.

3

"Fucking Nazi! Fucking Nazi! Fucking Nazi!"

The old man's shouted abuse is sprayed at unseen points around the room. He's in striped pyjamas, the cord-tied trousers hanging loose on his emaciated frame. There's a wet patch at the crotch. He waves his arms around in a shooing gesture as he shouts. Spittle flies from his mouth, dribbles over the grey stubble on his chin. Suddenly he stops waving, stops shouting, seems not to know where he is, runs a bony veined hand backwards through his thin white hair. His milky eyes lose focus, roll around aimlessly. Then, with an inarticulate screech, he comes to life and flings his right arm out and up in a semblance of the Nazi salute. It's only for a second, and the effort seems to exhaust him. He moans softly and gazes wildly around before realising there's a chair behind him. He flops heavily into it and sinks back, breathing open-mouthed, and his eyelids slowly slide shut.

Drawn by the noise, a nurse comes running into the room. By the time she arrives, the shouter is silent. She turns to the young man standing motionless beside the slumped form.

"I'm sorry, Untersturmführer. He sometimes does this. It's the uniform that sets him off." She hesitates, as people often do when they're talking to a Schutzstaffel officer. "Perhaps the next time you might be able to come in civilian clothes?"

Untersturmführer Walther Neumann inclines his head slowly, acknowledges the sense of what the woman is saying. He knew before he was accepted into the SS what effect the uniform would have on most people. Respect to an extent, if only the respect given to any government figure of authority, but the overwhelming effect is of fear. It might be mingled with dislike or even hate, but fear tramples on every other emotion. It's to be expected, and it's what Walther Neumann has always wanted. Now, newly out of his Schutzstaffel probation period and promoted to Untersturmführer, for the first time he is entitled to put on the fearsome black uniform. It's an entitlement he intends to enthusiastically embrace.

"Yes, of course. I will wear a suit next time, Fräulein . . . ?"

Walther would not normally be so obliging and polite, would not normally allow a common citizen to tell him his business. But this woman is very attractive. The Jews have a word for women like her – *zaftig*, 'juicy'. At least they got that right. She's not much older than his own twenty-seven years, her full figure barely disguised beneath the uniform of dark green Herbstkrankenhaus dress under a white pinafore apron and accompanying white cap. In any event, it is his father they are discussing, so Walther allows her some latitude. He can be charming when he chooses, and he chooses now.

The nurse tries polite but pointed dissuasion.

"Schellenberg," she says, "*Frau* Schellenberg".

Single or married, it means little to Walther, but this woman has yet to know that.

"Thank you, Frau Schellenberg. May I leave my father in your hands now? It is probably best I don't linger. Perhaps we might meet again on my next visit?"

Frau Schellenberg offers only a noncommittal "Perhaps" as she turns away to adjust the old man's clothing. Walther softly brings his heels together, gives the hint of a bow, then marches away down the corridor outside his father's room. He's relieved, glad to be leaving so soon, glad to escape the tedium of yet another session with a father whose moods swing unpredictably and wildly – sometimes not knowing who his visitor is, sometimes shouting obscenities or incomprehensible half-sentences, sometimes sitting slumped in morose dribbling silence. God in heaven, surely there's a better way than this. The government has cleansed the country of other defectives – the gypsies, the deranged, the half-witted dregs of society. Surely the system can accommodate an incontinent, mindless old man? Walther forces his speculation to a halt, takes a sharp breath, tries to put the visit out of his mind.

He steps through the building's guarded double glass doors and into Nollendorfstrasse, pauses briefly on the high steps to contemplate a row of four gutted buildings on the other side of the road, the now-extinguished fires which destroyed them courtesy of British bombers last month. Bastards. The stupid Englanders just don't know when to give up. When we've brought Russia to its knees, then we'll . . .

Walther shakes his head, scans the horizon. To the south-west, nearly two kilometres away across the affluent roofs of the Bavarian Quarter, he can just make out the tip of the enormous Rathaus tower. Finished just before the start of the last war, it embodies in stone the achievement, the confidence, the *power* of old Germany. And now that confidence is back, that power is once more on display, and it resides in men like him.

Walther unconsciously breathes deep, puffs out his chest, sets off east towards Nollendorfplatz and the S-Bahn station on its far side. This part of Schöneberg is hardly the haunt of high society, more like lower middle class, and the pinched buildings and dowdy pedestrians reflect the district's lack of status. Nonetheless, he strides erect and purposeful down the footpath, aware of the effect his black uniform has on others, gratified to see most of the oncoming foot traffic veering to give him clear passage. Good. He's who he wants to be, where he wants to be. He's a man to be reckoned with. Time to bring himself to someone else's attention.

4

In his tiny apartment on Ohmstrasse, Father Andreas Rochlitz sits alone, rests his head on the overstuffed back of a brown suede armchair. The chair and the priest have both seen better days, both well past their prime, equally threadbare. Father Rochlitz listens half-awake to the music of the Berlin Philharmonic. Tonight they're under Wilhelm Furtwängler, performing Schumann's third symphony, 'the Rhenish'. He'd rather be in the concert hall, of course, but his DKE38 radio is an acceptable substitute. Father Rochlitz calls the plain, cheap black box sitting on the sideboard his radio. The DKE38's official title is The People's Receiver. Many of its millions of other users call it a Goebbels Snout – but only if there's no possibility of a Gestapo informer in the vicinity to overhear. Father Rochlitz doesn't use the radio's slang name. Unless it's absolutely necessary, he refuses to speak the name of the Minister of Propaganda. Hasn't done since 1936 when, as Gauleiter of Berlin, Goebbels ordered all the beautiful trees of Unter den Linden ripped up and replaced with 10-metre tall fluted square columns topped by Party eagles. An abomination, in Rochlitz's view. Not the Party's worst, by far, just another of so many. He could fill a page if he listed them.

It's not long gone eight, fully dark outside, and he's tired. He thinks it's age that's responsible. After you reach 70, you slow down. Nature makes its demands of you. It can't be work that's making him so tired. A faint wry smile creases his mouth as he reflects on his current status – 'priest-without-portfolio', as the diocesan priest in charge of St Albertus Magnus, Rudolf Kroehl, is fond of saying. The supercilious young fool. Still, Father Rochlitz does what he can when he can. St Albertus Magnus caters mainly to the needs of the multitude of workers on the vast Siemens Electrical Company housing estate, nine kilometres west of central Berlin. The workers' accommodation surrounds his apartment building, over a thousand whitewashed brick houses full of employees and their families. Young Father Kroehl condescendingly lets the aged priest take confession sometimes, even less often lets him officiate at a burial or baptism. It's doing God's work, no doubt, but it leaves Father Rochlitz unfulfilled, incomplete. Even his voluntary 'work' as unofficial watch-repairer for the church staff and some of the parishioners leaves him incompletely satisfied.

His mind wanders back, as it so often does these days, to when he had his own church, when he was responsible for the church of St Lambertus in Moabit. Less than five kilometres from where he sits now, but a world away in his life. Were it not for a candle left unattended, for the hand of fate – or of God – to deal him a cruel blow, then his old church would be still standing, and he would still be . . . Ah, he sighs, but that was all when he was a younger man, a better man, when . . .

A double knock on the door jerks Father Rochlitz out of his nostalgic reverie, and he sits forward, blinking, momentarily confused. The knock is repeated, softly like the first time. The old priest gets stiffly out of his armchair, shuffles across the worn linoleum and unlatches the apartment door, apprehensive, wary. The man standing in the corridor is ordinary-looking, medium height, wearing a dark blue suit and soft grey hat. There's a small light brown leather case in his left hand. He looks like he's selling something. Father Rochlitz hesitates, starts to say he's not interested, but stops as the stranger raises his hat and speaks.

"Good evening, Father. I apologise for disturbing you at this hour. I am Herr Kempner . . ."

The priest starts to relax. His visitor's voice is polite, cultured, reassuring. Perhaps he is a new parishioner.

" . . . from the RSHA. Perhaps I might have a few minutes of your time?"

Father Rochlitz's throat constricts as his stomach lurches. His body is knotted tight with fear, cold, almost painful. The Reichssicherheitshauptant! The Reich Central Security Office! He tries to speak but can't, his voice gone. The terror grips him like a vice. The man from the RSHA just stares with cold grey eyes, doubtless familiar with the effect he has on those he encounters.

"We would be more comfortable inside, I think," the man says as he eases forward, past Father Rochlitz who has involuntarily taken a step backwards. The old priest is mute, his eyes wide with fear. His hands are shaking now.

Herr Kempner carefully shuts the door behind him, secures the latch, then places his leather case on the floor. As Father Rochlitz watches, transfixed, his visitor scans the small room before taking four steps to the open bedroom door and glancing inside. Then he turns and walks back to the priest. Without changing his neutral expression, he abruptly punches the old man hard in the face and quickly steps forward to catch him before he can slump to the floor. He lowers Father Rochlitz, dazed and semi-conscious, into the old armchair the priest left less than a minute earlier.

Herr Kempner retrieves his case and takes out a length of thin rope and a piece of cloth a little bigger than a handkerchief. He ties the rope around the unresisting priest's right arm, loops it tight behind the armchair, and ties the other end to the priest's left arm, painfully pinioning him in the chair. Then he stuffs the piece of cloth into Father Rochlitz's mouth before bringing a kitchen chair and placing it in front of the bound man. He sits, crosses his legs and lights a cigarette, regards his victim with what might be curiosity while he waits for the priest to regain his senses.

It takes a few minutes before Father Rochlitz looks like he might be in a position to understand what his visitor wants him to understand. The old man's left cheek is already swelling, his left eye puffy and beginning to close. Blood trickles from both his nostrils. His head swings abruptly left and right, as though seeking rescue, salvation. Fear is stamped all over him. His breathing is rapid, ragged, his chest heaves.

"Very well," says Herr Kempner, "we will begin. You are familiar, I presume, with the methods of the Inquisition. Is that not so, Father? Of course it is – you Catholics invented the thing. You will know, therefore, that when the inquisitors required a confession of sin, they did not immediately begin to inflict pain on the accused sinner. Such barbarous behaviour would not have been appropriate. No, they instead began by showing the accused sinner the instruments of torture, no more than that. As you will be aware, such was often sufficient to elicit a true confession, with accompanying repentance. A quite civilised procedure, would you not agree?"

Father Rochlitz's uninjured eye widens with naked terror as Herr Kempner speaks. His breathing becomes faster, more laboured, and small whimpering sounds creep out of his gagged mouth. Tears drip from both eyes.

The priest watches Herr Kempner lay his case on the floor beside the kitchen chair. He sees the man take out a pair of pliers, which he lays on the floor beside the case. Then a scalpel, laid next to the pliers. Then Kempner picks up a small brass cylinder with two knurled knobs near the top, from where a thin brass tube protrudes at right angles. Kempner holds the cylinder up directly in front of Father Rochlitz, now weeping copiously, his nose beginning to stream with snot over the blood.

"This is a gas blowtorch, Father. Very small, a tiny flame only, but sufficient for my needs. Do you know what happens to an eyeball when a pinpoint of blue flame is directed on to it? No? Well, I could tell you in considerable detail, but that hardly seems necessary at this point."

Kempner places the blowtorch on the floor next to the case, lights another cigarette, contemplates the terrified priest for a short time before he speaks again.

"I will ask you a question, Father, and you will answer it. I will remove the gag from your mouth for the purpose. Please nod if you understand me."

The priest's head slumps forward, once, twice.

"Very good. Now," he adds as he reaches into his coat pocket and brings out a photograph, holds it at arm's length so that Father Rochlitz can see, "you will tell me where I might find the original of this document."

The priest jolts as if electrocuted. His head snaps back, thrashes from side to side. His face is firebrick red, sweat glistening everywhere. His chest heaves as he struggles to breathe. Kempner reaches forward and holds his victim's jaw steady with one hand, removes the gag with the other.

"Yes?"

Father Rochlitz tries to speak through his tears, gasps for air, but his words are staccato, punctuated by the gasping, almost unintelligible.

"I . . . I . . . know . . . nothing."

Kempner's expression doesn't change as he abruptly stuffs the gag back in Father Rochlitz's mouth. He stands, moves to the side of the pinioned old man, holds his head steady with his left hand, then with his right takes the cigarette from his mouth and inserts the lit end into the priest's left ear. Father Rochlitz immediately jerks his head left and right violently, screams a muffled scream that continues as Kempner resumes his seat and waits until the old man stops screaming and thrashing.

"This is unnecessary, Father. You do not need to suffer. It will achieve nothing at all. I merely wish to know the location of the document. Then I will take it and be on my way. You must understand that you *will* tell me where it is – that much is certain. It is entirely up to you whether you tell me now or later. So, I will ask again. Where is it?"

Father Rochlitz has stopped trying to scream, has dropped his head forward onto his chest where it moves slightly up and down as he silently sobs behind the cloth filling his mouth. His breathing is raspy, spasmodic. Bubbles of blood and snot balloon and retreat in his nose, run down over his lip. He gives no indication he has heard what Kempner said.

Kempner reaches down, picks up the small blowtorch, turns one of the knurled knobs, lights the resultant gas with the tip of his still-glowing cigarette, then with the second knurled knob adjusts the flame to a pinpoint of blue and yellow. He stands, moves behind his bound victim and, with a hand beneath the priest's chin, pulls the old man's head up and back hard against the armchair. Father Rochlitz sees the blowtorch held in front of his face, arches his back fiercely, wrenches his head out of Kempner's hand, shrieks silently and ineffectually. His legs kick out wildly. Then, abruptly, he falls quiet, stiffens against the restraining ropes, his face white, waxy, contorted. Once, twice, he convulses, then goes limp, head falling forward onto his chest. His breathing has stopped.

Unhurriedly, Kempner moves to the front of the armchair, shuts down the blowtorch, regards the motionless priest with puzzlement. Then he puts two fingers on the side of the old man's unmoving wrinkled neck for a short time. He frowns, leans down, lays the side of his head on Father Rochlitz's chest for perhaps ten seconds, then stands erect again. A long sigh follows his grimace of frustration.

"Shit!"

Kempner sighs again, then stubs his cigarette out on the kitchen chair, takes a short sharp breath, and sets about his work.

5

Kurt Schneider's small one-bedroom apartment sits on Schwarzer Weg, about six kilometres west of the Alex, straddles the border of Charlottenburg to the south and Moabit to the north. His walking route to Hans Schmeling's boxing academy on Treseburger Strasse, south towards the Spree, is a winding one through the back streets. He has the choice of a few alternative routes, but usually takes the one past the old SA pub on Hebblestrasse, the Zur Alstadt. There's no SA thugs lounging around outside now, of course, not since the organisation was neutered in 1934 after the Night of the Long Knives, but the old Engelhardt Biere sign is still screwed to the wall, and a swastika still flies from the overhanging first floor's flagpole. Schneider doesn't miss the raised stiff arms, lecherous cat calls, drunken renditions of the Horst Wessel Lied.

To call Schmeling's joint an 'academy' gilds the lily – it's run out of a barn-like old wooden building previously used for warehousing paper. Fact is, it's no more than a gymnasium with a boxing ring. And Hans just adds more gilding by using the name Schmeling – he's no known relation to Max Schmeling,

Germany's world heavyweight boxing champion less than ten years ago. It hardly matters to Schneider. Fancy or rough makes no difference. He frequents the place for the exercise, for the camaraderie, for the change of pace from his policeman's duties, enjoys the smoky atmosphere of sweat, leather and liniment. Most of all he enjoys the boxing, the concentrated charge of adrenalin that surges as soon as he faces an opponent intent on battering him senseless. Not that he's battered senseless very often – Schneider's size and solidity usually keeps him out of harm's way, lets him absorb punishment as he dispenses it with interest. His size substitutes for style. Schmeling says he fights like a gorilla in gloves.

Schneider is preoccupied as he walks, his mind elsewhere. So he doesn't register the dog's head poking out of an entrance recess of the building he's passing until he's less than ten metres away. Then he sees it, stops dead. The dog's eyes are locked on his. It slowly moves out of the recess and onto the footpath proper, facing him. It's not big, about the height of a normal man's knee, but it's full of muscle. An indeterminate breed, short brown hair, a broad face and snout, powerful jaws. It stands motionless, its brown eyes never leaving Schneider's. He shifts his stance, moves his weight forward onto his left foot, right foot extended behind, lifts his hands so his forearms are parallel with the ground, doesn't break eye contact with the animal. Waits.

The dog half-squats for a moment before exploding forward, straight at Schneider. It accelerates furiously until it's a couple of metres away then launches itself towards Schneider's chest, his throat. He moves his arms in anticipation. Then the animal hits him square in the chest and Schneider wraps his arms around it, holding it close, pinioned to his body. He throws his head back as the dog lifts its snout up, thrusting towards his face.

"Good boy, good boy," he says, manoeuvring the animal's

body to keep its tongue from licking his face. He cuddles it with one arm, ruffling its neck with his free hand as the dog wriggles with delight, making small yelping sounds in its throat, its tail thrashing with pleasure.

"Good boy, Achilles, just calm down, alright? Here you go," he adds as he lowers the animal to the ground, holding the back of its neck with one hand, patting and thumping its chest with the other. He lets go, and Achilles starts skittering in circles around his legs, throwing its face up from time to time to make eye contact.

Schneider gives the dog some passing pats before looking up to scan the footpath. About thirty metres in front he sees a familiar figure in a dark blue Reichspost uniform pushing a small trolley with light wire mesh compartments. The postman looks like somebody's favourite grandfather, all white hair and beard, even the rosy cheeks and bulbous nose. Schneider raises a hand in salutation, receives a wave in response. The postman stops a few metres on, outside the entrance to an apartment complex, and Schneider hurries towards him, accompanied by the dog. The two men shake hands.

"I think Achilles likes you," says the Saint Nikolaus doppelgänger.

"It's not unrequited, Dolf – I'm fond of him, too." Schneider reinforces his declaration with a flurry of neck rubs as Achilles pushes against his legs. Neither man can remember exactly how Schneider's routine with Achilles started, but both participants fed off each other, and the mock-attack and subsequent cuddle and playtime became an established form of greeting for both of them.

"How are things at the Alex? Busy?"

"Always busy, Dolf, but I suppose that's what they pay me for. Like yourself, I would think. I never see you that you're not hurrying from one place to another."

"Off to Schmeling's?"

"Yes. A bit of dancing in the ring before I call it a day."

"Well, be careful. There's already enough blood around the place. I'd best be getting on. Come on, boy."

The two men continue on their different ways, Dolf Schliemann into the apartment complex accompanied by Achilles and the trolley full of letters and parcels, Schneider along Nordhauser Strasse towards the academy. As he walks he muses on the different ways in which Schmeling and Schliemann have appropriated names for their own purposes. Schmeling has looked to commercial gain from association with the former champion boxer. Schliemann, on the other hand, appears to be motivated by nothing more than eccentricity. Given that his namesake, Heinrich Schliemann, famously discovered the ruins of ancient Troy in the 1870s, it apparently amuses the postman to name his dog after the foremost Greek hero in King Agamemnon's army besieging that fabulous city. Schneider appreciates the touch of whimsy, particularly as it's in such short supply these days. He whistles as he walks, *Adieu Mein Kleiner Gardeoffizier*, an old Richard Tauber tune, wonders what Kriminalkommissar Neumann would say about his taste for romantic music.

6

A Kriminalkommissar of more than three years standing, as is Max Neumann, has the honorary SS rank of Hauptsturmführer, the equivalent of a captain in the British Army. The rank might terrify most civilians and impress the younger Kripo recruits, but it doesn't warrant anything as desirable as a dedicated secretary. Neumann shares Fräulein Helene Üffing with two fellow investigators, both of them younger and better looking than he is, and he's long resigned himself to them getting the lion's share of the young woman's attentions. So he's surprised to look up to her knock and see her standing smiling in his office doorway, even more surprised when she adopts a formality and deference normally absent.

"Excuse me, Kriminalkommissar. You have a visitor at the front desk."

"Yes? Who?"

"It is an Untersturmführer. He says he is your brother."

Neumann tries not to show the surprise he's feeling, instead offers up a small smile of acknowledgement.

"Thank you, Helene," he says as he gets up, "I'll go out."

Walther Neumann is standing by a worn wooden bench seat on one side of the cavernous entry hall, legs apart, hands behind his back, eyeing the four young women who sit at typewriters on the other side of the long public counter. They affect not to notice him, but cast surreptitious glances in his direction from time to time. One of them is blushing. The younger Neumann stops staring as his peripheral vision registers big brother Max's approach from the far end of the counter. He brings his feet together, raises his right hand in the approved manner.

"Heil Hitler!" he snaps, at parade-ground attention.

Max Neumann, against his inclination, but conscious the two men have an audience, briefly stops, returns the salute. Not crisply or energetically, but sufficient to satisfy what has now moved from convention to law. Then he steps up to his brother, extends a hand as his eyes run up and down.

"You look like you've stepped out of a recruiting poster."

Walther shakes the proffered hand, chooses to interpret the greeting as a compliment.

"Thanks. I was lucky enough to get a perfect fit from the Quartiermeister's." Walther holds out one black-clad arm, unnecessarily adjusts the sleeve length. "Probably from the Hugo Boss factory – they make the best ones." Max doesn't comment on the uniform.

"So, why the visit? I can't recall you ever coming here."

The visit is to show off Walther's new uniform, to impress the girls behind the front desk, to impress his brother. And anyone else he might encounter in the process.

"I was passing. On my way to HQ. I've been to see father."

Max braces for bad news from the nursing home, but Walther goes on without pause.

"We want to ask you and Irmgard to dinner next Thursday night. Anni hasn't seen either of you for weeks. We can all celebrate the end of my probation. And my first posting. Can you come? We'll get drunk. I've saved some Tattinger just for the occasion." In response to the flicker of dubiousness on his brother's face, he adds, "It's the real stuff, not what the Frogs are passing off on us these days."

"A posting already? To where?"

"All in good time, all in good time. Can you come?"

"Next Thursday? Of course. I'll bring some schnapps, decent schnapps – Prince Bismarck, if I can get it. The girls can have most of the champagne."

"Excellent!" Walther claps his brother on the upper arm, says "See you then," steps back before delivering another stiff-arm salute and leaving. Max Neumann decides one salute per meeting should be enough to satisfy any onlookers.

✠

"It was him?"

"Yes, sir. There is no doubt whatever. The handwriting examples in his room match the writing on the documents you received. And his typewriter was used also – I have compared the typeface of the machine with the notes. They are the same."

"But you did not find the document we want." Himmler permits himself slightly raised eyebrows.

"I did not. There was no indication as to its whereabouts."

"Nothing? Nothing to say where it is?"

"Nothing, sir. I was thorough."

Himmler nods distractedly, confirms his confidence in Standartenführer Schmidt's thoroughness. He rests both forearms on his desk and gazes off to one side for several seconds, towards the tall mullioned Gothic-arch windows and their view out onto Prinz Albrecht Strasse. Bright autumn sunlight floods through. Dust motes dance in the beams. In the distance, three small birds seem to cavort as they wheel and dive at one another.

"Then, clearly," he says as he brings his gaze back to his visitor, "the priest has secreted it elsewhere. Or entrusted it to someone for safekeeping." He stares at Schmidt's impassive face for a few moments before lowering his head and slapping the desk with his right hand.

"Damn!"

It's as demonstrative as Schmidt has ever seen his boss. He continues to sit and wait. A faithful servant. Himmler is collecting his thoughts, reining in his emotions.

"What are your next steps, Stefan?"

Schmidt answers slowly, methodically. It's in his nature.

"The immediate priority is to ensure the priest's death, this specific priest's death, does not draw undue attention. I will begin attending to that later today. Then I will seek out those closest to the old man and visit them. It may be necessary to conduct further searches." A brief pause before he adds, "There will be further casualties, of course."

"Yes, yes, of course." Himmler is unconcerned, his mind fixed on success, nothing else. "Thank you, Stefan. Please continue. I will await your report."

The two men exchange salutes and Schmidt leaves. Himmler sits for a long time, stares with blank eyes at nothing in particular before taking a deep breath as he sits up in his chair and reaches for his pen.

7

Kriminalkommissar Neumann shares a secretary with two other investigators of the same rank. Reichskriminaldirektor Gottfried Tanzinger, on the other hand, needs share with nobody. Outside his office on the fourth floor of the Police Praesidium on Alexanderplatz sit two assistants, an orderly-cum-bodyguard, Oberleutnant Albert Maschmann, and a secretary. It's the secretary whose refined Viennese tones spill out of Tanzinger's internal communication telephone when he responds to its rasping buzz.

"Yes, Lotte?"

"There's a call from the main switchboard, sir, someone asking for you personally. They tried to put him off, but he's very insistent. He says he knows you, sir."

"Has he given a name?"

"Yes, sir, Kroehl. Rudolph Kroehl."

"Kroehl? Kroehl? I don't know . . ." Tanzinger interrupts himself with a faint memory, more than twenty years in the past, sees a skinny shy kid who jumped at loud noises. Reinhard? No, Rudolph. The Kroehls senior come to mind, a warm and welcoming couple, good company despite their pervasive religiosity. He enjoyed their friendship as neighbours when he lived in Prenzlauer Berg, in the city's north-east. What does their kid want? Now, after all this time? Tanzinger hesitates. His inclination is to have Lotte make some kind of excuse. Ah, what does it matter, let's see what the kid wants. The Reichskriminaldirektor clears his mind, ready for whatever the call brings.

"I'll talk to him, Lotte. What line?"

"Three, sir. Putting him through now."

Tanzinger picks up the telephone's black earpiece, slides the base unit closer to him and flicks its third switch.

"Tanzinger."

"Thank you, sir, thank you for taking my call. It's Rudolph, sir, Rudolph Kroehl. We were your neighbours in Prenzlauer Berg, in Marienburger Strasse. I was just a boy . . ."

"Yes, I remember you, Rudolph. What . . ."

"It's urgent, sir," Kroehl interrupts. "There's been a murder! A priest has been murdered! A priest, sir! I found him. Please, sir, can you help me. Please . . ."

✠

Max and Walther Neumann climb the high flight of stone steps up from Nollendorfstrasse, push through the double glass doors of the three-storey building, the Herbstkrankenhaus, past the uniformed guard at his desk just inside. Until 1938 the Herbstkrankenhaus was home to a wealthy family of Jews. After they were thrown out by the Party the building was bought cheap and converted into a private hospital for those who could afford its services. Calling it 'Autumn Hospital' seems appropriate, given its clientele have all long since seen their summer days of youth and vitality fade into half-forgotten memory. Alois

Neumann's summer days have gone further, retreated far beyond memory's grasp, have almost entirely disappeared. All that remains are snatches of a life, brief confused glimpses through shifting fog, momentary shafts of light in near-perpetual darkness and misery.

The cost of keeping their father alive and cared for is crippling. Alois Neumann gets a pathetically small pension from a lifetime's government service, beginning with the Prussian state railway in 1901 and ending with the Deutsche Reichsbahn's creation in 1937, by which time his rapidly accelerating dementia could no longer be ignored. Alois' pension makes hardly a dent in what the Herbstkrankenhaus charges, and it's only what his sons contribute that keeps him here. It's that financial burden which lies behind the tension between Max and Walther as they enter the hospital, the angry silence that has settled over them. It started almost as soon as they had walked out of the S-Bahn station, just as they were starting to cross Nollendorfplatz.

"How do you think we can keep going? The fees are up another five percent at the end of the year. We can't keep doing this forever."

"We don't have to do it forever." Max speaks more sharply than he intends, tries to soften the words. "Father is old. He might not see out another year. Anything could happen in the meantime. The war might . . ." He catches himself. Walther isn't someone who wants to hear the war might be over within a year, not when the implication is that Germany will lose it. But the hesitancy isn't lost on his younger brother.

"What? The war might what?" Walther's anger is suppressed, but clearly present. "Be over? The Russians might win? Is that what you're saying?"

"No, all I'm saying is that . . ."

"Have you forgotten the last four months? Don't you read

the *Beobachter* any more? Our troops have crushed the Russians time and time again. We've killed millions of them, taken millions more prisoner, we're running around Russia as we please. Everybody says we'll be in Moscow for Christmas. It's a rout, Max, a total rout. The Ivans have got as much chance of beating us as I've got of . . . of . . . being promoted to Gruppenführer! Forget the war. It's over already. Like Father's life – it's over. Finished. We have to accept that."

"How can you say that? He's not a carthorse you shoot because he can't work any more – he's our father for Christ's sake, our father. You don't just throw his life away." Max's voice is louder than it should be, shriller.

"Listen to yourself, Max. He doesn't *have* a life anymore. He doesn't know where he is, who we are, what day it is. He doesn't have a mind any more. If he ever suspected he'd finish up like this he'd have begged us to do something about it. It's not just me. Other people, experts, doctors, say that . . ."

"Not that damned book again! I'm not going to argue with quacks. They're the ones who should be . . ."

It's not the first time Walther has fallen back on this argument. Twenty years now since Hoche and Binding published *Allowing the Destruction of Life Unworthy of Living*, twenty years for the seeds to grow and flourish. The eminent authors, one a lawyer, the other a psychiatrist, mounted a rational argument for eliminating the mentally incapable, putting to death those whom were adjudged to no longer have value to themselves or society. The book's argument has been seized, built upon, extended and codified by a small but influential coterie of thinkers within the Party, most radically by the odious Alfred Rosenberg, the Party's chief racial theorist. As far as Rosenberg is concerned, sub-humans include everybody from Russian citizens to Jews to mental defectives, and every one of them needs to be eliminated. His views attract widespread support, and not just within the ranks of the SS.

"No, not the book," snaps Walther, "it's gone beyond that. You should read *Der Angriff* more often. There was a piece in yesterday's edition about an asylum near Limburg. Ten thousand, that's how many defectives they've removed so far, ten thousand, a real achievement. There were speeches to mark the occasion, food and beer for the staff. It's not just me, Max, it's lots of others. Doctors, administrators, the government – are you saying they're all wrong? That we should throw every scarce resource at keeping these people alive? They're not even people any more, some of them, just empty mindless shells. Like Father. It would be a kindness, a release . . ."

"No! No it wouldn't!" Max spins around to face his little brother, thrusts his chin forwards. "It would be murder, as simple as that, bloody murder, and I won't have it. It won't happen while I've got breath in my body. Alright? Just forget it. If I have to, I'll pay all the fees myself. I'll find a way. You can walk away, forget Father, forget what we owe him, just . . ."

"We? *We*?" Walther is furious, indignant, his voice shrill. Passers-by stare, move around the arguing men. "For fuck's sake, it was never *we*, it was always *you*. Max the first son, Max the smart one, Max the golden boy who could do no wrong. Me? I was the afterthought, the accident, the spare. He wasn't my father, just some miserable drunk who ignored me unless I needed some slapping around. Do you know when I was happiest? Do you? It was when he was at work, or boozing, or chasing pussy in some cut-rate knocking shop. It was when he was nowhere to be seen! Now you expect me to say, 'Ah, all water under the bridge. I'll pay to keep you alive, Father. I'll make the sacrifices you never did.' Well I'm about up to here with it. I'm not going to keep pouring money into the old shit. You love him so much? You pay for him. Ah . . ."

Walther's anger consumes him, crowds into his speech, rips

apart his reasoning. He throws his hands up, shakes his head. The frustration is overwhelming. He increases his speed, stalks hurriedly ahead. Max has held his tongue in check. Now he lets the vicious beast off its leash.

"That's right, run away, forget where you came from. Go on, run. Just fuck off. And take your stinking ideas with you."

8

Kriminalkommissar Max Neumann isn't used to being examined, scrutinised like an insect in a jar. Usually, he's the one doing the scrutinising, making the object of his attentions wriggle with discomfort. He tries to project patience, calm, confidence, but isn't sure how well he's succeeding. He tries, with no success at all, to meet the steady gaze of the man sitting opposite, a man so powerful and so superior in rank that if he wished he could probably pick up the telephone and have Neumann taken out and shot.

Reichskriminaldirektor Tanzinger finishes his examination of Neumann, lights a cigarette with the Imco 'Trench' lighter on his desk and takes a deep pull before speaking.

"Well. You are wondering why you are here."

It's not a question. Tanzinger continues even as Neumann mutters a respectful 'Sir' of affirmation.

"It's straightforward enough. There's been a murder, and you're going to look into it." Tanzinger waves a quietening, dismissive hand as Neumann opens his mouth to speak. "Yes, yes, I know, Kriminaldirektor Becker would normally be doing this. Or your immediate superior, . . ." Tanzinger hunts for a name, finds it, ". . . Kriminalrat Böhm. I'll inform them later. The situation isn't normal. The son of an old family friend has reported the murder, and I've told him I'll put my best man on it." Neumann looks like he's about to say something, thinks better of it, swallows his unformed words of protest and waits as Tanzinger continues.

"You're that man, Neumann. Artur Nebe sang your praises before he handed over, and since then I've had good reports from other sources. They all confirm what I was told by Nebe, Gruppenführer Nebe as he is now, especially about your work on the S-Bahn murders. So the case is yours. You'll report directly to me. Here's as much as I know," he says, handing over a sheet of paper. "A couple of Orpos are keeping the place secure until you get there."

Neumann takes the proffered document, glances at the handwritten lines on it before he looks up in surprise.

"A priest, sir?"

"The very same," replies Tanzinger. "A Roman Catholic priest getting himself killed. We both know there are many among our colleagues who would find that neither remarkable nor undesirable. I'm not one of them, and you'd better not be. The man's dead, murdered, and some bastard out there did it. I don't care whether the corpse is a priest or a prostitute, just find out who's responsible and bring him in. Are there any questions?"

✠

It's only a twenty-minute walk from Trautenaustrasse in Wilmersdorf to Walther and Anni's apartment north towards the Berlin Zoo. A safe and comfortable twenty-minute stroll tonight. Thick low cloud is both a blanket over the day's warmth and a shield against any British bombers in the sky. Even so, there are few other pedestrians on the darkened streets, and they all keep their heads down as they go about their business. These days it doesn't pay to attract attention of any kind. You keep your head down, your eyes averted. A few bicycles pass by, fewer cars.

As Max and Irmgard reach Bundesallee a slope-nosed Kübelwagen carrying an officer and three soldiers splutters past, followed by an open truck with more soldiers crowded along the bench seats lining its tray. They look like tailor's dummies stamped from a mould – all upright, facing each other, grounded rifles aimed at the sky. At this time of night, they're probably heading off on a raid – rounding up some Jews or smashing a dissident cell. It's a familiar enough sight, one that doesn't warrant a comment. Not so familiar is the dark green Engelhardt Biere truck bringing up the rear, as though part of the small convoy. Max and Irmgard exchange a questioning glance, but neither remarks on the sight. The truck and its tarpaulin-covered load of barrels disappears down Bundesallee and is lost to view.

A few minutes later Max and Irmgard are outside his brother's apartment block on Eislebener Strasse, not far from the Kurfürstendamm. Max still can't entirely set aside the lingering bitterness of his recent exchange with Walther on the way to see their father at the Herbstkrankenhaus. The anger which burned in him at the time continues to hover like Banquo's ghost at Macbeth's feast, a shadow, but somehow tangible nonetheless. Max resolves to bury his emotions, force them down to where they can do no harm. He stares up at his brother's apartment block as though seeking inspiration.

Housing here is built to a formula, not an aesthetic. Maximum residents in minimum space must have been the instruction given to the architects or, more likely, to the cut-price builders. The five-storey building in front of Max and Irmgard exemplifies the point. Dull grey bricks crowd the edge of the footpath before soaring skywards unleavened by any highlights other than uniformly square and small windows. Anyone passing on the footpath could reach through an open window and shake the hand of a street-level dweller. But in this late autumn of 1941 nobody at street level leaves their windows open. Every one is either shuttered or barred, curtains closed, telling the world to keep out.

Max and Irmgard share a reassuring glance as they take a resolute breath and move through the double entrance doors. They ignore the waiting concertina-gated elevator, take the concrete stairs to Walther's apartment on the first floor, number 102, knock on the plain grey-painted door. It opens within seconds and Anni is there, arms extended, beaming, her freckled nose wrinkled with transparent pleasure.

"Max! Irmie!"

She steps forward into a hug with Irmgard, disengages and goes to Max. He gets a brushed kiss on the cheek and a waft of 'Arabian Nights' perfume before Anni takes his hand and pulls him into the apartment, calling for Walther as she does. Her husband appears from the direction of the sole bedroom and hurries forward.

"Hello Irmgard. So good to see you again." A look over her shoulder. "Welcome, Max, welcome."

Irmgard gives Walther a chaste cheek kiss before standing back to examine him. He's wearing his SS uniform. There's an uncomfortable silence. Max and Anni exchange a knowing glance. Walther's black uniform is at odds with the comfortable and casual dress of the other three. Anni tries to brush the awkwardness away.

"I've told him if he comes to bed like that I'm going back to my mother's."

"You might need to stay there for a few months," says Max. "Until the novelty has worn off. You know how it is – children with new toys . . ."

"You leave him alone," interrupts Irmgard as she steps forward and grasps Walther's shoulders at arm's length before smoothing down his jacket. She brushes away invisible fluff. "He's had to work hard to get as far as he has."

Everybody understands what she means. Not that many years ago, both of the couples had to jump through Party hoops to obtain a Certificate of Fitness to Marry, a certificate attesting they were racially pure, free from eugenic defects and hereditary disease, not displaying any 'asocial' defects. Everyone in the room remembers the degrading physical exams, the documentation, the labyrinthine bureaucracy. And everyone understands how much more laborious, lengthy and intensive has been the process Walther went through for acceptance into the SS. It's common knowledge that his years in the Army counted for nothing. Everyone knows how much effort it took to justify his 'German-ness', his Aryan unimpeachability, his ability to meet the stringent 'racial purity' standards laid down by the head of the SS, Heinrich Himmler. The interviews, the handwritten submissions, the dozens upon dozens of documents proving untainted ancestry stretching back for six generations, the parole and training and then, finally, months later, with clearance from the SS Racial Bureau, the authority to put on a black uniform. Nobody in the room underestimates the difficulty of the path Walther has trodden to get where he is.

Irmgard stops brushing Walther's uniform and takes a step back. "I think he looks very smart. Very manly. Take no notice of them, Walther." She hooks an arm around one of his. "Now, kind sir, please escort me to the best seat in your establishment."

Max and Anni exchange another look as Walther and Irmgard head towards the sofas, a look that shares slight embarrassment, mild concern, mutual understanding. But Max's thoughts go deeper, further back, to another man, to Irmgard's hand . . . He tells himself to stop – it's only his little brother. But the jealous beast within, ever-ready, starts to stir, prepares to rip his mind apart again. With an effort he forces it down, tries to lock the cage, turn his back on the past. It's always an effort, ashes in his mouth, but the ruinous alternative doesn't bear thinking about.

Anni draws Max towards the kitchen bench and a bottle of Tattinger sitting in a silver-looking 'Alpaka' ice bucket – nickel alloy rather than real silver. Max notices the embossed swastikas on the bucket's handle sockets, realises his brother has gone to some trouble and expense to procure the thing, says nothing. Anni asks him to open and pour, brings four glasses to him. They take the filled glasses to the others, sit facing the pair on the other sofa. Max raises his glass.

"My friends," he announces with mock solemnity, "tonight we celebrate a most notable achievement by the youngest of the Neumanns. He has laboured mightily and has been rewarded for his labours with appointment as an officer in the Schutzstaffel. Friends, I give you Untersturmführer Walther Neumann!" He strikes a dramatic pose before pillaging *Antony and Cleopatra*. "Upon your sword sit laurel victory, and smooth success be strew'd before your feet!"

Walther sits self-consciously as the others hold their glasses forward across the intervening low table, touch them lightly, then repeat 'Untersturmführer Walther Neumann!' before drinking. He takes a sip himself, mutters "Thank you," takes another sip as Irmgard leans forward.

"Max says you've already been posted. Can you tell us where you'll be going? When do you leave?"

As he responds, Walther's face is a puzzling study, a mixture of pride, recalcitrance, embarrassment, enthusiasm.

"I've been given command of a Special Action Group detachment. In Ukraine, Group B."

Anni and Irmgard are still smiling. The mention of a Special Action Group obviously means little to them. Irmgard asks again when Walther will leave.

"I'm to report back to HQ next Wednesday. Probably leave then, or perhaps the next day."

This is apparently news to Anni, and her smile immediately starts to slip, but she maintains her composure as Irmgard says, "Oh, so soon?"

Max doesn't smile. He knows what the women apparently don't. He knows that 'Special Action Group' is a neutered rendering of 'Einsatzgrüp'. Like Walther, he's well aware of what Einsatzgrüppen do. Max feels the tide of anger rising in him, fights against it, knows he shouldn't speak. But he does.

"He has to leave as soon as possible. The work is too important to delay." He swivels to face his brother, "Isn't that right, Walther?"

"That's right. Important work." Walther's tone is level, neutral, but he struggles to maintain his mood. He understands what Max is doing.

"Dangerous, is it? I hear some of those civilians can be ferocious. Still, it's not as though they've got weapons or anything. Unless you count teeth and nails. All the same, you'll need to be careful."

The two women are confused, their smiles gone, their understanding challenged. It's obvious something's happening, but neither of them know what. Their eyes flash back and forth between the brothers. Walther's face darkens with rage, with embarrassment, as he tries to remain calm. He is barely succeeding.

"Leave it, Max," he says tightly. "We do what we must do. I do what I'm ordered to. Just like you, so let's leave it at that."

Max feels like a puppet, like someone is pulling unseen strings, making him dance to a tune he doesn't want to hear, making him take steps he knows will end badly, making his mouth spout poison he wishes he could swallow instead.

"Yes, you're right, perhaps we should leave it. The girls don't want to hear about killing women and children, do they? Far too unpleasant . . ."

Walther is suddenly on his feet, hands clenched at his side in impotent rage, his face a reddened ball of fury.

"ENOUGH! NOT ANOTHER WORD, OR . . . I'll . . . I swear, I'll . . ." He fights to breathe normally, his chest heaves with emotion. His eyes swing wildly from side to side, taking in the startled, frightened faces of the two women. Then something inside him crests and breaks. His shoulders relax, his hands unclench. He locks eyes with Max. Then, with an inarticulate "Pah!" he stalks across the room and into the bedroom, slamming the door shut behind him.

Max hates himself for what he's said, can't meet the shocked and open-mouthed stares of Anni and Irmgard. He knows he's opened the floodgates of regret, fears he might drown in the resultant deluge.

9

The tail end of autumn can be bitter in Berlin. Icy blasts of northern wind can whip through the bone-bare trees, fling clouds of dead leaves into the faces of unwary pedestrians, send small children wailing into the arms of mothers or nannies. Not today. A still, sunny, surprisingly warm day. Pleasant enough at least for Walther Neumann to again call on his brother at the Imperial Police Praesidium and suggest they stroll home together from their S-Bahn station stop. Max suspects Walther's visit is less about the fine weather than it is a peace offering, that Walther is extending a fraternal hand to smooth over the tensions of last night. No matter either way – fine weather or the unspoken acceptance of an unspoken apology, Max welcomes the visit. His self-loathing has yet to abate.

As they round the corner into Pommersche Strasse the sound of raised voices reaches them, angry voices. About twenty metres ahead, in the recessed entrance to a pawnbroker's premises, a silver-haired old man in a faded grey overcoat is gesticulating, holding a scrap of paper in his right hand, jabbing the index finger of his left hand at it and repeating a phrase Max and Walther can't quite catch. The pawnbroker, or whoever he is, stands in the doorway making dismissive, shooing motions with his hand. He's much younger than the overcoated arguer, perhaps pushing forty, and much bigger. Dressed in dark trousers with braces and a striped shirt with rolled sleeves, he's running to fat. Misplaced vanity advertises itself in his back-swept and pomaded thick black hair and his extravagant Hindenburg moustache.

The old man suddenly stops gesticulating and stands with his hands at his sides. He seems to raise himself up as he says something to the pawnbroker. Whatever it is, it earns him a roundhouse slap to the side of his head, and he staggers sideways, nearly falling, a hand pressing against the hurt. The pawnbroker looks ready to launch another blow but hesitates at Max's shout.

"Kripo! What's going on here?"

Both men turn towards the noise. Both faces register first surprise, then naked fear. As the old man changes position, the yellow star sewn into the front of his coat comes into view. He drops his hand from his reddened cheek and ear, stands facing the approaching pair, but his eyes are locked on the young SS officer. The pawnbroker is staring open-mouthed at Walther, all belligerence drained from his features.

Now Max and Walther are right there, standing in front of the arguing men. Max's nose catches an unwanted waft of the pawnbroker's heavy pomade – violets, sickly.

"I asked what's going on. Why the shouting? Well?"

The pawnbroker drags his eyes away from the silent Walther to the less intimidating Max, swallows before speaking.

"It's nothing officer, nothing. This Jewish filth is trying to screw money out of me." The man hesitates, tries to read his audience. "Like they all do," he adds. "He wants to redeem a watch, that's all. Wants to pay less than we agreed. I've told him he either pays the full amount or he doesn't get his watch back."

"How much to redeem it?" Max hasn't paid any attention to the old Jew, has eyes only for the would-be Hindenburg.

"Two hundred marks. It's a fair price. Like I said, he's trying to screw me."

Max turns to the Jew, who's trembling, hands holding his hat in front of his waist, eyes down.

"Is this true? Well?"

The old man realises he's expected to say something. He takes a breath, raises his eyes, seems to find something in Max's face that gives him courage.

"No, sir, it is not. I have paid for the watch, but . . ." He points an accusing finger at the pawnbroker, ". . . this . . . this man has taken my money and refuses to return my property. I can not pay him twice, sir." Max is about to say something when the old man adds, defiant, "I *will* not pay him, sir."

"He has already paid you?" This to the increasingly confident pawnbroker, whose right hand fingers one waxed end of his moustache.

"Paid me?" he snorts. "The old cunt offered me a hundred marks. I told him to shove it up his arse. He pays the full price or he gets nothing."

Max turns to Walther, spreads his hands palm up.

"What can we do, Untersturmführer? How can we decide who tells the truth here? Perhaps you have a suggestion."

Walther frowns at first, unsure what his big brother is doing, what role he's expected to play. His frown fades as the events of last night are in an instant forgotten, sunk without trace in a flood of family bonds and shared experience, shared blood.

Both the pawnbroker and the Jew are holding their breath now, apprehensive, fearful, confused. If the SS is going to get involved, anything is possible. Walther's response justifies their fears. After initial hesitation, he plays along. By chance, his brother's behaviour presents an opportunity to once again parade the fear his black uniform generates.

"No need to decide, Kriminalkommissar," he says casually, as he waves his hand up and out. "Just shoot both of them."

Wide-eyed, the Jew and the pawnbroker flick their panicked gaze back and forth between Max and Walther. Max affects reluctance, conciliation, the voice of reason.

"That might be a little excessive in the circumstances, Untersturmführer. Perhaps there is a better way." He turns to the Jew. "Where is the redemption ticket?"

The old man is still clutching the paper stub, and he warily holds it up, allows Max to take it, waits for his reaction. Max stares at the small piece of paper as though it might give him the answers he needs. He hands it back to the Jew, turns to Walther.

"As he said, two hundred marks."

"Which the old bastard has to pay first," interjects the pawnbroker. "No money, no watch." He folds his arms.

"But I *have* paid, sir. I have. Please." The Jew is holding his hands together as though in prayer as he addresses Max. "I gave him the two hundred. Ten notes. It's all there."

"But this man swears you haven't paid," says Max. "How can we resolve . . ."

"It's in his pocket, sir! He put it there!" The Jew is pointing at the pawnbroker's chest. "In his shirt!"

Max slowly turns to the pawnbroker, whose eyes narrow, become wary, apprehensive.

"Show me what's in your shirt pocket," says Max evenly.

The pawnbroker blusters, panicked, evasive.

"This is . . . he's lying, officer. I don't have his money. I told you . . . the Yid's crazy. Surely . . ."

"The problem's easily solved. Empty your shirt pocket." Max takes a half-step closer to the man. Walther mirrors the action, moves off to one side, bracketing the pawnbroker between them. The man's eyes follow both movements simultaneously, darting back and forth. He's starting to sweat.

For a long moment everybody stands motionless, silent, all eyes on the hesitating pawnbroker.

"I won't ask again," says Max quietly.

Slowly the pawnbroker lifts his right hand to his shirt pocket, reaches two fingers in, and eases out a folded wad of red 20RM notes. Everybody can see Albrecht Dürer's distinctive portrait peering at them from the outermost note. The pawnbroker stands slack-jawed, staring at the notes as though they might suddenly attack him. The Jew points, starts to say something, but a raised hand from Max stops him.

"Count them."

The pawnbroker looks up to find Max's eyes boring into his. His hands are shaking as he lifts each note in turn, his voice is hoarse, quavering. He counts slowly, clearly, like a very small child trying to impress the grown-ups.

"One . . . two . . . three . . ."

He reaches ten and stops. There are no more notes. He holds the wad out towards Max, who takes it, stands staring at the terrified man for several seconds before speaking again.

"Get the watch."

The pawnbroker is deflated, defeated, his mind turned only to avoiding a beating, arrest, jail, any of the consequences which usually flow from a Kripo contact, let alone with an SS Untersturmführer along for the ride. He disappears into the darkened interior of the shop, is back within seconds holding a large silver pocket watch, well-used, with a gold or brass chain-ring at the top. He hands it to Max, who passes it to the Jew.

"Yours?"

The old man takes the watch, examines the scratched glass cover, turns it over and inspects the leaf-engraved rear, then looks up and nods.

"It was my father's."

Max hands him the wad of Reichsmarks. The old man frowns at the proffered notes, puzzled, hesitates to take them.

"Go on," says Max. "it's your money." Then, turning to the pawnbroker, "Alright?"

A resigned, sweaty nod, nothing more.

"Good. Then there is no longer a problem. You," he says, as he points to the pawnbroker, "back inside. You," this time to the Jew, "don't let me see you around here again. Go."

In seconds, Max and Walther are alone on the footpath watching the old Jew shuffling towards the gated entrance of the nearby Preussen Park. The pair resume their interrupted journey in silence. After fifty metres, Walther can no longer restrain himself. His voice is incredulous.

"Since when have you been a Jew lover? Has Kripo policy been turned upside down?"

There's a long pause before Max replies, his face thoughtful.

"There are some things I just can't let go unpunished, little brother. Hindenburg moustaches are one of them."

10

"I can understand why the Americans call their police detectives 'gumshoes'. They'd need them – doing this all day would be murder. It must be why Mickey Spillane's cops don't seem to get sore feet."

"Flatfoots," says Neumann.

"What?"

"That's what we are. Flatfoots. Cops are flatfoots, private detectives are gumshoes, like Mike Hammer. Gum, soft rubber on their soles, easy to walk, quieter than leather. My father calls them 'brothel-creepers'. Used to, anyway."

"Call them what you like, I'd still rather be in the car."

"Any more complaining and I'll make you walk all the way back to the Alex. Come on, it's only a couple of kilometres. The women won't steal the car."

Schneider doesn't bite back. He's the one who instigated their stop at a food stall set up on the side of the road, managing at the same time to bemoan the absence these days of all the Jewish bakers with their babka bagels and bialys. He settled instead for the pair of weathered old women with their ancient two-wheeled cart selling bratwurst, warm pastries and coffee, a tiny iron brazier slung beneath the cart to heat things up. Both men marvel at the women's resourcefulness in obtaining coal from God-only-knows where. After they finish their pastries and coffees in the Opel, it's Neumann who suggests going the rest of the way on foot – 'to walk off the food'. Schneider's protests are more about preserving his image than a serious objection. A token effort, just to maintain consistency of approach.

The pair head towards Ohmstrasse and a rendezvous with the dead priest, Rochlitz. Despite the slow segue from autumn towards winter, the day invites walking. A cloudless powder blue roof over Berlin, enough warmth in the lowering sun to take the chill out of a light wind from the west. They encounter a fat striped cat stretched out on top of a stone garden wall. Its eyes open and follow the pair until they pass, then close again. In Caspar Strasse, on the windowless side of an apartment building, they come upon a huge painted sign spruiking shoes by the Dorndorf-Schuhfabrik company in Zweibrucken. The central motif is a hiker with a backpack and conspicuously shiny Dorndorf outdoor boots, who smilingly proclaims 'They're the most comfortable of all!' to an invisible companion. Neumann and Schneider pass within touching distance of the sign. Neither man comments.

As they round the corner of Caspar Strasse and turn into Nonnendammallee, Schneider spots the familiar head of Achilles peering toward them from behind a rubbish bin. The dog's nearly fifty metres away, sitting stone still, watching, waiting. Another fifty metres or so further on, Dolf Schliemann and his trolley are disappearing into a clothing shop doorway. Schneider says nothing until he and Neumann are about fifteen metres from Achilles, when he abruptly flings out a restraining arm against Neumann's chest and stops dead.

"Hold it. Dog. There, up ahead. The thing looks vicious."

Neumann lifts his eyes, sees the dog, frowns.

"It's just a dog. Doesn't look savage to me. Let's . . ."

He starts to move forward again, and again Schneider raises a restraining arm.

"No, boss. Trust me, this one's a killer." As he speaks, Schneider stands legs apart, one foot back, lifts his arms half-up. "Get behind me, boss. I'll handle this."

"Come on, Kurt, it's not . . ."

Neumann's words die in his mouth as he sees Achilles emerge from behind the rubbish bin, stand for a moment with eyes locked on Schneider, then launch himself towards them. Neumann opens his mouth in surprise, moves to one side of Schneider, starts to reach for his pistol.

It's all over in a few seconds, and Schneider is spinning around clutching a slavering tail-wagging Achilles, rubbing the dog's coat, thumping its chest, man and dog both grinning with delight. Neumann's mouth is still open, taken entirely by surprise. He can't get out the obvious question, just watches in something close to amazement. Schneider puts Achilles down, keeps a hand on the dog's neck, continues to pat his chest.

"Meet my mate Achilles, boss. Go on, give him a pat. He's an old softie, no biting."

Neumann bends, rubs Achilles behind the ear a few times, runs a hand along his back. The dog's tail is thrashing. The two men raise their heads as postman Schliemann draws up. Introductions are made, Achilles is patted some more, then everybody continues on their journeys. Neumann waits until they've gone another fifty metres before speaking.

"There's a joke in here somewhere, isn't there? A postman called Schliemann with a dog called Achilles. Do you want to tell me the real story, or is the Reichspost recruiting only classicists these days?"

They're almost at the corner of Ohmstrasse before

Neumann finally but reluctantly accepts that there's nothing more in the situation than his partner has explained – just a Reichspostman with an idiosyncratic sense of humour. They turn into the street, quickly locate Father Rochlitz's apartment block nearly a hundred metres further along, number 156-162. In front of it, a couple of scarecrow boys about nine or ten are kicking a scuffed football back and forth. One of them sees the two Kripos approaching, gathers up the ball, and says something to his friend, who spins around to look. The pair dart into a nearby alley and disappear from view.

For several long seconds Neumann and Schneider stand on the footpath scrutinising the dingy brick building in front of them, momentarily silent as they absorb the depressing spectacle. A cheaply built apartment block on the Siemens Electrical Estate, the neglect of the war years evident in peeling paint, chipped plasterwork, green-tinged tarnish on the brass backplates of the entrance doors. Schneider lifts a huge right hand to quizzically scratch the top of his head.

"You'd think the company could afford to keep the place a bit better than this. They've got enough slave labour. Surely they could spare a few Ivans or Poles to tidy up."

"I doubt it. Too busy putting radios together, I expect. Or making sure the Panzers don't run out of dynamos and batteries. Priorities, Kurt, priorities. We don't want our gallant soldiers to run short of equipment, do we?"

"I'd be more concerned about our gallant equipment running short of soldiers, the way the Russian Front chews them up. How many Ivans have we killed or captured? One million? Two million? God knows. And they still keep coming. How many millions of them are there, anyway? The way things are going every woman in Germany will need to be popping babies out like kittens. Either that, or we run out of recruits."

Neumann slaps him on the back, starts towards the drab

entrance door.

“Cheer up, Kurt. We’ll be in Moscow before Christmas, Adolf says. So it must be true.”

Despite himself, Schneider casts a look around. The wrong person hears a remark like that, and you might find yourself on the receiving end of a formal Gestapo summons to attend their offices and explain your ‘asocial remarks’. That’s if you’re lucky. If you’re not, you’ll be heading for the Russian Front. Or taken into ‘protective custody’, a blackly ironic description of arbitrary arrest and incarceration from which few emerge alive. He follows Neumann into the building.

There’s no lift, so the two men trudge up concrete stairs into the familiar apartment fragrance of decay, mould and boiled cabbage. On the second floor there’s a small landing. Corridors extend in each direction, parallel to the street frontage. Near the end of one, on a couple of wooden crates, sit two Ordnungspolizei in their distinctive green uniforms. They’re Grüne Polizei to some, Green Police, but most people go for the easier and shorter Orpos. Call them what you like, they’re everywhere – emergency services, fire brigades, civil defence, coast guard. Even in some police battalions seeing active service, at least to the extent of guarding prisoners, ‘resettling’ Poles and Jews, exterminating undesirables. Nonetheless, Orpos still jump whenever anybody from the Reich Central Security Office appears, even if it’s only a couple of low-ranking Kripos. So at the sight of Neumann and Schneider the waiting men get to their feet, stub out their cigarettes, stand at motionless attention as the two investigators approach. The wooden truncheons hanging from the front of their belts continue to wobble about regardless, like wayward erections.

Neumann notices both Orpos have the same plain shoulder insignia. They are Unterwachtmeisters, pavement plodders. If this was London instead of Berlin, they’d be called Bobbies and be wearing tall cork helmets. Their respectful stance tells Neumann they know he's Kripo, but not how senior. It's of no importance.

"Good afternoon, boys. Everything all right?"

As he speaks, Neumann pulls out his warrant disc and holds it up for inspection. The two Orpos glance at it. They're both young. The older of the pair, although only by a few years, is the spokesman for both of them.

"Yes, sir. Nothing's happened since we came on duty. Our Wachtmeister told us to stand here and make sure nobody went in until you arrived."

"And nobody has been in yet? Not even you?"

"No, sir. The door was shut when we arrived. We haven't opened it." He leans forward, lowers his voice. "There's a body in there. Dead."

"They often are," says Neumann as he moves to the door and grabs the handle. "Stay here while we take a look." He pushes the door open, stands back to let Schneider past, closes it behind him, leaving two relieved Orpos standing in the corridor.

Now the aroma isn't of decay and cooking. Now it's the smell of death. There's no blood to speak of, just a few smears on the pale bruised face of the old man sitting bound in an armchair.

"Jesus Christ! Look at this!"

Schneider's exclamation isn't sparked by the sight of the dead priest – he's seen enough bodies to be unmoved by one more. But he hasn't seen any apartments in a state like this. Someone has methodically destroyed it. Every stick of furniture is in pieces, drawers removed, contents strewn, sideboard and dining chairs upturned. The armchairs are slashed along every seam, stuffing and fabric protruding like entrails. The remains of a half-assembled carriage clock lie on a small bare table next to an upturned jeweller's lathe. Everywhere the linoleum has been taken up to expose bare concrete, curtains pulled down and their linings slashed open. The priest's radio is in pieces. Every book in his small collection has been pulled from the bookcase and now lies on the floor, pages riffled. Hardcovered books have had their inside covers slashed and prised open. Even the light fittings are in pieces on the floor, only the bare bulbs still intact in the ceiling. At first glance, the sole undamaged object is a glass-domed skeleton clock on the mantelpiece, untouched presumably because it's incapable of concealing anything.

Neumann is silent for several seconds as he scans the scene, drinks in a spectacle unprecedented in his experience. "This," he finally says, waving his hand to encompass the room, "is what we in the trade call a fucking mess."

The pair move carefully across the debris littering the floor until they stand in front of the open bedroom door. The state of the room mirrors the rest of the apartment. Bed linen strewn about, the mattress cut along every seam and half its stuffing removed, the kapok clumps and strands settling on the floor like lumpy snowflakes. Two paintings have been removed from the wall, their backing papers stripped and ripped away. A bedside cabinet is upturned, its drawers out, contents spilled onto the floor, the cheap clock once on it now smashed and ripped apart on the floor. A glossy porcelain statue of Jesus on the Cross, apparently once hanging above the bed, lies in pieces underfoot.

Without a word, Neumann and Schneider turn around and move to the end of the main room which serves as the kitchen. Every utensil is out of the cupboards, on the floor. The oven is partially dismantled, its door removed, its shelves on the floor. Through an open door to the bathroom, the two men see a similar scene of disarray and destruction.

"You're more experienced than me, Kriminalkommissar Neumann," says Schneider, "so you might have a different view, but in my opinion someone was looking for something here."

“Seems that way,” muses Neumann, “seems that way. Question is, did he find it? Or does he now sigh the lack of many a thing he sought?”

The last remark earns him a reproving sideways glance from Schneider.

“One of the sonnets,” Neuman adds. “Number thirty.”

Schneider rolls his eyes, turns towards the dead man.

“Shall we take a look?”

11

Neumann pops two aspirin in his mouth, tilts his head back, gulps down a glass of water from the jug on his desk. He shifts position in his office chair, tries to lessen the sudden sharp back pain, glad Schneider's not there to crack his jokes about advancing old age or excessive matrimonial indulgence. A sudden knock on the open door catches him mid-position. There's a moment of embarrassment when he realises it looks like he's easing out a fart.

It's his shared secretary again, Fräulein Üffing, her demeanour almost respectful as she knocks. The second time in two days, it crosses his mind. Perhaps there's something he's unaware of. Has he suddenly acquired sex appeal? Gravitas?

"Yes, Helene? What is it?"

"A visitor for you, Kriminalkommissar. At the front desk. He says he knows you." She leans forward, lowers her voice, conspiratorial. "An American!"

For a few moments Neumann is disoriented, frowns. An American? He doesn't know any . . . His head jerks up. "Do you have his name?"

"The front desk says he is Herr Forbes."

Neumann is on his feet and moving towards the door, pushing past a startled Fräulein Üffing as he throws a 'Thank you, Helene' over his shoulder and heads downstairs at close to a trot. Reaching the passage door leading into the main hall he stops, composes himself, straightens his tie, buttons his jacket. Then he steps out into the hall, looks towards the waiting area, sees the man he is hoping is there. The waiting man spots Neumann at the same moment and raises both arms out and up as he starts forward.

"Max!"

It's Harry Forbes, the American who shared Neumann's Cambridge days for three years, two foreigners adrift in a foreign land as they struggled with the intricacies of Elizabethan England on their way to Bachelors of Arts. Harry Forbes, handsome, monied, athletic, irrepressible and popular. Neumann fell short at some of those hurdles, but Forbes carried him along regardless, and together they navigated the treacherous waters of academic discipline and English class structure. And now, here he is, here in the heart of the Alex, in the middle of a war, thousands of miles from home. The reason is unimportant for now. What matters is that he's here.

Neumann strides towards his visitor, and they meet in the middle of the public area in a handshaking backslapping greeting that teeters on the edge of becoming a hug. Forbes stands back, grabs Neumann's shoulders, holds him at arm's length as he runs an inspecting eye up and down. He still has his schoolboy's floppy fringe of dark hair falling over his eyes, still gives the familiar flick of the head to clear his vision. He's grinning as he gives Neumann a friendly shake.

"Just look at you! Max Neumann – Kriminalkommissar! We're a long way from Cambridge, Max."

Neumann responds in English, does his best to affect a

theatrical stage Englishman's diction.

"Now, Harry, whence come you?"

They've shared similar moments in the past. Forbes has heard the phrase before, hesitates a moment before snapping his fingers and replying.

"Henry the Fourth. Am I right? I am, aren't I? You haven't changed, Max. Whence come I? From the Embassy, of course. I've been posted. Goodbye Washington, hello Berlin!" He leans forward furtively. "Just in case you're thinking – I'm not a spy. Just a State Department cultural officer Grade Two. So your secrets are safe with me. Ah, Christ!" he exclaims, "where are my manners? I've got a present for you. Here."

Forbes lifts the midnight blue leather satchel he's carrying, a gold and paler blue embassy crest on its flap. Reaching in, he pulls out a heavy flat package in brown paper, about two hand spans square, offers it to Neumann with a grin.

"Nigger jazz," he says triumphantly, "Count Basie, Louis Armstrong, Duke Ellington, a couple of others. I know how hard it is to get that stuff here."

Neumann knows too. Knows how the Party abhors 'negro jazz', or anything else to do with negroes. The policy hardened after that black American athlete, Owens, won four gold medals at the Berlin Olympics five years ago, humiliating the 'Aryan' supermen pitched against him. Not that any of it matters to Neumann. He likes most jazz, still can't understand how you can tell negro jazz apart from any other jazz. He takes the proffered package as Forbes lays an extended finger along his nose a couple of times. "Diplomatic bag, of course."

Neumann opens his mouth to speak, stops as Forbes continues without a break.

"Can we go somewhere? We've got a lot to talk about, catching up to do. Have a beer or coffee or something. How long has it been, anyway?"

Neumann just nods, smiling. No need to speak – he's used to Harry doing most of the talking.

12

In any other circumstance, Kriminalrat Franz Böhm would think the situation risible, bizarre. About fifteen metres in front of him is a tall fat man seated behind an enormous carved oak desk, its front boasting hunters on horseback pursuing a deer through an intricately-detailed forest. The seated man is wearing knee-length black leather britches from beneath which thick dark grey stockings protrude and disappear into soft black leather shoes. A dark green collarless suede jacket, tightly buttoned, is matched by a green Tyrolean hat complete with brush held by a corded band. At least the hat is sitting on the desk, not on the man's head. Böhm assumes the outfit is meant to be traditional *Junker* hunting costume. Two blue-grey uniformed Luftwaffe NCOs stand stiffly beside the desk, slightly to the rear.

The fat man is preoccupied, semi-reclining in a high-backed swivel chair, a lion cub on his lap, its front paws held in his hands. The animal is as big as a bulldog, seems uninterested in anything but trying to lick the fat man's face. He taunts it, coming closer, then pulling back, holdings its paws to keep it at face level.

Just getting to this point, the inner sanctum of *Carinhall*, has taken over an hour of fast driving north-east from Berlin, the last kilometre or so along a winding track through more than 40,000 hectares of hunting estate surrounding the Minister's residence. Then an escorted walk through the central hall, baronial in the extreme with its huge oak beams supporting an A-shaped ceiling above suits of armour, mounted heads of deer and boar, massively solid furniture, tapestries and dark paintings lining the walls.

The room Böhm has just entered, much smaller than the central hall, is nonetheless cavernous, ornate, oppressive in its excesses. The high ceiling is coffered, carved in a vaguely Renaissance style, complemented with heavily scalloped cornices. The walls are covered in paintings, mostly oils, and Böhm thinks he recognises some Dutch masters among them. Huge marble sculptures line the wall behind the desk, bronze busts sit on pedestals in each corner of the room. The attendant who admitted Böhm shuts the office door behind him as he retreats. Böhm starts towards the desk. The carpet is so thick it feels like he's walking in beach sand. He's a few paces in when the seated man notices him, looks up, beams and bellows a greeting.

"Franz! My friend! So good of you to come."

Kriminalrat Böhm stops, stands to attention, raises his arm in the approved manner.

"Heil Hitler!"

The seated man repositions the lion cub as he stands, a hand beneath its chest, the other one holding the nape of its neck as he passes it to one of the Luftwaffe men who takes the animal and disappears with it through a side door. Lion-free, a still beaming Reichsmarschall Hermann Göring raises his right hand in something resembling an approved salute.

"Heil Hitler," he responds casually. "Now, then, my good man, come and sit with me. We will have coffee. Thank you for journeying all this way to see me. Come, come."

Göring moves to the left of the room where there are three burgundy sofas arranged in a 'U' around a low dark wood table with an inset stone top. He gestures to the remaining uniformed man, who immediately leaves the room. The Reichsmarschall flops heavily into one of the sofas, waves an inviting hand at the adjacent one.

"Sit, Franz, please. Talk with me, won't you."

Böhm is dressed in a sober brown suit, and he undoes the coat buttons as he takes the sofa next to Göring's, placing his hat beside him. He sits, knees together, hands on his thighs and waits for Göring to speak. He's known the Reichsmarschall since 1933, worked under him when Göring created the Geheime Staatspolizei, the Gestapo, in that year. His loyalty to his old boss hasn't wavered since then, despite the Gestapo and every other German police function falling into Heinrich Himmler's ravenous clutches. He's never felt anything other than affection and trust for the Reichsmarschall, and Göring has rewarded him with reciprocal loyalty. Göring is amicable, even jovial, in Böhm's company, but Kriminalrat Böhm is nonetheless always respectful, diffident, acutely aware of the chasm of rank which lies between the two men. So he waits.

Göring rubs pudgy hands together, leans forward and smiles at Böhm, raises his eyebrows.

"Your message said there was something I would be interested to learn. Tell me, Franz, what morsel have you for me? I know you won't disappoint."

At close quarters, Böhm detects the unmistakeable waft of Scherk's Tarr pomade. He knows it's also favoured by Goebbels, so, given Göring's frequent references to 'the Poisoned Dwarf' and 'the Crippled Megaphone', he's surprised that the Reichsmarschall is using the same concoction. He ignores his nostrils.

"Thank you, sir. It may be nothing. On its own, I would not have bothered you, but there has been a development . . . It may be the two things are connected. That is why I asked to see you."

Göring exudes geniality, interest, concern, sits back on the sofa and crosses his legs.

"You have my attention, Franz. Please tell me more."

"One of my informants contacted me yesterday. He was sizing up a house on Ohmstrasse a couple of nights ago, standing in the shadows, just thinking about the best way to break in. He saw someone arrive in a car. It was Standartenführer Schmidt."

The Reichsmarschall's head jerks up at the name. Schmidt the Creeping Death, Himmler's attack dog. The stories about him, rumours as much as anything, are legion. Even if only half of them are true . . .

"Schmidt! What did your man see?"

"Well, sir, that's the thing. He didn't see anything much, just Schmidt getting out of his car and going into a building, apartments. He had his case with him. As I said, if it had just been that sighting, I wouldn't have bothered you . . ."

"And there was nothing else? Schmidt just went into the building? Did he come out again?"

"I don't know, sir. My informant didn't stay there. He didn't want to be anywhere near whatever was going on."

Göring nods thoughtfully, agrees with the sense of that decision. If they have a choice in the matter, sane people don't go anywhere near Standartenführer Schmidt.

"You said there was something else."

"Sir. The apartments are where a priest was murdered that night. He was discovered bound, tortured."

"A priest? What would Schmidt want . . . Was he anybody of note?" Göring answers his own question. "No, I suppose not.

Not if he was living on the Siemens Electrical estate. So, why would the Creeping Death be bothering with a poor priest? Do you have any thoughts about that, Franz?"

The opening of a side door and the entry of a plump maid bearing a laden tray halts Böhm's reply. Göring turns towards the woman, waves a bejewelled hand at the serving table in front of the sofa.

"Thank you, Gerda, thank you. Here, please."

The two men wait while the woman sets the tray down, places two coffees on the table, milk, cream, sugar, and a small plate of pastries. She gives a hesitant bob as she leaves without a word. Göring gestures towards the cups.

"Take your coffee first, Franz. It won't be too hot. Gerda knows I don't like waiting for mine to cool."

As Böhm pours milk and stirs his coffee, Göring reaches into his inside coat pocket, brings out a small flat silver box, and takes from it a brown pill which he pops in his mouth before sipping his coffee. Böhm knows it's Pervitin. He's never felt the need for it, but hundreds of thousands of his countrymen do, apparently requiring extra energy, less sleep, and whatever other benefits the pills provide. These days you need a prescription to buy it, but that doesn't seem to have made a dent in demand. It occurs to Böhm that Pervitin became regulated under the Reich's Opium Law less than a week after the Wehrmacht invaded Russia, and he idly wonders about coincidence. He watches Göring, waits. Göring puts his coffee down, makes a rolling 'continue' motion with his hand.

"Yes, Franz. Your thoughts?"

"I don't know what to make of it, sir, but just the fact that Standartenführer Schmidt is involved . . . Well, that's enough to set alarm bells going. He must be acting on Reichsführer Himmler's authority, but as to what . . ." He holds up his hands, shrugs before continuing. "But then, just this morning, I found out that one of my men has been assigned to the murder, Kriminalkommissar Neumann. To investigate it. He . . ."

Göring interrupts. "You say he was *assigned.* By who? Don't you assign your own men?"

"That's the thing, I normally do. But Neumann was called in by Reichskriminaldirektor Tanzinger. He made the assignment, not me. I only found out about it when his adjutant told me this morning."

Now Göring is frowning, sits forward, elbows on his knees, coffee forgotten. He looks off to one side for a moment as though the answer to his queries lies there, then straightens and focuses on his visitor, rubs his chin with thumb and forefinger. For a moment he seems lost in thought, staring through Böhm as he ponders the implications of the Kriminalrat's report.

"This is . . . strange. Very strange." Göring brightens, sits forward and picks up his coffee. "Well, one thing is certain. If that devious bastard Himmler is behind the murder, it's going to be to nobody's advantage but his own. Let's see what the little man is up to. You can make some enquiries, Franz? Subtle, of course. We don't want Himmler finding out. Or Schmidt. Be careful, Franz. If Schmidt even thinks . . . Well, you know."

Böhm nods. He knows very well.

"I'll see what I can find out, sir. Leave it to me."

Göring smiles benevolently as he gets up from the sofa, prompting Böhm to do the same.

"Thank you, Franz," he says as he accompanies the other man to the office door. They exchange a Hitler salute, Böhm leaves, and Göring walks slowly back to his desk, sits, stares thoughtfully into space for a minute. Then he picks up the earpiece of one of the two black Siemens and Halske telephones on his desk and dials a number.

✠

Standartenführer Schmidt, as usual, has left his SS uniform in the wardrobe. He's dressed in a dark brown suit, white shirt, muted red tie, tan leather wingtips. There's a homburg on his head and a small leather case in his right hand. He stands outside the rectory of St Norbert's church in Schöneberg, sheltering under a tree from the light drizzle which has just started to fall. For a few minutes he is motionless apart from the sweep of his head back and forth along Reppichstrasse, looking for movement, for anything which shouldn't be there, or for something which isn't but should be. The street is deserted, dark, still. Near one end he can just make out the top of the Rathaus tower a few hundred metres away. Satisfied that all is as it should be, he turns to face the red brick rectory, scrutinises the vaguely Gothic façade with its tall narrow windows, steeply pitched slate roof, then walks to the studded black door and raps three times with the knocker.

Within a few seconds, steps from within the rectory come closer, a light flickers on in the entry hall, then the door opens to reveal a thin, grey-haired man in his fifties wearing a black cassock, a purple stole over his shoulders. He's not long since taken confession. He smiles uncertainly at his visitor.

"Yes, can I help you?"

Stefan Schmidt briefly lifts his hat from his head, nods towards the priest.

"Good evening, Father Dassler. I am Herr Kempner, from the Reich Central Security Office. May I be permitted to speak with you, please?"

Nearly a hundred metres away, standing just inside an alley running off Reppichstrasse, is a nondescript man in a dark brown trench coat and flat cap over thinning blonde hair. As Schmidt disappears through the doorway of the rectory, the man lowers a small pair of AEG night-vision binoculars. He slips the binoculars inside his trench coat, where they hang from a strap around his neck, then takes a notebook and pencil from a side pocket and writes for a minute or so. Replacing the notebook, he turns his collar up against a steady drizzle and slowly starts towards the rectory.

13

He's lost count of how many times he's done it, but every time it's as though he's never done it before. Every time, the stench is like a fist in the face, followed up by one in the guts, a vicious cocktail of odours – carbolic acid, chlorine, soap, urine, faeces, blood. And over it all, seemingly infused into the very structure of the room, is the smell of raw meat. Neumann steels himself, sets his jaw, and pushes through the glass-panelled door into the heart of darkness. Behind him, infuriatingly nonchalant, Schneider follows.

The police morgue in the basement of the Charité Hospital on Hannoveresche Strasse in Mitte is like morgues everywhere. A polished concrete floor with drain holes at regular intervals, glossy dark blue tiles lining the walls to ceiling height, banks of fluorescent lights grouped over four long stainless steel tables with their own drainage pipes running down to the floor. Gleaming metal implements hang along one wall above a room-wide stainless steel benchtop inset with taps and sinks. Depressing, unlovely, practical. This is a room dedicated to one purpose only – the investigation of death.

Neumann's entry makes a dry door hinge squeal in protest, and the noise in turn triggers a raised head from the man writing on a clipboard next to one of the stainless steel tables. He's small, perhaps a hundred and sixty centimetres on his tip toes. He has to be at least sixty, but he carries himself like a young man, moves fluidly, erect, alert. Thinning light brown hair, a studious thoughtful face and a trim greying beard and thick moustache combine to make him look like what he is, a Professor of Medicine. Were it not for the fact that since the first of January 1939 Jews in Germany have been banned from practising medicine, or anything else for that matter, Neumann would swear he was looking at that famous Jew, the psychiatrist Sigmund Freud. It would have been a coincidence too far, Neumann thinks, if the man had looked like his even more famous namesake, the Renaissance painter, Albrecht Dürer.

Professor Otto Dürer's face comes alive when he sees who's in the doorway, and he raises a hand in greeting.

"Max! Come in, come in. And Kurt also! This is most pleasant." He beams at the men, says, "God's greeting to both of you" in the traditional Bavarian way. No Hitler salutes today from anyone in the room.

Neumann and Schneider offer up their own greetings, walk over to the professor and shake his hand. Both of them keep their eyes averted from the cadaver on the table behind Dürer, avoid looking at the gaping Y-shaped incision running from both its shoulders down to the groin, ignore the black emptiness beneath the incision. Neither man wants to contemplate what indignities have been visited upon Father Rochlitz since they last saw him.

Professor Dürer understands the effect of his trade on civilians. As soon as hands have been shaken he extends his arms and shepherds the two Kripos towards double brown doors with portholes at the far end of the room.

"Come, gentlemen, we'll be more comfortable in my office.

You know the way," he says. He doesn't need to hear their sighs to know their relief.

As they walk away from the dead priest, Professor Dürer shrugs off his grey laboratory coat, revealing a black satin waistcoat tightly buttoned over his crisp white shirt and plain red bow tie, black trousers with grey pinstriping beneath. Everything is fitted, tailored, immaculate. Dapper doesn't even begin to describe it.

The professor's office reflects its occupant – small, organised, tidy, stylish. There are two unpadded Biedermeier wooden chairs in front of the leather-topped desk behind which Dürer moves as he motions to the others to sit. He leans back in his swivel chair, contemplates the two men.

"I regret that ours will be a short meeting, gentlemen. In part it is because I am required elsewhere in just a few minutes. Were it not so, I would welcome the opportunity to share with you some real coffee I have come by." He taps an extended finger on the side of his nose as he speaks. "A friend of a grateful friend. Alas, it can not be. The other reason behind my ungracious haste is that I have very little to tell you about the late Father Rochlitz. As you will already have surmised, he was struck quite hard on the left side of his face not long before he died. I doubt the blow was sufficient to render him unconscious. Dazed, certainly, given his age. The rope tied to his arms you already know about. But you may not have seen the burn in his left ear. It is . . ."

"In his *ear*?" It's Schneider, his voice questioning, sceptical.

"Indeed, in his ear. The inner ear has suffered a significant burn, second-degree in my opinion."

Neumann is frowning. "It doesn't sound accidental. So . . ."

"No, most certainly not accidental. Someone inserted something hot into the ear. It burned the perimeter of the auditory meatus, the ear canal, but did not reach as far as the tympanic membrane. In the absence of any evidence to the contrary, it is my surmise someone inserted a lit cigarette into the priest's ear and held it there. I can think of no other source of the injury."

"I take it that neither the blow to his face nor the burn would have killed him, Professor."

"Quite so, Max. He died of, if one might say it in these circumstances, 'natural causes'. A heart attack, nothing more, nothing less. He was living on borrowed time, and that time ran out. Without inflicting Latin terms upon you, I can say that his heart was already severely compromised by hardened and thickened arteries. In one of them part of the wall broke away, a large clot, and it completely blocked the artery. Death was inevitable. It would have been almost immediate."

"The cause of the attack, sir?" Schneider's eyebrows are up.

"Ah, that is more difficult. It may have been pure chance. These things are quite unpredictable. It may have been physical exertion, psychological stress, shock if you will. Certainly there is a reasonable possibility that being struck and subsequently tortured would have played a role." Dürer spreads his hands, palms up. "Beyond that, however, there is nothing useful I can add. Whoever tied him up and injured him may not have intended to kill the poor man. He may have been as surprised as the victim. And now, I do beg your pardon," he says as he rises to his feet, "but I must leave you. Please," he adds, waving a hand in a downwards motion, "sit awhile to think your thoughts. There is no need for you to leave until you are ready."

The professor moves picks up a folder from his desk, moves to Neumann and Schneider and shakes their hands in turn.

"Until next time, gentlemen, thank you. Goodbye."

✠

"It's good of you to see us at such short notice, Father," says Neumann unctuously. "We realise that a man in an important position like yours has many other calls on his time."

Neumann continues the shameless flattery and false deference he and Schneider have been laying on with a trowel since arriving at the rectory of St Albertus Magnus. Father Rudolf Kroehl seems oblivious to mockery or sycophancy. He basks in the warmth of attention from the two Kriminalpolizei, plays the gracious host who deigns to deal with his inferiors.

A sour-faced old woman has grudgingly acceded to the priest's request for refreshments and brought in three coffees and a tray of small plain biscuits. Everybody present knows the 'coffee' will have been brewed from anything but actual coffee beans. To Schneider the biscuits look suspiciously like communion wafers, but he eats several of the crumbly dry offerings anyway.

Both Kripos have independently reached the same conclusion about Father Kroehl as had the late Father Andreas Rochlitz – he's a supercilious young fool. Kroehl is not unhandsome, with thick black hair cut short, a regular if bland face, and a thirty year-old's athletic build and movement. Yet he effortlessly manages to infuse both his words and his facial expressions with condescension, arrogance, sufferance.

"One can always put aside important work to help the police, Kriminalkommissar," says Kroehl patronisingly. "We men of God are here to serve, you know."

"Of course, Father, thank you," says Neumann, stifling both a smile and a desire to slap the priest. "We will try not to take up any more of your valuable time than is necessary." He ignores Kroehl's hand gesture of gracious acquiescence. "Perhaps you could tell us something of the late Father Rochlitz. What he was like, who were his friends and family, that sort of thing."

"Yes, of course." Father Kroehl steeples his fingers under

his chin and gazes heavenwards for several seconds before responding. Neumann thinks someone must have told him the pose looks dignified, thoughtful, mature. It doesn't. Schneider takes another of the thin flavourless biscuits. His 'coffee' is getting cold.

"Father Rochlitz was a model priest – hardworking, devout, modest in his habits and demeanour, a lovely man. I really can think of no reason someone would wish to hurt him. None at all. He was, after all, as am I, a man of peace. A man of God."

"And yet," says Neumann, "someone *did* hurt him. Kill him. Can you think of any reason why that might have happened?"

"I can not, my son. It is one of God's mysteries, sent to test us, I am certain."

Neumann tries to waltz around the useless platitudes. "Did he have friends or family? Anyone who was close to him?"

"I understand his parents are long dead, Kriminalkommissar, and I am unaware of any siblings." Father Kroehl again steeples his fingers in contemplation before continuing. "No, I believe his only close friends were myself and Frau Konrads." Seeing the incomprehension in his visitors' faces he adds, waving his hand towards the interior of the rectory, "She brought us refreshments."

"Had he been here very long, your worship?" Schneider has stopped eating, deliberately uses the flatteringly wrong form of address. Kroehl either doesn't notice or chooses to accept it.

"For only a few years, I am afraid. Would that it could have been longer. Ah, but it was not to be." Kroehl sighs theatrically, lifts his gaze towards the ceiling.

"And before that?"

"He was . . ." Kroehl hesitates, concentrates. "He served in various roles. I would need to look in our records to be precise about locations and dates."

Neumann and Schneider swap glances. The insufferable priest's touted 'close friendship' with Rochlitz apparently doesn't extend to knowledge about the old man's past. Kroehl brightens before he continues.

"Of course, he was something of a wandering gypsy since the terrible fire at Saint Lambertus. The one in, let me think . . . in twenty-eight. Yes, it was in nineteen twenty-eight. After that, sadly, we struggled to find him a suitable home." Kroehl makes it sound as though for the past thirteen years he has personally wrestled with the problem of relocating Father Rochlitz.

"Saint Lambertus?"

"In Moabit, Kriminalkommissar. It was totally destroyed. Only by God's good grace were Father Rochlitz and the others spared. But the building itself, all its beautiful works, its treasures, its records, everything was lost to the flames. Rebuilding has not been possible, I'm afraid. The government, the war, other considerations . . ."

Kroehl trails off, perhaps wondering if it is impolitic to refer even indirectly to the oppressive anticlerical actions of the Nazi government, the creeping subordination of the Church to Party needs, the increasing persecution of the Catholic clergy.

"So there is nobody Father Rochlitz would have turned to, nobody close to him, nobody he would confide in. Is that the case, Father?"

Kroehl sighs, world-weary, caring, saddened. "Only me, I am afraid. It may sound strange, but I believe he thought of me as a sort of father figure, a confessor perhaps."

It's all Neumann can do to choke down a snort of disbelief.

"Yes, of course. And did he confide in you anything that might have a bearing on his death?"

"Ah, well, here I must ponder for a moment." Kroehl's face assumes a look of beatific concentration for several seconds before he speaks again. "You understand that anything said in formal confession is sacrosanct, Kriminalkommissar. I am unable to reveal anything of that nature. Outside of the confessional, however, I can inform you that Father Rochlitz did not tell me anything which could possibly have been connected to his death."

"And did you offer him formal confession, Father?" Schneider's face is open, ingenuous, artless.

"Ah. Yes, I see . . . Well . . ." Schneider stifles his satisfaction as Kroehl's face colours with embarrassment. The priest struggles to find the words he wants. "Not . . . perhaps not as such. But it was always . . . That is, Father Rochlitz knew I was always available, always prepared to assist him in any way I could. Yes, I am sure he knew that."

Schneider can't help himself, can't resist the temptation that tugs insistently at the coat of his better judgement.

"But he never sought confession?"

Father Kroehl hesitates for a moment, weighs the merits of further equivocation before accepting he is defeated.

"No," he says spiritlessly, "he did not."

14

Neumann and Schneider telephone, walk, drive, trawl newspaper archives – the *Berliner Tageblatt*, the *Völkischer Beobachter*, even old issues of Goebbels' *Der Angriff* and Julius Streicher's semi-pornographic Jew-hating *Der Stürmer*. It takes them days. Nothing. Father Rochlitz appears to have led a life in the shadows, a life that didn't extend beyond the parishes in which he worked since being admitted to the priesthood.

In 1896 the call of God had caused Rochlitz to abandon a watch-making apprenticeship in Munich and enter the Freising seminary in Bavaria. He'd gone from Freising straight to the bottom of the hierarchy ladder at the church of St Lambertus in Moabit, and there he'd stayed until fire destroyed the building in 1928, by which time Father Rochlitz was the priest in charge. As it turned out, that was the pinnacle of his career in the church. Afterwards, his employers shuffled him from parish to parish, never in anything more than a subordinate role, a charitable attempt to give a little meaning to the life of someone who'd never amounted to much, and never would.

Neumann and Schneider have visited or telephoned the

other temporary repositories for Father Rochlitz's minimal talents, the handful of churches where he was successively placed after the fire at St Lambertus. They've interviewed clergy and lay staff alike, but to no avail. The dead priest trod lightly on the earth, and the faint trail now discernible comprises little more than expressions of vague regret and polite half-compliments. The last throw of the investigative dice is the only surviving member of those on the staff at St Lambertus before the 1928 fire, a lay worker, Frau Gabriele Steinert. She still lives in Berlin, in Gesundbrunnen now. Her apartment is about four kilometres to the north-east of Moabit, on Gustav-Meyer Allee. She's in one of the ubiquitous 'rental barracks' thrown up in the early days of the Nazi ascendancy, when Germany was girding its loins to take on economic depression before tackling the rest of the world.

The apartment is on the top floor, the sixth. As Neumann and Schneider get out of the elevator and step onto the cramped landing for the floor, they are rewarded with a spectacular view of the enormous flak tower on the edge of nearby Humboldthain Park. The dirty grey behemoth is seventy metres square and forty metres high, has walls of reinforced concrete over three metres thick. For a moment, the two men stand speechless, transfixed by the tower's silent menacing bulk. Both of them know that, although they can't see it from here, only a kilometre to the north-east sits the equally gigantic AEG Turbine Hall complex. There's something vaguely unsettling about an apparently modern compulsion to build on such a scale. Schneider breaks the spell.

"Those English and their Stonehenge!" A snort of derision as he gestures towards the flak tower. "If the Wehrmacht made a circle of these fuckers, people would come from all over the world to see. We could charge admission."

"Now there's an idea," replies Neumann. "All those rich

Americans. And we could have Adolf stuffed and put in a glass case. No need to wait until the war's over . . ."

Neumann's voice abandons his train of thought, leaves implications floating in its wake. Schneider shoots him a look. He's not disagreeing with the sentiment, but you never know who might hear a remark like that. Both men are well aware the Gestapo cultivates the ears and eyes of universally despised apartment block wardens. Schneider has no desire to tour the Russian Front or to find himself in an Einsatzgrüp pulling the trigger on women and children. He peers at the numbers painted on the concrete wall of the landing, sees an arrow pointing to numbers 61-73, starts towards the narrow railed pathway which will lead them to number 67 and Frau Steinert.

The apartment's exterior is like every other one in the building. A central entry door flanked by large square windows either side. Plain, solid, functional, uninspiring. Schneider raps three times on the small glass panel inset into the door at shoulder height, and a few seconds later a fleeting shadow heralds someone inside.

The door opens. It's a man in his early thirties, slim, light brown hair cut short and neatly parted, a serious scholar's face with a trim goatee beard. He's in casual trousers and a grey cardigan over his white shirt. His eyes flick between the two visitors for a few moments until he decides he doesn't know them.

"Yes?" Wary, noncommittal.

"Good afternoon," says Neumann, holding up his warrant disc to the young man. "I'm Kriminalkommissar Neumann. Is this where Frau Steinert lives?"

"She is my mother. What is this about?"

"Perhaps we could come in for a moment." Neumann is already moving forward. The young man takes a step backwards. Most people do when a Kripo detective wants to come in. Schneider follows in Neumann's wake, smiling as he enters, making eye contact, non-threatening. At least, as non-threatening as someone his size can reasonably be.

They are in a spacious room running away from them to the other end of the apartment. Doors are set into each of the side walls, presumably leading to bedrooms and a bathroom. At the far end is a kitchen bench and cupboards, a table with four chairs in front of it. The end of the room nearest the entry door is furnished simply but tastefully with fabric armchairs and a two-seat sofa, small sideboards and a low table with dried flowers in a vase. In one of the armchairs sits a woman, her legs covered with a patterned rug.

She is perhaps sixty years old, grey starting to claw its way through her once-blonde hair, her face showing the inevitable ravages of time and gravity. Neumann and Schneider take a few seconds adjusting to the change in light before they realise she's there. When they do, both men face her, smile, give a slight nod.

"Frau Steinert?" asks Neumann.

"Yes, I am Frau Steinert." Her voice is cut crystal, precise and strong, the voice of a much younger woman. As she speaks, the two men realise that her old age only thinly disguises the beauty she must have been as a young woman. It's in the bone structure, the erect posture, the clear blue of her eyes. A beauty, now growing old, a but a beauty still.

"I apologise for our intrusion into your home, madam. My name is Neumann. This," a half-turn and gesture, "is my colleague, Kriminalassistant Schneider. We would like to speak to you if that is convenient. About your time at the church of Saint Lambertus."

Neumann's words seem to spark something in the woman's eyes, and she gives a small start before recovering herself.

"Of course, Herr Neumann." She turns her face to the young man hovering behind the two Kripos. "Allow me to introduce my son, Jürgen." The three men lock eyes, nod towards each other. "Please be seated," Frau Steinert adds, extending a hand towards the vacant armchairs. "Forgive me if I do not stand, gentlemen. These," indicating her covered legs, "have abandoned me, I fear." She turns back to her son. "Jürgen, perhaps we could have some coffee for our guests?"

"Of course, mother." Jürgen gives a half-smile and goes into the kitchen. Frau Steinert puts into words the inevitable thoughts of her two visitors.

"Ersatz, of course. These days, you know . . ." She doesn't need to elaborate. Neumann and Schneider, like all but the Party bosses and profiteering industrialists, know that they'll be drinking roasted barley, oats, chicory and acorns. It's rumoured a sprinkling of Pervitin is sometimes included to enliven the brew, but that seems unlikely in this setting. They nod and smile politely, understanding, wistful. Coffee, real coffee, now at 200RM for a half kilo, is becoming a distant memory, joining cream, chocolate and oranges. "So, you wish to know about my time at Saint Lambertus? Yes?"

"I understand you worked there for many years."

"I did, Herr Neumann. From early in nineteen hundred and two until the fire. In twenty-eight. It was a very happy time in my life."

"And your duties there? What were they?"

"They varied. At first I was the housekeeper for the priest and his assistants. Father Schiller – he was in charge. Father Hanke and Father Rochlitz assisted him. I cooked and cleaned for them. As the years went by, I was given increased responsibilities, assisting them in preparations for ceremonies, doing clerical work, anything that was required in fact."

"Did you come to know Father Rochlitz well in that time?"

Frau Steinert seems taken aback, frowns. "Yes, of course. I came to know all of the priests quite well. We all lived together for many years. Father Rochlitz was there when I arrived and he stayed on, but the others came and went. Father Schiller died, so another priest replaced him."

"Can you tell us what Father Rochlitz was like, Frau Steinert? What sort of man he was?" It's Schneider, smiling, doing his cuddly toy impression.

"He was a quiet man, thoughtful, considerate. A gentleman, you might say. He loved the life at Saint Lambertus. It broke his heart to leave there. He was . . ." Frau Steinert pauses, thinking. "Why are you asking all these questions? Has Father Rochlitz done something wrong?"

Neuman throws Schneider a sideways glance.

"I am afraid Father Rochlitz has been murdered, madam."

Frau Steinert gasps, throws her hands to her mouth, jolts upright, eyes stretched open with shock, just as her son arrives with a tray. He drops it to the small table with a thud and rattle, quickly kneels by his mother's chair and puts and arm around her shoulders.

"Mother! What is it? What?"

Frau Steinert shakes her head several times, lowers her hands to snatch a handkerchief from her sleeve, dabs her eyes. She takes a few deep breaths before patting Jürgen's comforting hand and lifting it from her shoulder as she looks to Neumann and Schneider.

"I apologise for my outburst, gentlemen. Please . . . It is just such a surprise. It has been a long time . . . Please. Continue. May I know what happened? When it was."

Neumann surrenders the explanation to Schneider. He's the one who made the old lady cry.

"It was the week before last, on the Friday. We do not know what happened, only that someone assaulted Father Rochlitz in his apartment. We are trying to find out who did that. Can you think of somebody who would have reason to harm him? Did he have any enemies that you know of?"

"Enemies?" The suggestion seems to surprise her. "I would not think so. The Father Rochlitz I knew was a gentle, caring man, a man of God. A man such as he does not make enemies. Surely there has been a mistake."

"We do not think so," says Neumann. "Whoever was responsible searched his apartment. Very thoroughly. They were clearly looking for something, but as far as we can establish nothing was stolen. Can you think of anything Father Rochlitz might have possessed which others would value? Something small, precious. Gold, perhaps, or a jewel?"

Frau Steinert seems taken aback before she regains her poise and almost scoffs openly. "A valuable possession? No, he had no valuable possessions, no money, very little in the way of worldly goods. He lived a life of modesty bordering on poverty. I can think of nothing he owned which anyone would want to steal. Nothing."

"Is there anyone else who would have known him at the time? Your husband, perhaps? Your son?" Schneider again.

"My husband died long ago, Herr Schneider. In the first war, in 1914, at the battle of the Marne. He was in the 18th Infantry Division under General von Quast. Jürgen remembers nothing of his father."

The young man, so far sitting silent in his chair, nods his agreement.

"That is so. I was barely three when he went off to war."

"And Father Rochlitz?" asks Schneider. "Did you know him well? As you got older, I mean."

Jürgen brightens at the memory. "I have fond memories of him, Herr Schneider, even as a small child. He played with me often. Even as I grew older he was loving and attentive. We went hiking, boating, that sort of thing. He taught me to fish, how to make rods, lures and so forth. And he tried to teach me about watches and clocks, but I am afraid I was a poor student. Sometimes he would accompany mother and me when we visited the zoo, or attended a concert. I have only happy memories of him, right up until the fire when I was seventeen, after which he was transferred to . . . to . . ." Jürgen glances at his mother.

"Saint Peter's. In Schwerin," she answers for her son. "After that, we did not see Father Rochlitz again."

The two Kripos nod, understanding. Schwerin's more than 150 kilometres to the north-east. Not an easy or cheap journey to make, especially for a penniless priest or a low-paid housekeeper.

"Was there any correspondence afterwards, perhaps when Father Rochlitz returned to Berlin?" Neumann asks.

"No," she says with finality, "there was not."

15

"And so, when the posting came up, I jumped at it. Right now, Berlin's the second most important embassy we have. Well, okay, perhaps the third. London and Tokyo are getting a lot of attention. But there's opportunity here to do well, Max. Promotion. Recognition." Harry Forbes is about to stop talking when he realises he's forgotten something. "And of course, there's you. I wasn't going to get another opportunity like this one to combine business with pleasure."

Neumann lifts his beer off the table, inclines his head in acknowledgment, takes a sip. There's no food on the table, just beer. Forbes tentatively suggested a plate of sausage and sauerkraut, but Neumann said he wasn't hungry, as he often isn't these days, and the American seems content to go without.

They're in the gigantic domed Haus Vaterland, on the southwest side of Potsdamer Platz. Before the war, the enormous dome would be lit nightly with thousands of electric bulbs, visible from all over Berlin. No lights now, though – they would provide a perfect aiming point for British bombers. Neumann wonders if he'll ever see them lit again.

He's brought his friend to the Löwenbräu bar, on the fourth floor, a reproduction bierkeller with a painted backdrop of the Zugspitze mountain. Every day, patrons can watch an artificial 'sun' set behind the snow-capped peak. Forbes is more impressed than Neumann, who thinks the whole Haus Vaterland complex overwrought, childish, gaudy, a profusion of silver paint and fake 'old world' European nostalgia. Still, the beer's good, and Harry Forbes is enjoying himself. They could have been in a bar nearer the American Embassy on Bendlerstrasse in the Tiergarten district, but Forbes said he wanted to go somewhere other Americans normally didn't go. So here they are on Potsdamer Platz, less than a few kilometres away in distance, but a world away in authenticity.

"And are you still a single man, Harry? Marriage still that elusive goal?"

Harry's appetite for women, and his ability to attract them without trying, was legendary at Cambridge. Neumann guesses from the absence of a ring on Harry's finger that not much has changed since those halcyon days of youth.

Forbes gives an enigmatic grin. "Single, my friend, still single. Haven't found a girl that'll put up with me for more than a few weeks. Haven't stopped trying, though. And you? No, no, don't tell me. Let me guess." He affects deep thought, chin on clenched hand. "I'm thinking about all those holidays we took, all the visits back to see your folks. I'm thinking about the girls you used to chase then, the types you liked. Ah, yes, I see your wife now. She's a blue-eyed blonde, a long plait in her hair, wears a dirndl around the house, big-chested. Don't tell me, her name's . . . yep, her name's Brunhilde. And you've got three kids, another one on the way. I'm right, aren't I?"

Neumann affects surprise, amazement.

"How do you do it, Harry? How can you tell all that without seeing her? You should go on stage. Really. Make a fortune."

"So I'm right, yeah?"

"Very close, very close indeed. Just missed a few details. Her name's Irmgard, she's got short dark hair, she's slim and athletic, brown eyes, dresses like everybody else these days, and we've got no kids. Apart from those small details, you're right on the money. I'm impressed."

"Ah. No kids, eh. Guess I got that wrong."

"Only just. We're trying. If we can churn out eight, Irmgard will qualify for a gold Mother's Cross. Worth the effort, wouldn't you agree? More soldiers in the making. Do you know Goebbels has proclaimed a new patriotic slogan – 'Fuck For The Fatherland'. Catchy, don't you think? Should be popular."

Forbes gives the awkward grin of someone who's not entirely sure that what they're being told is a joke, then changes the conversation's direction. "Tell me about your work. Is it what you wanted? We never talked about it at Cambridge. You were too busy spouting Shakespeare and chasing girls."

"Chasing girls? Hardly. You were the master – I was just along for the ride." Neumann waves his arms theatrically. "I did but follow there in the chase, not like a hound that hunts, but one that fills up the cry!"

Forbes pretends to clap his hands together. "Bravo, good sir. What, Romeo and Juliet?"

"Close again. Missed it by a whisker. Roderigo. In Othello. The one who lusted after Desdemona. Why does he remind me of you? And yes, the police work is what I wanted. Not then, but after. In the twenties, it seemed the right thing to do. Be a policeman, I mean. The Weimar Republic was a shambles. Right-wing and communist gangs in the streets, assassinations, the Kapp Putsch, the Nazi Putsch, billions of Papiermarks to buy a loaf of bread, a trillion to buy one Rentenmark. You know what it was like. Nobody in their right mind then thought that the Nazis would one day be running the country."

"Hitler did. Imagine it."

"I said 'nobody in their right mind', Harry."

Even though they're at a table well away from the smattering of other customers, even though he's speaking quietly, force of habit makes Neumann swing his eyes back and forth as he speaks. Forbes is suddenly sober, serious.

"That bad, huh? I'm told it's not just the man himself. Is that right? The others are just as crazy, I hear."

Neumann lowers his voice even further, reflexively leans in towards Forbes.

"Crazy? Perhaps, but it's worse than that. Let me give you an example, just one. Have you ever heard of the Charitable Patient Transport Company?"

Forbes frowns, "No, should I?"

"Probably not yet, but give it time. You don't often see their vans – they usually wait until late at night to go out. They're a front, Harry, a front for murder." Forbes jerks his head back in disbelief as Neumann goes on. "The programme name is 'T4'. I've got no idea what that stands for, but I know what happens. They kill people. Crazy people, prisoners sick in the head, madmen. The vans transport them to be gassed – stuck in a room with carbon monoxide pumped in. It's murder, Harry, organised, official, government-controlled murder."

Forbes stares at Neumann. His mouth is agape.

"It's like this," adds Neumann. "We hear about your gangsters all the time – Dillinger, Baby Face Nelson, Capone, Machine Gun Kelly, Bonnie and Clyde. Alright, think of them, all of them and their kind, in control of your government. Running the treasury, the police, the army. Well, that's what Germany is now, a country run by gangsters. Some of them are mad, but most of them are just plain bad. Corrupt, evil, murdering bastards who . . ."

Neumann stops abruptly, aware his voice is rising, aware

his face is contorting with passion, disgust. He gulps a mouthful of beer, sits back in his chair, tries to control his breathing. Forbes watches without speaking as he sips his beer. There's a long pause before he eventually speaks.

"Christ, Max. I knew it was bad, but I didn't think . . ."

"Almost nobody does, Harry."

"So what's the answer? What do you do?"

"I do what I can. We all do."

✠

The woman sitting behind a desk and a Continental Silenta typewriter raises her eyes as the outer office door opens. A smile shoulders aside her frown of concentration and she lifts her hands from the machine's keys, sitting up straighter than before, eyes locked on the visitor. She is in her twenties, small, trim, shoulder-length brown hair, a pleasant, open, friendly face.

"Good morning, Fräulein Braunwald. Made better by seeing you, of course. It is always a pleasure." Neumann plunders a sonnet, holds up both hands in mock wonder. "How like Eve's apple doth thy beauty grow!"

"You are so predictable, Kriminalkommissar Neumann," she replies, maintaining the mock formality, "but please do not withhold your frivolous compliments on my account." Her elegant Viennese accent suits the formal tone.

Neumann steps up beside her and lowers his voice.

"Do you know what he wants?"

"No, but I can tell you that Becker is with him."

Neumann involuntarily tenses in response. He assumes Reichskriminaldirektor Tanzinger wants to talk to him about the Rochlitz murder. That doesn't bode well, given there's no progress of substance he can report to the chief. The fact that Kriminaldirektor Becker, 'The Little Accountant', is in there too doesn't bode well either. Neumann steels himself, nods to the young woman.

"Thanks, Lotte. Better let them know."

She picks up the handset and flicks a switch on her internal communication telephone, receives a 'Yes' in response, says "Kriminalkommissar Neumann is here, sir". The reply sounds like a grunt, but she apparently knows it means 'Send him in'. She conveys the message to Neumann with a sideways flick of her head. "Good luck," she adds, as he heads for the door of the inner office.

He knocks once, opens the door, sees Tanzinger and Becker sitting together on a sofa against one wall. Neumann comes briefly to attention, delivers the obligatory salute, waits. Tanzinger waves him in, points to the sofa opposite. Neumann sits, waits again.

As expected, Tanzinger wants to know about Rochlitz. Neumann tells him. It doesn't take long – there's not a lot to tell when you've drawn a blank every time you've asked a question. Tanzinger and Becker listen in silence. To Neumann's surprise, it's not Tanzinger but The Little Accountant who speaks next, in his usual precise and tedious way.

"I have this morning informed Reichskriminaldirektor Tanzinger that another priest has been found murdered."

Neumann stares at him, nonplussed, temporarily perplexed.

"The dead man is in Schöneberg," Becker continues, glancing down at a sheet of paper beside him. "At Saint Norbert's church. A Father Dassler, I believe. The report of his death indicates he was tortured before being killed and that his rooms were nearly destroyed at the same time, apparently in the process of a search for some item unknown. You can see, Kriminalkommissar, that there are unnatural similarities with the murder of Father Rochlitz. That is why Reichskriminaldirektor Tanzinger has decided your investigation of that matter should now be extended to encompass the second murder."

Neumann opens his mouth to speak, decides not to.

"I have informed Kriminaldirektor Becker of my views," says Tanzinger. "He agrees it would be best if your investigation of both deaths was conducted in the normal way. Kriminaldirektor?"

Becker is on firm ground now. Tanzinger is backing him, and Neumann is left in no doubt that the Kriminaldirektor's in charge again, occupying his rightful place in the hierarchy. Becker drives the point home. "You will henceforth report any progress directly to Kriminalrat Böhm, in the usual way. He will decide whether any developments warrant my involvement. And I in turn will inform Reichskriminaldirektor Tanzinger as appropriate. Do you have any questions, Kriminalkommissar?"

Neumann has more questions than he can accommodate. Why another priest? Is the second one connected to the first? Why is Tanzinger shuffling this one off when he wanted to oversee the first one himself? What are the killers looking for? What is this information, this thing, this valuable commodity suddenly in the hands of parish priests?

"No, sir. No questions."

"Good," says Tanzinger as he gets to his feet, Becker following. Neumann is quick to join them. "That will be all," says the man in charge of the Reich's Kriminalpolizei.

Still mystified, his head swimming, Neumann gives the required salute, receives two in return, and leaves the inner office. He barely registers Fräulein Lotte Braunwald's presence as he walks through the outer office and back to his desk.

16

St Norbert's church sits squat and dominant in the Schöneberg landscape. Solid Romanesque Revival arches and thick-walled towers support conical roofs. Columns and pilasters encrusted with spiral and leaf carvings soar heavenwards. It's a church fit for fat rich burghers, for moustachioed Junker aristocrats and their entitled offspring. And when it first sprang into being in the nineteenth century, its worshippers tended towards that end of the social scale. But now fields and farms have been squeezed out of the vicinity, replaced by industry and workers, the proletarian base of a modern military power. A few of the old mansions remain along Hauptstrasse's broad avenue, but for the main part industry and commerce have swamped the district's previous incarnations, a transformation cemented in 1920 when Schöneberg officially became part of Greater Berlin and country became city.

Neumann and Schneider park their Opel directly outside the church rectory, walk ten metres to the door, knock and wait. Only a few seconds later it's opened by a small, thin, severe-looking woman with tightly-pinned shortish brown hair. A pair of dark eyes peer over her hawkish nose.

"Yes? What is it?" She seems as angry as she is impatient.

"Kriminalpolizei," says Neumann, and the two Kripos flash their identity discs, what Schneider calls their 'beer tokens'. The woman barely glances at the offerings.

"You're here about Father Dassler. You'd better come in. There's another one of your lot with him."

Neumann and Schneider exchange a puzzled look – as far as they know, no Kripo officer is detailed to be here. They follow the thin woman into the rectory, wait for her to slam the door shut, follow her as she leads them through the main entry and front room into a short passage which bends right. As they turn the corner they see further along an Orpo on a stool, an Unterwachtmeister, apparently dozing, his back and head leaning on the door behind him. The noise of all the footsteps awakens him, and he springs to his feet, tries to stand at sleep-addled attention.

"I'll leave you to it," says the woman, and disappears back into the rectory proper. Neumann and Schneider walk up to the silent Orpo, show their discs. He stares, but doesn't move.

"It's all right, son, we'll take it from here," says Schneider. The fuzz-lipped Unterwachtmeister, barely eighteen by the look of him, nods vigorously, steps back against the wall. "Nobody's been in?" Schneider says to the youth. Another vigorous shake of the head as the young man stutters an answer.

"N . . . no, sir, nobody."

The pair open the door to Father Dassler's room, go in, shut it behind them. It's dim, almost dark, thick blackout curtains drawn across the only window on the far wall. The familiar heavy sweet smell of blood fills their nostrils. Neumann fumbles around for the light switch, flicks it, and lets out an involuntary groan of shock when he sees the room clearly. Beside him, Schneider throws a hand up to his mouth, grips his jaw fiercely.

There's a long, stunned pause before either man can speak.

"Mother of God!" Schneider shakes his head in disbelief, horror, bewilderment. "What have they done to him?"

Both men realise they'll have little need of Professor Dürer's services this time – there's no question of how the priest died. He's tied to an armchair, as was Father Rochlitz. And the room in which he sits has been destroyed, torn apart like Father Rochlitz's apartment. But that's where the similarities end. Father Dassler is facing them, his head sunk onto his chest. Where his eyes once were, there are only blackened depressions, a trickle of blood and other fluid from each one congealed on his pale cheeks above a slack, gaping dead mouth. His face resembles a Japanese mask from the *Noh* theatre, almost white, dark eyes, dark mouth. A sodden wadded cloth, presumably once a gag, lies in the dead man's lap.

Wordlessly, Neumann and Schneider move carefully forward, one to either side of the armchair in which the priest's body is bound. As they step closer, the size of the blood puddle pooling on the linoleum behind the armchair becomes apparent. The reason reveals itself as they arrive behind the body. Father Dassler's wrist veins have been carefully opened with a very sharp knife or scalpel, the incisions running longitudinally down his arms. His body has been virtually drained of blood. If the destruction of his eyes didn't kill him, without question this would have done so. Both men have seen death before, seen the messy aftermath of murder in all its kinds, but neither one has seen this or anything like it. Their eyes meet across the divide of the armchair as they share mutual incomprehension, revulsion. And fear. What sort of man are they dealing with who can do this?

17

The Reichsluftahrtministerium edifice, the Ministry of Aviation's administrative headquarters, is the largest office building in Europe, and looks it. Two hundred and fifty metres of frontage along Wilhelmstrasse, seven stories high, it's as though several large apartment complexes have been glued together before being set down as a single entity. It's no coincidence the building's architect was Ernst Sagebiel, the man responsible (criminally, in Max Neumann's view) for the hideous monstrosity of Tempelhof Airport. The Ministry is a good example of the Party's 'scare-the-people-shitless' building style in Kurt Schneider's view, but he's careful about who he shares that opinion with.

A Reichspost delivery man in his military-style uniform of peaked cap, dark blue trousers and tunic jacket with wide leather belt walks down the Wilhelmstrasse pavement, past the building's vast forecourt, his leather satchel slung over one shoulder. He pays no heed to the grandiose behemoth beside him, maintains a steady pace as he passes by column upon column of uniformly square windows stretching to the top floor.

As he nears the corner of Leipziger Strasse he's confronted by a uniformed Hitler Youth member, a boy of about fifteen. The boy has a Winter Relief tray of tiny glass badges suspended from his neck by a leather strap. He thrusts his red collection box in front of the delivery man, rattles the coins already in it. The delivery man ignores him, keeps walking, knocks the collection box aside with one swinging arm as he passes. The boy stares at the disappearing figure, open-mouthed. Winter Relief collectors are never ignored. Everyone knows it's State-sponsored blackmail, but nobody is prepared to risk retribution from Party thugs if they refuse to purchase one of the little glass badges.

The postman reaches Leipziger Strasse at the northern end of the building and turns right past yet more columns of windows until he reaches the Ministry's north-east corner, when he turns right again and into the deliveries forecourt. There are service ramps, loading docks, steel girders with chain hoists protruding from notches in the walls on the first floor. Trucks come and go, unload, sit idling doing nothing of consequence. Trolleys of boxes are wheeled about, men are shouting orders, complaining, enquiring, laughing. Someone is hammering metal loudly. Everything is movement and noise, ordered and purposeful activity. The man in the Reichspost uniform winds his way through the throng towards a small door next to a loading ramp, nothing on it to distinguish it from any other door except that it is kept locked until it is needed. He walks up to the door, knocks sharply three times, hears the lock turn before the door is opened inwards. He moves through the opening and into a blind corridor. Behind him, the door is shut and locked again.

An Oberleutnant in a Luftwaffe uniform offers the small man a deferential nod, says, "This way, please sir," and heads off down the corridor to a small caged lift at the end. He slides the cage door open, steps back to allow the other man to enter first, then closes the gate and moves a wooden-handled lever to number seven on the arched dial behind it. When the lift reaches its destination, the top floor of the building, he steps out first and holds the cage door for the other man, who gives him a nod of acknowledgment before stepping across the corridor and knocking on a plain wooden door opposite the lift. A voice behind it tells him to enter, and he pushes the door open.

He's standing in a large square office lit by huge rectangular windows facing east, out over the rear of the Ministry. A wide rosewood desk sits in front of the far wall, on which hangs a portrait of Hitler by Franz Triebsch, the one showing him in full field uniform at the bottom of a flight of stone steps, one foot raised on the lowest tread, hand on hip, peaked cap in his other hand, staring seriously into the middle distance. The painting radiates authority, vision, gravitas, power. The man sitting behind the desk is also in uniform, one of his own design, loosely based on a Luftwaffe officer's dress ensemble. This one is a hummingbird blue, with black facing on the extra wide lapels, which are decorated with embroidered silver oak leaves and swastikas. Ribbons and medals festoon the left breast of the jacket, silver aiguillettes hang in loops from the right shoulder. Featuring prominently on the man's right coat lapel is the treasured Golden Party badge, held by only those whose unbroken membership started before 1933. A blue and black officer's hat sits on the desk. The outfit resembles something that might normally be seen on a heroic character in light opera.

Hermann Göring rises beaming from his chair as the Reichspost messenger enters the office, strides across to his visitor, hand extended. The small man is about to raise his arm in salute, but Göring stifles it with a downward motion of his hand. His fingernails are painted a pale blue.

"No need for that," he says, grasping the other man's hand and shaking it vigorously. "Come, sit. You will have coffee? I have been given a present by Fritz Todt, straight from Costa Rica, he tells me, a delicious drink. Come, come."

Göring steers his visitor away from the three mahogany Zopfstil chairs directly in front of the desk, ushers him towards one of the four black leather armchairs set a little further away. The visitor smiles politely as he places his satchel and cap on the floor. Göring moves to his desk, presses a button on it, then sits down facing the other man. A waft of 4711 cologne envelopes them both. From a side table next to his armchair Göring picks up a small cedar box, opens the lid, proffers the cigars in it to his visitor, who declines with a wave of his hand. Göring takes a cigar for himself, lights it, sinks back into his chair and contemplates his visitor for a moment. The other man sits silent, hands in his lap.

"What have you to tell me, Tadeusz?" asks Göring as he exhales a cloud of smoke.

Tadeusz Zebrowski gives a small nod, as though confirming the chasm of authority existing between the two men. Zebrowski is Polish, from Pultusk near Warsaw, and he's been working for Hermann Goering since 1936, when he started providing intelligence on Polish targets and subversives, when he helped to pave the way for the German onslaught three years later. His identity papers say he is Friedrich Heyse, holds the Wehrmacht rank of Oberstleutnant, a Lieutenant-Colonel. He speaks slowly and softly, nearly a monotone. His German is without accent, faultless.

"As you required, Herr Reichsmarschall, I observed the activities of Standartenführer Schmidt. He was not aware of my presence, of course. All of yesterday he remained in his apartment in Kreuzberg, on Riemann Strasse. I was unable to observe his activities during that time, but on three occasions I passed by his door and on two of them I heard what I believe was gramophone music – Schubert's Eighth Symphony on the first occasion . . .”

“The ‘Unfinished’,” interjects Göring, playing his role as knowledgeable patron of the arts.

“Quite so,” Zebrowski says before continuing. He does not refer to notes – his report is from memory. “On the second occasion it was Wagner, from *Tannhäuser*. On the third occasion, Standartenführer Schmidt was playing a violin. I was unable to identify the piece. He left the apartment at eight twenty four in the evening carrying a small case and travelled in his car to Saint Norbert’s church in Schöneberg, on Reppichstrasse. There, still carrying his case, he knocked on the door of the rectory and was admitted by a priest who I now know to have been Father Erwin Dassler. The Standartenführer remained in the rectory until ten thirteen, when he left, returned to his car, and drove away.”

“Away? Where did he go?” Göring seems puzzled.

“That I do not know. I adjudged it best to remain and establish what had occupied him for nearly two hours. To that end, I went to the Rectory. Being unable to determine anything of consequence outside, I entered the building. Father Dassler was tied to a chair, dead. A gag was in his mouth. He had been tortured. Several of his fingernails were missing, and . . .” Zebrowski pauses a moment as though gathering his strength. “And both eyeballs had been severely burned. Destroyed.”

Göring is upright in his chair, frowning, incomprehension swamping his face. “Destroyed? You mean . . .”

“Completely, Reichsmarschall, gone. There was minimal burning of the facial flesh, of the eye sockets. I surmise that the Standartenführer must have used a very small, very intense flame. It was sufficient to melt or burn away all of the eyeballs. The Father must have been in unimaginable pain before he died. It is almost certain he was alive when the veins in his wrists were cut – the amount of blood on the floor surrounding his chair suggests it came from a beating heart."

"Good God," sighs Göring, "I did not think . . . How can a man, even a man like Schmidt . . ." He rubs his forehead, presses his bejewelled fingers hard, as though trying to erase the image from his mind. He brings his attention back to Zebrowski. "Go on please, Tadeuz."

"The rooms occupied by Father Dassler had been thoroughly searched. Drawers had been emptied, clothes cut open, carpets lifted, paintings and photographs removed from their frames. It is clear the Standartenführer was looking for something, something small enough to be concealed within a painting frame. I believe such a small space would allow the concealment of only documents or photographs. I am unable to say whether or not the search was successful."

A brief knock on the office door is followed without pause by a plump middle-aged woman in a dark blue skirt and blouse carrying a tray with a coffee pot, cups, milk, cream and sugar. Without a word, she puts the tray on a small table between the armchairs occupied by the two men and disappears back through the door.

Göring is lost in thought, his mind somewhere far away. His cigar hangs unnoticed from his hand, and he makes no move towards the tray on the table. Zebrowski leans forward, pours coffee for both of them, marvels at the ability of the Reichsmarschall to obtain cream, pours some into his own cup, sits back and sips his coffee while he waits. A hooded crow lands on the ledge outside one of the windows, pecks at something it sees on the glass, flies off again. The noise snaps Göring out of his thoughts, and he seems surprised to find a cup of coffee in front of him. He leans forward, adds milk and sugar, sits back with the cup and saucer in his hands.

"Yes, thank you, Tadeusz, thank you. You have done well. I think it best to continue your observations." A thought occurs to him. “Is it possible to search Schmidt’s apartment without him knowing? Can you do that?”

“It is not possible, Reichsmarschall. The Standartenführer’s apartment is on the third floor, so entry from a window would be ill-advised. The only other entry point is the main door, and that is secured with a combination dial lock.” Seeing Göring’s brows knit, Zebrowski adds, “Like the one on a safe. It can be bypassed by smashing the dial away and driving out the central spindle, but such a method would hardly escape the occupant’s notice. I can do that if you require it, but would advise . . .”

“No, no,” says Göring hurriedly. “Schmidt must have no idea you are watching him. No, for the moment, just keep him under observation. I want to see what his next move is. Let me know when you have more to report.”

The audience is finished. Zebrowski drinks the remnants of his coffee, picks up his cap and leather satchel, gets to his feet. Göring stays in his seat, lifts a farewell hand.

“Thank you, Tadeusz. Be careful.”

Zebrowski nods, puts his cap back on, leaves by the door opposite the lift in the corridor. Standing next to the lift is the Oberleutnant who escorted him earlier. The two men get in.

18

In 1906 Pope Pius X granted the Church of St John the Baptist, on Lilienthalstrasse in Neukölln, the status of 'Minor Basilica'. To Kurt Schneider the bestowed appellation is as ridiculous as it is incomprehensible. Neumann explains as best he can given his sketchy knowledge of things ecclesiastical, that to be granted the status of Minor Basilica involves the Pope being satisfied about things like a church's size, renown, the fulfilment of certain liturgical rites, and other conditions Neumann can only guess at.

"In other words, it's all bullshit, right?" Schneider has never had anything remotely resembling orthodox faith. His gods are facts, logic, practicality, satisfaction of the senses.

"When you craft your argument as persuasively as that, I can't help but agree," replies Neumann. "But it's still a fairly impressive pile of rocks."

The two men are standing on the Lilienthalstrasse footpath, surveying the pale grey stone-clad church from across the road. It's big, with a soaring spired tower placed centrally between a pair of two-storey wings. A huge circular stained glass window dominates the tower, about halfway up, sitting below a pediment surmounted by a clock face and yet another pediment, all of it leading to a pierced hexagonal tower base beneath the spire proper. It looks vaguely Swiss provincial.

Schneider's unconvinced by his colleague's assessment of the structure. "Impressive? Yeah, I suppose so. But I reckon a cuckoo's going to jump out when the clock strikes."

"Ah, Kurt," sighs Neumann melodramatically, "thou wast ever an obstinate heretic in the despite of beauty."

"No, stop, don't tell me!" says Schneider quickly, playing the game, "I know this one. It's Henry the Fifth, right? His speech to the troops before Agincourt."

"As usual, my large and uncouth friend, you are very close. Don Pedro, in Much Ado About Nothing. Now, let's get on with our job. There's a body waiting to not see us."

The body used to be Father Paul Gantz, priest-in-residence at St John's, now a murdered corpse awaiting their inspection somewhere in the depths of the huge building across the road.

The pair stand in silence while a convoy of covered trucks pulling field artillery and munitions trailers clatters and rumbles past. Bored soldiers in the backs of the trucks stare listlessly at the two pedestrians.

Neumann and Schneider have already exhausted discussion and speculation about the sudden spate of murdered priests, three in less than a fortnight. There's nothing more to say. All they have at this point is questions. Why priests? Why the barbaric viciousness of the attack on Father Dassler? What could he or Father Rochlitz have had that the killer wanted? Why has Reichskriminaldirektor Tanzinger taken a giant step away from his original interest in the murder of Father Rochlitz? Is there a link between the first two priests and perhaps now this third one? Nothing is normal, nothing makes sense. Neumann feels like he's being dragged into a deadly game against an opponent he can't see. A game he doesn't know how to win, and where only his opponent knows the rules.

The convoy of trucks eventually ends, taking its noise with it. Relative silence spreads its soothing caress upon the world. Neumann realises with a start that he's drifted off, finds Schneider looking at him expectantly. He gives up an apologetic half-grin and heads off across the road, his partner following. After ten metres of road surface, another ten of cobblestones, and a metre of thick coir mat, the pair enter St John's through the church's arched double doors. It takes a long time for the change in light to settle their eyes before they see a young priest in a black soutane walking quickly towards them from the vicinity of the altar. Behind him soars the huge arched half-dome above the Sanctuary, with its figure of Christ bestowing a blessing, his right hand lifted, palm open and facing down. Neumann stifles the tempting thought that if Jesus lifted his hand a little higher and held his arm a little straighter he would be delivering a Hitler salute.

The young priest is agitated, red-faced. His thick black hair is dishevelled, and it's obvious he hasn't shaved yet. The silver cross and chain hanging from his neck sways and rattles as he hurries up to Neumann and Schneider.

"Are you police?" His voice is high-pitched, anxious.

"We are, Father . . ?"

"Lindemann. I am Father Lindemann. There has been a murder, here, in the church. One of our . . ."

"Yes, Father, we know," interrupts Neumann, "that's why we're here. I am Kriminalkommissar Neumann and this is Kriminalassistant Schneider. Perhaps you could direct us to the scene of the crime."

"Yes, yes, of course. Follow me please."

There's relief in the priest's voice at the prospect of being able to leave the two Kripos to do their job. He strides towards a door at the end of the church's right-hand transept, and the three men make their way along the uncovered wooden floor of a long bare passage before arriving in living quarters at the end, at the rear of the church. They are in a communal kitchen and dining room. Father Lindemann points to a closed door on the other side.

"Father Gantz's room is through there, at the end of the passage. A Green Policeman is waiting for you." He steps back a little, hesitantly asks, "Do you require me any further?"

"Not for the moment," says Neumann, sparking a visible moment of relaxed tension on the part of the priest, "But we will need to speak to you later. And to everyone else on the staff. Please ensure they are all available."

"Yes, yes, of course Kriminalkommissar. I will attend to it now." The priest can barely contain his desire to be anywhere else but where he is, and he bustles away towards the church proper. Neumann and Schneider exchange a look, say nothing, move towards the closed door across the other side of the room.

19

This part of Ukraine, almost as far south as the Black Sea, near the small town of Balta, is rich land, part of the 'black soil' zone stretching across half the country. Gentle swells and plains of fertile earth, stands of thick wood winding along the shallow depressions. On some of the slight rises sit thatch-roofed farmhouses, barns, livestock pens, occasionally a lemon or apple tree beside the farmhouse. Thriving, fruitful country. Bare now, but six months ago, near the height of summer, it would have been idyllic, with shimmering fields of wheat and barley ready for harvest, rugged peasantry tending the fields, the men in cord-tied trousers and short coats, their squat women with scarves over weathered heads – the kind of scene that Pieter Brueghel might have painted.

The young man feels the tug of his childhood here, of the rare visits to his uncle's farm in Michendorf near Potsdam, echoes of a timeless routine, of a partnership between the workers and the land. Except that in these fields, on this land, there are no workers to be seen in the offing, no rugged peasantry to give life and meaning to the soil.

Although face-on to the late afternoon sun, he is in the shadow of a woman standing in front, her back to him, slightly higher on the slope of freshly-turned earth. Perhaps in her thirties, she is wearing a long coarse-textured skirt and a blue blouse. The raking light illuminates a golden halo of wind-ruffled blonde hair around her head. It reminds him of a sunflower in full bloom, its dark centre within a garland of yellow petals. It reminds him of the medieval fresco in the Michendorf church near his uncle's farm, a saint's face ringed by divine radiance. Images and echoes of those long gone times reverberate, wash briefly over his mind and disappear, a world lost forever.

Within a fifty-metre radius of where he stands there are dozens of people, but the young man hears nothing, sees nothing except the woman in front of him. No birds sing, no machines clatter, no voices reach his ears. It's just him and the woman.

She stinks. She hasn't washed for days, and he wrinkles his nose against the stale sourness of her sweat and accumulated dirt. A new and acrid smell abruptly assaults his nostrils – she's lost control of her bladder. He was warned. They told him what it would be like. Always hard the first time, they said. But you'd be surprised how quickly you get used to it. After a while, it's nothing at all. Just remember who they are, why we're here, what this is all for. You'll be alright, you'll see.

He takes a sudden deep breath and clenches his jaw as he raises his right arm, rigid, and holds it steady. The muzzle of his pistol is less than a metre from the woman's head, which is moving back and forth in small jerks as she sobs. He pulls the trigger. The force of the shot topples the woman forwards as her legs give way beneath her and she half-slides, half-falls down the dirt slope in front. He watches her disappear from view, slowly lowers his arm to his side, stands motionless for a few seconds, then takes a side step to his left and halts.

It's an old man this time, his bald sweating head reflecting the sunlight like a glazed bowl. He seems to be talking to himself, praying perhaps, but there's no sound. The young man raises his arm again, pulls the trigger of his pistol, and the old man is gone. Another side step, another shot, and he moves slowly down the line. Step, shot. Step, shot. The others were right – it gets easier. Before he's even half way along the line, it's easier. He reloads with steady hands, continues. One, another, another. The third-last in line gives him pause, but for less than a heartbeat. A young woman holding a child no more than a few months old. She clutches it tightly to her chest, her protective arms around it, the infant's teary dirt-streaked face poking above her left shoulder. A thought bursts into the young man's brain – is this a test? Have they set this up? The thought disappears as quickly as it arrived. Test or not makes no difference. Two shots in quick succession. One into the baby's face and, before the mother can react, another one into her skull.

Another side step, another shot. Another step, another shot, and it's over. He's done it. The rite of passage is completed. From out of the enveloping numb silence, sounds and movement resurrect themselves, and he's conscious of the warming sunlight on his face. Then the others are around him, hands on his shoulders, slaps on the back. Someone passes him an opened bottle of vodka, and he gulps a mouthful. His men cry, 'Well done, Sir!' and 'Good man!' Everybody is grinning, laughing. With surprise, Walther Neumann realises he is too. They were right. They were right. You soon get used to it.

20

The Orpo guarding the crime scene gets to his feet from a plain wooden chair as Neumann and Schneider come through the door to the living quarters of the St John's priests. He's surprisingly old, at least sixty, silver hair and trim moustache, ruddy face and the paunch of a man who enjoys food and beer with the best of them. His face registers surprise, then pleased recognition and he steps forward as the two Kripos approach. Schneider reaches him first, holds out a hand to shake, and the old Orpo grabs it enthusiastically.

"This is a surprise, Baby Bear. How are you, my boy?"

Schneider affects sadness and regret before he replies, grinning, "Still missing your wise counsel, Joseph. Struggling to bring villains to justice." He turns to Neumann, who holds back, curious, puzzled. "Joseph was my boss when I joined up," explains Schneider. "Took me under his wing for nearly a year." He waves an introductory hand between the other two men. "Joseph, this is my boss, Kriminalkommissar Max Neumann. Boss, this is Unterwachtmeister Joseph Kohl."

Neumann and Kohl shake hands, nod at each other, mutter

greetings. Neumann frowns as he speaks, his gaze fixed on Kohl.

"Baby Bear?"

"That's how I thought of him, sir. As my baby, someone to look after, bring up, teach them about the world. The 'bear' part speaks for itself."

"You were Kripo?"

"I was. Vice. Stationed at Spandau, across the road from the prison. I had Kurt in my section until I retired." Kohl sees a flash of scepticism in Neumann's face at the mention of retirement. "Had to get out early. A pimp put a bullet through my ankle. That was the end of being a Kripo. Doesn't seem to matter now, though. Old, half-crippled, but still good enough to be an Unterwachtmeister." There's no bitterness in his voice. If anything, it's wry amusement.

Kohl doesn't need to elaborate. Everybody present knows the young and fit are needed elsewhere these days, grist for the insatiable Wehrmacht mincing machine. Old or crippled or both, you're still good enough for the Ordnungspolizei.

"We all do what we can, Joseph. You're well out of it, believe me. Being a Kripo isn't what it used to be, believe me." Neumann pauses, waits for Kohl's acknowledgement before jerking his head towards the closed door off to their right. "Have you been in?"

"Only to confirm that there's a body in there. I didn't go in as such, just opened the door and poked my head around the side. It isn't pretty, sir. Hope you've got a strong stomach. I can vouch for Baby Bear's."

"We'll find out soon enough, I suppose. It's going to take us a while. Why don't you see if the fathers can't provide you with a coffee and something to eat while we're in there?"

The old Orpo nods gratefully. "Thanks. I could do with a change of scenery." He sets off towards the kitchen and dining hall, the limp from his damaged ankle now clearly evident. The two investigators watch his retreating form until it disappears. Delaying the inevitable.

Neumann rolls his shoulders, glances at Schneider, takes a sharp breath.

"Ready?"

"Ready."

Schneider doesn't bother covering his hand before grabbing the doorknob and turning. By now, with whoever found the body already smearing their prints on it, and with Joseph Kohl following suit, and who knows who else, any useful fingerprints that might once have lurked there are long gone. He pushes the door carefully open, all the way. The smell rushes out to attack his nostrils.

"Holy fuck!"

Schneider covers his nose with a handkerchief even as he speaks. Neumann echoes the big man's move with his left hand as his right searches for the light switch. He finds it, flicks it up, and two bare ceiling bulbs burst into life. Their yellowish glow illuminates a scene from hell.

Father Gantz, like Fathers Rochlitz and Dassler before him, is seated in an armchair, painfully backstretched arms bound together by thin cord. Like Father Dassler's, Father Gantz's eyes have disappeared, in their place only two weeping black depressions. What appears at first glance to be a pile of wet clothing or rags sitting in his lap is his entrails, spilled from a huge vertical slash in his abdomen. The smell is horrific. Blood, guts, faeces, urine. It's agricultural, animal, the stench of the slaughterhouse.

Neumann and Schneider have no words. They unwillingly drink in the abomination, each man deep within his own thoughts and imaginings, temporarily pushing aside the things of polite society – shopping and children, ice cream on a hot day, birds singing, a warm bed, the touch of a loved one. There is no place here for such things. This is beyond them, a different world, a world of unimaginable pain and inhuman depravity, the world of the beast. Neither man speaks, wants to be the first to speak. They force their eyes from the despoiled dead man, take in the rest of the room. As with Father Rochlitz and Father Dassler, so it is with Father Gantz – his room has been systematically destroyed. Slashed, broken, ripped, snapped, reduced to the aftermath of a search for something. The contents of the room are as ruined as the man sitting dead in the middle of them.

Minutes slide by unnoticed. A heavy black mantel clock, its case and glass both smashed and detached, lies on the floor but still clunks and thumps the seconds, the sound unnaturally loud in the otherwise complete silence. Each man can hear the other's breathing, hear his own heartbeat. Nothing moves. It's Schneider who eventually drags them back to reality.

"We'd better make a start."

Neumann doesn't speak, just nods. The two men begin to move slowly around the room, examining, analysing, thinking, looking for some hint, some insight, some . . . some . . . unknown thing, something that will help them understand. Even as they do, both men silently struggle with the same unspoken, desperate, despairing thought – this is beyond understanding.

✠

Kriminalrat Franz Böhm exits the lift at the rear of the Reichsluftahrtministerium building, steps across the top floor corridor and knocks on the door to the Reichsmarschall's office. He's surprised when the door is almost immediately opened from the inside by Hermann Göring, who breaks into a broad smile as he extends a hand, forestalling the Hitler salute Böhm had intended. Göring's other hand is engaged in slipping a small flat silver box into his left side coat pocket. A Pervitin pill popped before the meeting begins.

"Franz! So good of you to come. Please, enter. I have arranged for coffee and cake. Come, come."

Göring takes a step back to let Böhm through the door, and in the process catches the eye of the Luftwaffe Oberleutnant standing at attention next to the lift. "Thank you, Günther," says Göring as he closes the door again.

Inside, ever the genial host, Göring ushers his guest to one of the black leather armchairs set away from the Reichsmarschall's desk. Today he's eschewed the comic opera uniforms he frequently favours, choosing instead a beautifully tailored three-piece dark grey suit, a suit so well-cut it almost manages to disguise his enormous girth. It's the look of a prosperous businessman, a man of affairs, a man of substance. Even Göring's usually heavy application of 4711 cologne is restrained, although Böhm notices the Reichsmarschall's fingernails are still painted. A pale grey, in keeping with the suit. As fashionable and tailored as it is, the suit is nonetheless a costume too. Böhm has heard all the jokes about Göring's predilection for dressing up. Göring's heard them also – he always laughs the loudest, sees the jokes as a sign of affection, a measure of his popularity. Böhm was there when Göring heard the one where the Reichsmarschall was sent by Hitler to depose the Pope and sent back a telegram – 'Mission successful. Pope defrocked. Tiara and pontifical vestments fit perfectly.' Göring nearly wet himself at that one.

Böhm is not in uniform either, not for this kind of visit. Like Göring, he's wearing a suit, although it's one off the rack from Wertheim's department store, getting on for three years old now, bought in the days before the store's Jewish owners were kicked out. In different circumstances, he'd feel shabby, cheap, inferior, but Göring's geniality steamrollers everything in its path. The

Reichsmarschall holds out a cedar box with its lid open, offers a cigar, insists that Böhm try one.

"They're genuine Cuban. A friend of mine arranges it. Usually he can get Black Wisdom, but lately I'm afraid . . . No matter – these are excellent. Have you tried the Clear Havana before? No? Then please, . . ."

Göring bends forward to light Böhm's cigar, then sits back to light his own. A knock on the office's other door precedes the entry of the usual plump middle-aged woman, Gerda, pushing a trolley with coffee, milk, cream and sugar accompanied by several slices of cake. Without a word she places everything on the low table between the two men, gives a slight nod, and retreats with the now-empty trolley.

Göring pours coffee for each of them, gestures expansively at the table's contents.

"Try the apple cake, Franz. The Führer's own pastrycook makes it for me as a favour."

Böhm is aware of Hitler's fondness for 'Führer cake'. He eyes the plateful before him, astonished at someone's ability to source the raisins and nuts which populate it. He dutifully forks a mouthful, chews appreciatively, nodding and making genuine 'Mmmn' noises as he does. He swallows, says "Delicious, thank you," as he leans forward to take up his coffee. Göring beams with unfeigned pleasure before speaking, rubs his fat hands together in anticipation.

"Well, my friend, to business. You have some news, yes?"

Böhm has sipped his coffee, puts the cup down. "Yes, a little, Herr Reichsmarschall, although I'm not sure what to make of it all. The situation is far from normal."

"We live in times that are far from normal, Franz. Tell me."

"You have heard about the other dead priests? The two more recent murders?"

"I have. Are they connected to the death of the first priest?"

"It seems likely, sir, but in what way isn't clear. My man reports that he's . . ."

"Your man," interrupts Göring. "Are you now in charge of the investigation?"

"Yes, sir, I am now. The investigator, Kriminalkommissar Max Neumann, reports directly to me. He tells me . . ."

"What has changed? When we last met you told me Tanzinger had taken control of the investigation."

"He had. But that was when only one priest had been murdered. When the second one was killed, Tanzinger handed the whole thing back to Kriminaldirektor Becker, and he's put me in charge. That's what would normally happen."

The news seems to puzzle Göring. He sits back in his chair, smokes his cigar, seems to have forgotten Böhm is there. Suddenly he gestures with his free hand, points at Böhm.

"Himmler must have told Tanzinger to back off. He's the only one who could put that sort of pressure on him." Göring hesitates, realises he might have unintentionally slighted Hitler. "Apart from the Führer, of course. No, it must have been Himmler. But why? Why wouldn't the little shit want Tanzinger close to the action? Do you have a view, Franz?"

"I can't think of why, sir. All I know is that Becker's dumped the whole thing in my lap. Even he doesn't seem that interested in what's going on."

"And are *you*, Franz? Interested?"

"Of course, sir. I'm following the investigator's progress closely. Not that there's been a lot of progress. We have no witnesses, no obvious leads. Neumann and his partner have been probing every possibility of a connection between the three murdered men, but with one exception, beyond the fact that they were all priests, there's nothing to link them. As far as we can tell, they didn't even know each other."

"You said there was an exception."

"Yes. In each case, the rooms where the bodies were found had been searched, thoroughly searched, nearly destroyed in the process. Somebody, almost certainly Standartenführer Schmidt, was looking for something. The fact that three priests have died suggests he didn't find it. At least not the first two times. And perhaps not even on the third occasion. We may have to wait and see if another priest . . ."

Böhm lets the sentence hang, lets its implication waft and settle. Göring nods thoughtfully before responding. He knows the answer to the question he's going to ask, but it will do no harm if Böhm thinks otherwise.

"And we're sure . . . you're sure it's Schmidt each time?"

"We think so, sir. It was obviously him the first time, with Rochlitz. And the injuries, the other priests' deaths . . . There is no possibility of coincidence. It has to be him."

"And your investigator, . . . ah . . ."

"Neumann, sir, Kriminalkommissar Neumann."

"Yes, Neumann. Does he know about Schmidt? Have you told him what your informant saw?"

"No sir. I thought it best that for the time being only you were given that information."

"Yes, yes, of course, let us keep some of this to ourselves for the moment. If the time comes when Herr Neumann needs to know about Schmidt, well, we'll cross that bridge when we get to it. My only concern at the moment is that we need to find out what Schmidt is looking for – and get our hands on it before anyone else does. If we're not already too late."

Göring doesn't dwell on his last thought. Instead, he claps his hands together and beams, sits forward in his chair, points to the 'Führer cake' on the table in front of them. "For now, however, we have more important things to think about. Have another slice, Franz. With cream." He leans forward to serve his visitor.

21

Standartenführer Stefan Schmidt exchanges a 'Heil Hitler' with his boss, takes a chair in front of Himmler's desk. He's in his dark blue suit, white shirt, grey tie. A soft grey hat rests on his lap. The two men sit without speaking, wait as Himmler's adjutant, Hauptsturmführer Ernst Knoechlein, collects the documents he was showing the SS chief and leaves the room.

Himmler leans back in his chair, removes his rimless spectacles and cleans them with a handkerchief from his trouser pocket. He's the only member of the SS able to perform such an action – anyone else who needs to wear spectacles is automatically prohibited from joining the Schutzstaffel because of their demonstrable 'genetic weakness'. Nobody wants to be first to point out the hypocrisy.

"Very well, Stefan," he says, rubbing the lenses, "proceed."

"I regret, sir, that there is little progress to report. Since we last spoke I have interviewed a great many people who knew Father Rochlitz, but they have not provided any insight into what he might have done with the certificate. Not that I have alluded to the existence of such a document, of course. The process continues, and I am casting my net wider, further back in his life. There are another three or four of his friends and colleagues I have yet to see, but it does not look promising."

"Interviews? You said you interviewed them."

"I put questions to them, Reichsführer. Led them to believe I represented the Ministry of Propaganda, gathering information for an article about the late Father. As far as I can tell, all of them were truthful in their responses. If the interviews of those I have not yet contacted also prove fruitless, I may have to revisit the people I have already seen and adopt a different approach. A more insistent approach."

Himmler doesn't ask the nature of Schmidt's proposed 'more insistent approach'. The Reichsführer knows all he needs to, knows that Schmidt's methods achieve results, which is all he wants. But one small matter causes him passing curiosity.

"The other two priests? How are they connected?"

"There is no connection, sir. I was unable to determine any link between them and Father Rochlitz, which is primarily why they were chosen. The deaths of three priests in quick succession removed the spotlight from Father Rochlitz. There is no cause for anyone to think he was singled out. As far as the Kripo are concerned, he's just one of a string of murdered priests whose rooms have been searched. There is no reason for a Kripo investigation to focus on only him."

Himmler rests his chin on steepled fingers as he listens, ponders. A slight frown creases his forehead. As Schmidt finishes, Himmler reaches over and picks up a gold and silver Pez Spezial tin on his desk, opens it and extracts a breath mint. He pops the mint into his mouth and sucks for a few seconds before he responds.

"Yes, I see, of course. I have made sure the three deaths are all being handled as a routine investigation. That fool Tanzinger got his hands on Rochlitz's case and wanted to pursue it personally for some reason. I told him I'd heard he was wasting time on a routine death, said I wasn't prepared for my top policeman to be dealing in trivialities, told him to throw it all back into the pool. That should be the end of it."

"And yet, sir, the document is presumably still in existence. Either secreted somewhere by Father Rochlitz, or entrusted by him to other hands. I am inclined to the former possibility."

"Your reasons?"

"Simply that more than a month has passed since the document was brought to your attention, and there has been no attempted public release of it. That suggests it may yet be hidden. I think it less likely that a person holding it on the priest's behalf would not realise its significance. Either way, it has not been revealed to a wider audience."

Himmler sucks his Pez mint, drums his fingers on the desk top, thoughtful and preoccupied. He stops as Schmidt finishes speaking.

"Hm," he grunts. "That might be an impediment, but one to our advantage. Revealing it to a wider audience. There's not a newspaper or radio station in the Reich which would make such a thing public. So, how is he . . . how is whoever's behind this going to achieve publicity?"

It's a rhetorical question, and Schmidt doesn't respond. Both men know the almost non-existent chances of public dissemination through news outlets subject to ferocious Party control. The most likely avenue would be printed flyers distributed anonymously around the capital, a dangerous but effective means of spreading prohibited information. The possibility exists that the document might find its way into the hands of a foreign power, but that poses little threat. If the foreign power is in the enemy alliance, then the document can easily be dismissed as a clumsy forgery dreamed up to discredit the German government. Not so easy if the foreign power is neutral – although such a country would be as likely to lose as to gain by allowing a public revelation. So, a possibility only, and a threadbare one at that. Nonetheless, one Himmler can't allow to play out. He locks Schmidt in his gaze.

"It is no matter. Please continue your endeavours, Stefan."

22

The third-floor apartment is modestly affluent in its dimensions and furnishings, neither the home of a struggling factory worker from Kreuzberg nor an industrialist's villa on Schwanenwerder commanding a desirable view over the Wannsee. Irmgard Neumann has homemaking taste and ability, both freely acknowledged by her husband, who just as freely acknowledges his shortcomings when it comes to choosing curtains, tableware, decorative art. A generous space off the small but adequate entry hall doubles as a dining and sitting room, looks through a Romanesque arch to the kitchen. Doors lead from both sides of the dining room, two bedrooms off one, bathroom and toilet off the other. Tonight, through nothing short of magic, Irmgard has from somewhere managed to acquire red and white cornflowers to decorate the dining table and walnut Biedermeier sideboard. The best porcelain and silver are set beside blue linen napkins. The new bakelite Philco Transitone on the sideboard is tuned to a popular music station, softly plays an Evelyn Künneke song. The overall effect is restrained, solid, middle-class, comfortable.

An ice bucket sits next to the table, produced at the last minute when Harry Forbes arrives with a bottle of Pol Roger 1939 and insists they drink it that night. Forbes doesn't comment as Max uses his first sip of wine to down a couple of aspirin, and Max doesn't ask how his friend came by a bottle of genuine champagne. Max suppresses a smile at the irony that the three of them will be drinking what the British Prime Minister, Winston Churchill, famously drinks every day.

It's obvious Irmgard is impressed by Forbes, by his handsome face and trim body, by his smooth East Coast accent and studied politeness, by the sheer exoticism of him simply being American. She warms to him immediately, and he to her, the two of them chatting as though Max was in another room. As happens every time, Max's stomach churns to see Irmgard's attraction. It's all he can do not to break into their conversation, disrupt the situation, pull his wife away from their guest. She's wearing perfume tonight, 'Mystikum', and Neumann interprets the unusual occurrence adversely. In his mind's eye he sees again Irmgard's hand on his little brother's arm during their dinner at Walther and Anni's apartment. He silently berates himself, curses his schoolboy jealousy. Like Othello, he needs an Iago to warn him against 'the green-eyed monster which doth mock the meat it feeds on'. It's only willpower that keeps the roiling emotions down, maintains a smile on his face.

Most of the champagne has disappeared by the time dinner is ready. Max tells Forbes to sit at the table as Irmgard carries in soup plates from the kitchen.

"Bring your glass," he says to Harry. "There's enough left in the bottle to go with soup." He retrieves Irmgard's half-full glass from beside the armchair she was sitting in, puts it on the dining table. She sets the last soup bowl on the table and takes her seat, smooths her dress beneath her. As she does, Harry gets to his feet, glass raised, beaming.

“A toast to my friends! To Max and Irmgard, who have shown kindness and hospitality to a stranger in their country.”

He waits until the couple raise their glasses in response, throws his head back, downs what’s left of his champagne, sits.

“Irmgard,” he says, taking a spoonful of soup, “this is delicious, really good. I’m impressed that you can conjure up something like this when . . . well, the shortages, the rationing. It must be difficult.”

There’s a small moment of silence. The Neumanns are already painfully and continually aware of demands made by the government’s stringent rationing regime – it’s brought home to them every day. Meat, butter, cheese, eggs, chocolate have become delicacies for all but the wealthy or the well-connected. What was once an abstract possibility has for so long been a harsh reality that Max and Irmgard are fleetingly surprised to be reminded that the situation is abnormal. And surprised also to be reminded by a newcomer to their country.

“Thank you, Harry,” responds Irmgard. “It *is* difficult, but we manage. Like everyone else, I suppose. We’re lucky to have friends who help.” She waves a hand towards the soup bowl in front of her. “If it wasn’t for old Herr and Frau Hilfiger in the next block, we wouldn’t be having French onion soup, I’m afraid. It would have been potato instead – they’re not rationed.”

“The Hilfigers grow onions on their balcony,” explains Max. “Herbs, too. We help them out with a few things, and we get a few things in return. Everybody’s doing it. Times like these, you have to survive as best you can.”

Forbes smiles understandingly.

“And we’ve got the Hilfigers to thank for our main course, too,” adds Max. “They’ve donated one of their balcony pigs. We don’t get them very often.”

Forbes smiles again, but this time uncertainly, frowns, opens his mouth to speak. Irmgard forestalls him.

"Rabbits," she laughs, "rabbits. At least, one rabbit. The Hilfigers breed them on their balcony. Quite a few people do. It stretches the meat ration – every little bit helps. We're lucky Max isn't a big eater these days. More for you and me."

Forbes smiles, but then he's suddenly serious.

"When will it end? The rationing. The fighting. All of it."

Max and Irmgard exchange a sharp look, stop eating, sit motionless. Nobody asks that question any more. Not in public, at least. But this is different – it's not in public, but among friends. The moment passes.

"It depends on who you ask," responds Max guardedly. "If you listen to Mahatma Propagandhi or the Fat Man, then our brave troops will march gloriously onwards until all our enemies are crushed. Russians, British, communists, Jews, homosexuals, socialists, *Untermenschen* of every kind. The lot."

"Sure, but Goebbels and Göring aren't going to say anything else, are they? What do ordinary people think, people like the Neumanns? What do you think, Irmgard?"

She looks surprised to have been asked for an opinion, takes a moment to consider it before replying.

"I can only go on what the Führer has already achieved. Everyone can see his record. France, Belgium, Holland, Norway, Denmark, Poland – all subdued. The English are beaten but won't admit it. The Russians are on their knees. We'll be in Moscow for Christmas. Our troops are in control all over Europe." She takes a breath, pauses. "It's difficult to see how all that can be undone. We just need to see it through."

Forbes' face gives away his agreement with Irmgard's assessment. He turns to Max.

"Is that how you see the future?"

Max could see this moment coming. He's prepared. Cautious, even though he's known Forbes for so long. It's a narrow path to be steered between his wife and his guest.

“I’m a bit less confident. Irmgard’s right – we’ve already achieved a lot. If it was anybody else but the Ivans, I’d be happy to put money on outright victory. But they’re tough customers. Tough enough to hold on to Moscow. And they seem to have an inexhaustible supply of troops – no matter how many we kill or capture, they still keep coming.” He sees Forbes peering intently at him. “We’re going to need some luck. A lot of it. If we don’t get it, well . . .” He shrugs, throws up his hands in a ‘Who can tell?’ gesture.

Forbes continues staring at him. The silence stretches on. It’s broken when Irmgard abruptly gets to her feet and gathers up the empty soup bowls.

“Max, some more wine for our guest. I’ll serve the rabbit.”

Neumann moves to the sideboard, wrestles there with a corkscrew and bottle before bringing the wine and three fresh glasses to the table. He pours for Forbes.

“There’s at least one thing in favour of our Italian friends,” Max says. “Even with all our science there’s no way we can produce anything like this in Germany. Nature just won’t let us grow . . ,” he holds the bottle up, studies the label, “Nebbiolo. Or any other decent red grape for that matter.” He pours a glass for himself, one for Irmgard.

Forbes leans forward.

“I hope I wasn’t out of place there,” he says quietly. “I don’t want to set you and Irmgard at odds.”

“You won’t. You haven’t,” replies Neumann with a dismissive gesture. “We both know the same facts, or as close as you can get to facts these days. We just interpret them differently. What about America? What’s the feeling there?”

“Back home? I guess ‘mixed’ describes it. A lot of people think Germany’s going to come out on top. Even so, they don’t want anything to do with another war in Europe – not after the last time. They don’t really give a damn who wins, figure it won't affect us. But there's a lot of others who think we should get involved on the side of the Brits, stop Hitler before it's too late. They think there's still time."

Forbes listens intently, concentrates, takes a moment to gather his thoughts.

"And you?"

"I've got to say that I incline towards Irmgard's view of the situation. A lot of the guys at the Embassy are on board with it, too. Your soldiers are a long way from being beaten. There's no finer fighting force in the world, in my opinion. And I include my fellow Americans. We just can't match your guys. The Waffen-SS in particular. Hell, they . . ."

"Thugs, the lot of them." Neumann bursts into Forbes' flow, fixes him with a hard look. "Just thugs. Don't let the scary uniform and the Goebbels bullshit fool you. They're vicious bastards, nothing less, just . . ."

Irmgard's voice stops her husband dead.

"Don't believe everything you hear, Harry."

Back at the table, she sets down two plates of rabbit stew, potatoes and carrots on one side. She throws a quick glance at her husband as she continues.

"Max is biased. He has been ever since the Kripo became an unwilling SS bedfellow. They're not such a bad bunch, in my experience, no better or worse than any other security force. Did you know Max's little brother Walther has joined the SS? He's an Untersturmführer."

She turns and goes back to the kitchen for the third plate of stew, throws over her shoulder, "Is Walther a thug too, Max?"

Forbes is obviously surprised by the revelation. "You didn't say anything," he chastises his friend. "Are you unhappy about it?"

Neumann takes a moment or two before replying, still negotiating the narrow path between candid and polite.

"I'd be happier if he was a policeman. Or he'd just stayed in the Army. Walther's alright, but some of the company he keeps . . . Nobody's going to deny the SS has more than its fair share of bullies and psychopaths. And they're all infected with the rubbish about pure blood, Aryan racial superiority, that sort of stuff. Even Walther. He had it rammed down his throat during training. He . . ." Max breaks off, realises he's about to go too far. Irmgard steps in.

"Tell us something about yourself, Harry. Max says you live in a penthouse in Washington. I've never been in one. It must be wonderful to come home to luxury like that."

"Ah, yes, well . . . There's a bit of a story there," says Forbes. A shadow of something falls on him. Neumann can't pick it for a moment, studies Forbes as he tries to choose his words. Then he realises his friend is embarrassed. Forbes hasn't flushed red, but he's clearly uncomfortable. He takes a sharp breath before continuing.

"It's true – I *used* to live in a Washington penthouse. But now I live in . . . at least before I was posted here, I had an apartment in Anacostia." Forbes gestures helplessly. "It's south-east of the Capitol, over the Anacostia river. Not too far, and the bus route ran right outside, dropped me nearly at the front door of the office."

Neumann struggles to accommodate the information. The Harry Forbes he knew at Cambridge was always flush with funds, as befitted the only son of a wealthy newspaper owner. His father ran the *Boston Gazette*, the *Philadelphia Record*, and a handful of smaller regional publications on America's east coast. Harry's clothes, his books, his car – everything shouted wealth handled with taste. Now Neumann is hearing about the man taking buses, living outside of Washington proper in a neighbourhood notorious for its depressed inhabitants. Something has changed. He's about to pose the obvious question

when Forbes forestalls him.

"The crash of twenty-nine. That was the start of it. The papers took a hard hit, nobody advertising, nobody buying, job cuts . . ." His words fade away as he momentarily relives the downfall of his family's fortunes. Then he's back. "Anyway, Dad tried to hang on, trade his way through the crisis, poured in a lot of his own money. For a couple of years he kept his head above water, just, but by thirty-two things finally fell apart. The papers had to close. The *Record* went first, the *Gazette* not long after. Then the rest all at once. That was the end. Nobody realised how bad it was, how much it affected him. Ma took it hard. We all did."

Max is dumbfounded by the revelation, speechless. Irmgard is saddened, solicitous. She lays a hand on Forbes' arm.

"What does your father do now, Harry? Is he still in the news business? Papers, magazines?"

A slow shake of the head in response.

"No, he's not with us anymore. Losing the papers . . . well, it had been his life. He didn't leave a note or anything, but that had to be the answer."

The silence, awkward and sudden, stretches on. Irmgard keeps her hand on Forbes' arm, squeezes it once or twice.

Abruptly, Forbes reaches across and briefly lays his free hand on Irmgard's, then sits up straight and swings his gaze between the two Neumanns.

"Enough of the downcast looks, my friends! I refuse to be anything but happy tonight. Another toast!" He lifts his glass, beams at the others. "To good friends and good times, yes?"

Dutifully, Max and Irmgard follow suit, offer up weak smiles, but their hearts aren't committed.

23

"Yes? Kriminalkommissar Neumann."

In the middle of unloved paperwork, he sounds more impatient and annoyed than he means to.

"There is a call for you, Kriminalkommissar."

Neumann instantly regrets his brusqueness, recognises with pleasure the voice from the switchboard. It's that new girl, the young one. Olga? Helga? Something like that. Looks like an advertisement for the *Bund Deutscher Mädel*, BDM, the League of German Girls, all long blonde plaits and a sunny freckled smile. He's aware that BDM is increasingly being thought of as short for *Bund Deutscher Matratzen*, the League of German Mattresses. It's not the first time the new girl has been in Neumann's mind, dressed in her uniform of short dark blue skirt, white blouse straining across the chest. Even as he thinks the thought he chastises himself – she's young enough to be my daughter. Still, when . . .

"It's a Frau Steinert. She says you know her."

The name hesitates at the entrance to his brain for a moment before his memory lets it in. When it does, he recalls there was no telephone in Frau Steinert's apartment. Either he missed it or she's capable of getting out and about, perhaps as far the nearest public telephone.

"Yes. Yes, I do. Put her through, please."

Neumann imagines those smooth young fingers manipulating the telephone jacks, pulling one out, inserting it elsewhere. He waits for the static and clicks to stop.

"Herr Kriminalkommissar?"

"Yes, Frau Steinert. What is it?"

"I apologise if I have bothered you unnecessarily, but something has happened." Then, as though she's read his mind, "Frau Beckenbauer, my neighbour. She has allowed me to telephone from her apartment. Someone was here yesterday asking questions. About Father Rochlitz. This man, he . . . I was frightened. I did not want to bother you, but all day I have been thinking about it . . . I'm sorry, but . . ."

"Please, Frau Steinert, try not to distress yourself. I'm sure there's an explanation. Was he a policeman? Perhaps one of my colleagues?"

"No, not *Kriminalpolizei*. He was from the Ministry of Propaganda. But he didn't . . . He frightened me, Herr Neumann. I thought it best to let you know."

"Of course, of course, I understand. Perhaps I could call on you again with Kriminalassistant Schneider. Then we can work out what this is all about. Would that be of assistance?"

Even over the telephone, her relief is tangible.

"Yes, yes, thank you, Kriminalkommissar. A visit would be most helpful."

"We have already arranged to speak to another person later today, so we will not be able to call on you until after our appointment. Would that be convenient? About six?"

"Thank you, thank you, Kriminalkommissar. I will look forward to your visit."

✠

"We're running out of customers, boss."

"Not enough good Fathers left to murder, you think?"

Schneider's as aware as Neumann of the extent to which the Catholic Church's priesthood has been denuded since the Party took power in 1933. Lumped in with all the other discontented, the other 'asocial' elements and crypto-communists, priests occupy many a hard bed in the concentration camps. The camp inmates might be considered lucky, given the number of priests who have vanished without trace into the night and fog.

"That too, but I'm talking about witnesses, people who'll talk to us."

Schneider's comment resurrects the thought Neumann has been forcing down for the past fortnight or more. Three dead priests, interviews with dozens of the dead men's friends, family and work colleagues, trawling through newspaper and archive records. And it all amounts to nothing. There's no connection to be found between the three murdered priests, no suggestion that any of them possessed something valuable enough to warrant what has happened. No witnesses, no clues, no possible starting point. And yet there's a disquiet that refuses to go away. Neumann feels uncomfortable, sure he's missed something important, something that doesn't sit right, and he's irritated, frustrated that he can't put his finger on it. It's the feeling you get when you know there's something you need to remember but can't remember what it is.

The pair are standing outside the rectory of Sacred Heart church in Tegel, about ten kilometres north-west of Berlin centre, at the northern tip of the Tegeler See. The rectory sits like an afterthought at the rear of the soaring Gothic Revival building that is the church itself. One of the late Father Gantz's fellow priests at St John's has pointed them in the direction of a former housekeeper there, Frau Hoffmann. Father Gantz and she were particularly friendly, it appears, friendlier that he was with anyone else at St John's. If he divulged any information or secrets, it's possible Frau Hoffmann was the recipient. It's not much of a lead, only a possibility, but in the absence of anything else it's a lead that needs to be followed up. Neumann steps up to the blackened timber door and thumps the iron knocker a few times before turning back to Schneider.

"There's always customers, Kurt. Just that some of them aren't keen to come out from under their rocks."

As Neumann speaks, the rectory door opens to reveal a stooped bald old priest who studies them through watery pale eyes. He keeps a hand on the edge of the door for support. The two policemen produce their identity discs, hold them out.

"Kripo, Father. We'd like to talk to Frau Gertrud Hoffmann."

The old priest leans forward, cupped hand to his ear.

"Who?"

Neumann raises his voice.

"Frau Hoffmann!"

The old man stares at him for a moment before replying.

"No. You. Who are you?"

Schneider steps in close, still holding his disc out, bends down to be level with the priest.

"We're cops, Father. Can we see Frau Hoffmann?"

There's a few seconds pause before the old man slowly turns back into the rectory and disappears from view. The door is still open. Neumann and Schneider exchange glances, wait. A minute or so passes before they see a shape emerging out of the darkness of the interior. A thin, bird-like woman in her sixties appears in the doorway brushing damp grey hair from her forehead. She's in a shapeless brown dress on top of which is a bib-fronted faded blue apron. Her shoes are badly scuffed at the toes. Above them are thick wrinkled grey stockings. In one hand she holds a damp yellow cloth. She peers at the two policemen over half-moon spectacles, her eyes flitting back and forth, curious rather than hostile.

"I'm Frau Hoffmann. What do you want?"

After a brief exchange on the steps of the rectory, Neumann and Schneider find themselves sitting at a kitchen table strewn with altar vessels, some dull, others polished and shiny – a silver chalice, two gold patens, a silver ciborium, various other lesser items. The men look across the table and its contents to Frau Hoffmann on the other side. She sits with knees together, hands folded in her lap, straight-backed and controlled after her initial shock on hearing about Father Gantz's death. Neumann explains why they are there, and she tells them as much as she can about the late priest. There's nothing new in what she says, nothing that takes their investigation any further – the late priest was quiet, polite, humble and devout, a 'lovely and kind man'. Frau Hoffmann can not conceive of a reason he would have anything valuable in his possessions, nor of a reason anyone would want to harm him. He was, she insists, universally loved and respected. She has no adverse comment about any of the other priests or lay staff at St John's.

"They were some of the nicest people you could imagine. I was happy there, and you can't always say that about the places you work. I could tell you some stories about St Sebastian's, for instance. But that was an exception. I've enjoyed my work almost everywhere. Some lovely people, you know. The AEG factory in Moabit, the . . ."

Neumann is about to interrupt the old lady's stream of consciousness. She's told them all she can, and only politeness is keeping him and Schneider at the table. But then she says something which stops him dead.

". . . the people at Saint Lambertus, and the boys at the

Hackescher Markt. I've had some . . ."

"Excuse me, Frau Hoffmann. Did you say Saint Lambertus?" Neumann is as puzzled as he is surprised. The name Hoffmann hasn't surfaced in connection with Father Rochlitz or St Lambertus. Is there another church of the same name in Germany? Or in a different country?

Frau Hoffmann is mildly irritated at being interrupted. She peers sharply at Neumann before replying.

"Yes, Saint Lambertus. Why do you ask?"

"The church in Moabit?"

"Yes, in Moabit," she snaps.

"Forgive me, Frau Hoffman, but we have asked about the staff at Saint Lambertus, and been given their names. Yours is not among them. Do you know why that would be?"

"No, I don't. Perhaps it's because I was there only a short time. For a few months in twenty-two, not long before Christmas. Why? Is it important?"

Neumann explains about the murder of Father Rochlitz, asks if Frau Hoffman knew him. It's clear from her face's reaction to the question that if she did, it wasn't well.

"Rochlitz? Ah, yes, the young one. I remember him a little. A shy one, or at least he didn't talk much. I don't think we said more than a few words to each other. It was the other woman there who did his cleaning and such. Steiner, Schindler, something like that."

"Was it Frau Steinert? Frau Gabriele Steinert?"

"Yes, Steinert, that's the name. A friendly woman, I liked her. But it was Fräulein, not Frau. She was single."

Schneider can't hold back, blurts out in surprise. "It must have been someone else, then, Frau Hoffmann. Frau Steinert was married, had been married. To a soldier. He died in the Great War. She was a widow."

"No, it wasn't someone else, it was her. Gabriele Steinert.

She wasn't married. Never had been."

"But she had a son," Schneider persists, "a young boy called Jürgen."

"Just because you've got a child doesn't mean you're married, young man," says Frau Hoffmann primly. "Do I need to spell it out for you? Everybody there knew she wasn't married. They knew about the boy. Why do you think she was working for the church? Who else would have her?"

24

In a drab brown suit and hat to match, worn grey overcoat with collar turned against the cold, Tadeuz Zebrowski looks like any one of the thousands of workers thronging the miserable wet streets around the Reichsluftahrtministerium. A leaden sky, biting north wind, spatters of rain – there's no pleasure to be found in the threatened onset of a Berlin winter, and the workers streaming home with heads bent reflect the weather's joylessness. When he reaches the rear corner of the Air Ministry building, Zebrowski peels away from the masses on Leipziger Strasse and makes his steady way to the loading ramp and unmarked door next to it which will take him to Göring's office.

No words are spoken as Zebrowski is admitted, escorted to the elevator, taken to the seventh floor. He leaves his escort behind, knocks on Göring's door, and from within is told to enter. Göring rises from behind his desk, shakes hands in greeting, ushers Zebrowski to a chair. The Reichsmarschall today is in a plain but well-cut deep grey suit with matching silk waistcoat. His clothes reflect his mood. He is less than his usual ebullient self, preoccupied, worried, all bonhomie seemingly stripped from him. Zebrowski makes no comment, waits, thinks the deteriorating situation on the Russian Front might well be behind the fat man's sombre spirits.

"It's good of you to come, Tadeuz," says Göring mechanically, as he reaches into the side pocket of his jacket and pulls out a slim orange and blue metal cylinder. It's Pervitin. Zebrowski knows the main ingredient is something called methamphetamine, knows the stimulant's effects, knows that hundreds of thousands of citizens are regular consumers. The Wehrmacht, too, dispensing 'tank chocolate' to the Reich's soldiers in vast quantities. Zebrowski doesn't need stimulants. His work is stimulant enough. He waits while Göring takes a sip of water with two of the pills before addressing his guest again.

"So!" Göring claps his hands together, summons up a beaming countenance, sits forward in his armchair. "You have something to report, I'm sure. Please, let me know all you can."

"Of course, Herr Reichsmarschall. I have been observing Standartenführer Schmidt, as you require. He has been very active these past days, very peripatetic. So much so that on two occasions I was unable to follow him to his destination. On several other occasions my observation of his activities was achieved only with considerable difficulty."

Göring becomes animated. "You don't think he . . . Did he realise you were following him?" There's a note of alarm in Göring's voice. Perhaps fear.

"No," says Zebrowski quickly. "He was unaware of my presence, of that I am certain. The speed and suddenness of his movements were for other reasons. He appears to be acting in some haste. Perhaps he is under pressure from Reichsführer Himmler. Whatever the reason, he has questioned a great many people in a short time."

"Questioned? What, arrested?"

"No, merely questioned. He visits their home or place of

work and asks them questions. There is no evidence of violence or coercion. His approach is to be expected if he seeks the location of something one of the dead priests had possessed. From the little I have been able to discover, he seeks information from friends, work colleagues, family members."

"Yes, it's to be expected," says Göring ruminatively, pursing his lips in concentration. A thought occurs to him. "There must be a great many people involved. How does he expect to . . ." His voice trails off, leaving Zebrowski to pick up the unspoken intimation.

"Indeed, yes, that is the thing. He appears not to be questioning everybody. Only those connected to Father Rochlitz. He has made no enquiries concerning the other two priests. Dassler and Gantz."

Göring sits forward, not understanding.

"No enquiries? But why? Surely if he is looking for something the others will . . ." Again he leaves the sentence dangling in the air.

"Indeed, sir, that would be the logical course of action. If he is not questioning those persons associated with Fathers Dassler and Gantz, the only reason which makes sense is that he knows they will have nothing to tell him. And that in turn means that the dead priests have no relationship to whatever it is the Standartenführer is seeking. Which of course means their deaths are to a degree unrelated to the murder of Father Rochlitz. I . . ."

"It makes no sense," interrupts Göring, spreading his arms in frustration. "None at all. What are you saying, Tadeuz? That someone else killed the other two priests?"

"No, Herr Reichsmarschall, we know with certainty it was Standartenführer Schmidt who killed them. And I believe he did so for a reason. Allow me to explain."

The explanation doesn't take long, and Zebrowski leaves the office immediately afterwards, exhorted by Göring to continue his surveillance and enquiries without putting himself in danger. For several minutes after Zebrowski departs, Göring sits at his desk, head propped up by his forearms, staring vacantly into space as his mind grapples with the implications of what he's been told.

✠

Despite his seniority, the office of Kriminalrat Franz Böhm is scarcely bigger than Neumann's. With Neumann and Schneider sitting on the other side of the desk from him, the room seems uncomfortably tight, an impression not helped by the towering bulk of Schneider who occupies almost as much floor space as two normal men. Böhm waits until both his visitors are settled before speaking. He doesn't waste time with idle pleasantries.

"What's happening about the priests?"

Neumann tells him. Outlines the similarities of the murders, the attempts by him and Schneider to find a common thread between each death, their questioning of everybody connected to the three men, their fruitless search for a plausible motive or common denominator.

Böhm listens without interruption, but nonetheless taps his fingers impatiently on the arms of his chair. He needs something to tell Reichsmarschall Göring, something the man doesn't already know, something which will explain why Himmler has set his attack dog loose.

Neumann reaches the end of his account, waits in silence for Böhm's response.

"So, what you're telling me is, we've got nothing. The only thing we know with any certainty is that whoever killed these priests was looking for something. Is that a fair summary of the situation, Max?"

Böhm sees no need to enlighten Neumann about the involvement of Standartenführer Schmidt. That information can be held in reserve for the moment.

"It is, boss. I know it's not much, but Kurt and I have chased every rabbit we can find down its hole. The only good news is that there haven't been any more dead priests turning up."

"What's your reading on that? Does it mean the killer has found what he's looking for?"

Neumann resists the urge to shrug. "Hard to say. It could mean that he found it when he killed Father Gantz, but . . ."

"But what? Do you think he's still looking?"

"I think he is, yes. There's nothing at the scene, in Gantz's room, to suggest the killer found whatever he wants. The place was completely turned over, just like the other two."

Even as he explains, Neumann can't shake the feeling he's got it wrong, that there's something he's missed. It worries at his brain, an itch that can't be scratched. He can't articulate his hesitancy, can't identify the worm burrowing away in his subconscious, tries to sound more confident than he feels.

Böhm isn't convinced.

"If the killer didn't find the thing, then presumably he's still looking for it. But you said yourself that no more dead priests have turned up. Any thoughts on that?" He swings his gaze to Schneider. "What about you, Kurt?"

Schneider glances at Neumann, gets a silent go-ahead.

"I can't add much, sir. But I agree with Kriminalkommissar Neumann – I think the man's still out there, still looking. There might not be any more dead priests, but perhaps he's got someone else in his sights." A quick look at Neumann. "We might need to widen our search. Check any other murders. Ones after Gantz. See if there's some connection with any or all of the priests."

Böhm raises his eyebrows at Neumann.

"Is that how you see it, Max?"

"It is, boss. We need to start looking further afield, see if there's anybody else been killed, tortured, had their place turned over. It's the only shot we've got left."

Böhm ponders briefly, then gives a sharp nod, places both hands palm down on his desk.

"Right. Better get on with it, then."

The two investigators mutter their thanks and leave, closing the door behind them. Böhm sits back in his chair, runs a hand through his hair, closes his eyes and thinks. If Neumann was told about Schmidt, what would happen then? Would Neumann be so foolish as to try and arrest the man? Surely not. Even Max would baulk at the prospect of trying to cage Himmler's pet rottweiler. But to let Schmidt continue unchecked . . . Well, there's the dilemma, isn't it? Are others going to go the way of the priests? And how many? And, most of all, for what? What is it that's apparently important enough to unleash Schmidt?

25

As they emerge from the lift onto the sixth floor of the Steinerts' apartment block, Neumann and Schneider glance without speaking at the darkly-silhouetted Golem of the flak tower in Humboldthain Park. As always, it seems immovable, permanent, a force of nature destined to forever menace its surroundings. It's what the Party would look like if it were made of concrete, thinks Neumann. He stamps on the thought, leads his partner towards the Steinerts' door, knocks.

Today Jürgen Steinert is in a cheap brown suit, white shirt and tie, no doubt the clothes of his working day. He greets them politely, briefly, holds the door open for them to enter. His movements are jerky, agitated. Motioning the two policemen into the apartment, he closes the door behind them as they walk over to the armchair in which his mother sits.

"Good day, gentlemen," she says, smiling at each in turn. "Thank you for coming. It really is very good of you." She waves an inviting hand. "Please, sit, sit. Will you have some coffee? Or we have tea if you prefer."

Neumann and Schneider accept the offer of chairs, decline

the drinks, thank Frau Steinert for both. Her son remains standing, moves beside her armchair, places a protective hand on its back.

"You said that you have had a visitor, Frau Steinert. One who caused you concern. Can you tell us about that, please?"

Neumann's tone gives nothing away.

"Of course, Kriminalkommissar. It was yesterday, at about this time. Jürgen was home." She glances at her blanket-covered legs, adds, "I am always at home, of course. The man said he was from the Ministry of Propaganda. Herr Wagner was his name. He said he was writing an article about Father Rochlitz. To be published in the *Völkischer Beobachter*, I think. Or perhaps *Das Reich* – I'm afraid I can't remember which one."

"I don't think he was specific, Mother," interjects Jürgen.

"No, no, you're right. Perhaps I assumed . . .

"What did he want to know?" Schneider asks quietly.

"He asked about Father Rochlitz. Everything. What he was like, who were his friends, his past, his hobbies, everything. He was insistent, Herr Schneider. He wanted to know things which should never be published. I did not like him at all. He scared me." She seems to run out of breath for a moment, but then suddenly adds, "And he threatened Jürgen."

Her son immediately throws up a hand, as if he's preparing to ward off an imminent threat.

"Mother, please. He didn't threaten me. He just asked some questions." The young man's appearance and manner don't match his words. He looks and sounds like someone who has been threatened. To Neumann he says, "It was not a threat. The man asked me about things I did not know, and even when I told him so he did not stop."

"Things? What sort of things?" asks Neumann.

"Where Father Rochlitz had visited. Whether he knew other priests. Ones other than at Saint Lambertus. If he had children.

Those sort of things."

"Children? A priest?" Schneider manages to feign both surprise and indignation in his question.

"I know," replies Jürgen, "and I told him as much. It seemed to make no difference. He was a strange man. And, the strangest thing of all was that he did not make any notes about what we told him."

"Nothing at all? Did he have a notebook?"

"No, nothing. It was as though he didn't care what we said."

Neumann and Schneider both look thoughtful, hesitate before speaking again. Frau Steinert's blue eyes flicker between the two men as she and her son await whatever's coming. After a long silence, Neumann speaks.

"Yes, thank you," he says to Jürgen. "Perhaps you could provide Kriminalassistant Schneider with some details of the man, what he looked like, sounded like, that kind of thing." He exchanges a look with Schneider. "Kurt, would you speak to this gentleman outside, please?"

Jürgen looks startled at the suggestion they should leave the room, begins to open his mouth to speak, but shuts it as Schneider takes his elbow and starts moving him towards the door. He throws a last glance at his mother before disappearing outside with Schneider. Neumann turns to the old lady. She seems less startled, as though she knows what's coming. He meets her eyes.

"I thought it best to speak to you alone about this matter. It concerns your son. And perhaps your husband. Could you tell me something of him, please? Of Herr Steinert."

She holds Neumann's gaze, apparently confident, even defiant, but the impression is momentary. Slowly her shoulders begin to sag, her head droops, and she ages beyond her years.

"How much do you know, Kriminalkommissar?" There's weariness in her voice, resignation.

"I know there is no Herr Steinert. I've checked the records of the 18th Infantry Division. Who is Jürgen's father?"

Frau Steinert seems to ponder the question. Her eyes are pools of retrospection. The seconds tick by. Then she focuses, stiffens with resolve.

"It was him, of course. Andreas Rochlitz."

As she speaks, Frau Steinert searches Neumann's face for something. Understanding? Absolution? Whatever it is, she seems to find it there, and it fortifies her.

"We were both young, Kriminalkommissar, both young people then. It was . . . you understand, I am sure. Nobody could know. I could tolerate being a fallen women, but Andreas . . . It would have ruined him. The Church does not easily forgive, you know. Andreas and I . . . we decided it was best this way. Even though we could not publicly declare our love, we had many happy years together. The three of us. Just like any family."

Her eyes lose focus again, turn inwards, conjure up visions of the past, of family idylls, different and better times.

"And Jürgen," asks Neumann softly. "Does Jürgen know?"

"No. No, he is unaware." Her voice is dreamlike, rooted in the past. Then it snaps back to her audience.

"It is better this way. After Andreas was transferred to Schwerin, to Saint Peter's, it would have been impossible to follow him. To tell Jürgen then would have been intolerable. I could not risk losing him. Andreas agreed – we would never tell him. Jürgen had seventeen years, both of them did, seventeen years of warmth, affection, joy. It was a wonderful friendship. Even love. Yes, love, Herr Neumann. Neither Andreas nor I wanted to jeopardise that, to risk it all for no discernible gain."

Frau Steinert pauses, seems to suddenly think of something.

"You must not tell him!" she bursts out, her eyes wide. "Please, you must . . ."

Neumann's placatory hand is already in the air.

“Of course not. I see no reason to say anything at all on the subject. What you have said will stay with me. Me and Kriminalassistant Schneider.” He sees the momentary flash of alarm in the old lady’s eyes, quickly adds, “And he will tell nobody. Not another living soul. You have my word, madam.”

Frau Steinert’s relief washes over her. She smiles and nods her gratitude, reaches forward and puts her hand on Neumann’s knee, pats it twice before sitting back again.

Neumann surprises himself, recognises his reaction – it’s embarrassment, the more so as he doesn’t think he’s done anything to deserve praise or thanks. He coughs nervously before speaking.

“We can put that subject aside for the moment, Frau Steinert, but I need to ask you about something else.” He pauses, gathers his thoughts. “When we spoke the last time, you told me that after Father Rochlitz was transferred to Schwerin you never saw him again, and you did not exchange letters with him, is that correct?”

“Yes, that is correct,” she says without hesitation. “Andreas and I made that decision before he left Saint Lambertus – or what remained of it after the fire.”

“Did he ever send you anything? Perhaps a memento, a photograph, a document, something of that nature?”

Frau Steinert seems momentarily puzzled, seems to think Neumann is asking her the same question in a different way. Then she realises it’s a different question altogether.

“No, nothing. We have received not a thing from him.”

26

Neumann's eyes move listlessly over yesterday's issue of the *Illustrierter Beobachter* propped up in front of his breakfast Bauernomelett and coffee. The omelette has a lot less bacon than it should, and the eggs in it have used up half the week's rations, but extra onion and herbs almost make up for the deficiencies. Neumann forks it up, savours the treat, enjoys the remembrance of good times past.

In normal circumstances, he'd barely glance at this particular newspaper, certainly wouldn't contemplate buying his own copy. But this one comes gratis, sent by Frau Hilfiger from the next block with one of her freshly-slaughtered balcony pigs. The rabbit will be on the dinner table tonight after Irmgard has worked her culinary magic on it and any vegetables she can lay her hands on. As Neumann eats, Irmgard is at the kitchen bench, jointing the animal, rolling it in flour and seasoning, ready for the evening's roast.

The *Illustrierter Beobachter* is being studied over breakfast, although 'studied' overstates Neumann's desultory perusal. His eyes wander here and there without either purpose or much interest. He flicks past the usual stories of heroic deeds and military successes, past the photos of stalwart soldiers and dashing Luftwaffe pilots. If you believe the newspaper, and few do, you'd think that ultimate victory is only a few months away, as soon as those subhuman Ivans have been brought to heel.

One photo takes his eye. It's a Waffen SS private, supposedly beating back Russians in the Wehrmacht's attempted encirclement of Moscow. The soldier is preparing to throw a Model 39 'egg' grenade over a low brick wall. Everything about the picture shrieks deception, broadcasts that the soldier has been carefully posed in his arm-back position, a steely determined look on his face. Neumann idly contemplates the likelihood that even the dumbest soldier in the Wehrmacht would stand so far above the wall, would expose so much of himself to the enemy. He barely suppresses a guffaw of disbelief as his eyes roam further down the page.

The bottom quarter of the page is taken up with two drawings, side by side, apparently identical. They depict a German tank firing on a Russian one, destroying it in a ball of flame and debris. The caption beneath invites the reader to 'Identify the five differences between the drawings', says the answer is to be found on page 27 of the paper. Neumann registers the simple puzzle without interest, starts to turn the page, then stops abruptly.

He flicks the page back, stares at the two drawings. Somewhere in his subconscious a spark ignites, flickers, starts to flare its way into the world. The drawings mean something. Something more than a children's puzzle. Something important. Neumann's world shrinks to the page in front of him. He stares fixedly as his brain churns, works through the myriad possibilities, the implications, hints, connections. He sees nothing else, hears nothing, sits as though frozen solid. Irmgard turns, opens her mouth to speak to him, stops as she sees his unnatural stillness.

The spark arrives in his consciousness, but now it's an inferno, roaring, searing, obliterating everything else but the message it carries. Neumann slams his palm down on the table, rattling the plate and cutlery, startling Irmgard.

"Yes! That's it! They're different!"

✠

The desk has been cleared of everything but the telephone, now pushed to one corner. Spread across the surface are photographs of disorder, devastation, ruin. They are all black and white, all the same size – the British and Americans call it 'eight by ten', and German photographers have set aside their metric system and informally adopted the convenient shorthand. It's much easier to say than 'twenty point three centimetres by twenty-five point four'. The Kripo photographer has done his usual thorough job and produced several prints of each of the murdered priests' rooms.

Kurt Schneider bends over the desk. His eyes roam back and forth across the photographs, stopping here, moving on, flicking back and forth between two or three images. His brow is furrowed, lips pursed in concentration. He's been at it for a few minutes. Then he straightens, shakes his head.

"Can't see it, boss. They look the same to me. Dead man, room torn to pieces afterwards, stuff smashed everywhere. Alright, different men, different rooms, but apart from that they look the same. I'll bite – what's different?"

"Ah, Kurt, it seems you want me to be like Ford in the Merry Wives of Windsor. Very well, 'I shall discover a thing to you'. Look, here."

Neumann points at one of the photographs of Father Rochlitz's room, to a framed print ripped from the wall and thrown face down on the floor. It's been slashed open behind, the thin cardboard backing peeled away from the frame, the interior revealed.

"And here, too." He moves to another photograph, this one showing Father Dassler's room, points to another framed print torn from the walls, slashed, lying face down on the floor. "Right there. And this one," as he points to a photograph of Father Gantz's room. "Here," he adds, hands Schneider a magnifying glass, "you might find it easier with this."

Schneider takes the glass, gives Neumann a dubious sideways glance as he bends again, peering like Sherlock Holmes at each photograph in turn, back and forth, back and forth. Each inspection takes longer than the preceding one. After repeated inspections the magnifying glass is held unwavering for long seconds over the scene in Father Dassler's room. Schneider straightens, eyes narrowed. He hesitates.

"Whoever killed Dassler and Gantz didn't care . . . He wasn't really looking for something, was he? It was for show. Is that what we're looking at?"

Neumann slaps Schneider on the back, conjures up *Hamlet* in his excitement. He's in a good mood.

"A hit! A very palpable hit! Well done, Kurt. Show me."

The two men bend forward over the photographs. Schneider runs a finger around the image of the destroyed framed print in Father Rochlitz's room.

"This one is slashed on three sides, right down to the corners. So the killer could make sure nothing was hidden inside." Schneider shifts to the photograph of Father Gantz's room. "This one, slashed on three sides, but not all the way along. Same here," he adds, pointing to the scene in Father Dassler's room. "Whoever did it wouldn't have been able to see everything behind the print." He jabs his finger on the last photograph. "There. There's still some of the backing intact.

Could have been a photograph in there, a document, something small, but the killer wouldn't have been able to see it."

Schneider is energised now, gliding the magnifying glass back and forth across the photographs. He focuses on the Rochlitz scene for a few moments, then swings the glass to a Dassler photograph, holds it steady for a few seconds before jabbing his finger down.

"And here! Father Dassler's statue of the Virgin Mary. There's still a part of it intact, big enough to hold something small. Look!"

Although he's already seen it, and more, Neumann looks. Father Dassler's porcelain statue is smashed, probably stamped on. It's a reproduction in miniature of Michelangelo's *Pieta*, and the majority of it is in small pieces – the adult Christ's body broken completely, Mary's legs and voluminous dress in small pieces. But her head and upper left shoulder are intact. Enough room in the remaining hollows to secrete a jewel, a key, a folded piece of paper. Neumann points to one of the Rochlitz photographs, to the one showing the dead priest's bedroom, and the broken statue of Jesus on the Cross. This statue has been smashed in its entirety. Not even Jesus's head has escaped. There is not a scintilla of a chance that something might have been secreted in the intact statue and have escaped notice by the killer. Schneider follows Neumann's finger, nods, scratches the back of his head.

"Fuck me." He pauses, still scratching the back of his head. "What's going on? Why would this character . . ." Schneider's voice fades away as the thoughts flooding his brain take over. Then he sees it.

"He's trying to divert us. He wants us to think there's nothing special about Rochlitz, wants us looking in the wrong direction. It all fits. Ask yourself, why aren't the friends and family of Dassler and Gantz getting visits from this mysterious stranger? It has to be because he's not interested in them, in the last two priests. It's only Rochlitz that interests him. But he doesn't want us to know that."

Both men stare at the photographs, thinking. Reassessing.

"But . . ." Schneider's still processing the information, the implications, struggling with them. "But if it's only Rochlitz, then it means . . . what does it mean – he's killed two people just to muddy his tracks? Jesus, what are we dealing with?"

"I don't know, Kurt. But whatever it is, it must be important, big, huge. Big enough, important enough to warrant two murders for nothing more than distraction. How a simple parish priest could justify that is beyond me – if that's all he was, a simple parish priest. Nothing we've seen tells us anything different, but I still can't believe that's the case. There's something else going on here. Something well beyond what we can see."

27

Neumann and Schneider sit uncomfortably on ill-shaped wooden chairs in the rectory of St Albertus Magnus. Opposite them, in a tan leather armchair, is Father Rudolf Kroehl. The two Kripos share the same unspoken thought – nothing's changed since the first time they were here. Still the same prune-faced old harridan serving coffee, on this occasion with some thin slices of stale cake. Still the same Father Kroehl, still supercilious, patronising, stupid. Neumann sighs silently as Kroehl babbles on. He wishes he could just close his eyes and drift away.

". . . so it was with some trepidation, Kriminalkommissar, that I learned you wished to further question me about our departed Brother in Christ. I trust there is nothing untoward in this, nothing to suggest any shortcoming in the Church's actions. Such a suggestion would of course be . . ."

"No, Father, nothing like that," Neumann interrupts. He wants to get this over with as quickly as possible. Schneider's on his third piece of dry cake, apparently in no hurry to leave. "We are simply following up a new development. Your assistance would be most valuable in helping to find Father Rochlitz's murderer."

"But of course." A condescending wave of the hand. Kroehl confers on both officers what he imagines is a beatific smile. "It is my Christian duty, as you will appreciate."

"We do, Father, thank you," says Neumann, shooting a warning look at Schneider, who is eyeing the remaining two slices of cake in front of them. "Might I ask if there have been any further enquiries about Father Rochlitz? Since the last time you spoke with us. Has anyone else contacted you?"

For a moment, Kroehl seems puzzled. He lowers his head and frowns as though Neumann has unexpectedly asked him to recite a passage from Goethe. Then he lifts his chin, back in control again.

"Yes, as a matter of fact there *was* someone." He frowns again. "It was some weeks ago, the date I am unable to recall. A charming gentleman, from the Ministry of Propaganda and Enlightenment. We had a very civilised discussion."

Schneider ignores the cake now. He and Neumann stare at Kroehl as he speaks. Both of them doubt the priest will later describe this discussion as 'very civilised'. Kroehl continues to sing the praises of the other visitor.

"What was his name, Father?" interrupts Schneider.

Kroehl seems startled at being questioned by a junior policeman, but quickly recovers his poise.

"Herr Wagner was his name. I am afraid I was not made aware of his first name. He was most . . ."

"Can you describe him? His appearance. His clothes." Neumann pauses before adding, "Please."

"I am able to do so. The accuracy of my memory in these matters has been remarked upon by others. Herr Wagner was very well dressed." A thoughtful pose before continuing. "He wore a pin-striped grey suit. And a dark blue tie. His shoes were polished. I would estimate he was perhaps forty years old. He was about my height, which is to say medium, fair-skinned, an unremarkable but not unhandsome face." Father Kroehl seems about to conclude his description, but then suddenly adds, "And he had unusually pale grey eyes. A well-spoken man, clearly an educated and discerning one. We spoke for some time . . ."

"About what?" asks Neumann bluntly.

Kroehl seems once again taken aback by the question. Perhaps he thinks he's on the receiving end of impertinence or rudeness. Regardless, with a slightly sorrowful shake of his head, he indulges his visitors further.

"About Father Rochlitz. Herr Wagner wanted to know all about him. For an article in the newspaper, or perhaps it was a magazine." The thoughtful look again. "Or perhaps the gentleman did not specify precisely where the article would appear. Is it important?"

Neumann bites back the desire to grab Kroehl by the throat.

"It may be, Father. Can you recall what kinds of things this gentleman asked about?"

"Of course. He wanted to know everything he could about Father Rochlitz. His parentage, his family, interests, possessions, health . . . everything. Herr Wagner was most thorough, most thorough. A professional gentleman."

"And he wrote down all that you told him, yes?" Schneider mimics a pen and notebook. "Kept a record of your discussion?"

The question appears to surprise Kroehl yet again. He gives a small start, as though something obvious has just struck him.

"A record?" Kroehl asks himself. "No, I do not believe he made a record."

✠

Schneider reclines in the visitor's chair, puts his huge feet up on his boss's desk. He lights one of the foul-smelling smokes bought from a dark-yellow cigarette vending van encountered as he and Neumann were walking back to the Alex. Before the war Schneider smoked Trummers, Manolis if he couldn't get them, and Muratti Ariston Gold from Loesser & Wolff if he was feeling extravagant. The pale grey thing between his fingers now is unbranded, rough, filled with something resembling tobacco. Nobody in their right mind would confuse it with a quality cigarette. Still, when rationing limits a man to three a day, you take what you can get. The boss isn't so desperate that he accepts Schneider's offer of one.

Neumann lifts the earpiece from his desk telephone, dials a number, waits several seconds for the switchboard to pick up.

"Good morning, Liesl. Put me through to the Ministry of Propaganda and Enlightenment, please. Main switchboard. Yes, thank you." He sits back in his chair, waits.

"Good morning. I wish to speak to Herr Wagner." A pause. "No, I am afraid I do not know that. He is probably in your publications department. A writer, I think." Another pause. "I'm sorry, but that is all the information I have. The matter is important, so I would be grateful if you could make the appropriate enquiries. Yes, I will wait." This pause is longer. Neumann sits back, rolls his eyes at Schneider, waits.

Almost a minute goes by before Neumann sits forward.

"Yes, I am. Have you . . . My name? Certainly. I am Oberst Joachim von Manheim. I'm calling from Wehrmacht High Command." A short pause. "There are no other Herr Wagners in the Ministry? Frau Wagner? No, not her. Yes. Thank you."

Neumann covers the mouthpiece with his hand. "They've got one. He's in the Publications Section." Schneider raises his eyebrows, is about to say something, stops when Neumann speaks again.

"Yes. Is that Herr Wagner? Good morning, sir. My name is

von Manheim. I am calling from Wehrmacht High Command. Perhaps you could be of assistance. Yes, thank you." Neumann's words are smooth, but his face isn't. His brow is furrowed, his eyes narrowed with concentration. He listens to Herr Wagner at the other end of the line. His frown deepens.

"Forgive me, Herr Wagner, but I fear there may have been a mistake. May I ask how long you have been with the Ministry?" Another pause. "I see. And before that? Where were you employed?" Neumann exhales, lets frustration and disappointment out before speaking again. "Yes. Yes. And would you tell me your age, please? Yes. I see. Yes. Herr Wagner, please accept my apology for having bothered you. Yes, it seems someone has made an error. Thank you for speaking to me. Yes. Thank you, sir. Good morning." He replaces the earpiece on its cradle with a solid clunk.

Schneider takes his feet off the desk, sits upright, waits. Neumann seems lost in contemplation until Schneider speaks.

"And?"

"It seems," says Neumann slowly, "that we have barked up the wrong tree. Either that, or Herr Wagner is a master of disguise. The man's been a compositor at the Ministry for the last four years. Before that he did the same work at Westermann's for more than twenty years. He's seventy-two and sounds it. Hard to imagine he's been impersonating a smooth-talking forty year-old."

Schneider takes a few seconds to absorb this, mull it over.

"We've only got what he told you on the blower. It could still be him. Disguised voice and all that."

"I don't think so. I know an old man's voice when I hear it. Anyway, all it's going to take is a call to Westermanns. If he was there for twenty years, like he says, there's an end to it. Give them a ring, please Kurt. I'm going to see Böhm."

28

The church of St John the Baptist in Neukölln sits as before, impassive, immovable, solid, reliable. Outwardly, nothing has changed since Neumann and Schneider attended upon the despoiled body of Father Gantz. Only a month or so ago. It seems like a year.

Neumann and Schneider get out of their little Opel Olympia, walk straight across the road and into the darkened interior of the church. They head straight for the altar, their shoes clacking loudly on the parquetry floor. The noise attracts attention, and a boy about fourteen emerges from a room behind the sacristy and scurries towards them. He's wearing a dark blue uniform of some kind. Not Hitler Youth, but similar. Whatever it is, he looks like something from the colour pages of *Wille und Macht*, all tousled light brown hair and angular features.

"May I assist you, sir?"

Schneider pulls out his brass police disc, holds it up so the boy can see. It looks like a coin sticking out of a Christmas ham.

"Kripo, son. We'd like to speak to Father Lindemann."

"Yes, sir." The boy gestures to the pews. "Please be seated.

I will bring him." He heads back the way he came.

Within a minute Father Lindemann appears in the doorway, slightly dishevelled and red-faced as before. He hurries up to greet his visitors.

"Good afternoon, officers."

"Good afternoon, Father. May we speak with you?"

"Of course. What is it?"

"We may have only one question for you, Father," says Neumann. "It is a simple matter, but possibly important. Since our first visit, after Father Gantz was murdered, has anyone else visited and asked questions about him? Any other police, perhaps? Or an official? A newspaperman?"

The priest seems puzzled, surprised. "Visited here? About Father Gantz?" He shakes his head emphatically. "No, nobody has come to us. Nobody has asked any questions about him."

✠

They've been here only once before, but you don't easily forget the timeless solidity that is the church of St Norbert. The Schöneberg landmark seems rooted in antiquity, destined to last forever, to let transitory fashions like Nazism and a world-wide war wash over it without leaving a trace. Neumann and Schneider pause before the rectory door, now out of the incessant drizzle of an early winter sky, shake their hats free of water, brush their coat sleeves. They exchange a glance as Schneider knocks loudly.

"Second time lucky, boss?"

"We'll be like Henry the Fifth – 'Once more unto the breach, dear friends, once more.' Who knows? Perhaps the termagant from last time has been replaced by a Bavarian milkmaid. Something for you there, Kurt? Long blonde plaits and a dirndl?"

Before Schneider can answer, the door swings inwards. It's the same severe thin shrew from last time.

"Good morning," says Neumann as he lifts his hat. "My colleague and I were here at the time of . . ."

"Yes, I remember. What do you want?"

Nothing's changed, thinks Neumann.

"We would like to speak to Father Grönemeyer again, please . . ," Just in time, he recalls her name, "Frau Esslinger."

She swings dark bird-like eyes back and forth as though he's asked her to remove her clothes.

"I'll take you to him," she says after several seconds. "Wipe your feet,"

They obediently shuffle their feet back and forth, feel like chastised children, then step inside and follow the woman's retreating form down a long central passage. She stops as she reaches the open door to the kitchen.

"Those two Kripos are here again," she announces through the doorway before turning and pushing past the visitors back towards the front of the rectory.

Father Grönemeyer emerges from the kitchen. He's wearing a red and white striped apron over his cassock, holds a heavy knife in his right hand. He beams with apparent pleasure.

"Gentlemen! Good morning! This is something of a surprise. What brings you back to our humble place of worship?"

"Good morning, Father. We have just another question or two, if that's convenient."

"Of course, of course. Come in." He extends his free arm toward the kitchen. "I'm preparing for our evening meal."

The kitchen table is littered with bowls, vegetables, and a chopping board on which is a partially-sliced leek. The priest moves to the edge of the table, starts slicing the leek again.

"Please, ask your questions. I dare not stop or I will be in trouble again with Frau Esslinger." He's smiling as he says it.

Neumann returns the smile, the knowing look.

"Thank you, Father. It's about Father Dassler. We are still investigating his death. We have reason to believe we may not be the only ones conducting an investigation. Other men, perhaps another organisation, may also be involved. That is why we are here. Has anybody else been making enquiries? About Father Dassler."

Father Grönemeyer continues slicing the leek.

"Nobody has asked any questions about him. Only you."

✠

The dilapidated Kaiser Hotel on Kochhannstrasse is not far from the Friedrichshain cemetery, and only a little further from the Böhmisches Brewery, so there's usually the inviting smell of hops in the air. The neglected state of the hotel seems to Neumann at odds with the big poster mounted in a new glass-covered frame near the street entrance. It depicts a rugged soldier in his uniform and coal-scuttle helmet facing the viewer. He's holding aloft a billowing war ensign, its large black swastika prominent above his head. *Sieg Um jeden Preis*, reads the message printed below, 'Victory at any price'. Neumann catches a raised eyebrow from Schneider as they both think the same thought – we still don't know how high that price is going to be.

Past an uninterested desk clerk and up the threadbare carpet of the staircase, the room they find themselves in is small. There's hardly enough room for a single bed, two unpadded metal chairs, a washbasin and stand, and a wardrobe barely big enough to hold a week's change of clothes. Thousands of similar rooms across Berlin mirror these run-down lodgings, echo the peeling wallpaper, fading paint, cracked cornices, thin linoleum.

The workers who inhabit these places are very near the bottom of the social and economic ladder, cling to its lowest rung by their fingertips, know that an injury or week's lost work will loosen their hold and drop them into the mire. Desperation isn't a passing sad song for such men – it's the background music to their entire lives.

"Do you want to tell us about it, Lotar? Who did this?"

Lotar Olias is sitting on the single bed, slumped against the wall. He looks tired beyond exhaustion, stubble-faced, pallid, hair awry, a man worn to the bone by circumstances. His left eye is swollen, blackened, nearly shut. There's a nasty purplish bruise on his forehead. His breath comes in ragged, shallow gulps. If his ship of life had run aground before, now it's washed up on the beach and waves are battering it into oblivion.

"He said he was Kripo."

The words are slurred, a thick Berlin accent heavy with misery. Olias groans as he puts his left arm down to help shift his weight on the bed. A grimy bandage shows below the shirt sleeve. Neumann nods, tries again.

"When was this?"

"Three days ago. Sunday. Second time he's been."

That grabs Neumann's attention.

"He's been twice?"

"Yeah. First time not long after you came. Couple of weeks. Then again Sunday." A thought strikes Olias. He pauses, gulps in air. "First time he was polite. Like you two," he adds.

"What did he want?"

"Same as you two."

"About the priest, Father Rochlitz? Is that what he asked about both times?"

"Yeah. Same stuff. What Rochlitz was like, who his friends were. Where he went. He just kept on and on. Bastard."

The effort of speaking seems to diminish the man, and he

slumps even further down the wall. Neumann and Schneider exchange a look. Schneider steps forward, silently offers an open pack of cigarettes, waves aside Olias's attempt to return it after he's taken one. He lights the cigarette for Olias, steps back.

The first time the pair saw this man, he was on his lunch break at the nearby Bosch factory, where he assembled generator switchgear. Years earlier, in better times, he'd been the groundsman at St Lambertus. There wasn't much he could tell them about the murdered priest – his groundskeeping and Father Rochlitz's duties seldom crossed paths, but Neumann and Schneider needed to cover every possibility. That was several weeks ago. Even then, Olias was a man barely surviving hard times. Now, survival is beginning to look like an hourly proposition. The last thing he needs is a beating, but he's been given one anyway.

Schneider follows through on his gift of cigarettes.

"Did you tell him anything different from what you told us, anything we don't know about?"

A slow shake of the head precedes the bitter words.

"Nothing. You all got everything I know." A pause, then a vehement outburst as Olias unthinkingly tries to spread his arms for emphasis. "The truth!" The minimal effort makes him gasp in pain, drop his left arm to the bed. His breathing becomes fast, erratic. Neumann and Schneider wait for the man to settle, get his breathing under control. Neumann points.

"The bandage?"

"Used his cigarette. Fucking caterpillar line up my arm." He winces, either from the memory or a fresh jolt of pain.

"Can you describe him? What he looked like, the sort of clothes he wore?"

"Yeah. Bit older than you. Average height, looks. In a suit. Good one, expensive. Talked like a lawyer or a professor."

The two Kripos exchange a glance of recognition, of

affirmation.

"Did he have a name?"

"Could have. Can't remember."

"Anything else?"

"No, not that . . . Wait. Eyes. His eyes were dead. Grey. Dead. There was nothing there. Nothing."

Neumann and Schneider have heard all they need to. Olias is the third person in as many days to tell this story. Someone, obviously the same man in each instance, has been following in their earlier footsteps. He's visited the same people, asked the same questions about Father Rochlitz, echoed their own endeavours. But he's done it with a trail of casual viciousness that defies comprehension. Whatever he's looking for, he's prepared to make everybody suffer in the process.

It's time to go. As they thank Olias for his help and start moving towards the door, Schneider stops, turns around.

"Can you still work, Lotar? Are you going back?"

Despite his injuries, Olias snorts with painful derision.

"Back! I never left. Turned up Monday like normal." He reads the surprise in their eyes. "Don't work, don't eat. Simple as that."

There's silence for a while as Neumann and Schneider digest the scenario, process their thoughts. Then Schneider digs in his coat pocket, brings out his wallet and removes a dull red banknote. The 20 Reichsmarks is probably more than a day's wages for Olias. Schneider lays it carefully on the wash stand. Olias's eyes track every movement, but he says nothing. Schneider moves towards the door, follows Neumann through, catches Olias's gaze as he turns to shut the door. They exchange a brief nod.

29

Kriminalrat Franz Böhm doesn't look like everyone's idea of a senior and experienced policeman. More a middle-aged Ministry official, or a newspaper editor, something of that nature. Average height and build, a bland but friendly face surrounding brown eyes, thinning swept-back brown hair. Nothing to upset or frighten good citizens. Even in his Kripo uniform, as he is now.

Max Neumann and Kurt Schneider aren't fooled by appearances. They know Böhm is a good cop, a no-nonsense pragmatic boss who lets his investigators get on with their job. If they can't, he'll step in and make sure they can. Neumann is cautiously thinking of that possibility now. He and Schneider have decided to let the boss a little further into what they've found out.

" . . . and we can't see any other explanation for it. Whoever killed the second and third priests wasn't as thorough as the first time. He was trying to make it look as though he was, but it was a bluff, a smokescreen. He *wanted* us to think Father Rochlitz wasn't as important as he obviously is. And now, on top of that, someone's been leaning on the people who knew Rochlitz, only Rochlitz. The people who knew the other two priests, the people we interviewed, this thug hasn't been near them."

Böhm listens without interruption to Neumann's detailed report, a deepening frown of concentration the only indication he's absorbing the flood of new information. He sits motionless, gaze fixed on his desk, hands folded in his lap. Neumann finishes. Slowly, Böhm nods. Once, twice, as though affirming he understands what he's being told. His eyes shift to meet Neumann's.

"Two obvious questions. First, who is this man? Second, why is he trying to minimise the importance of the first priest? Rochlitz. What's your thinking?"

"We're up against it, boss. We've got a pretty good description of the killer, or at least of the thug who's been terrorising the people who knew Rochlitz. But it could be anybody. There's nothing to pin him down to any organisation that we can find. The names he's using, Kempner, Wagner, they're obviously false. He's not in uniform, nobody has a phone number or an address, nobody's seen his car – if he's got one. He could be anybody."

Böhm looks on, impassive. Behind his expressionless facade he debates the usefulness of telling Neumann about Standartenführer Schmidt, dismisses the idea until he's heard Göring's views. Decides instead to throw in a red herring.

"Gestapo? It's the sort of thing they do."

"True, but they usually operate in pairs. And they're not shy about making sure their victims know who's beating them up. It's almost their calling card. Besides, our man dresses like he's off to a society wedding at the Adlon Hotel. If he was Gestapo, he'd be in a fedora and leather trench coat."

"Security Service, then?"

"Hard to see it, boss. The SD fries big fish. Rochlitz was a sardine. I can't see him as part of a major spy ring, or a foreign agent of some kind. Nothing we've turned up says he was anything more than an old parish priest."

"So, a lone wolf's behind this, you think. But why? What's he after? Why all the mayhem?"

"Ah. That's the big question. Right now, it's one we can't answer. We're still chasing down some of the people who knew Rochlitz, second interviews, but we're struggling. If we can't come up with something, something new, we'll have to let it go. I know the other boys are up to their ears. We might be better off taking on some of their work."

Neumann thinks this is what Böhm wants to hear – the thing's never going to be solved, so put it aside and get on with something else, free up scarce investigators. After all, Böhm's got a squad to run, more than a dozen men under his command. He needs all the hands he can get. Especially two reliable ones like Neumann and Schneider. It's not what Neumann and Schneider want, but they can't come up with a half-decent argument for keeping the case open, so why not buy a bit of goodwill from the boss with an easy option. But that's not what happens.

"No," says Böhm decisively, "it's too early yet. Keep on it. Talk to the rest of your people, tease out whatever you can. Give it another couple of weeks at least, then we'll talk again. Alright?"

Neumann and Schneider try not to appear stunned as they simultaneously mutter, "Yes, boss," and leave before Böhm changes his mind.

✠

The early morning north wind howls down Schwarzer Weg as Kurt Schneider steps out of his apartment block and onto the footpath. His overcoat is tightly buttoned to the top. One gloved hand holds his hat down. Swirling sprays of dead leaves dart about the street – sycamore, maple, elm, horse-chestnut, lime, others Schneider can't identify. Their incessant spattering against his legs reminds him there's a price to pay for Berlin's abundant spring and summer greenery.

It's only a few hundred metres to the S-Bahn station, and in less bitter weather he wouldn't have a dilemma – walking to work would win the day. He pauses for a moment, debating the wisdom of leaving one hand exposed to the elements, reaches a decision. He jams the Homburg down hard over his ears, shoves both hands deep into his overcoat pockets and strides out into the near-gale, heading for the station and then the Alex. The streets are sprinkled with others following his example, heads down, eyes on the dusting of snow beneath their feet, shoulders reflexively hunched up into collars and scarves.

The first shout doesn't penetrate his shivering concentration or the whistling wind, and Schneider keeps walking. Then it comes again, louder, insistent.

"Kurt! Wait!"

He swivels his eyes to the right, towards the sound. It's across the street. Dolf Schliemann in his Reichspost uniform, pushing his trolley. Schneider swivels his gaze left and right, but can't locate Achilles the dog. Schliemann starts across the road, his trolley jolting and clattering over the paving blocks. He bumps over the kerb and draws next to Schneider, puffing, stamping his feet, wraps his arms tightly around his chest.

"Shit of a day to be delivering, Dolf. Where's Achilles got to? I can't see him."

A watery-eyed sharp nod of agreement, then a pause before Schliemann speaks.

"Too cold for him – he won't come out in this weather." Another pause, then, "Something I need to ask you about."

Schliemann glances around. “Let’s get out of the wind.” He jerks his head sideways, towards the recessed entrance of a jewellers shop a few metres further on. “There.”

They silently move to the boarded-up front of the closed business, Baumgartner & Kleist, huddle as close to the entrance door as they can, now both with their hands in their coat pockets.

“What is it, Dolf? Is there a problem?”

“I’ve seen something. I’d like your advice.”

“My advice? I’m flattered – not a lot of people ask for that. Advice about what?”

“It’s about that priest, the one on the Siemens estate. The one who was murdered a while back.”

In an instant, the cold and the wind are forgotten. Schneider stares at the postman, astonished, expectant.

“He’s got a private box. At the Charlottenburg post office. It’s paid for until next Friday, the last day of a six-month rental. If he doesn’t renew it, then I’ll have to close it down. I saw the name in the rental register. It’s my job to make sure the boxes are reallocated. I don’t know what to do . . . I mean, he’s dead now, isn’t he? Rochlitz.”

“Hold on, Dolf. Just slow down a bit. First of all, how did you find out about this.”

“Like I said, it’s my job to make sure the rented boxes don’t go over time, transfer them to new customers if the old ones don’t want them any more. Yesterday I checked the register, saw that an old woman in Heilmannring was coming up for renewal. While I was checking the entry for her box I noticed that next Friday the box for Father Rochlitz is up for renewal too. I know the name. It was in the paper. And I’ve seen him a few times on our side of Spandauer Chaussee. So I know he’s dead. Won’t need a renewal.”

Schneider’s mind is racing to keep up with the unexpected rush of information, to assess its importance, plan a response, understand. For several seconds there's silence.

"What advice are you looking for, Dolf?"

"Well, that's just it. I'm not sure. I don't know what to do."

"What would you do if the box holder hadn't been murdered? If it was anybody else but Father Rochlitz? "

"I'd visit them, ask if they wanted to renew. Leave a note if they weren't home. I do it all the time."

"Alright. You won't be doing that now, I suppose. So, what *will* you do?"

"Well, strictly speaking, I should tell young Ferenbach. The Postmeister. He decides what to do if the box holder has died. I just thought . . . you know, because the box holder was murdered and everything . . ."

His voice trails off as he waits for Schneider to pick up the thread, to solve the dilemma for him.

"You're right, Dolf. Best to handle things a bit differently. Can you leave it all with me? I'll go and see my boss. He's the one you met a while back, when he was with me. He'll know what to do. How does that sound?"

"Yes, good, that's good. I'll let you handle it. Thank you, Kurt, thank you. That's a weight off my mind. Thank you." Schliemann takes his hands out of his pockets, moves towards his trolley.

"One thing," says Schneider quickly. "Not a word, alright? Not even to the Postmeister. For the moment, this is just between you and me."

"Of course. Just between us. Thank you again."

30

Postmeister Ferenbach's cubbyhole is exactly what you'd expect of a small city post office like Charlottenburg in the middle of a war – cramped, dim, functional and cheerless. On the wall behind the seated Postmeister hangs a copy of the ubiquitous official Hitler portrait by Heinrich Knirr, the one with the Führer in a severe drab brown jacket staring with hand on hip at limitless horizons and opportunities situated far behind the viewer. And underneath is the nearly-as-ubiquitous printed injunction, 'Always remember to give the Hitler salute!'

Neumann and Schneider have followed the self-important young Postmeister into his office and closed the door behind them. His youth, his awkward gait and the calliper protruding from the bottom of his left trouser leg tells them he was probably one of the unlucky ones when the polio epidemic of 1913 struck. It explains why he's sitting in front of them and not wielding a rifle somewhere on the Eastern Front. The man's been dealt a shit hand by fate, and that fact restrains Neumann for the moment. He watches and waits as Ferenbach takes the seat behind his desk, leaves his visitors standing. Schneider pulls up a couple of chairs from against the office wall, and the two Kripos sit down.

"I understand this comes as a surprise, Herr Ferenbach. Let me assure you we are seeking information only to assist us in finding the person who killed Father Rochlitz."

"That is as may be, Kriminalkommissar, but I have a duty to those who place their trust in the Reichspost. Before I can provide you with information about a box holder, I will need to know why you require the information. The box holder may not wish his or her information released to a third party."

Schneider opens his mouth to speak, shuts it in response to a glance from Neumann, who's still soft-pedalling.

"I regret that I am not in a position to reveal specific evidence of a criminal investigation. But surely, Postmeister, the fact that the box holder is dead removes any considerations of privacy or confidentiality. The man is dead. Murdered."

"So you say, but I have only your word for that, sir. Otherwise, there is nothing of which I am aware to indicate Father Rochlitz is either dead or would wish you to have access to his private information. Accordingly, Kriminalkommissar, I must decline to release the information you seek."

Neumann sighs wearily and lowers his head for a moment. Then lifts it and meets Schneider's eye. The big man gets out of his chair and takes a step towards the Postmeister's desk, puts his hands on the edge, leans forward so that his face is less than half a metre from Ferenbach's. To the seated man, it looks like a wardrobe is about to fall on him.

"Herr Ferenbach, please listen to me. If you cooperate with our enquiries, we will finish our work here within a few minutes and be on our way. Do you understand?"

A subdued "Yes", one that nevertheless still carries echoes of defiance, still asserts a degree of authority.

"However," continues Schneider, "if you choose not to

cooperate, we will arrest you, put you in handcuffs and call for a van to take you to the Alex. There you will be closely questioned about your motives for refusing to cooperate with the police. A report will be sent to your superiors explaining the reason for your arrest. In such circumstances, no doubt your superiors will have certain action they wish to take."

Schneider straightens up but remains at the edge of the Postmeister's desk, spreads his hands apart, beams at the wide-eyed occupant. "Please, Herr Ferenbach, consider what I have said. Take your time. We are reasonable men."

Silence. Ferenbach stares vacantly at his two tormentors sitting expressionless in front of him, runs competing scenarios through his mind. Every scenario but one falls headlong into an abyss of unwelcome discomfort, even pain. It doesn't take long before only one scenario is left standing and available for selection.

"Very well." Ferenbach musters the little dignity he has left, reaches into a shallow drawer in the centre of his desk, selects a key from a tray of numbered slots. "This is the key you need." He presses a button on the desk as he passes the key across, prompting the office door to fly open and an excited plump dark-haired girl to appear. "Anke will show you the box."

They follow the girl down a long corridor leading to the delivery side of the wall of private post boxes. She keeps glancing behind as though fearful of losing her charges.

"What I don't understand," says Schneider, "is what Rochlitz did with his key. He must have kept it hidden somewhere, or he wouldn't be able to access his box.'

"It's possible the killer found it. Possible he's already used it. If he has, we're not going to find anything in the box. If he didn't find it, we might be in luck. Ah, here we are."

Anke stops at the end of the corridor, stands smiling at Neumann and Schneider as she points to one of dozens of locked boxes. “This is the one, sir.”

Neumann returns her eager-to-please smile, steps forward, opens the box and peers into its dark interior. He reaches in, pulls something out and shows it to Schneider.

“There’s our answer, Kurt. He didn’t find the key.”

31

Heinrich Himmler stares at an invisible point somewhere on the ceiling of his office, his head resting on the back of his chair. An unlit cigarette sits unnoticed in his right hand and he absentmindedly fiddles with the distinctive dark green packet it came from. Lucky Strikes. The Americans provide what a German war economy can not.

Concentration, worry, puzzlement and annoyance all jostle for supremacy on the Reichsführer's normally bland countenance. From the secretary's room behind a closed door the clack, clack, ping of a typewriter intrudes only slightly into the near-silence. The office wall clock thunks out dull mechanical seconds like a heartbeat. Outside the windows, heavy grey clouds scud and tumble in a biting wind. From time to time the panes shimmy, momentarily distorting Himmler's view of the Berlin skyline. Both men in the room think the same unspoken thought – if this weather holds, at least the bombers won't be here tonight.

Slowly, Himmler lifts his head, leans forward and puts his forearms on his desk, scrutinises Stefan Schmidt, who sits on the other side of the desk with his hands in his lap and an unreadable expression on his face. Himmler takes off his glasses, polishes them with a handkerchief, his unlit cigarette cast aside.

"I could arrange for you to take over the investigation, or perhaps to join the investigating officers. An additional resource, perhaps. Something of that kind. That would enable you to find out everything they know. Your thoughts?"

Schmidt breathes deeply before answering.

"In my view, such a strategy would be unlikely to succeed, Herr Reichsführer. I am aware the two investigators have spoken to the same people I have interviewed. By now they will have my description. Even if I altered my appearance and put on a Kripo uniform, I believe it likely I would be recognised. The risk would in my opinion not be justified at this stage. It seems improbable the Kripo officers have uncovered any information I have not."

"Yes, yes, I suppose so." Himmler seems distracted, still thinking of alternatives, other plans, a solution to the problem. He continues to fiddle with the pack of Lucky Strikes. "But there must be a way to . . ." His voice drifts and fades.

"May I suggest, sir, that for the moment I do nothing more than follow the Kripo investigators to see where they go and to whom they speak. Such an approach would allow me to identify any lines of enquiry that have so far eluded me."

"For the moment, you say." Himmler's frustration shows in the sharpness of his voice. "And if what you suggest does not achieve our ends? What then?"

"In that case, I suggest I be permitted to interrogate the officers under duress. Whatever they know will then be forthcoming."

Himmler sees no reason to question Schmidt's judgement, understands that answers will doubtless be forthcoming. His concerns are elsewhere.

"Certainly, although . . . My concern is that such an action would raise questions. Awkward questions. It would inevitably cause Reichskriminaldirektor Tanzinger to become involved. The suspicious death of a Kripo officer might prove counterproductive. Two of them even more so."

"I understand, sir. The problem might be ameliorated, however, if one or both of the officers simply disappeared. It would raise questions, of course, but a disappearance is much more easily explained than a death, a murder. Rumours could be put about suggesting links with the Resistance. Or perhaps flight to a neutral country. Like that Gauleiter in Ostpreussen, the one who ran to Portugal – I believe his name was Scherwitz."

Himmler meets Schmidt's eyes as though seeing him for the first time. He nods twice.

"Yes. That might well be . . ." His voice drifts for a moment, then sharpens. "Very well, Stefan. For the moment, please follow the Kripos, see what you can learn. If we need to go further, we will. Let me know your progress." He leans forward, picks up a pen. The audience is over. Schmidt immediately stands, hat in his left hand, right arm and stiffened right hand raised at the required angle.

"Thank you, sir. Heil Hitler!"

✠

One feature excepted, the envelope sitting on Max Neumann's office desk is unremarkable. Just a dull whitish coarse-textured envelope of the size and type used in offices everywhere across the Reich. Big enough to hold a standard sheet of typing paper folded twice across its width. It's sealed, gummed shut in the normal way of something sent through the Reichspost. But, although thirty minutes ago it was sitting in the late Father Rochlitz's private post box, it didn't arrive there through the post. There is no stamp, no postmark, no name or address. Just a plain, sealed envelope.

Neumann and Schneider sit on opposite sides of the desk, stare at the envelope. They've turned it over, back and forth, scrutinised it, found nothing to excite their interest. There's clearly at least one document inside. The envelope needs to be opened, its document or documents examined. Yet neither man makes a move, both of them aware this could be a pivotal point in their investigation, a hinge on which the future turns. Whether for better or for worse is an open question.

An envelope apparently placed in a private post box by the now-dead holder of that box, an envelope apparently unknown to anyone else, a private post box apparently unknown to anyone other than the Postmeister at Schöneberg, no sign of a key or any documentation showing Father Rochlitz's possession of the box. Whatever he put in that box, it's something he didn't want in his apartment. Or anywhere else. But what it is, and why . . .

"Can't put it off any longer, boss."

"I know. You do the honours."

Schneider picks up a brass letter-knife on the desk, slides the tip beneath one end of the gummed flap, slits open the top of the envelope. He puts the knife aside, spreads the envelope slit apart with his left hand, reaches in and removes a single folded piece of paper. It's cream-coloured, heavy linen quality, greying with age, brown mottling at the edges, folded so that whatever's written on the other side is concealed. Schneider unfolds it carefully, smooths out the creases, turns it over so that both men can see the writing.

The heading is printed in large Fraktur font of the kind popular a century ago and now resurrected by the Party as part of the new 'pure' Germany, the traditional Germany. But this isn't a modern relapse into nostalgia – this really is from a century ago. 'Certificate of Wedding' is in thick black letters at the top. A wedding that took place in Berlin in 1841. Heavy black printed headings on the certificate provide for handwritten insertion of the usual details: names of bride and groom, names of parents, birthdates, occupations, religions, places of residence, and so on.

The faded spidery handwriting on the certificate challenges concentration. Neumann and Schneider unconsciously bend further forward to decipher the words, their eyes closer to the document. It records the marriage at the Church of St Lambertus in Moabit on Sunday, 3 May 1841 of Gebhardt Franz Himmler and Hani Malka Bleiberg, aged 27 and 22 respectively. The groom's name leaps up, grabs both men. Their eyes meet.

"Is it . . . Do you think it's him? His family?" Schneider's eyes are dragged back to the name on the certificate.

"Could be," says Neumann slowly, returning his gaze to the document. "Probably is. I think Himmler's father was called Joseph Gebhardt, or Gebhard, something very similar, so the name could have been passed on. And the family history is definitely centred on Moabit."

Schneider looks doubtful, surprised, something approaching incredulous. His eyebrows are up.

"I'm sure I read it somewhere. *Wer Ist's*, probably," adds Neumann. "There's no need to look at me like that. It's not a common name. Probably why it stuck in my mind."

They turn back to the certificate. Gebhardt Himmler's occupation is recorded as 'Book-keeper', Hani Bleiberg's as 'Domestic'. His residence is in Moabit, hers in Reinickendorf, five kilometres to the north. It's all very ordinary, very urban Berlin. But the names of the bride's parents arrest the two men's attention. Taub and Sara Bleiberg. German names, and yet, somehow . . . not. Simultaneously, both men turn to the next line on the certificate, the religion of the bride and groom.

He is 'Roman Catholic'.

She is ‘Jew’.

An abrupt silence. Neumann and Schneider stare at the word, the single word, the word that suddenly brings recent events to a focus. Jew. Heinrich Himmler’s grandmother was a Jew. Implications, ramifications, reasons floods their minds, an avalanche of understanding released by the word.

Jew.

Schneider is the first to speak.

“Holy fuck! This . . .” The words won’t come. He shakes his head in exasperation, astonishment, throws his hands up.

Neumann continues to stare at the document on the desk, his face rigid, concentrating, thinking. Suddenly he gets up, gives a sharp groan of pain as he straightens, puts one hand on the side of his waist, then on the small of his back for a second. Fully straightened, he quickly goes to the closed office door and locks it before returning to the desk and his chair. Schneider stares at him.

“We’re in trouble, Kurt. This,” he gestures towards the wedding certificate, “could get us killed. If the Gestapo burst in right now, or any of Himmler’s hatchet men, we’d be dragged outside and shot on the spot. It’s as good as a death warrant.” He slumps back in his chair, runs a hand over his face. “Christ!”

“What do we do? We can’t just . . . we can’t ignore it.”

“We can. We can ignore it. We can pretend that we’ve never seen it. Burn the damn . . .”

Abruptly, Neumann stops. He frowns with concentration, narrows his eyes, sits motionless for several seconds. Then he abruptly sits forward in his chair and slaps the desk hard.

“Of course!” he exclaims. “It should already be burned. The fire. The one at Saint Lambertus. Back in twenty-eight. The church burned down, destroyed everything. That’s the story everybody tells. But this,” a wave at the document, “this didn’t burn. Rochlitz must have saved it, pulled it out of the flames.

And if he did, he must have known . . ."

"Or he grabbed it before the fire," interjects Schneider. That would make more sense. He didn't need to rescue it because he already had it. Kept it somewhere safe."

Neumann is nodding thoughtfully.

"You're right, that makes more sense. But why keep it all this time? What was . . .?" Neumann answers his own question. "Insurance. He must have seen which way the wind was blowing, held on to it just in case. He saw it might one day be valuable, might be a bargaining chip. Give him some leverage."

Both men silently absorb the newly-upended situation, consider the implications of the dead priest's actions. Neumann suddenly shakes his head.

"It doesn't matter. It doesn't matter. We have to get rid of it. Now. Burn it before it burns us." Neumann erupts out of his chair, grabs his back again, paces back and forth. "Fucking Himmler! He has to be behind this. He knew Rochlitz had the certificate. If the priest hadn't dropped dead they'd have dragged the information out of him. He was dead either way." Neumann throws up a despairing arm, "Christ Almighty!"

Schneider starts out of his seat.

"You want me to get rid of it, boss?"

"Yes! Burn . . ." Neumann stops, gets his breathing under control, sits down again and lifts his face to a standing Schneider. "No. No. We need to think this through. There might be something we can do with the thing, some good we can wring out of it. It's evidence. Forget Himmler for a second – it's evidence, it shows motivation."

"Fine," says Schneider, clearly unconvinced, "it's evidence of motivation. That begs the question – motivation of who, and to do what? We're back where we started. It motivates Himmler to murder whoever has the certificate. If this became public knowledge, he'd be finished. You can't beat your chest about being the purest of the pure if you've got a Jewish body in the cellar. He'd be lucky to get away with his head still on his shoulders. Hitler would have him strung up with piano wire."

"I know, I know. But there's no getting away from the facts. It's almost certain Himmler's behind whoever did this. He might not have bloody hands, but he gave the orders."

"So what do you have in mind? We front up to his office and bring him in for questioning? That ought to be interesting. I've never had the experience of measuring my life span in minutes. You'll have to tell Irmgard you probably won't be home for dinner."

Neumann holds up his hands in mock surrender.

"You're right, Kurt. Of course you are. Still, there might be a way . . . There might be something we can do. Even if we can't arrest Himmler, we might still be able to get to his errand boy. Or boys. Someone killed those priests. The certificate might be the way to them. I don't know how, but . . ."

"Are you forgetting we can't tell anybody about it without putting our heads in a noose? It's never going to end up in an investigation file. We're never going to produce it as prosecution evidence. It's not evidence, it's a bomb. The minute we tell anyone else about it, the fuse starts counting down. Let's . . ."

"That's it!" interrupts Neumann. "You've put your finger on it. We don't tell anybody. Think, Kurt. The only reason we've got this is because it was lying in Rochlitz's private box. It's obvious nobody else knew it was there. If they had, they'd have grabbed it. Whoever killed the priests didn't know it was there. We are the only two people in the world who know. And there's your answer – we don't tell anybody else. What we do is put this where nobody but us can find it. We keep it safe. And then, when we decide what to do, we use it if we need to." He throws his hands up. "For what, I don't know. Insurance. Something like that. This thing has . . . it has *potential*, it's a weapon we might be able to use."

Schneider looks doubtful again. "Alright," he says slowly, "We put it somewhere safe. There's another problem straight away. Where is it going to be safe? Rochlitz put it somewhere he thought was safe, and look what's happened."

"Exactly. But don't forget, someone knew Rochlitz had the certificate. Someone knew he had to have hidden it somewhere. That's where we've got an advantage – nobody knows it's in our possession. There's no reason for anyone to look for it. So we hide it in plain sight, pretend it's just another document, nothing special about it."

Schneider is still doubtful, pulls a doubtful face. "In plain sight? Here, in the office?"

"It's as good a place as any. If nobody knows we've got it, nobody's going to look for it. We just need to put it where nobody but us will ever look." As he speaks, Neumann scans the office. His eyes settle on one of the gunmetal filing cabinets lining the bottom half of the wall behind his desk. "There!" He's pointing to a slide-out drawer with a green paper label on the front: 'Regulations'.

Now Schneider brightens. "That should do it. Nobody's ever going to look there." He watches as Neumann smooths the Marriage Certificate, opens the cabinet drawer, and slides the document into a hanging file marked 'Discipline'.

"Done." Neumann shuts the drawer. "Now it's just you and me, Kurt. Just you and me." Schneider just nods, both men suddenly serious, contemplative.

32

The bitter cold and oppressive sky of dirty ragged clouds driven by a wind straight off the North Sea echoes the mood of the two Kripo officers – sombre, mute, determined. Not even the massive flak tower in nearby Humboldthain Park draws their attention as they trudge up the stairs onto the sixth floor and head towards the Steinerts' apartment, number 67. Neumann is angry, at the world at large, but mainly at himself. He should have come here first. He should have realised. That bastard, Wagner or Kempner or whatever he's calling himself.

They've called the few who have a telephone connected, warned them, or tried to warn them. Too late, in every case. Now Neumann and Schneider are nearly at the end of their list, visiting every other person they've already spoken to, much of the day spent driving, walking, chasing down every quarry, and always with the same result. The well-spoken and impeccably-tailored man has left in his wake a trail of injury, damage and shattered self-possession. He's walked the same streets as Neumann and Schneider, knocked on the same doors, encountered the same people, but now he's abandoned his former pretence of polite enquiry.

The lights are on in the Steinerts' apartment. In response to Schneider's knock, the door is opened after several seconds by Jürgen Steinert. His face is drained, fearful. With his left hand he holds a folded napkin against his forehead. A trickle of dried blood shows below. At the sight of Neumann and Schneider he visibly sags with relief, seems on the edge of tears. Without a word he steps back and opens the door wide. Inside, the pair can see Frau Steinert sitting in one of the armchairs, her head in her hands, crying softly. Neumann takes two steps into the room, turns to Jürgen.

"He was here again?"

A vestigial nod from Jürgen. "He's only just left." The young man's words are slurred, his voice thick. His revelation makes Schneider stiffen, whip around back towards the outside landing and the stairs. Neumann moves too, snaps at Jürgen, "When? When did he leave?"

Neumann's halfway through the door, Schneider already on the landing, gun in hand, when they hear "About ten minutes ago. Not long." Both men stop. Schneider re-holsters his gun, and they return to the apartment. Unless the assailant's a complete fool, which he clearly is not, he's long gone by now.

Inside, Jürgen Steinert has slumped into an armchair next to his mother's. His left hand continues to press the napkin to his forehead. The other one rests lightly and reassuringly on his mother's shoulder. She's stopped crying now, just, but still dabs at her eyes with a crumpled handkerchief. Neumann kneels in front of her, goes to take her hand. As he does, he sees one sleeve of her coat is pulled back, exposing her forearm. Three ugly, weeping, circular burn marks disfigure the mottled pale skin. Neumann's stomach instantly lurches with revulsion and anger. He chokes it down hard, forces his voice to project calm and authority as he holds the old lady's hand in both of his.

“I am so sorry this happened, Frau Steinert. Did he hurt you?” He nods towards her injured arm. “Otherwise.”

His sympathy, or perhaps the tone of his words alone, seems to give the old lady strength. She swallows with effort, attempts a thin smile as she speaks.

“Thank you, Kriminalkommissar.” Her head swivels sideways towards her son. “Jürgen has . . . the swine hit him with a pistol. Is . . .”

Neumann sees that Schneider has already started tending the young man’s injury. Jürgen’s skin has broken in a jagged line across his left temple, and already a huge angry bruise is starting to swell. Schneider has found a cloth somewhere and some disinfectant, is cleaning the dried blood. The giant is surprisingly tender, his huge fingers suddenly transformed into deft and gentle instruments of care. For his part, Jürgen seems content to lie back in his chair, eyes closed, and let someone take care of him and his mother.

“Your son is in good hands. My colleague has had some experience in these things. But you . . .” He raises his eyebrows. “Have you anything to put on . . . your injuries?”

“It would be best to leave them uncovered. They will heal faster. I will put a bandage on later.” Frau Steinert’s voice has recovered some of its strength. She speaks with more confidence, authority, but it’s clearly a struggle. “Perhaps something to ease the pain. I have aspirin. In the bathroom.” A waved hand towards her legs. “Would you be so kind, Herr Neumann?” Then a gesture towards the far corner of the room. “That door. They are in the wall cabinet, on the top shelf.”

Neumann gets to his feet, grunts as a jolt of discomfort courses through his lower back when it takes the strain of rising. He goes to the bathroom, finds the tablets, brings two of them and a glass of water to the old lady. She thanks him with her eyes, slowly washes the aspirin down, settles back in her chair.

Her burnt arm is gently lowered onto the chair's padded side. She closes her eyes for a few moments before opening them again and looking at her son. Schneider has finished cleaning Jürgen's wound and is applying a pad of cloth with some adhesive plaster. Jürgen looks as though he's asleep. Neumann recognises the signs of recent concussion. He pulls a footstool over and sits in front of Frau Steinert, faces her.

"What did he want?"

The old lady shakes her head slightly, sorrowfully. "The same as before. About Father Rochlitz. He insisted we had received something from him, a letter, a document. I told him we had not, but it made no difference." She glances at her burned arm, turns her eyes back to Neumann. "I think he enjoyed it. Hurting me. There was evil in his eyes. Pleasure."

Neumann nods. He understands.

"We will find this man, Frau Steinert. He will pay for his crimes." After a pause. "Did you tell him anything?"

"I did not. Only what I told him the first time."

"And," Neumann silently indicates Jürgen, who still has his eyes closed, "about . . .?"

"Nothing, Kriminalkommissar. Nothing."

33

He's lost count of how many. Walther Neumann's Einsatzgrüp squad has been operational for only a short time, but already the days swirl with indistinguishable ragged edges, each one much like the one before and the one after. First comes the roundup – shouting and wailing and rifle blows the invariable accompaniment to loading the trucks. Then a bumping grinding journey from some pig-shit village, along muddy tracks, and on to the destination. By the time he and his men arrive, an earlier load of villagers, Jews or undesirables at gunpoint will have dug the trench they'll soon be occupying. Walther, officer that he is, can stand back and smoke while he watches more shouting and wailing and rifle blows as the cargo is corralled until it's time for the first batch to be sent out.

He stands back now, lights a cigarette, watches as a dozen or so men and women are forced at a trot towards the fresh ditch about ten metres in front of him, the bodies of those who dug it lying still warm at the bottom. The men who will do the shooting are standing in twos and threes chatting, smoking, laughing, waiting for the line to form up before taking their places and shouldering their rifles.

There's still morning frost on the ground. No wind, but shoulder-hunching cold even so. The few trees in sight are bare, having completed their skeletal preparation for what's to come. There'll be snow soon enough. Walther keeps his free hand inside his greatcoat pocket. Even with gloves, his cigarette hand is nearly numb. He swings his gaze along the line now moving into position.

These peasants have a sameness about them that is depressing. Unkempt hair, grubby hands and faces, most of them stinking as though they've abandoned washing themselves for other pleasures. And the clothes. Always patched, always dirty, always mismatched, clothes that belong on a scarecrow instead of a human being. It looks like the cold has forced this batch to put on everything they possess. Thin ragged coats over even thinner ones, scarves wrapped tight around scraggy throats, old worn boots stuffed with straw or paper in a pathetic attempt at insulation.

The line is almost in position now, almost ready to stop, turn and face the ditch. Walther scans the faces of the doomed with distaste. The women, no matter their age, are uniformly haggard, ugly, with sunken eyes, hair awry, teeth missing. The men share a near-universal look of simian stupidity, of dull-witted peasant ignorance – apparently their Ukrainian heritage.

As usual, the faces of both men and women are those of bewildered sheep, their eyes swivelling back and forth in vacant apprehension. But one man stands out. Like the others, he's trotting forward. But unlike the others, his eyes are not unfocused, not vacant. He seems to be concentrating. He looks towards Walther, the only officer in sight, and for a moment their eyes meet before the man jerks his gaze away. Walther's curiosity is aroused. He looks more closely at the man. Young, hatless, under thirty, beanstalk-thin, swaddled in layers of clothing against the cold. There's little to distinguish him from the others. He's no cleaner, no better dressed, not bigger or smaller or anything of note. Just another peasant. Walther looks away, watches the work of his squad as the line is ordered to halt and turn towards the ditch.

The groups of riflemen break up now, start moving to their positions to start the day's work. Cigarettes are cast aside, rifles are cocked, chattering dies out. Walther lifts his eyes, turns his head away from the line, ready to give his go-ahead to the detachment Unterfeldwebel. A sudden noise stops him. Like a shout or a scream, but both at once, fuelled by urgency, fear, alarm. Before Walther can even react, other shouts and screams join in. As he whips his head around towards the cacophony he sees the young man from a few seconds ago. The look of concentration is back, a fierce focus. Walther barely registers what others have seen. A pistol has appeared in the young man's hands. It's pointed at him. Before Walther can move, there is a staccato roar of rifle fire as the young man is cut down by half a dozen guns. It's too late – he's fired the pistol. In the infinitesimal fraction of a second between Walther seeing the raised pistol and its bullet striking his head, his single stunned thought is simply, 'How can he have a gun?'.

34

Between the two seated men a hospitality table holds a circular silver tray bearing cups, coffee pot, cream, milk and sugar, spoons and small forks. On either side are two smaller trays, one with shortbread biscuits, the other with thin slices of Weihnachtsstollen. A pair of Meissen plates, part of the 18th century Swan Service, sit next to them, their scalloped low-relief depiction of paired swans amid bulrushes complementing the baroque flamboyance of their owner. It's all been delivered without a word by the plump middle-aged and apparently voiceless woman who always attends on Göring in his Reichsluftahrtministerium office.

Kriminalrat Franz Böhm is astonished at the availability of the food – he doesn't see cream, shortbread biscuits and cake outside of these visits to the Reichsmarschall. God knows where the man can obtain raisins and nuts for the Weihnachtsstollen, the Christmas cake. Cake made at home, as his wife used to bake every Friday, is a distant memory. And their occasional outings to a konditorei for mid-afternoon apfelstrudel and hot chocolate are now consigned to a fabled past. Rationing has sunk its claws into the world, reduced all but the wealthiest and most influential citizens to a diet of bread, potatoes and monotony.

Hermann Göring leans forward, picks up the silver coffee pot by its saucepan handle and pours for both of them. Today he's in his dove-grey uniform, made, like all his clothes, by the famous Viennese tailor, Berndt Tiller. Although the gold epaulettes are florid extravagances, the uniform is, for Göring, relatively restrained, with only minimal amounts of gold braiding around the gorget tabs. The Reichsmarschall waves an inclusive arm towards the laden table.

"Help yourself, Franz. I recommend the Stollen. Emmy tells me I must take only one slice a day." He pats his huge paunch. "My wife wants to see me skin and bones, I think." Göring reaches out and helps himself to two slices, sits back with a knowing, conspiratorial wink towards Böhm.

Böhm smiles dutifully, takes two of the biscuits onto his plate and places it back on the table. He pours cream in his coffee, sits back to savour the moment, his eyes on the Reichsmarschall. For a minute or so they sit in silence, Göring eating his cake, Böhm sipping his coffee. Göring finishes, wipes his mouth with a napkin, sips his coffee before speaking.

"Ah, the simple pleasures, eh? But we cannot sit here all day eating and drinking, can we? To business, Franz. What can you tell me about Himmler and his mongrel?"

Böhm's hopes for a Cuban cigar like last time are dashed. He tries to keep his eyes away from the cedar box sitting on Göring's desk, off to the right. He lays out for Göring the state of Neumann and Schneider's investigation, such as it is, emphasizes how extensive the enquiries have been, how time-consuming, how fruitless. Göring nods understandingly as Böhm sets out his officers' inability to locate the mysterious man who is apparently pursuing the same lines of enquiry in connection with Father Rochlitz. Only Rochlitz. He explains that

Schmidt is assaulting almost everybody he speaks to. Böhm finishes his exposition by relating how Neumann and Schneider's investigation has run into a brick wall, says they have asked if they should shelve the whole thing.

"If it were any other murder, I'd tell them to file it away and get on with other work. But in view of your interest, sir, I thought it best to buy some time so I could seek your views. I've told the investigators to keep the case active for another two weeks to see if anything turns up."

Göring has listened without interruption, an occasional grunt or murmur the only indication he's listening at all. His chin is sunk almost to his chest, eyes staring at the table in front of him. Now he lifts his gaze to Böhm.

"Yes, I see. It appears likely Standartenführer Schmidt, and presumably the chicken farmer himself, are the only people who know what he's trying to find. That puts me . . . us . . . in an invidious position, Franz. I was hoping to remain at arm's length in this matter. To let Himmler think the Kripo investigation was a routine one. And as far as your man is concerned, it *is* routine, just another murder. You and I know different, of course." Göring drums his fingers on the arm of his chair. His gaze wanders as he thinks the problem through.

"The question is, what do we do now? We can scarcely point your man towards Schmidt – he'd be dead within a day, and we'd still be none the wiser. And I'm not in a position to take any direct action myself, throw some rank and weight about. Himmler would just throw his own around, and both of us would finish up in front of the Führer like a couple of brawling schoolboys. It pains me to say this, Franz, but I fear we may have come to the end of the road. Whatever Schmidt and Himmler are looking for . . . Well, there's no way we can get there ahead of them, it seems."

Böhm knows better than to express surprise that Göring is

prepared to drop his interest in Himmler's activities, but it's an effort to restrain himself.

"It appears to be the case, Herr Reichsmarschall. If he has Reichsführer Himmler behind him, Schmidt is unassailable. I can't think of any way around the problem."

"No. The problem is one we will have to set aside." Göring is beaming now. The discussion is over. He reaches out and takes a third slice of the Weihnachtsstollen. "Come, Franz, have some cake. Look," he points, "you haven't even eaten your shortbread. More coffee?"

✠

Adolf Hitler's familiar steely-eyed stare lances across the enormous rosewood desk, out over the heads of the two men seated in armchairs on the other side, out into the furthest unseen reaches of the Reich he is building. Even in oil and canvas, courtesy of Franz Triebsch, the Führer dominates the room, a constant reminder to its occupants that in this brave new Germany he is the repository of all authority, all power. It's unlikely Hitler is acquainted with French history, but if he was he'd heartily embrace the view of Louis XIV – *L'État, c'est moi.* I am the State.

Tadeuz Zebrowski is in familiar territory. He receives the undivided attention of Reichsmarschall Hermann Göring, who leans forward to pour coffee, offer cream. Zebrowski mutters his thanks, sits back in his armchair, cradles the cup and saucer on his lap. He's already politely declined Göring's offer of a Lebkuchen from the piled plate between them – he can't abide gingerbread. Politely declined, too, his host's offer of a Pervitin pill, which hasn't stopped Göring from downing two of them himself with a sip of water. Not for the first time, Zebrowski briefly wonders how much of the man's relentless energy is innate and how much driven by chemicals. Not that it matters either way – their relationship is a long, trusting and mutually advantageous one.

The Reichsmarschall's office in his Ministry building is as always, but Göring himself is not. Zebrowski detects a vague tension underlying the usual ebullience, something worming its way into Göring's speech patterns, his movements. He's worked for Göring long enough to know that there's nothing to be done but wait until the source of the tension is revealed at a time of the big man's choosing. So he blows on his coffee, takes a tentative sip or two, listens to his boss extol the virtues of the gingerbread biscuits. And waits. After a few more desultory remarks by Göring, the source of the Reichsmarschall's behaviour is revealed.

"About this priest, Tadeuz," Göring says tentatively. He takes a mouthful of his coffee before continuing. "The first one killed by Schmidt. I had thought the matter might by now be resolved . . . by other means. Which is why I asked you to cease your activities." He sips his coffee again. "The situation has changed, however. I would like you to renew your efforts. To renew pursuit of the Standartenführer." Despite Zebrowski's attempt to appear unperturbed by the request, Göring immediately senses the man's apprehension. "From a distance, of course," he adds hurriedly.

Zebrowski silently considers the matter for a few seconds before responding.

"May I ask with what object, sir?"

Göring waves a vague hand. "To find out what he's doing about the priest. This thing isn't over. I still want to know what it's about. Can you help me, Tadeuz?"

"Of course, sir, but . . ."

"Yes, I know – it might be dangerous. That's why I will be relying on your judgement. Your judgement about how far to go, how closely to observe Schmidt. I do not want you taking unnecessary risks, Tadeuz – only risks that you think warranted in the circumstances. Your safety is important to me."

There is real concern in Göring's voice. For all his egocentric flamboyance, his cultivation of an image of everybody's friend and all-round good fellow, he has genuine affection for the modest, quiet, loyal employee who has been with him for so many years. Zebrowski is keenly aware of it, values it, has never tried to take advantage of it, and he does not do so now.

"I understand, sir. Of course. I will pursue the Standartenführer with diligence but care. My safety is important to me also."

Göring smiles with gratitude, even amusement. It's as close as Zebrowski ever gets to a joke.

35

Neukölln, less than five kilometres to the south-east of central Berlin, on a night like this one, is a darkened deserted maze of grimy streets. In the years before the war Neukölln was the reddest district in Berlin, a Communist stronghold, full of working-class agitation and malcontent resistance. That ended when the Party had finished scourging the capital and the unions, despatching followers of the red flag to oblivion one way or the other. Tonight, the threat to the Third Reich comes from a different quarter. British bombers are back, taking full advantage of the scattered light cloud, raining down their fury. The drone of their engines seems to fill the skies, to arrive from every direction. To the north and west of the city centre comes the staccato rack-a-rack of massed 20mm anti-aircraft guns. The less frequent deep whump of 88mm Flak 37s lends a rhythmic bass note to the deadly melody of the smaller guns. But no bombs have fallen here in Neukölln. Yet.

Tadeuz Zebrowski pauses in the entrance to a filthy alley, next to a foul-smelling broken barrel of something unwanted. He can just make out his quarry, now almost a hundred metres ahead, turning the corner into Fulda Strasse. As soon as the man is out of sight, Zebrowski hurries on light feet up to a darkened watchmaker's shop on the corner and cautiously peers around it. This is far from the best way of following anyone, but Zebrowski has opted for extreme caution over all else. If Standartenführer Schmidt thought somebody was following him, well . . . Those are not consequences Zebrowski wants appearing on his doorstep. The Reichsmarschall has made it abundantly clear he does not want Zebrowski's mission to endanger his life. It's a desire shared by both men.

He sees Schmidt has slowed, is now less than seventy-five metres ahead, has crossed the road. Now Schmidt slows even more. Zebrowski pulls his head back from the corner of the shuttered watchmaker's which shelters him so that only one eye is exposed, stands unmoving. Schmidt has come to a stop outside an apartment building with a high brick-arched entrance, as dark as every other doorway in the street. But this doorway is different. Outside it, against the kerb, are four cars. Two are big Mercedes-Benz saloons, empty. Another, a huge Duesenberg, has a uniformed chauffeur sitting in the driver's seat, his face intermittently illuminated as he smokes a cigarette. The fourth vehicle, incongruously, is a small light brown Opel spattered with mud.

Schmidt slowly turns his head and shoulders, briefly looks both ways along the street before he steps up to the door in front of him and knocks. There's the faintest of glows for a moment as the door is quickly opened and shut again, then nothing. The street is entirely deserted, dark, quiet. Only the cacophony of gunfire, engine droning and intermittent 'crump' of delivered bombs in the north-west disturbs the night.

Zebrowski waits. In the rooms above the watchmaker's a chink of light shows beside a closed curtain. From within, the music of Zarah Leander drifts moodily out into the street. He recognises the tune – *Tiefe Sehnsucht*, Deep Longing. Five minutes go by. Nothing. Nothing moves, no noise is heard beyond the faint singing from above, no lights appear. Nothing. Further ahead, about a hundred metres past the door opened to Schmidt, Zebrowski can see silhouetted the recently-constructed Church of Martin Luther, its elegant clock and bell tower pointing a defiant finger at the cloud-peppered night sky. A thought crosses his mind – how appropriate it is that a church dedicated to a famous enemy of Catholics should be here, in this place, the haunt of a killer of those very same Catholics.

Zebrowski starts slowly forward, towards the doorway through which Schmidt has disappeared. As he approaches the brick-arched entrance, now less than five metres away, the faint sounds of unidentifiable music reach him. He steps up to the entrance, sees a black studded door with a small shuttered grill at head height. Now the sounds are clearer – music and the rising-falling susurration of a crowd enjoying itself. The occasional shout or burst of laughter rises above the clamour before falling back again. Zebrowski hesitates. It's apparently a club of some kind, and well-patronised by the sound of things. He knows it's a risk, following Schmidt here. The man could easily spot him, despite the crowd. On the other hand, Schmidt doesn't know Zebrowski is dogging his footsteps, has never set eyes on his shadow. Zebrowski decides the risk is small when weighed against the possibility that Schmidt, a dedicated loner, is here for a purpose that would interest Reichsmarschall Göring. He steps up to the door and knocks.

The grille is opened a few centimetres and a pair of sharp eyes scrutinise Zebrowski before flicking back and forth to the darkness behind.

"Good evening, sir. Are you a member?"

Zebrowski expected this, or something similar. He takes another calculated risk.

"No. The Hauptsturmführer asked me to meet him here."

The man behind the grill doesn't ask, as Zebrowski expects, 'Hauptsturmführer who?', or 'which Hauptsturmführer?'. Perhaps it doesn't matter. Or the man doesn't care.

"Of course. One moment, please."

The dull light behind the face at the grille becomes even duller as the grille is snapped shut and the door swings inwards. Zebrowski takes two steps inside and the door closes behind him. The doorman, tall and elegant in a dark grey suit, slicked-back hair and an unfashionably thin moustache, flicks a switch and the entry hall lights up again. It's long and narrow, a door at the far end and one on each of the long sides. Lacking only an extra door on one of the long walls, the hall is typical of the crowded apartment blocks scattered around Neukölln. But, where there once would have been rows of mail boxes screwed to the wall, where the door to the caretaker's room would have been flanked by pasted-on lists of rules and prohibitions, now there are ornate plaster cornices, rich burgundy wallpaper, two small chandeliers. This is not somewhere frequented by the factory workers and low government clerks who still call Neukölln home. The doorman turns to Zebrowski.

"The entry charge for non-members is twenty marks, sir."

Zebrowski pulls out his wallet, hands over the fee to the doorman, who folds the dull red note and drops it into a slotted metal box on a side table before turning back.

"Your coat, sir?"

The biting cold of the street has been replaced by the kind of smoky, humid warmth generated by hundreds of bodies in close quarters, and Zebrowski's already feeling uncomfortable in his heavy overcoat. He shrugs it off and hands it to the doorman, who gestures towards the door at the end of the hall and mutters something about a pleasant evening. Zebrowski straightens his coat and tie as he heads to the door.

He walks into a wall of music, smoke and animated conversations, almost gasps with surprise. The room is enormous. Someone has demolished what must have been several apartments and converted the space into a double-height theatre. Half a dozen slim columns substitute for the original supporting walls. There are perhaps a hundred small tables occupied by couples, threesomes, foursomes. Everywhere there is laughter, drinking, talking. A wooden counter lined with bottles and glasses occupies a corner of the room, a barman behind, two waiters with trays on the other side. On a brightly lit stage at the other end of the room a girl of twenty or so with long blonde plaits is seated on a three-legged stool. Her only clothing is a pickelhaube from the last war, perched back from her forehead. Her nakedness is concealed, although only partly, by the piano accordion she is playing. Zebrowski recognises the tune as *Das Kuftsteinlied*, the folk song all about madeira wine and holidays in the mountains. He wonders how the girl avoids getting her nipples caught in the accordion's bellows.

There are no empty tables in the room. Zebrowski can't immediately see Schmidt, casts his eyes around for somewhere he can sit down. Off to his left is a table for two with only one occupant, a fat bald middle-aged man smoking a thin cigar. In front of him is a bottle of wine and a single glass, partly filled. Zebrowski walks over, bends towards the fat man so he can be heard over the noise of the crowd.

"May I be permitted to sit here?"

The man swivels his head slightly, registers Zebrowski, waves a nonchalant hand towards the vacant chair and shrugs his agreement before turning his attention back to the girl with the accordion. Zebrowski sits, and within seconds a waiter is next to him. He orders beer and sausage, sits back, slowly scans the audience looking for Schmidt.

Onstage, the girl has come to the end of her performance.

She stands to scattered polite applause, choosing to cover the top half of her body with the accordion. Despite himself, Zebrowski looks, notes with approval the natural blonde of the girl's hair, lets his gaze linger for a few moments as she performs a half-bow and walks offstage. He turns back to the audience and immediately spots Schmidt, sitting against the far wall at a table with two other men. Like Schmidt, they are both in suits. The three men each have a glass of beer in front of them. Zebrowski watches out of the corner of his eye, pretends to be focused on the stage. The three men at the table also appear to be engrossed in what's happening there, intermittently sipping their beers. There is no conversation, just drinking and watching. Zebrowski can't decide whether they know each other or are, like him and the fat man, strangers thrown together by circumstance and a shortage of chairs.

From somewhere offstage a drum roll sounds, with piano accompaniment, and two suited men walk onstage. They are perhaps thirty or a little more, both slim, athletic. Unsmiling, they survey the crowd. Then one walks a few steps backwards, the other turns around so his back is to the audience, and they simultaneously reach into their coats and produce wicked-looking knives, the blades a hand span long. A knife in each hand, the men theatrically extend their arms sideways to ensure the audience sees exactly what they're holding. Then, another drum roll, and the men start juggling the knives, spinning them up and over, catching the handles every time. After several seconds, the men flick the knives towards each other, so that four knives are in constant motion, swapping back and forth, blades flashing in the myriad lights. A swell of applause rewards the performance, increasing as the man with his back to the audience starts spinning around between throwing and catching his knives. A catch, a spin, a throw, a catch, a spin – over and over and over. The applause is raucous, genuine. It dies as the men retrieve their own knives. With each man still juggling, the one in front turns to face the audience before he steps backwards to stand next to his partner. For a few seconds they continue to juggle the whirling blades then, at an unseen signal, they fling their knives high into the air, move sideways around each other, and each catches the knives thrown by the other. Except one of them doesn't.

The man who earlier was at the front of the stage fails to catch one of the knives, and it falls to the stage at his feet, clatters, bounces, lies still. The other man, having caught both his knives, looks across at his hapless partner and sniggers, lifting his chin arrogantly as he strides to the front of the stage and acknowledges the renewed applause, his arms spread wide. Behind him, furious, his partner picks up the fallen knife and, in an instant, flings it into the other man's back.

A huge intake of breath sweeps the audience. A woman sitting near the stage screams. Stunned silence envelops the crowd as the man at the front of the stage staggers forward, stiff-legged, the thrown knife protruding from his back. He sags at the knees, his eyes sweeping the room as though searching for something. Then, abruptly, he springs up and stands erect as his partner strides to his side. The two men are motionless for a few seconds before the one with the knife in his back slowly turns around. This is the first time the audience has seen his back. And now everyone can see the outline of a thick slab of something under his coat, a thick slab into which the knife is embedded. The man spins around, grinning, to join his also-grinning partner, and they lock arms, bow to the audience, then run off stage pursued by cheers, shouts, clapping.

Zebrowski, like everybody else, is impressed by the theatricality of the performance. In front of him now, delivered unnoticed, is his beer and sausage. He lifts the glass, drinks, and sees over the rim that Schmidt is doing the same thing. He puts the glass down, forks a slice of sausage into his mouth, chews slowly as he continues to surreptitiously watch Schmidt. Even now, none of the three men at the Standartenführer's table have spoken. Each is an island, separate and silent.

Without warning, Schmidt rises from his chair, moves towards the far corner of the room, towards an open corridor above which are a pair of silhouette signs, one a man in evening dress, the other a woman in a long gown. Schmidt disappears into the dimly-lit corridor as a man and two women emerge from it. Onstage, a fat woman on a unicycle appears, pursued by a dwarf in a jester's costume waving a huge dildo. The spectacle is lost on Zebrowski, who momentarily debates whether Schmidt is visiting the toilet or engaged in some other activity. Not knowing what else might lie at the end of the corridor, Zebrowski gulps down some of his beer and goes in pursuit.

The corridor is perhaps twenty metres long, a plain unmarked door on the left, about halfway down, and a pair of doors at the end, each with another silhouette sign denoting men or women. Zebrowski ignores the plain door, heads straight into the men's toilet, steps aside as a man emerges from it. Inside, there's the usual row of porcelain urinals along one wall, four cubicles against the other. None of the cubicles are occupied, and Schmidt isn't one of the three men at urinals. Zebrowski steps back into the corridor. As he does, a man emerges from the plain unmarked door halfway along and walks back into the theatre. Zebrowski debates the wisdom of entering an unknown room, decides he can risk it, given Schmidt doesn't know he's being followed, has never set eyes on his pursuer before. A small risk, set against the potential to uncover something significant in Schmidt's visit to this place, and to whatever's behind that door. As Zebrowski runs the problem through his mind, a small fashionably-dressed old man appears at the theatre end of the corridor and walks straight up to the unmarked door, opens it without knocking, and disappears inside.

Zebrowski prepares himself mentally, quickly rehearses an 'I'm afraid I'm lost' explanation if challenged, takes a short sharp breath and opens the plain door. He's in a short corridor, with another door at the end. There's an acrid taste in the air. It gets stronger as he walks towards the second door. He's about to grasp the handle when it's opened from the other side and a young man with a bad limp emerges, half-smiles at Zebrowski, hold the door open for him as he walks through. Zebrowski nods his thanks, catches the edge of the door before it swings shut, and goes in.

Now the smell hits him, stronger, pungent. It's urine. He's in a tiled room perhaps eight metres across and four deep. Along the far long side is a full-length tiled trough set about half a metre below ground level. Standing in it, facing into the room with his arms spread above his head and held there by manacles fixed to rings bolted into the wall, is a dark-haired youth in his late teens. He is naked. Standing in front of him, urinating, is Schmidt. His stream strikes the youth in the face, about the head and shoulders, runs down his body and joins the pool collecting in the tiled trough. The youth splutters and spits, turning his head this way and that, his eyes tightly closed. His penis is erect, swollen, nearly purple with engorging blood.

Off to the right, two men are standing close together, one smoking a cigarette. The other, the old man who entered less than a minute earlier, is lighting up. Their focus is on the youth in the trough. They momentarily glance at Zebrowski as he enters, then return their attention to the youth. Zebrowski wills himself not to hesitate, not to show doubt. Instead, he moves off to the left, assumes what he hopes is a nonchalant stance, awaits developments.

Schmidt finishes urinating, shakes, bends his knees slightly as he returns his penis to his trousers, then wordlessly turns as he buttons up and walks to a small basin near the door. He pays no attention to Zebrowski, but the two smokers do. Now both their eyes are on him. He reads expectation into their gaze. There is nothing else for it – he'll have to piss on the youth. He walks the few steps to where Schmidt stood moments before. Behind, he can hear the man washing and drying his hands. He's aware the two smokers are still watching.

Pushing aside the desire to flee, resolving to see this through, Zebrowski unbuttons his trousers, pulls his penis out, and summons up a stream. The youth's eyes have blinked open for a few seconds, but they screw shut again as Zebrowski's modest stream strikes him. Zebrowski aims at his shoulders rather than his head, but the youth seems determined to maximise the humiliating experience and ducks his head as far into the stream as he can, again spluttering and spitting. His erection stands as before, makes small jerking movements up and down. Zebrowski forces himself to stay calm, tries to bury his revulsion, slows his actions to a semblance of normality and casualness. He finishes, turns to wash his hands at the basin. Schmidt has gone but, unnoticed, two other men have entered, and now stand slightly apart, apparently waiting their turn. Zebrowski washes and dries his hands before slowly walking out, back into the corridor, then the theatre, and back to his seat. He gratefully slumps into his chair, gulps a draught of beer, realises he is breathing hard, sweating. He can scarcely believe the events of the last several minutes. A glance across the room. Now there are only two men at Schmidt's table. His beer is still there, but Schmidt has gone.

36

"Yes, yes, of course. I understand. We will not stay long. Thank you, Doctor, thank you. Yes, we will come directly. Perhaps an hour. Thank you."

Neumann replaces the telephone earpiece on its candlestick cradle, puts the instrument down on his desk, runs a hand back through his hair. He suddenly feels tired, battered, old. For a moment he closes his eyes, savours the transitory pleasure of nearly falling asleep. He forces his eyes open, takes a sharp breath, and gets up for his hat and coat. On the S-Bahn, he can be home within half an hour. Another half an hour will get him and Irmgard to the SS hospital in Lichterfelde, a little more than ten kilometres south, on the other side of Schöneberg. He leaves his office, heads down the long corridor to the stairs and the street. Halfway down the stairs, on the second floor landing, he encounters the dapper Freud look-alike pathologist, Otto Dürer, heading upstairs. Neumann is preparing to offer a greeting in passing, but Dürer has other ideas and stops directly in his path.

"Max!" His face is serious. "I have been informed about your brother's injury. Please accept my best wishes for his speedy recovery."

Neumann isn't in so much of a hurry that he can dispense entirely with civilised behaviour. He comes to a halt.

"Thank you, Professor. I'm on my way to see him now. He's awake, out of surgery."

"Excellent, excellent. That is pleasing news. Who has performed the surgery, do you know?"

"Ah, yes, . . ." Neumann has to gather his scattered thoughts. "It's a Doctor von Pettenkofer. He telephoned a few minutes ago."

"Then your brother is in good hands. Helmut is one of the best. Now, be off with you. My wishes for Walther's recovery."

The professor continues on his way upstairs, Neumann in the other direction.

✠

The massive hospital building at 44-46 Unter den Eichen in Lichterfelde sits next door to a much smaller building which houses the Liebstandarte SS Adolf Hitler, the Führer's personal bodyguard. Since May 1941, the huge former Municipal General Hospital has admitted only one kind of patient. To get through the doors now, regardless of your injury or illness, you have to be a member of the SS. These days, the hospital's services are in high demand accommodating a steady stream of casualties, most from the Russian Front and North Africa. There's an additional if desultory intake of patients from places like Finland, Poland, France, the difference being that their injuries are almost exclusively sustained at the hands of partisans and resistance fighters. Plus, of course, on all fronts, those injured by faulty equipment, drunken escapades, overturned vehicles. It makes no difference whether the SS patients have been attacked by regular troops or amateur warriors, or otherwise injured – if they can't be successfully treated at one of the hundreds of remote field hospitals, this is where they end up, among more than 700 other inmates. Like Walther Neumann.

As Max hurries with Irmgard through the entrance, he can't avoid the thought that the hospital sits uncomfortably among the substantial Wilhelmine structures and moneyed apartments all around. That said, the hospital's architecture perfectly reflects its purpose and its clientele. Everything about it is brutally severe, from the huge rectangular stone blocks framing the four wide entrance doors to the layered stories of grey granite and brick above, reminiscent of a jail for the most vicious of criminals. No jail, perhaps, thinks Neumann, but undoubtedly it houses some of those criminals. He pushes the thought aside as the couple enter, pause to get their bearings, then head towards a large alcove on their left. In front of it, spanning the entire recess, is a dark wood reception counter, behind which three women sit at typing at desks. One of the women rises, comes to meet Max and Irmgard as they approach.

"We're here to see Untersturmführer Neumann."

She nods as though they're expected, asks them to sit on the bench nearby while she sees if Doctor von Pettenkofer is available. They sit, watch as the woman picks up a handset and flicks a switch on the internal communication telephone. She says a few words to someone at the other end, replaces the handset, flashes a thin smile at Max and Irmgard, then returns to her typewriter.

The two Neumanns sit without speaking for a few minutes, each churning through their own thoughts. The cavernous room is silent apart from the intermittent clack-clack-ping of the typewriters and the slow thud of a large railway clock on the wall above the reception counter. Then comes the sound of footsteps on the polished wooden floor of a corridor next to the counter. They steadily grow louder until their source appears around the corner.

Doctor Helmut von Pettenkofer looks nothing like either of the Neumanns was expecting. The name alone conjured up visions of someone tall, probably handsome, self-possessed, even arrogant, the product of a long line of Junker aristocracy used to riding roughshod over peasants and other inferiors. But the doctor is no more than middling height, running to fat, in his forties, thin greying hair swept straight back, clean shaven and bland-faced. He's in a white coat over what appear to be grey workman's overalls. The bell end of a stethoscope protrudes from a side pocket of his coat, the rest of it apparently stuffed inside. He spots Max and Irmgard, breaks into a smile, hurries forward to shake their hands and introduce himself. He gestures towards the bench they have just vacated.

"Please, sit, sit. Perhaps I could explain a little before you visit the Untersturmführer. Your brother, Herr Neumann."

The pair sit down again. Von Pettenkofer sits too, next to Irmgard. Max and Irmgard swivel on the bench to half-face him. He's not smiling now. Now he's someone about to deliver news the recipients don't want to hear.

"First, I must tell you that Untersturmführer Neumann's life is not in danger. The surgery went well, and I see no complications arising. He will recover from his injuries, but it will take some little time, and he will be in discomfort to some extent. There is no reason he can not live a full and long life."

Irmgard stares at the doctor, frowning slightly, as though unable to understand what it is she's being told. Max speaks for both of them.

"Thank you, Doctor. But . . . his injuries. I have been told only that . . . that . . . A head wound, they said. Is . . ."

"Yes, exactly that, a head wound. I understand he was attacked with a pistol at quite close range. He came near to death. A few centimetres to one side, and . . . well. Of course, a few centimetres the other way, and we would not now be speaking."

"So the wound is superficial?" Irmgard grasps at the straw.

"Unfortunately not, Frau Neumann." The doctor breathes deep before continuing. "The bullet grazed his left temple as it passed. Even so, it caused a significant degree of damage." He spreads his hands, a universal sign of events beyond control, of helplessness. "The shock wave from the impact, you see. We have been able to save a good portion of his ear, and in time it will heal, but there was nothing we could do with . . . The bullet carried much of the ear with it." Von Pettenkofer looks hard at both of the Neumanns in turn before continuing, preparing them.

"I regret to say we could not save his eye." He shakes his head slowly. "The damage was too great. I am sorry. We have removed it. Again, the injury will heal, but . . ."

Max and Irmgard don't hear the rest. Irmgard's hand is on her mouth as though holding something in. Her eyes swing wildly between her husband and von Pettenkofer, imploring one of them to help, to make things right again. A small whimpering noise comes from her throat. Max stares unblinking at the doctor, but in his mind sees only Walther. Damaged, disfigured Walther, lying somewhere upstairs. A broken body and broken dreams.

Neither of the Neumanns register von Pettenkofer's final words or of his departure back down the corridor. For long minutes they sit, stunned, angry, confused, worried. The emotions swirl and merge, shut words out. There is nothing to say. Max holds Irmgard's right hand, resting on her thigh. Her left hand dabs at her eyes with a crumpled handkerchief. The minutes stretch and break, and others arrive to take their place, in silence. After a time, Max straightens, puts his left arm around Irmgard's shoulders.

"We'd better see him." They both stand, resolute.

The woman they first encountered takes them to Walther's

bedside, leading the way up the steep flights of stairs. She apologizes for the inconvenience.

"The lift is broken. I'm sorry, but you know what it's like trying to get anything repaired these days." She seems unconcerned that her comment teeters precariously on the edge of outright criticism of the Party. Either that, or the sentiment is freely shared even by those in the SS hospital. Max and Irmgard don't respond. They know what it's like.

Onto the third floor landing, and right into a long corridor. The woman stops at an open door near the end, holds an arm out towards the room beyond.

"In here, sir. Last bed on the left."

Max and Irmgard stand facing the doorway, hesitant, fearing what lies within. A subconscious signal passes between them, and they start forward. The room holds eight beds, four each side, separated by dull blue curtains suspended from rails in the roof. The pair try not to look at the occupants of the beds, but can't resist. They see a young man apparently without his lower legs, laying back, eyes closed. A grey-haired man in his fifties is sitting up in bed reading, one arm encased in plaster. He lifts his eyes as they pass, shoots an uninterested glance, goes back to his book. Two men in adjacent beds are swathed in bandages around their head, apertures for their eyes, nose and mouth. Burnt flesh is apparent at the edges of the bandages. There's an unpleasant smell.

Anni sits next to Walther's bed, one hand on his arm. She looks up as she hears Max and Irmgard. Her eyes are puffy, red, her face the colour of pastry. A sodden handkerchief is wadded into her free hand. She gets to her feet, half staggers towards Irmgard, and they fall together, arms locked around one another. Anni sobs silently. Irmgard strokes her head, her hair, makes soothing sounds.

Max is rigid, staring at Walther. The left side of his head is heavily bandaged. It's impossible to see what remains of his left ear. It's impossible not to think of his left eye, the one that's no longer there. Max tries to force from his mind an image of suppurating nothingness, of a hole where an eye should be. Has always been. Images of Fathers Dassler and Gantz crowd their way unbidden into his consciousness. He pushes them out again.

Walther seems asleep, his right eye shut, his breathing slow and regular. Max turns to Anni, now standing back from Irmgard, takes a step forward and chastely hugs her.

"Is he . . .?"

"He's been awake. He keeps drifting off. I . . . The doctor said it will . . . he will . . ." Her words float aimlessly and disappear. She looks back to Irmgard, her eyes imploring, begging for help. Irmgard steps up and takes her hand, guides her back onto the chair by the bed. All three fix their eyes on Walther's silent form.

37

Tadeuz Zebrowski is a cautious man. Adaptable, inventive, persistent, thorough, dedicated – all of those things, but all of them underpinned by his innate caution. It's caution that has enabled him to survive when so many of his countrymen have not, that has propelled him into the service of one of the most powerful men in the Reich, a man he considers a friend. Caution has kept Zebrowski alive for many years. Still, he ponders, as he walks slowly down Biedenkopfer Strasse towards his Reinickendorf apartment, on this occasion caution might not have been the best policy. His assignment, the wish of the Reichsmarschall, is to keep Standartenführer Schmidt under observation, to establish where he goes and who he sees and why. But for two days and nights now, the man has apparently vanished. Not at his apartment, not seen going into or out of the Reich Central Security Office, nowhere. Zebrowski has spent hours tonight watching the club where he last saw the man, but without a result. Wherever Schmidt is, it's apparent he wants to remain unseen, but the reason is unknown. Zebrowski does not like not knowing, being in the dark. He silently berates himself, hunches deeper into his collar as he turns the corner into Sterkrader Strasse. The razor wind drives Schmidt from his thoughts. They turn instead to home comforts and some wine with a late dinner. In his mind's eye, he's already in his apartment, warm, comfortable, relaxed. Less than fifty metres to go. Somewhere up ahead, a dog barks.

"Excuse me, friend. Do you have a light?"

Zebrowski starts. The voice is behind him. Close. He stops, turns, and is jolted by the sight of Stefan Schmidt less than three metres away. Even as he asks himself where the man has come from, he realises Schmidt must have been standing in a recessed doorway. Waiting. The Standartenführer is overcoated, hat covering his head, scarf around his throat, hands deep in his overcoat pockets. He regards Zebrowski coolly, expectantly, apparently relaxed. Unthreatening.

Heart pounding, Zebrowski stamps hard on his rising fear, affects nonchalance as he responds.

"I regret to say I do not smoke, sir."

Schmidt gives a half-smile. It is not a friendly one. Even as his lips curl his right hand whips out of his overcoat pocket and Zebrowski is looking at a Steyr Mannlicher 9mm pistol with a sound suppressor screwed to its short barrel. Zebrowski is not a fighting man, not a trained killer. He's not armed, and even if he was there is nothing he can do but stare. To run or to leap upon his assailant would be an exercise in futility – he'd be killed before he'd taken a single step.

"Please do not make a sudden movement. If I must, I will shoot you here in the street. We will continue, you and I, to your apartment. You will walk ahead of me and you will not turn around. If you do, I will shoot you. When we arrive at your apartment, you will put the key in your door and then stand still. Do you understand? Answer, please."

In the short time it takes Schmidt to issue his instructions, a dozen scenarios flash through Zebrowski's mind. None of them bear close scrutiny. None of them offer a glimmer of hope. He tries desperately to control his fear, to keep thinking, to look for any opportunity to fight or talk his way out of the situation. In the immediate short term, though, he has no options available.

"Yes," he replies, "I understand." The words sound to his ears as though they're being said by an actor in a play.

"Very well, turn around and proceed."

The two men walk slowly on down Sterkrader Strasse until they reach Zebrowski's apartment building. Then in through the single half-glassed front door and up the stairs to the first floor. Zebrowski does as he's been told, takes the key from his inside coat pocket and inserts it into the deadlock, then stands and waits. As Schmidt has been throughout, he is three metres behind, his pistol levelled. For the first time on their short journey, he speaks.

"Good. Now, move two paces to your right and lie face down with your hands behind your head."

Zebrowski does as he's told, lies face down on the cold linoleum of the corridor. Behind, he hears his apartment door unlocked and opened, the rustle of clothing as Schmidt moves a step or two and back again, the click of a light switch, then another two footsteps as Schmidt moves back into the corridor.

"Get up. Walk slowly through the door and stop in the middle of the room. Lie down there as you have done here."

Zebrowski's hopes slide towards nothingness with every movement he makes. Schmidt clearly knows exactly what he is doing, offers not the slightest glimpse of an opportunity. He maintains his distance, keeps his pistol aimed at his captive, remains cool, unhurried, confident.

As Zebrowski comes to a slow halt and lies down in the middle of his already-illuminated apartment he hears behind him the door being closed and locked. There's a rustle and a metallic clank and some clicking. He twitches in surprise as something thuds onto the floor next to his waist. He looks sideways. A pair of handcuffs, each cuff fully disengaged, ratchet teeth exposed.

"Do not turn around. Remain lying on the floor. Put your hands behind your back and secure them with the handcuffs. Do that now, please."

Zebrowski's disappearing hope turns into resigned despair as he goes through the motions called for. By the time he has secured his own hands and his nose is hard against the musty carpet, he has abandoned any expectation of either mercy or escape. He has seen what Schmidt is capable of, can think of no consideration or circumstance which will deflect the man's actions. He has known for years that, for a man like him, a situation like this is how the end would come. It is a strangely comforting thought, the realisation that his life will soon be over, a life he chose to live, knowing all the while its likely consequences. Zebrowski's thoughts turn towards the people and the things he values. He barely registers Schmidt's footsteps moving carefully towards him, hears the gentle swoosh of trouser material and air only a moment before a fierce kick to his head knocks him unconscious.

✠

"I regret to report, sir, that the man resisted my efforts. He refused to divulge any information at all. Nothing. Not even his name, real or assumed."

"Nothing?" Reichsführer Himmler's eyebrows are up. He is not used to hearing that Stefan Schmidt has failed to elicit information. First there was that bastard priest, Rochlitz. Now this man, whoever he was. Himmler scrutinizes Schmidt more closely than usual, asks himself if the Standartenführer is slipping, perhaps allowing his penchant for inflicting pain to override his judgement.

"Nothing," repeats Schmidt, apparently unperturbed by his boss's examination. "It is regrettable, as I say, but the man was able to withstand the most severe pain without succumbing. I have not encountered such a man before." There is a note of something approaching admiration in Schmidt's voice.

"So you know nothing at all about him? Why he was following you? Who he was working for?"

"I was able to ascertain some few facts about him, sir. His name, or at least the one he was using, was Tadeuz Zebrowski. A Pole, of course. That is the name in his ration book. I found two identity cards. One is in the name of Zebrowski, and I am inclined to believe it was his given name. It says he was born in Silesia, near Wroclaw. The other card identifies him as Friedrich Heyse, an Oberstleutnant in the Wehrmacht. I have checked – it is false. There is nobody of that name and rank listed. Whoever the man was, he appears to have been unmarried. There was nothing at his apartment to suggest anyone else lived there. Nor was there any evidence of where he worked, or for whom. He possessed three uniforms, however. One of a Reichspost delivery man, one of a BVG employee, a tram conductor I believe. Both were well used. The other was a Wehrmacht uniform, an Oberstleutnant's, presumably used in conjunction with his false identity card. I have to assume the other uniforms were part of false identities also. It was . . ."

"Was he Kripo? A detective?"

"It is doubtful, sir. I found no Kripo or SS uniform, nor any regulation issue equipment. Nor did I locate a weapon of any kind."

"What about his income – where did he get his money from? Nobody can live on air." Himmler is unaccustomedly energised by this shadowy figure who has confounded Schmidt.

"I have made enquiries of the local bank branches, but there is no record of him held there. His landlord informs me that Herr Zebrowski always paid in cash. I found this . . ," Schmidt pauses, reaches down into his briefcase on the floor next to his chair, pulls out a bundle of banknotes secured with string and puts it on the desk in front of Himmler, ". . . hidden behind a wall panel. There is a little more than six thousand Reichsmarks."

"Mmm." Himmler nods distractedly, slides the bundle back towards Schmidt. "No, you keep it, Stefan." He pauses, concentrates for a few seconds as Schmidt replaces the money in his briefcase. "It seems unlikely he was acting independently, would you not agree?"

"Yes, it is unlikely."

"Then someone must have sent him to follow you. Or perhaps to kill you. It has be related to that damned priest"

Schmidt is less certain than Himmler. He instantly thinks of the dozens, even hundreds, of people who would kill him without blinking, the legacy of his years of carnage in the Reichsführer's service, but he lets the point slide by without comment. After a short silence, Himmler speaks again. His tone is insistent, peremptory.

"Is there a possibility the Kripo have learned of the missing document? Are we under scrutiny?"

His frustration and agitation are showing. Schmidt tries to lower the temperature.

"I do not think so, sir. Only you and I are aware of the document, and we have told nobody. The Kripo investigators will have deduced someone is looking for something, but they can not possibly know who is looking, or what is being sought. I am certain we have nothing to fear from a Kripo investigation. However, to make sure, I propose interrogating one of the investigators." He meets Himmler's eye and holds it. "We discussed this course of action at our last meeting."

Himmler nods thoughtfully, thinking. "Yes, of course." He studies his desktop for a few moments before returning his gaze to Schmidt. "Please proceed, Stefan. As we discussed."

38

It's one of the oldest restaurants in Berlin, tucked away on Waisenstrasse, hard by part of what remains of the city's medieval wall. Nearly four hundred years old, Die Letze Instanz was originally the brandy room of a residential building and still looks like one. As they head towards the blackened oak front door Neumann tells Harry Forbes that less than a hundred years ago the surrounding area was where butchers would gather their cattle ready for slaughter or an overnight reprieve.

"So, it really was 'The Last Instance' for the cows. It can't be all bad, though, or Leland wouldn't have recommended it. C'mon, let's live dangerously."

Neumann gives a half-hearted grin wrapped in doubt and follows Forbes through the door. Neither of them notices the fashionably-dressed but otherwise unremarkable man casually strolling past, heading towards the northern end of Waisenstrasse. Standartenführer Schmidt's head doesn't turn as he passes, but his pale grey eyes have seen all they need to. He increases his pace back to his car. He'll need to act fast.

Neumann and Forbes are in a long, low, dark room

dominated by massive wooden beams on the ceiling. Wood-panelled booths of different sizes line each long side, leaving a corridor down the middle for the waiters and arriving patrons. On the wall of each booth is a framed print of some famous German – Gutenberg, Bach, Goethe, Mozart and, of course, Hindenburg with his fearsome moustache. As usual these days, a large print of Hitler features most prominently, this one a full-length portrait hung at the far end of the long room. The table in each booth boasts a candle-holder on a red-and-white check tablecloth. Only one candle is lit, at a table near the back wall occupied by a middle-aged man and woman.

The owner bustles forward from behind the small counter near the front door. It's clear he's a man who enjoys his food, looks vaguely like a short version of Hermann Göring. He's in black trousers and a white shirt, over which a black waistcoat strains at the buttons. His round face breaks into a welcoming smile at the sight of two customers.

"Good-day, gentlemen. A table for two?" No Hitler salute here, whether by omission or intent isn't clear.

"Thank you." Forbes points to a booth about halfway along the room. "There, perhaps?"

"Of course, sir, of course. This way, please." Prompted by the obvious American accent, the owner asks Forbes if a countryman has recommended the restaurant.

"My boss said I should come here. He's the Charge d'Affaires at the American Embassy. I think he's been more than a few times."

The fat man claps his hands together like an excited child. "Ah, of course. Mr Morris has honoured us with his patronage on several occasions. He is well, I trust?"

"Sure is."

Forbes is already studying the menu – he doesn't want the conversation to drag out. He forestalls a renewed question from the owner by quickly pointing to the drinks list and asking for two Weihenstephaners.

Neumann waits until the owner has gone to get the beers before speaking. "Are you any nearer to getting an Ambassador? It's been a couple of years."

"I doubt it. The President doesn't seem to be in any hurry to fill the seat. He probably thinks we'd lose face. You can't withdraw an Ambassador in high-minded protest if you replace him even though nothing's changed."

Neumann nods thoughtfully in agreement, silently scoffs at the futility of the whole charade. America wanted to signal to the world that Germany's treatment of Jews, Kristalnacht in particular, was unacceptable, so it recalled its Ambassador in protest. And that achieved . . . well, it achieved fuck all. The Party's treatment of Jews didn't improve, it got worse. The death and destruction surrounding Kristalnacht, only three years earlier, was just for openers. Since then, the Jews have . . .

"Anyway, enough about the State Department." Forbes has gone back to the menu. "What will we have?"

The offerings on the menus are limited. They expected that. What they didn't expect to see on offer was lake trout with green beans and potatoes. Ordinarily, only Party grandees and war profiteers would have such a choice. Both men settle on that.

"Our host must have a very good contact somewhere," observes Neumann. "Black market if he does. Either that or we'll be palmed off with something like cod or sole. I don't expect the genuine article, but you never know. Ah, our beer."

The beaming owner puts down two small tankards, says he hopes his guests will enjoy them, foreshadows a fifteen minute wait for their lunch, then disappears through to a back room.

Neumann and Forbes raise their tankards, exchange a 'Prost' and a 'Salut' and each takes a mouthful. Neumann's is barely more than a sip.

“Not good?” Forbes raises his eyebrows.

“No, no, it’s fine. I like wheat beer.” Neumann is unexpectedly sombre for a moment, then brightens and declaims theatrically, “If the drink you give me doth touch my palate adversely, I make a crooked face at it.” He forestalls Forbes’ jibe in response. “Coriolanus,” he says, as the solemnity returns. “It’s just . . . I don’t know. These days it doesn’t have the same appeal it once did. I’m not drinking much at all. Middle age, probably. The body tells you to slow down or die. Something like that.”

“Yeah, sure,” scoffs Forbes, lifts his chin. “I’m not buying that, my friend. We’re close enough to the same age, and my body isn’t talking back to me. Besides, you could do with a bit of fattening up. Irmgard thinks you’re not as cuddly as you used to be. Beer’s just the thing for that, trust me.”

Neumann chokes down the green-eyed monster that rears up unexpectedly, doesn’t want to dwell on how Harry knows what Irmgard thinks. “Anything to keep the peace,” he replies as he takes another sip. “And to keep my lady happy.” He immediately realises he’s put undue emphasis on the ‘my’. A pause. “But you didn’t invite me here because I needed feeding. Call me a cynical old Kripo bull if you like, but I get the feeling there’s an ulterior motive sitting on your shoulder. So, out with it – what’s up?”

Forbes affects an outraged look, sits back in his chair.

“Me? Ulterior motive? How dare you, sir!” He holds the pose for a moment then drops it. “Alright, officer, you’ve got me. I’ll make a full confession.” Forbes is suddenly serious. He leans forward, forearms on the table. “I’m in a bit of trouble, Max. From over in the States.” He breaks off, gulps his beer.

“Trouble? What kind of trouble?” Neumann realises the theatrics have finished, that his friend isn’t fooling around.

Forbes breathes deep, lets it out with a loud sigh.

“The usual, I suppose. Money. I owe some guys. They don’t

take kindly to people not paying them back."

"How much?"

"A lot. Nearly three grand US."

"Jesus, Harry. How? How did you get into this?"

"Ah, well, you know how it is. I thought I was a better card player than I am. Lost a little at first, couldn't cover it. Some friends said they'd stand me . . ." A contemptuous snort. "Friends? Ha! They sucked me right in, Max. A bit more, a bit more, play a few more games, your luck has to change some time." Forbes mingles shame with bitterness as he continues. "It all added up. I never hit a winning streak. Then suddenly I'm in there right up to my neck and my so-called friends want the money or else . . ."

"But you're here. In the Embassy. What can they do all this way from home?"

"Sure, we're a long way from Washington. But it doesn't make any difference, Max. These guys, they're . . . they're animals, thugs." His shoulders sag, and extra years appear on his face. "I got a letter yesterday. From my mother. They've been to her house. Frightened her. Said what they'd do to her if I don't pay." Forbes runs a hand across his face. There's a wild look in his eyes. "For Christ's sake, Max, my mother! They've threatened my mother!"

"Isn't there anyone who can help? Can you get a bank loan? I can help, but it wouldn't be much . . ."

"No!" Forbes snaps it out. "No, that's not why I'm telling you. I don't want charity, I want to work for the money. Anything, anything at all. I thought you might know someone. Someone in business, someone who needed . . . I don't know. Just anything. I'd do the black market if I had to. I really need the money. There isn't anyone else. Dad's dead, I haven't got any brothers or sisters. And the banks. Jesus, they won't even let me in the front door. I need some extra work, Max, it's as simple as that. If I can at least start paying back what I owe, make some regular payments . . ." There's no need for Forbes to spell out the implications.

Neumann concentrates hard as he listens, prepares to speak, but is forestalled by the arrival of the restaurant's owner bearing two plates covered with silver cloches. He places a plate in front of each man before theatrically whipping the cloches up simultaneously to reveal their lunch. He asks if they would like more beer. Forbes drains what's left of his tankard in a gulp, says please. Neumann gives the owner a thin smile as he shakes his head. For the moment, the mood is broken, conversation suspended as the two men contemplate the food in front of them, breathe in the rich odours. Forbes takes the first mouthful, blows on a chunk of fish at the end of his fork.

"Mmmh," he mumbles as he chews and swallows. "This is good. The real McCoy. They're not trying to sell us a pup. Go on, try some."

Neumann does, mimics his friend's assessment. It's real lake trout, no question. For a few minutes, they eat in silence. The owner returns with another Weihenstephaner for Forbes, leaves, and the meal continues. It's Neumann who stops eating first, takes a sip of his beer.

"I'm sorry to hear about your mother, Harry. I'd like to help, but . . ." He shrugs, spreads his hands. "Just look around. Jobs are hard to come by unless they contribute to the war effort. Poles and Ivans are doing all the donkey work, some of the skilled stuff too. Your talents are . . ." Neumann breaks off suddenly as a thought strikes him. "Translation. Your German's still good. Good enough to translate. There are government departments who could use you. It's not the best-paying job in the world, but . . ."

"I could do that," says Forbes eagerly. "But how would . . . Do you know anybody? In one of the departments? Could you get me an introduction?" Forbes puts down his knife and fork, ignores his beer. He's interested.

"I don't know anybody. Not as such. But that isn't a problem. I can ask around, work out who to see, that kind of thing. It shouldn't take me more than a day or two." Neumann's tone changes. "But can you do it? What about the Embassy? I don't imagine the State Department wants its diplomats working for a foreign government."

Forbes brushes the problem aside, waves his hand nonchalantly. "I'm the lowest of the low when it comes to diplomats. Besides, the Embassy won't know, will they? As far as anyone's concerned, I'm just a visiting American looking for a few extra bucks to help pay for my holiday. Yes?"

Neumann isn't convinced, but doesn't want to strangle his friend's new-born hope at birth so he agrees, and both men go back to their meal. Forbes attacks his enthusiastically. Neumann pushes his food around the plate, takes a small mouthful, has another sip of beer – he's had enough of both.

39

Kurt Schneider works through lunchtime, sits at Neumann's desk and compares lists of stolen property against seizures from illegal pawnbrokers. He welcomes the mind-soothing repetitive nature of the small task, a favour for one of his hard-pressed colleagues. As he works he munches periodically on a pile of sliced sausage and chunks of a dark rye kommissbrot loaf sitting on an old issue of the *Beobachter*. He's already polished off the two thick slices of Westphalian ham which accompanied them.

From time to time he makes a mark against one of the listed items, a tick or a question mark. The sausage and the bread are good, filling, but Schneider's a big man and loves his food, and he'd much rather be sitting in Die Letze Instanz like the boss. His mind wanders to thoughts of what Neumann and his friend are probably eating – rabbit fillets with creamed horseradish, side plates of vegetables, pickle and sauce boats. Perhaps strawberries covered with real cream . . .

He starts at the peremptory shrill ring of the telephone on the desk, snatches up the earpiece and leans forward to speak.

"Kriminalassistant Schneider."

It's the switchboard. That young blonde one he ogles every chance he gets.

"There's a call for Kriminalkommissar Neumann. Is he available?"

"He's out for an hour or two. I'll talk to them, take a message."

"Yes, of course." She sounds doubtful, uncertain. "It's a lady. She's very upset. I'll connect you."

There's a dull click, a burst of static, then a breaking tear-filled voice erupts from the earpiece.

"Herr Neumann? Please . . . please help . . ."

He's heard the voice before, knows it, but not like this.

"Frau Steinert? This is Kurt Schneider. Kriminalkommissar Neumann isn't here. Can I . . ."

"Please help me, Herr Schneider." Her voice teeters on the precarious edge of hysteria. "That man . . . that man has been again. He has beaten Jürgen, he . . . I thought he would kill us. I don't know what to do, please . . ."

"I will help, Frau Steinert. But first, does your son need an ambulance? Is he badly injured?"

"He . . . no, I do not think so. Frau Beckenbauer is with him. My neighbour. I am frightened, Herr Schneider. Of that terrible man . . . he might return. Please, can you help?"

"I will come immediately. It will not take long. Please lock your doors until I arrive. We can talk then. Are you alright, madam? Did he . . . did he hurt you?"

"No, I am unharmed. Jürgen . . . Jürgen is . . . Please hurry."

Schneider hurries, bread and sausage forgotten, takes the stairs three at a time, all the way into the Kripo garage in the basement. He guns the little Opel out of Alexanderplatz and on to Kaiser-Wilhelm Strasse, curses the motor's sluggish response as it struggles with BV Aral – the low-octane petrol is all that's available these days. With siren wailing, Schneider heads north for Gesundbrunnen barely four kilometres away. He's there in minutes, runs his car up onto the footpath outside the Steinerts' block and races up the stairs to number 67. He knocks rapidly and loudly.

"Frau Steinert! It's me," he bellows between gulped breaths. "It's Kurt Schneider. Open the door please. You have nothing to fear now."

Out of the corner of his eye he sees the front window curtain move slightly, then a few seconds later the door is opened wide. A woman he's never seen before narrows suspicious eyes at him. She's about fifty, solidly built, holds a carving knife in her hand, down by her side. Without taking her eyes off Schneider she calls to someone behind her.

"Is this the one?"

"Yes, it's him. Let him pass please Frau Beckenbauer."

The woman steps aside, still wary, still holding the knife. Schneider walks into a room in disarray, furniture displaced, a small side table overturned, the flowers once on it now lying wetly next to their smashed vase. Rugs are awry, framed photographs knocked from the mantel, two chairs overturned. Jürgen Steinert is lying on the sofa, his mother in a wheelchair beside him, one hand resting on his shoulder. Her son's eyes are both closed, one involuntarily because of the bruising and swelling around it. Jürgen's shirt is ripped at the front, spattered with blood. A gash across his forehead looks like it needs stitches, still weeps fluid. There are red welts on both sides of his neck. Beside the sofa is a stool holding a shallow bowl of water, a few cloths, some with blood showing, and a roll of gauze bandage.

Schneider moves quickly to the wheelchair, goes down on one knee in front of it.

"Did he hurt you, Frau Steinert? Are you injured?"

“No, no, I am alright.” She clearly is not alright. Her hair is disordered, her face pale, eyes puffed and red-rimmed. Even so, there is steel in her voice. “It is Jürgen,” she adds, turning her face to her son. “That man, that, that . . . animal. He beat Jürgen. Hit him with a gun.” She reaches forward, clutches Schneider’s upper arm. “I am frightened, Herr Schneider. I thought Jürgen might be killed. I do not know what to do. Please . . .”

“There’s no need to worry. It’s over. He can’t hurt you now. But we must make sure your son is . . .

“I will look after him.” The sharp voice comes from behind Schneider. It’s the neighbour, Frau Beckenbauer. He starts to stand as she speaks again. “I’m a nurse. At the university hospital. Step aside and I’ll continue tending to him.” Her tone is peremptory. She is used to being obeyed. Schneider moves backwards, and the woman kneels by the sofa and continues cleaning Jürgen’s wounds. As Schneider watches, Frau Steinert wheels her chair backwards, towards the kitchen area, and with a jerk of her head motions for him to follow.

She waits for him to join her.

“May I have a glass of water, please?” Her voice is strong, but Schneider can see her hands are trembling. He fills a glass sitting on the kitchen bench, hands it to her. She holds it in both hands, sips at it before resting the glass in her lap. Her head droops and she stares at her hands.

“I have not told you the truth,” she says flatly, without lifting her head. “Please do not judge me harshly. I thought it was for the best, that it might keep us safe. I am so sorry, Herr Schneider. I have brought us only pain . . . Jürgen . . . This might not have happened had I not been so foolish.”

Schneider is on his knee again. He reaches out and lays a hand on the woman’s wrist. He doesn’t speak, but the expression on his face conveys his thoughts.

“I told you, you and your colleague, that Father Rochlitz

had not contacted us since we left Saint Lambertus." Her voice is barely above a whisper. "That is not true. I am sorry. Some weeks ago I received a short letter from him. There was a key with it. He said it was for a private box at his post office, that the box held something valuable. Valuable and dangerous. He asked me to do whatever I thought best with it if he . . . if something were to happen to him."

Now Schneider is staring at her in open astonishment. He takes long seconds to form his words.

"What did you do? With the letter and the key."

"I burned the letter. As he asked me to." Her eyes are filling with tears. "The key . . . I hid it. Until someone could take me to the post office. Without Jürgen . . . in case there was something about . . . " She lets the implication speak for itself, points to an overturned earthenware jar on the benchtop, dried lentils spilling out of it. "There. I had to tell him. He was hurting Jürgen. I just wanted him to stop."

Schneider pictures the scene even as she speaks. The unknown assailant raining blows on Jürgen, his mother hysterical with fear, Father Rochlitz's wishes and interests forgotten as she desperately tries to save her son. There's not a gram of blame or censure in his thoughts, only concern.

"Did he take the key?"

A nod. "Yes. He made me tell him what was in the letter." Her eyes drill into Schneider's. "Forgive me. There was nothing I could do. Nothing."

Schneider knows. Of course there was nothing she could do. But there is something that can be done now, something he can do. He gets to his feet.

"Forgive me, Frau Steinert, but I must leave immediately. I know where this man will go. If I hurry, I might be able to get there before him. Lock your door, answer to nobody." He's already halfway across the room. "I will send someone to stand guard as soon as I can."

Then he's out the door, starting to run towards the stairs. If he can get to the Charlottenburg Post Office in time, he might be able to stop this man. He hurtles down the stairs three at a time, using the handrail to swing around the landing corners. In full flight, he reaches the ground floor, out through the entrance arch, and up to the Opel still parked on the footpath. He fumbles in his trouser pocket for the keys as he wrenches open the unlocked driver's door and throws himself into the seat. As he jams the key into the ignition he becomes aware of a shadow to his left, a movement. Instinct turns his head, and past the still-open driver's door he's looking at the barrel of a silenced pistol aimed at his face from less than two metres away.

"If you move I will kill you."

For one or two seconds Schneider is incapable of movement, frozen by the suddenness, the unexpectedness of what has happened. It's not fear as such, but the need to reassess the world around him, to accommodate this startling new reality. The moment passes, and for a split second his mind races through courses of action still open to him. He could try to start the car and speed off, try to grab the pistol, try to draw and fire his own . . . Another split second of thought tells him nothing is going to work. The stranger's gun isn't close enough to grab – he'd be dead before he could get the car started. He has no options left. None at all. He sits motionless, hands on the steering wheel, eyes on the man holding the pistol. The grey eyes tell him that this is the man he's looking for, the one behind the killings. For a few moments there's only the sound of Schneider's laboured breathing.

"Very good. You have made the sensible choice. Now, slowly, take your hands from the steering wheel and get out of the car. Keep your hands where I can see them. Bring the key with you, please."

Schmidt steps back as he speaks, putting an extra metre between himself and the open driver's door as Schneider steps onto the footpath. The big man stands still, awaits the next move, desperately assesses the changing situation for an opportunity, an advantage of some kind. But the man with the gun knows his business, leaves no windows of opportunity open.

"Very slowly, please, take out your pistol and place it on the ground in front of you. Hold it only with your fingertips."

Schneider does as he's told, places his Walther P38 on the paving, stands erect again.

"Place the key on the roof, close to the door."

Schneider complies, moves slowly, still searches for any advantage he can utilise. There is nothing.

"Good. Now walk to the rear and open the trunk."

Again, he follows his instructions, opens the lid of the trunk, awaits whatever's coming.

"Please get in."

Even as he faces imminent death, Schneider can't avoid thinking for a moment how farcical the situation is. He is enormous. The trunk is tiny. It will be like trying to stuff a gorilla in a suitcase. His eyes flick to meet those of his captor. There is neither threat nor amusement in them, just focused determination. Schneider has little choice – he clambers in, folds his body into a foetal position, head and feet pressed hard against the side panels.

Stefan Schmidt peers at the huddled figure lying on the floor of the trunk for a few seconds. Then, without another word, he slams the trunk lid closed. He retrieves the key from the roof, locks the trunk, then walks a few metres from the car to retrieve his small leather case from beside a lamp post. He returns to the car, gets in, puts his case on the front passenger seat. As he settles in and puts the key in the ignition, Schmidt makes a mental note to despatch someone to retrieve his own car. He starts the Opel and moves cautiously off the footpath and onto Gustav-Meyer Allee, heading south-east towards the industrial districts of Kreuzberg and Friedrichshain.

✠

Neumann returns from lunch to find his office deserted. On his desk are the robbery lists Kurt Schneider was working through, and there are some slices of kommissbrot and sausage sitting on newspaper. Although he's eaten very little, drunk even less, the smell of the sausage churns his stomach, and he swallows hard against a heave of nausea. There's no note on the desk to say where Schneider has gone – his hat and coat are still on the rack in the corner, so it's not likely he's out. Neumann mentally shrugs, assumes his partner will return shortly, hangs up his hat and coat and settles down into his chair. He carefully wraps the remnants of bread and sausage and puts them out of sight in a side drawer.

It's less than ten minutes later, as Neumann trudges his way through the latest set of directions from the office of the Reichskriminaldirektor, that the phone on the desk rings.

"Kriminalkommissar Neumann."

"A call for you." It's a voice he doesn't recognise, brusque and coarse, sounds like a gypsy hawker. A new girl on the switchboard, apparently. "Says he's Orpo. Unterwachtmeister Joseph Kohl."

"Thank you. Put him through."

The usual static and clicking, then a hesitant voice.

"Hello? Kriminalkommissar Neumann?"

"Yes, speaking."

"It's Joseph Kohl, sir. Unterwachtmeister Kohl. I'm a friend of Baby . . . of Kriminalassistant Schneider. We met when you and him were investigating the dead priest, the one at Saint

John the . . .”

“Yes, of course. I remember. How can I help you?”

“Well, sir, I might be able to help you. We’ve found a body. It’s like the priest at Saint John’s. His eyes are gone. I thought you and Baby Bear would be interested, seeing as how . . .”

Neumann’s upright in his chair, senses jangling. “We are. I am. Interested. Where is the body?”

“It’s probably in the morgue by now. I haven’t seen it myself, but one of the boys told me it was fished out of the Landwehr Canal, near the Bornholmer Strasse bridge. They called the Alex and a couple of Kripos came and had a look, then the morgue van took it away. From the sound of things, it’s like the priest – eyes gone, guts hanging out. I thought you would want to know, that’s all.”

“You were right to think so, Joseph. Thank you for being so thoughtful – you’ve done well. I hope I’m able to repay the favour one day. Don’t hesitate to call on me if you need anything. Thank you again.”

Neumann ends the call, stifles a groan as he leaps to his feet, presses his hands against his side and back until the pain subsides. Grabbing his hat and coat he hurries towards the stairs, heading for the basement. He emerges into the underground car park, starts towards the spot allocated to his and Schneider’s little Opel, but stops short as he sees only an empty space. He takes a few seconds to reconcile the facts that the car is gone and that Schneider is nowhere to be seen. He can’t readily come up with an explanation, shakes his head and turns around to look for the transport supervisor, Unterfeldwebel Erich Kroos.

The man is in his half-glassed cubicle near the elevator doors, the cubicle thick with smoke from the pipe permanently jammed between his teeth, jutting out beneath an unfashionably thick walrus moustache. The pipe is carved briar, a huge bowl in the shape of a snarling dog’s head – Neumann can’t decide whether it's sinister or just ridiculous. As he gets nearer he can see Kroos is hunched over a chart showing car and truck movements in and out, a red pencil in his left hand making marks on some of the ruled squares. Kroos looks up as Neumann opens the cubicle door. He doesn't speak, doesn't take the pipe out of his mouth.

"Erich." Neumann's greeting elicits a silent nod. "I'm looking for the Opel. Has Kurt taken it out?"

Kroos reaches forward, plucks a clipboard leaning against a WW1 mortar shell on the desk, consults it. He removes the pipe from between his teeth.

"Left here at twelve thirty seven." His speech is Low Saxon, German with an unsettling echo of English in its pronunciation. "Didn't say where he was going. Or when he'd be back." Speaking over, Kroos again clamps his teeth around the pipe.

"And you haven't seen him since?" Even as he says it, Neumann realises the inanity of his question. A shake of the head gives him an answer anyway. "Then I'll need another car. What's available?"

The Unterfeldwebel flips up the first two sheets of paper on the clipboard, studies the third one. Slowly, as though reluctant to part company with it, he takes his pipe out of his mouth again. "There's a BMW free for a few hours, a 303. It's old, runs a bit rough, but still serviceable."

"Right. Where is it?"

Kroos is smoking again. He lifts a key and ring from a board covered in numbered hooks hanging by his desk, passes it to Neumann and points with his other hand to a marked bay directly opposite his cubicle. Neumann immediately sees the old BMW, mutters his thanks as he takes the proffered key and heads towards the car.

40

The attendant Neumann encounters in the Charité reception area has not long left Professor Dürer, he says, opines the pathologist will probably still be finishing up an autopsy. He suggests Neumann uses the entrance near the storage room in case Dürer has already left the autopsy, in which case the professor will be in his office nearby. Neumann heads in the direction of the basement mortuary, his heels beating a tattoo on the tiled floor of the corridor. He reflects on the unintentional irony of the morgue's location in the basement of the Charité Hospital in Mitte. Above, the living, being cared for, cured, comparatively in heaven. Below, the souls of the damned in hell. I'm like Orpheus, he thinks, descending to the underworld – to retrieve not Eurydice but the story of a dead man, a journey driven not by love but by the obligation of duty.

He passes Professor Dürer's office in the corridor, the door shut and the light off, continues on to the end. A pair of solid brown doors guard the entrance to the autopsy room, each one with a glass porthole at eye level. Neumann stops, peers in. There's only one person in the room. One living person. The diminutive pathologist is washing his hands at one of the sinks on the long stainless steel benchtop adjoining a wall. Professor Dürer looks up as Neumann shoulders through the double doors, breaks into a smile as he recognises his visitor.

"Max! God's greeting to you." His smile quickly segues into concern as he speaks again. "How is your brother? Is his recovery proceeding well?"

"Thank you, Professor. He is well enough, I suppose. His wounds are healing." A moment's hesitation. "The injuries . . . I think he will take some time to return to normal. His mind, I mean. He harbours bitterness, anger. He seems . . . changed."

"It is to be expected, perhaps. He was literally within millimetres from death. Such things can change a man, can lead him to view the world differently." Dürer's face lightens slightly. "It is unlikely to be a long-lasting phenomenon, Max. I have seen other men in similar situations who recover both in mind and body without permanent impairment. Your brother needs to be patient. As indeed do you – these things must take their own time."

Neumann manages a wry smile. "Of course. It's just that it was so sudden. It's a cliché, I know, but one minute Walther was so young, full of life, full of promise, and now . . ." He lets the obvious implication make its own case as his voice trails off. A few seconds of silent understanding connects the two men before the pathologist breaks it.

"Now, you wish to see the man your Orpo colleagues found this morning, yes? One moment, please."

Dürer walks to a panel and grille set on the wall at the far end of the room, leans into it as he presses the black button beneath the grille. Neumann hears muted sounds coming from the grille before the professor says, 'Yes, please. I'll see him now,' and walks back to where Neumann is standing.

"Is there any identification?" asks Neumann.

"I understand not. Your colleagues searched his clothing, I am told, but there was nothing to be found. No wallet, no identification, no keys, nothing that we would expect to find if you or I were suddenly murdered." Dürer pauses for a moment as though contemplating the likelihood of such a thing. "I do not intend a full examination just yet. An external examination should be enough for your purposes, I think. I will be conducting the autopsy tomorrow. Something more helpful may emerge from that, although I think it unlikely. Ah, here is your man."

As Dürer speaks, Neumann hears the bump of a cadaver trolley against the portholed doors on the far side of the room, looks up. A grey-coated grey-haired attendant wheels the trolley up to the two men, locks its wheels in place and nods curtly before returning the way he came. The body on the trolley is covered by a patched khaki sheet showing dampness in a few places near the middle. Professor Dürer leans over the front of the cadaver trolley and grasps both corners of the sheet.

"I don't think we need to have him on a dissecting table just yet. We will be able to see what we need to."

Dürer peels the sheet back, all the way down to the dead man's feet. Despite knowing what he's about to see, despite having seen similar things in the last couple of months, Neumann can't stifle a wave of revulsion and nausea as he sees the blackened skin, the missing eyes, the slashed stomach with its glistening internals open to the world. He gasps involuntarily.

"As you see, Max, this is very much like the others. The damage to the eyes, as far as I can tell at the moment, is identical. The abdominal slash too." He waves a hand above the corpse. "Our people have temporarily replaced his viscera. For reasons of transport and storage, you understand. You may be interested to see, here, however." He points to the man's left hand. "The nails. Gone."

Neumann bends over to examine the hand. Only the

thumbnail is intact. The four fingers have each had their nails removed completely, leaving swollen red pulpy ends. Neumann bends further over, looks more closely, studies the apparently intact thumb.

"These marks, Professor." He points to a few small indented striations on either side of the first joint. The skin isn't broken, but reddened. Dürer bends forward, his head level with Neumann's, as they examine the marks. The professor moves his head back and forth, seeking a better view.

"Yes, it seems someone has . . . It would appear pressure has been applied to the interphalangeal joint. From both sides, probably simultaneously. I expect the joint is damaged, but I will need to open him up to be certain." He straightens up and breathes deeply. "I would venture someone has applied pincers or pliers to this man's thumb. Such a thing would cause great pain. I expect . . . Max! What is it?"

Neumann, rising from his examination of the corpse's thumb, gasps at the searing brief jolt in his side and back, whips his right hand around to press on the spot. He stands erect, gets his breathing back under control.

"It's nothing. Just a bit of back pain I get sometimes. I must have strained it somehow. It isn't usually a problem."

Neumann's dismissive words don't convince Dürer.

"It seems somewhat more than the 'nothing' you describe, judging by your expression when it occurred." He bends forward and replaces the sheet on the body before turning back to Neumann. "Come with me, please, Max. To my office. Come." He starts walking towards the double doors. Not certain what's happening, Neumann follows in his wake.

Professor Dürer's office is, as always, impeccably tidy, orderly, spotless. Neumann briefly ponders whether its occupant does all the cleaning and tidying himself. Dürer closes the door behind them, directs Max to sit on one of the unpadded wooden chairs before he seats himself behind his leather-topped desk.

A change appears to come over him, affability exchanged for authority, friendship for professionalism.

"Now, Kriminalkommissar, I am going to examine you."

Neumann shifts uneasily in his chair, starts to rise before an extended hand from the other man directs him back down again.

"What is it? You think that a pathologist is not the man to conduct an examination of someone who is still alive?" Neumann opens his mouth to speak, but Dürer doesn't pause. "I may cut bodies up every day, but I am still a doctor. Accordingly, I am qualified to examine patients. Now, enough. Tell me the nature of your pain, please."

Neumann realises only rude and unfriendly action on his part, action he's not prepared to take, will avoid what's coming. A small sigh of acceptance escapes him.

"As I said, it's nothing. I get a jab of pain from time to time. I'm sure I've pulled a muscle doing something or other."

"You say 'from time to time'. Daily?"

"No, no, only . . ." Even as Neumann starts to speak he realises that, yes, it does happen every day. "Well, probably every day. I don't keep a tally."

"Always in the same place?"

"Always. Here, and here." He points to his side, his lower back. It's over in a second, just a stab, then it's gone."

"And your health generally. It is good? No other aches, nothing else to cause you concern? Or Irmgard."

"Not really. Everything else is fine. I get a bit tired sometimes, but that's just age creeping up on me."

Dürer looks sceptical, this coming from a man yet to reach forty, but he lets it pass. "I see. Very well. Stand up, please. I will do a little prodding and listening." As he speaks, the professor reaches into one of the desk drawers, lifts out a stethoscope, stands, then moves around the desk.

For the next five minutes Neumann bends and twists and positions himself as directed by Dürer, who repeatedly asks variations of 'Does this hurt?' as he places his hands on various bodily locations. The pathologist listens to his patient's heart and lungs, looks in his mouth and ears, then peers into his eyes with a small but powerful light. He takes Neumann's blood pressure and temperature before sitting down and writing on a slip of paper, speaking as he does.

"It may be a muscle strain, as you say, but it's best we exclude other causes. I'm going to give you a note to see Doctor Telemann. He's a good man, very experienced. Fortunately, you won't have to go very far – he's upstairs. He'll have a closer look at you than I can, and probably arrange an x-ray. Perhaps some other tests, too."

Neumann is taken aback, frowns. "What, now? You want me to go now? Why the urgency?"

"If you can go now, it would seem to be convenient. After all, it will save you an additional trip. Of course, if Doctor Telemann is not available, then you will have to make that trip at some later point. Best not delay too long, however. These things are best treated early. I will telephone his secretary when you leave – if he is here, he may be able to see you now." Dürer passes the note to Neumann. Then, with a smile and a shooing motion, "Now, be off with you, Max. Go, get yourself better."

Professor Dürer watches Neumann open the office door and disappear through it. His smile fades in tandem with his visitor's fading footsteps in the corridor. With an abrupt intake of breath, he reaches for the telephone on his desk, dials a number.

"Ah, Monique. It's Otto Dürer. How are you, my dear? That is excellent. Is Johann available, perhaps? Ah, I see. Well, when he has finished, could you please ask him to call me. It's rather urgent. I wish to speak with him before he sees a Herr Neumann, whom I have just directed to his office. Yes, yes. Thank you, my dear. Goodbye."

✠

Kriminalrat Franz Böhm hears the rapid knocks, looks up from his desk, sees Neumann standing in the open doorway barely restraining himself from bursting in.

"Max. What is it?"

Neumann pulls out a chair on the visitor's side of the desk, sits without invitation.

"There's been a development with the dead priests. Another death. Another murder."

"What? A fourth priest?" Despite himself, Böhm is startled by the news. He doesn't have to feign genuine interest.

"No, no. At least there's no indication it's a priest. There's another body. It was pulled out of the Landwehr Canal earlier today. It's like two of the other ones, the priests. Eyes gone. It has to be connected. Dürer says the eyes are the same, the belly slash too. Apparently he had no ID on him. Could be anybody."

As Neumann speaks, Böhm's mind races ahead to assess what all this means. He realises that it's almost certainly Standartenführer Schmidt's work again, wonders whether Reichsmarschall Göring knows about it. And he worries about how he, Böhm, should handle it. He thinks on the problem for several seconds after Neumann finishes, expressionless. Then he shakes his head, lifts his hands.

"Jesus. What the hell is going on?"

"That's what we're trying to find out, boss. We need to handle this one too. If we . . ."

The words trigger something in Böhm's mind, make him interrupt Neumann.

"Where is he? Schneider, I mean. Is he still working on the original murders?

"I don't know. He's out somewhere. I'll chase him up. The reason I'm here is to ask if we can have this new one. It makes sense for us to be across all four deaths."

"Yes, yes, agreed," says Böhm distractedly. His mind is running ahead of events again, Göring's views uppermost in his thoughts. "I've got no problem with that. Who's handling the thing now?"

"Two of Schaeffler's boys are on it. They went to the canal after the body was found. I don't know what they've done about it since then."

"Alright, it's yours. I'll call Schaeffler and smooth it over. It shouldn't be a problem – his team's got a big caseload already. Anyway, he owes me more than one favour. Acceptable?"

"Yes, boss. Thanks." He gets to his feet. "I'll get moving."

Neumann is nearly through the door when he hears Böhm's parting words.

"Keep me informed!"

41

Finally, mercifully, the jolting and noise comes to a stop. Schneider's legs and shoulders are on fire. His foetal position in the trunk of the Opel is now as much from pain as it is from necessity. He's aware he's been badly affected by the exhaust fumes – there must be a hole somewhere, letting in more carbon monoxide than it should. His head pounds, he can't think straight, and his stomach feels like it's about to discharge his lunch. He tries, with little success, to focus, to be ready for whatever opportunity might come his way. Even as he tries, his mind drifts away, muddied by pain and nausea. He feels the car lurch as someone gets out and shuts a door. Seconds later, his senses are dragged back into focus by a loud thump on the bodywork above him.

"Listen to me, please. I will unlock the trunk and open it. You will not move until I tell you. Not a single movement. If you so much as lift a hand I will shoot you. Do you understand?"

Schmidt's voice is muffled, as though coming from a great distance. Schneider almost laughs at the idea of him making a sudden movement, chokes down the lurch in his stomach as he does. Then the voice again.

"Do you understand? Answer."

Schneider concentrates, steels himself.

"Yes," he rasps. It's all he can manage, but it's enough. After a few seconds he hears the lock being turned, then the lid of the trunk flies up as Schmidt takes two rapid steps backward, his pistol trained on the opening. A rush of cool, clean air into Schneider's face makes him close his eyes in gratitude as he breathes it in. For several seconds there is blissful silence.

"Get out. Slowly."

Schneider is powerless to move in any other way. He painfully slides his legs over the lip of the trunk, gritting his teeth against the burning sensation as blood starts to flow freely again. Legs now extended, he half-falls out of the car, landing on his hands and knees, whimpering with pain like a wounded animal. He grabs the bodywork, tries to haul himself upright. He's almost there when another wave of pain strikes him, and he slumps against the car. His chest heaves with effort. Sweat pours out of him. The exhaust fumes have played havoc with his thinking, his movements. Dimly, he realizes the car has stopped in a huge covered space, a dark and derelict building of some kind, perhaps formerly a factory or warehouse. The Opel is inside, near one of the supporting steel pillars. Schneider looks up as Schmidt speaks.

"Walk to the chair."

His eyes follow Schmidt's pointing arm, see about five metres away a wooden straight-back chair against a pillar, tied to it with rope. He stares, struggles to think clearly what is required of him.

"Walk now. If you do not move I will shoot your kneecaps."

He levers himself away from the car, staggers as his legs take full weight, manages to balance himself. Each step is agony. He stumbles and staggers forward like a crippled, sick old man, then half-falls onto the chair.

Keeping his pistol unwaveringly aimed at Schneider, his captor reaches inside the Opel's open window and lifts out a small case. He puts it on the roof of the car, opens it with one hand and lifts the lid. With the same hand he pulls out three pairs of handcuffs and moves to within a couple of metres of where Schneider is slumped on the chair.

"Look at me!" The sharp command forces Schneider to focus, and he lifts his head, meets Schmidt's pale grey eyes.

"I will throw a set of these at your feet. Put one end around your ankle, the other around a leg of the chair." Then, it's as though he's read Schneider's mind. "Do not contemplate throwing them at me. You will achieve nothing except a bullet in your stomach. Do you understand?"

Schneider understands, and the understanding suddenly makes him feel very tired, as though he's come to the end of a long and exhausting day. Even his pain seems to recede, replaced by a combination of futility and resignation, an acceptance that the world he knew has been transformed, upended, reshaped. It feels like he's an onlooker, someone watching another's life being obliterated. He says, "Yes". It's little more than a drained sigh. Schmidt throws the first set of handcuffs at his feet.

With laborious slow movements, Schneider gets the handcuffs onto the chair leg and then around one ankle. The circle of steel is barely big enough to fit his leg. He's only just clicked the ratchet into place when a second pair of handcuffs lands on the floor next to his feet.

"Now the other leg, please."

He repeats the process as he pants and sweats with the effort, the concentration, the pain. Then he slowly levers himself upright to find Schmidt has moved closer. A third pair of handcuffs lands heavily in his lap.

“You will put them on one wrist, please, then put both hands behind you. Keep your head facing forward. If you attempt to turn around you will be shot.”

Schneider complies, and Schmidt moves warily around behind him, out of sight. Schneider feels his cuffed wrist take the strain of movement as the handcuffs are grasped, feels a hand on his other wrist. Then, in an instant of astonishing pain his arms are wrenched together and his free wrist is locked into a steel circle. He roars with pain, with frustration, with anger. Momentarily, the agony clamps his eyes shut, contorts his face. By the time he opens his eyes again his tormentor is standing in front of the chair, impassive, surveying his handiwork.

“Good. Now we may begin. I am Standartenführer Schmidt. I report to Reichsführer Himmler. He seeks a document which was in the possession of the priest, Rochlitz. It is a document which, if it were made known in certain circles, would mean the certain downfall of the Reichsführer. Perhaps even his death. As you will understand, he is anxious to obtain it. I have been directed to achieve that end. Until only a few hours ago, I believed you and your Kripo colleague might have led me to it. But now, thanks to that old woman and her useless son, I no longer need whatever knowledge you possess. Instead, after we have conducted our business here, I will proceed to where the document is currently located and remove it.”

Schmidt pauses, peers intently at Schneider, who has painfully lifted his face.

“It may be that you are asking yourself why you are here if you have nothing I require.” A tight, mirthless smile. “Partly, it is because otherwise you might have thwarted my endeavours. Primarily, however, it is because I intend to torture you.”

The lethargy and exhaustion smothering Schneider’s mind is momentarily thrust aside. His eyes widen, focus, his mouth involuntarily starts to open.

"Ah, yes, that shocks you. It always does. Civilised people, officers, men of honour – they do not speak of such things. And yet, and yet . . . Well, as you see, they do. Please be aware, you will die in this godforsaken place." He sweeps his eyes and arm around as he speaks. "Were it not to be so, I would of course not have divulged who I am and what I am doing. However, for better or worse, I have, and you can not continue to live with that knowledge. I'm sure you understand."

Schmidt continues to study his captive as he slips his pistol inside his jacket, into its holster. He takes out a pack of cigarettes, lights one, and stands smoking silently for a short time. Schneider's head has drooped, his eyes on the ground. His laboured breathing is punctuated by moans of pain sparked by his wrenched and pinioned arms. Schmidt slowly walks up to him, hears the low indistinct sounds of speech. He half bends, brings his head closer to Schneider's.

"Is there something you wish to say to me?"

Schneider's reply is slow in coming, the words forced out between erratic breaths.

"Eat . . . my . . . shit."

Schmidt's expression gives no indication he's heard the words, much less been affected by them. He straightens up and moves to Schneider's left side.

"Very well. We will begin."

He draws long and deeply on his cigarette.

42

Untersturmführer Walther Neumann strides purposefully along Nollendorfstrasse, turns right when he reaches the high steps of the Herbstkrankenhaus and pushes through the double glass doors. The uniformed guard inside rises from his desk, snaps to attention and raises his right arm.

"Heil Hitler!"

Walther returns the salute as he passes. He is in uniform, and an SS uniform of any kind, regardless of the rank it proclaims, triggers instant attention. Fear lies behind it, of course, and Walther knows that. Knows it, welcomes it, and now uses it as a shield, something to thrust his ruined face into the background, to set aside the mutilation visited on him because he did his duty. He tells himself he is deserving of respect, of gratitude, of fear. He holds his head high, defies pity or shame, takes the stairs at speed.

On the third floor landing the administration desk is occupied by two uniformed attendants. One is a pale thin woman younger than him. He hasn't seen her before. The other is an older, senior attendant, flecks of grey in her dark hair. She knows him from other visits. The rapid clack of approaching boots on the floor makes them both look up simultaneously. Only the younger of the two women momentarily displays shock or revulsion. It's the other one who speaks, her face professional, neutrally welcoming.

"Good day, Untersturmführer Neumann. You wish to visit your father?"

"Is he in a fit state?"

She affects not to notice Walther's brusque rudeness.

"I believe so. Would you like me to accompany you?"

Walther snaps a "No" over his shoulder as he marches towards his father's room.

Alois Neumann is lying on the bed in his pyjamas, staring at a length of wool yarn held between his hands. He alternately tugs at it and then releases the tension so that it sags. Over and over he says a single word, 'Penguin'. His pyjama pants are damp at the crotch, the padded underwear he now wears apparently overwhelmed by his wayward bladder. Walther's appearance in the room goes unnoticed by the old man, who continues fiddling with the yarn, continues mumbling 'Penguin'. Walther walks to the bedside, stands over his father, watches, says nothing. Still the old man fiddles, mutters, seems oblivious to his son's presence.

His face wrinkled with distaste, Walther reaches over, roughly shakes his father by the shoulder.

"Father. It's me. Walther."

Alois Neumann slowly lowers his hands to the bedside and turns his head towards the noise. He stares blankly at Walther for several seconds, running his eyes up and down. It's as though he's searching the heavens without intent or result. Then abruptly, he hawks something into his throat and spits hard. A clump of phlegm and saliva lands on the thigh of Walther's trousers, hangs there momentarily before it slowly drips and runs downwards. Expressionless, Alois turns his head away, lifts his arms again, and continues to mumble 'Penguin' as he fingers the length of yarn.

As his lips curl in disgust, Walther reaches down, lifts a corner of the bedsheet and uses it to wipe off the globule of muck on his trouser leg. Setting his jaw against the impulse to remonstrate, he looks around, picks up a chair by the adjacent wall and sits down at the bedside, his head now nearly level with his father's. If the old man hasn't seen his son clearly before, he will now.

"Father." There's no response. "Father, look at me." Walther's voice is louder now, imperative. Something gels in Alois Neumann's addled brain, and he slowly swivels his face towards his visitor. For long seconds he seems to study what he sees, then turns his head back, his expression unchanged. Dropping the yarn, he lets his hands fall to the bed before lifting his right one and sliding it under his pyjama cord, down to his genitals, where it starts to rub back and forth. In a grotesque parody of singing he tunelessly mumbles a song from somewhere his past.

"*Lovely maiden . . . mmmm . . . pure and sweet and kind,*
Let me lift your skirt . . . mmmm . . . see . . . we can find.
Your . . . fuck . . . a . . . little maiden . . . fuck . . . mmm."

The words fall away into unstructured muttering and dribbling throaty sounds. The old man's eyes are closed, his hand continues to rub away at his genitals. The incoherent mumbling drones on.

Walther's eyes never leave his father's face. His own is suffused with revulsion, anger, indecision. The wreckage on the bed in front of him was barely a father from the outset, more concerned with chasing skirt and boozing with his mates than acknowledging his youngest son, a remote cold figure whose role centred on routine and discipline. Walther remembers the 'mother's boy' taunts, the slaps, the almost total lack of interest. And now, now that the boy is a boy no longer, now that he is a man in Schutzstaffel uniform, a man disfigured in the defence of his country – what? What has changed? No slaps now, just spit. That's as far as the old man's interest goes, just enough to register his disgust, his continued rejection of his youngest son. Max wouldn't have to put up with this. Not Max, the first-born son, the son to make any man proud, the son who can do no wrong . . . Christ! What have you done, you old bastard? What have *you* done for your country? Fuck all, that's what. Nothing. Nothing compared to what I've done, and will do again. Nothing compared to what I've suffered. Worse, not only have you contributed nothing, you suck the life out of everything and everybody around you, drain the time and money and energy of everyone who keeps you above ground. You don't deserve what you've got, what we're paying for. Don't deserve a damn thing. Scum. Parasite.

Walther's face is a mask, but his mind whirls and races. Maelstrom thoughts churn as he revisits the past, assesses the present, piles recrimination upon recrimination, weighs the suffering and the neglect all the way back to his childhood. His missing eye hurts. Bolts of pain pulse in the empty socket. His brain feels like it's being squeezed in a vice. Then, in an instant, everything stops. All around is silence, clarity, as though a great light has been shone into the darkness. Walther feels calm enveloping him like a fresh bathrobe. It soothes, warms, lets him think clearly, absorbs his pain, his doubts, gives him strength.

He gets out of his chair and walks to the door. It's slightly ajar. Carefully, quietly, he closes it before returning to his father's bedside. Alois continues to rub his crotch, both eyes closed, makes small grunting noises. Spit bubbles in one corner of his mouth. Outside, a siren sounds briefly as an ambulance speeds by. Walther picks up the chair he sat in and places it back where it came from before returning to the bedside. He picks up a spare pillow sitting at the head of the bed and firmly grips a short edge in each hand. For a moment he stands motionless, looks down at his father, observes, thinks. Then, in a fluid single movement he leaps astride the recumbent old man and jams the pillow across his face, thrusting the edges down as hard as he can. For a second there's no reaction at all. Then a faint screaming from under the pillow as the frail and ancient body arches and convulses. Alois Neumann tries to free his hands, to claw at the thing killing him, but the right one is trapped still in his pyjama pants, held hard beneath Walther's buttocks, and Walther's thigh presses tightly against the other one.

The old man's life-or-death struggle doesn't last long. After less than a minute he stops moving. Walther maintains pressure on the pillow. Another minute. Then another.

It's over. Walther eases himself from the bed, smooths the pillow he's used and replaces it on the bed, makes sure the side wet with saliva and snot is underneath. He repositions his father's arms, places them by his side, smooths the bed coverings and his father's rumpled pyjamas. Stepping back two paces, he runs his eye over the room, makes sure everything is as it should be. Then he rearranges his clothes, tightens his tie and passes a smoothing hand over his hair. He stands on the spot for a few more minutes, gets his breathing under full control. Then he walks to the door and opens it before stepping into the corridor. His face is blank.

"Help! Nurse, nurse! Help!"

43

Once more, Kriminalrat Franz Böhm is on the top floor of the Reichsluftahrtministerium, sitting in one of the Reichsmarschall's armchairs. He hopes for the usual coffee and cake, perhaps another Cuban cigar, but the small table between the two men is bare, and Göring is in no mood for pleasantries. It's a rare thing, to see the big man subdued, even worried, less than his normal voluble self. He's ushered Böhm in, shaken his hand and asked him to sit, but it's the bare minimum of welcoming politeness. Böhm decides to wait out the mood, not break the long silence after they're both seated. He sits with his hands in his lap, hat on the arm of his chair. He waits. Göring seems preoccupied, mind only half on his visitor. The Reichsmarschall absentmindedly fingers the material on his suitcoat, unnecessarily adjusts the way the lapel lies. Then he raises his eyes.

"Yes, Franz. There is something you wish to ask me?"

"Er, no, Herr Reichsmarschall, not really. I wanted to let you know of a development in the matter of the priests. The actions of Standartenführer Schmidt." Göring sits up, lifts his eyebrows. Böhm mistakes the action for surprised annoyance, hurriedly adds, "I know you said we should not pursue the investigation, but . . ."

"What is it, Franz? What has happened?" Göring comes alive, leans forward in his chair, eyes alight. Böhm is taken aback. He wasn't expecting this.

"Another body, sir. Like the priests. The man's eyes were gone, burned away, and his stomach . . ."

"Who is it? Do you have his name?" Göring fires the words at his visitor, impatient, peremptory.

"We . . . there is no name, sir. We can't identify him. He had nothing on him to . . ."

Göring won't wait, wants his answer now, interrupts again.

"What does he look like? A description, Franz, give me a description."

Böhm is mystified by the Reichsmarschall's agitation. He expected interest in what he revealed, yes, but not this thrusting interrogation, this headlong burst of tense impatience.

"He . . . the body is in the morgue, sir. I have not seen it, but my men say the man is small, in his mid-forties, blonde hair going bald. Fairly nondescript, apparently. His clothes were cheap, a little shabby. I don't know . . ."

Böhm breaks off, unsure of what's happening as Göring sinks back in his armchair, eyes closed, hand over a face turned pale. The big man sits motionless, slumped, for several seconds. He takes his hand away from his face, now a tightly-drawn mask. His breathing is rapid, shallow. His next words are forced out, suffused with dread.

"Does he have a tattoo?"

For a few seconds Böhm is unable to reply as he digs around in his memory of what Neumann told him, tries to recall the description he was given.

"A tattoo? Ah . . . I think yes. My investigator says there

was one on his upper arm, an imperial eagle."

Göring brings both hands up to his head, drags it down as he lets out something between a groan and a wail. He rocks slowly back and forth on the seat of his armchair, makes small whimpering noises. When he finally stops, lowers his hands and looks again at Böhm, his eyes are full of tears. He fumbles in his trouser pocket, drags out a white handkerchief and clumsily wipes his eyes as he tries to compose himself. His breathing is ragged, wet. Böhm says nothing, stunned into uncomprehending silence by the Reichsmarschall's reaction.

"Forgive me, Franz . . . A shock. The man, this man, I know him. He is . . ." A pause, as Göring's emotions again threaten to engulf him. He coughs wetly. "He is a friend."

Göring can't say any more. Böhm watches as the big man's throat tightens and he shakes his head back and forth, raising a hand that says 'Wait. I can't go on.' Böhm waits. It takes a couple of minutes before Göring settles, gets his anguish under control. He stands, walks to his desk, takes a flat oblong tin from one of the drawers, opens it and puts two brown pills in his mouth. After swallowing them with a glass of water from the carafe on his desk, Göring returns to his chair.

"This is a shock, Franz. A shock. The dead man is someone I knew quite well. For a long time. That animal Schmidt is responsible, of course. Bastard!"

Göring slams his fist down hard on the arm of his chair. There is fire in his eyes. He leans forward, closer to Böhm.

"Set your men on him. On Schmidt. I want him dead. Not arrested, Franz – dead!"

Böhm's mind reels, chases a situation that outstrips his ability to keep pace. When he walked into Göring's office it was with the understanding that the Kripo would abandon the investigation into Schmidt's killings. Now, the investigation is to be resurrected. And resurrected with the aim of killing

Standartenführer Schmidt. Böhm can hardly believe what he is hearing, has a multitude of objections clamouring at his brain. He wants to tell the Reichsmarschall that Kripo officers aren't assassins, aren't a tool to be used to murder people. He wants to point out that if Himmler learns the Kripo have killed his pet rottweiler, heads will roll. Literally. Böhm does not want his to be among them. A lesser, but still important, consideration is the possibility that any Kripo officer who goes after Schmidt will be the one who ends up dead. But even as these thoughts chase themselves around in his head, he knows he can't refuse the Reichsmarschall's request. If Göring wants it to be this way, it will be this way. All Böhm wants now is to survive the conflagration which is coming.

"Understood, sir. I will . . . it will be difficult, of course. The Standartenführer is a dangerous man. And he has the total backing of Reichsführer Himm . . ."

"I'll take care of Himmler if need be," snaps Göring. "If we play our cards right, the little shit will never know who's responsible. Your men need to be careful, that's all. If Himmler looks like causing trouble, I'll make sure it doesn't happen."

There's hard determination in Göring's words. Böhm hasn't seen the big man this angry, this resolute. He takes a few grains of comfort from it. Already, his mind is turning to the question of how he can motivate Neumann and Schneider to do what's necessary.

✠

The desk telephone rings, an unwelcome insistent intrusion into Neumann's contemplation of a kaleidoscopic mix of knowns, unknowns and possibilities. Part of him ponders the mystery man hauled out of the Landwehr Canal, the man with no eyes. He knows there has to be a connection between this most recent victim and at least two of the murdered priests, but he's damned if he can see any logical way to construct one.

Another part of him mulls over Kurt Schneider's absence. Not a word since before lunchtime yesterday. It's unlike Kurt to disappear without explanation. Neumann glances at the clock. Not even ten yet. Still time for Kurt to show up today, wherever he's been for nearly the last twenty-four hours.

Yet another part of him broods over his visit to Professor Dürer's colleague, Dr Johann Telemann. The specialist doctor was almost everything the little professor was not – overweight, dishevelled, uncommunicative and barely articulate. Only his thoroughness matched the professor's. Neumann spent well over half an hour in Telemann's office being quizzed about his diet, weight stability, bowel habits, about his health in general. Miniature dirty snowstorms of falling ash accompanied the shambling Telemann as he chain-smoked his way through the physical examination, prodding here, pressing there, making his patient adopt various positions sitting and lying. Neumann could get little from him beyond noncommittal grunts and, at the end, a vague assurance that the x-rays he'd ordered 'will tell us something. Or not. Wait. That's what we do now.' With that, Neumann was despatched to the Radiology Department on the floor below armed with an illegible note from Telemann.

The three streams of thought, about the dead man in the Landwehr Canal, about Kurt's disappearance, and about the implications of Dr Telemann's actions, criss-cross within Neumann's consciousness, merge and diverge as each one struggles for precedence. They push away the everyday world, fill up the space it leaves behind, until Neumann becomes so disconnected with his surroundings that the ringing telephone on his desk makes him start visibly. He gathers his senses, concentrates, picks up the earpiece and leans forward.

"Kriminalkommissar Neumann".

“A call for you, Kriminalkommissar.” It’s the young blonde switchboard operator again. Neumann’s earlier thoughts step briefly aside to allow in a fleeting one about the girl. “He says he’s the manager of the Herbstkrankenhaus, a Herr Sauckel.”

“Put him through, please.”

Even as he speaks, Neumann’s brow furrows. The only times he has spoken to Alfred Sauckel previously has been when financial matters needed to be addressed. Surely that’s not the case now, given the accounts have all been paid on time, so if it’s not that, then . . . it can only be something’s wrong.

“Herr Neumann?”

“Yes, speaking. Good day, Herr Sauckel.”

There’s a pause. Neumann can hear the man breathing.

“I am afraid I have some unpleasant news for you,” says Sauckel without preamble. “It is with sorrow I must inform you that your father has gone to God. I am most sorry. We did everything we could, but to no avail. If you wish . . .”

Neumann barely registers the prepared recitation as it drones on. He has known without articulating it that death stalked ever closer to his father these last years. And now it’s happened. Inevitable, of course, but still there is surprise mixed in with the grief. And, truth be told, there’s relief. From worry, from financial burden, from . . . Hard to say. Perhaps from the frustration and pointlessness of one-sided ‘conversations’ that went nowhere and meant nothing to an old man who didn’t even know who he was, let alone know who was speaking to him. Gone to God? Perhaps, but unlikely, unless God has now decided to admit . . .

Neumann is jolted out of his speculations and back to reality by something Sauckel has said.

“ . . . very suddenly. Your brother was with him, and called for assistance immediately, but by the time the . . .”

“My brother was with him? When he died?”

Sauckel is speechless for a moment. People do not usually interrupt when he is offering his condolences. He attributes it to grief, makes allowances.

"Yes, that is correct. The Untersturmführer was at his bedside when it happened. A sudden event. Your father's heart, you understand, he was old, it was not strong."

Neumann can't explain the feeling, why it has arrived, or even what it is, but he feels unease, discomfort. The director's words don't sit well, the situation he is explaining seems only part of the story, as though he's intentionally left something out, or doesn't know something crucial. Abruptly, Neumann intrudes once again.

"I will come immediately."

"There is no need, Herr Neumann. We will make the necessary arrangements. You may rest assured that . . ."

"I will come now, Herr Sauckel."

Neumann ends the call before the manager can respond.

44

Neumann's slow progress up the steep steps of the Herbstkrankenhaus and through its glass doors is born not of weariness, but preoccupation. His mind is elsewhere, wading through a swamp of emotions and doubts. He can't cast aside the feeling that something unwholesome is dogging his steps, that some foetid abomination is closing on him with evil intent. He gives a distracted nod to the uniformed guard as he passes, disregards the man's Hitler salute, heads for the stairs.

The door to his father's room is open. As he reaches it, Neumann sees his brother Walther slumped in a low chair in the far corner of the room, his gaze fixed on the ceiling. Two white-coated attendants are fussing around some kind of wheeled trolley positioned next to his father's bed. Alois Neumann's body is still in the bed, covered by a faded sheet. A nurse in a dark green Herbstkrankenhaus uniform is standing to one side, her back to the door, apparently supervising. Neumann's seen her before. Schellenberg, he thinks, Frau Schellenberg. She senses his appearance in the doorway and quickly turns, recognises him, steps forward. She locks onto his eyes before she speaks.

"I am most sorry, Herr Neumann. This is . . . this was not to be expected. Your father showed no sign of . . ."

"Thank you." Neumann nods, starts to move forward, to go to Walther, who has so far not acknowledged his brother's arrival, but Frau Schellenberg won't release her hold on his eyes. There's an intensity there he can't place.

"Do you wish to see your father before . . ?" She waves a hand towards the two white-coated attendants. Her gaze hasn't shifted from his face.

This isn't what Max had in mind. He's never been one of those who want 'one last look', who think a lifetime of looking and touching and talking isn't enough, that just one more time is needed to fulfil some kind of moral obligation or social imperative. Dead is dead. Gone. The life is what matters. But this is different. The woman is almost willing him to look.

"Yes, please."

Frau Schellenberg turns away, motions to the two attendants who are adjusting the height of the wheeled trolley. They step back, stand with hands clasped in front of them, eyes lowered, like professional mourners at a funeral. Neumann moves up to the bedside. Frau Schellenberg picks up the top edge of the covering sheet and slowly peels it downward, exposing Alois Neumann's head and shoulders.

Neumann gasps involuntarily. He was expecting to see his father lying dead, but he wasn't expecting the old man's eyes to be open. They stare, unseeing and lifeless, at a point unknown. Neumann absorbs the image, consciously fixes it in his mind, takes out a small insurance policy against the inevitable decline of memory. He feels Frau Schellenberg's continued scrutiny and turns his head to again meet her eyes. She flicks a glance towards the silent form of Walther before returning her gaze to him. It isn't wavering. Neumann is uncomfortable, attributes the feeling to embarrassment, turns back to his father, scans the old man's stubbled grey face again. He tries to avoid the eyes. There's something unsettling about returning the gaze of a corpse.

Then he sees something that shouldn't be there. His body goes rigid. For long seconds he stares fixedly at his father, his jaw clenched tight. He closes his eyes for a moment, takes a sharp breath, then opens them and leans forward at the waist, brings his face to within half a metre of his father's. As he peers intently downwards his breathing becomes deeper, more rapid, and his hands gradually clench into white-knuckle balls. Abruptly, with a small grunt of pain, he stands erect. Frau Schellenberg is still focused on him, stands silently as he meets her look. She realises he's seen the same thing she has. He knows. She drops her gaze and slowly steps back a few paces.

Neumann's been around enough dead bodies to know petechiae when he sees them – small dark spots on the whites of the eyes of those who've been strangled or suffocated. He sees them now. In the unmoving open eyes of his dead father. He knows it's not proof absolute, knows that petechiae can appear for a host of other reasons. But he knows too that Walther was with their father when he died. The same Walther who is now slumped mute and motionless in a chair in the corner of the room. And he knows that the nurse, Frau Schellenberg, thinks something is wrong.

His head feels like it's being slowly crushed by huge invisible hands, the heaving emotions within being compressed into an ever-tighter ball of rage, grief, doubt, frustration. He knows he's teetering on the cusp of exploding, erupting into verbal or physical violence, but there's nothing he can do, nothing is within his control any more. Four rapid strides put Max directly in front of Walther, glaring down at him, breathing heavily, unable to speak.

Walther register's his brother's appearance, shifts his gaze from the ceiling to meet Max's eyes. Something passes between them. An infinitesimally brief moment of understanding, of mutual knowledge. Walther raises a languid hand as though to brush something aside. His voice is flat.

"It happened suddenly. He was gone in an instant."

The words light a fuse. Max jerks further upright, blood rushes to his face, and he lifts his right hand, contorted into a clenched fist, takes a half-step towards the seated Walther. Unchained rage gurgles in his throat. Not words, but a shapeless groan or bellow. Frau Schellenberg starts moving towards the two men.

Then it's over. Max lets out an incoherent roar of fury, turns on his heel and barges out of the room and into the corridor. The angry thud of his boots on the floor quickly recedes, fades to nothing as a door slams somewhere. Both attendants stand motionless near the bed, ashen-faced, apprehensive. Walther turns his head towards the nurse, aware she's staring at him. It's impossible to mistake the depth of contempt he sees. He returns his gaze to the ceiling.

✠

Neumann feels as though the world has flipped over, upended his stability, introduced new and bizarre parameters into his life. In any normal circumstance, an eldest son whose father had just died would be attending to the funeral arrangements, not sitting at his office desk. He would be at home offering comfort to those who needed it, a stable and strong focus at a time of family grief and uncertainty. Neumann knows what is expected, knows what he should do, but he can't bring himself to go through the motions. The Herbstkrankenhaus staff have been left to take care of the funeral arrangements – they know what they're doing. He's not needed. And he's not needed to comfort his only other family. Walther's behaviour has thrust him outside the orbit of Max's concerns. At this moment, Neumann never wants to speak to his brother again. Walther is lost to him, a stranger. If he died this instant, Max would shed no tears.

Half an hour at home with Irmgard was enough. Her defence of Walther, her preparedness to disbelieve what Max was telling her, drove him out of the apartment. He knew that if he stayed with her there would be words he didn't mean, angry, bitter words, ones that could never be unspoken. So he's back in his office. The office has become sanctuary, a place where he can avoid confronting what would otherwise be the inevitable and irretrievable.

Despite the crippling uncertainty and anger pulsing in his head, Neumann is still capable of worry about Kurt Schneider. There continues to be no sign of him. The Opel is still missing, and nobody has heard from Kurt for well over a day now. Nobody Neumann's talked to since yesterday has seen him or knows where he might be. First thing this morning Neumann checked with the transport supervisor in the basement, Unterfeldwebel Erich Kroos, but came away with nothing – neither the Opel nor Schneider has been sighted. Now, Neumann debates with himself whether to go to Schneider's apartment on Schwarzer Weg, see if he's sick in bed, injured, anything. The thoughts crowd in upon themselves, blocking out anything else, so Neumann doesn't realise there's someone standing in his office doorway until two soft raps on the open door make his head jerk up.

His surprise is immediately elevated to something resembling astonishment when he sees it's The Little Accountant. In any normal course of events, Kriminaldirektor Karl Becker wouldn't cross the room to speak to Neumann. If Becker wanted his subordinate for any reason, he would have him summoned upstairs. Neumann is caught open-mouthed. Before he can recover his wits he gets another surprise.

"May I come in, Max?"

The Little Accountant never asks to come in. And he never calls Neumann anything but Kriminalkommissar. Something must be wrong. Becker's countenance confirms the suspicion. His face is set, held fast in a neutral expression, not a hint of the usual disapproving look. Neumann manages to resurrect his faculties as he half-stands in deference.

"Of course, sir."

Becker slowly closes the door before pulling up one of the hard chairs and sitting across the desk from an increasingly concerned Neumann. He looks down at his knees for a few seconds as though what he wants to say is written there. Neumann is tempted to break the silence, but something tells him to hold back, wait and see what this is about. Becker lifts his face, locks eyes with his subordinate. There's a look there that Neumann's never seen there before.

"It's about Kriminalassistant Schneider."

For a fleeting instant Neumann's spirits leap, but Becker's tone and his rigid expression crush the moment. He steels himself against whatever's coming next from the Kriminaldirektor.

"I am most sorry, Max. It is bad news." Becker takes a deep breath as though to fortify himself. "I regret to say that our colleague has been killed."

Neumann's world freezes in a heartbeat. Time ceases to exist. He sees no movement, hears no sound. The world has collapsed around him, shrunk, solidified, concentrated in its entirety on his small office. For long, long seconds he stares unseeing at Becker. His brain has turned to jelly, incapable of thought, sensation, function. Then, far away through a fog, as though someone else in the room is talking, he hears a voice.

“What happened?”

Neumann realises the voice is his.

“We do not know all the facts yet. He was found earlier this morning at Sennheisers, the smelters in Kreuzberg. He was concealed in a wagon of copper scrap, ready to be tipped into the furnaces. If one of the workmen on the shift hadn’t seen a hand sticking out . . . well, we would never have known. One of the officers who attended recognised him.”

“An accident?” Neumann hears his own voice again.

Becker hesitates, looks down, then up, his face chiselled with effort as he fights to control himself.

“No, not an accident. He has been murdered, Max.”

Neumann listens, hears the words, understands them individually, but he can’t assemble their meaning into a coherent whole. A barrier has been thrown up inside his head, something stopping normal thought processes from penetrating his consciousness. He stares blankly at Becker, struggles to formulate an emotion which will accommodate what he’s hearing. Kriminaldirektor Becker is speaking again.

“I am very sorry, Max, but . . . there is more. He was abused before he died. Tortured. It is very bad . . . I . . . I do not know how such things can be. We will find who did this, I swear.”

‘Tortured’ explodes into Neumann’s consciousness, shatters the barrier shielding him from what he’s being told. A strangled groan of despair bursts from deep within, a groan of anguish, anger, shock, grief. The pain is physical, a knife twisting in his chest. Neumann doubles over in his chair, head nearly hitting the desk, sits erect again as his clenched fists rise uselessly in front of him. His eyes are clamped tight, shutting out everything but the agony that is consuming him. For almost a minute he sits, motionless except for the working of his clenched jaw, the jagged rise and fall of his chest.

He opens his eyes to see Becker still on the chair, watching him. For the first time, Neumann views the Kriminaldirektor as something more than an object of ridicule and contempt. Becker displays a hitherto-unknown expression that Neumann realises is sympathy and concern. The boss has set aside petty differences and personal slights in the face of tragedy visited upon one of their own. The realisation prompts Neumann to nod slightly as he affirms to himself this new side of Becker.

"I want to see him."

Even as he speaks, Neumann realises he didn't want to see his dead father. But now he wants to see Kurt. He can't explain why it's different.

Becker doesn't register surprise or raise an objection.

"Very well. He is at the Charité. Do you wish to go there now? I will take you."

Neumann gets out of his chair by way of acknowledgement, walks over to fetch his hat and coat. He turns back to see Becker has risen and now stands regarding him with an unfathomable expression. Neumann's quizzical look triggers what comes next.

"Before we go . . . I must inform you . . . Kriminalassistant Schneider has been grievously injured. Whoever . . . whoever did this, tortured him . . ."

All at once Neumann knows what's coming. His chest tightens, his entire body tenses in anticipation. Through the thumping roar of his own heartbeats he hears Becker finish what he has to say.

"They took his eyes, Max. His eyes. They are gone."

45

Kriminaldirektor Karl Becker turns hard left out of Hannoveresche Strasse into the car park at the front of the Charité Hospital, rolls to a smooth stop next to a large bare-branched beech, turns the ignition off. For several moments he and Neumann sit staring ahead in silence broken only by the metallic ticking of their car's cooling engine. Four stories of the red brick hospital tower above them. Near the top of the severe tiered facade, above the Roman-arched entrance, the huge clock at the centre is getting ready to strike noon. Thick dark scudding clouds overlay everything. It seems appropriate. Becker turns towards his passenger.

"Are you ready, Max?"

A nod before Neumann opens his door and steps out into the bleak grey world of early winter, pulls his coat tightly around him. The two men walk slowly along the path leading to the twin doors of the entrance, then through them and down the main hall's stairwell leading to the basement and the morgue.

As he has more than once before in this place, Neumann feels like he's making the long slow descent into hell – Orpheus, on his fated journey to the underworld. But this time is different. This time, for the first time, Neumann's journey is driven not by duty but, like Orpheus was driven, by love. The realisation gives him pause. Is it love? Does he love Kurt Schneider? And he answers his own question in an instant. Of course he does. He loves Kurt in the way that men, comrades, love one another without ever saying it. Kurt is a friend, a comrade, a man he would trust with his life. A man he loves.

With a start, Neumann realises they have arrived. The entry door's dry hinge squeals its protest at being opened, the way it has done for as long as he can remember. He looks up, sees the familiar dark blue tiles, banks of fluorescent lights, glitters and reflections everywhere on the polished stainless steel tables and benches. Next to one of the tables is Professor Dürer, immaculate in a herring-bone dark suit and waistcoat. Beside him, incongruously thickset and battered, stands Reichskriminaldirektor Gottfried Tanzinger in full dress uniform, blue eyes moist and shining as he turns to greet the newcomers. He steps forward and wordlessly shakes the hands of Becker and Neumann in turn before placing one hand on Neumann's shoulder and squeezing it briefly. Professor Dürer doesn't move, doesn't offer a hand, but his face says more than any words or actions could. He holds Neumann's eye for a few seconds before turning around and walking over to the two brown doors at the far end of the room. Dürer motions through a porthole to someone on the other side then rejoins the trio beside the table.

He's only just reached the table when the double doors swing open and an attendant pushes a wheeled cadaver trolley through. Briskly the attendant rolls the trolley up to the four waiting men, locks its wheels in place, then disappears back the way he came.

Everybody stares at the trolley. Everybody knows that the

mounded shape under the dark grey sheet covering it is what's left of Kurt Schneider. And everybody knows what they're about to see. As though by prior arrangement, Becker and Tanzinger step back a little, leaving Neumann and Dürer the closest to the table. Dürer steps forward, grasps the topmost corners of the covering sheet, turns his head to Neumann. He receives in return a slow, almost imperceptible, nod. Dürer sets his mouth tightly, then gently peels the sheet down, nearly down to Schneider's waist, before taking a step back.

For a moment, there is only silence. Then out of Neumann's closed mouth comes a low rising moan of anguish, pain, loss. His body is rigid, his fists clenched, his face contorted and drained. Like a wax statue he contemplates his dead partner. Schneider's eyes are gone, nothing there now but blackened oozing pits. Neumann expected that, had half-prepared for it. He hadn't expected the myriad of cigarette burns on Schneider's face and arms, the missing fingers, the bloodied swollen mouth. He can't wrench his eyes away from the mouth, a ragged slash splitting it from the left side to halfway across Schneider's cheek. He points to it, raises his head to look at Dürer. The professor steps closer.

"It appears his assailant wanted him to open his mouth and met with resistance. It was forced open with an implement of some kind. The laceration probably resulted from that."

Neumann has turned back to stare at Schneider's body while he listens to Dürer. Now he looks at him again. His eyes ask an unspoken question. Dürer purses his lips, lowers his head.

"I'm sorry, Max. They took his tongue." He lays a hand on Neumann's upper arm, leaves it there.

Neumann's face betrays nothing. For several seconds he doesn't move, doesn't make a sound. Then, his gaze fixed and level, he slowly turns away from the trolley and walks out the way he came in. The soft slap of his shoes on the floor is the only sound in the morgue.

✠

Kriminalrat Franz Böhm is aware The Little Accountant took Neumann to the Charité morgue earlier in the day. He's heard what happened to Kurt Schneider, heard about his injuries, needs little imagination to know what this will mean to Neumann, how badly the man will be suffering. Now is the time to tell him about Standartenführer Schmidt.

Part of Böhm rebels against what he's going to do, but with an effort he rationalises his actions, tells himself Reichsmarschall Göring's grief over his murdered friend is hardly less worthy of respect, convinces himself that the destruction of Schmidt justifies casualties along the way. Even so, the thing sticks in his throat. He likes Neumann, respects his work, his ethics, doesn't want him to suffer unnecessarily. But there's nothing else for it. He knocks on Neumann's closed office door. There's a long pause. He's about to knock again when he hears noise on the other side. A word, perhaps, but indistinct. He draws a sharp breath and opens the door.

Neumann is at his desk, sitting on the edge of his chair, elbows on the desk. He's obviously had his head in his hands. His forehead is pressure-red, but the rest of his face is grey, sick, sapped of life. Dark moist eyes stare up at Böhm as though at an apparition. Böhm closes the door and sits across the desk from Neumann. For a moment, he hangs his head.

"This is a bastard of a thing, Max. A tragedy. Kurt was one of the best – a good policeman, a good human being. I . . . I don't know what to say . . ." Böhm spreads his hands in a gesture of hopelessness, helplessness. "We will get the animal who did this, make him suffer . . . No matter what it takes."

Neumann keeps staring, but his expression doesn't change.

It's hard to tell if he understands what Böhm is saying. Böhm shifts uneasily in his chair, unsure, discomfited. He's about to break the silence when Neumann speaks. It's barely more than a whisper.

"Yes." For a few seconds he lapses back into silence. But then his eyes seem to focus, and he meets Böhm's. "We have to find him," he adds. "Find him."

Böhm nods, affirming what both of them have said, reinforcing the imperative now driving their thoughts.

"I think I can help, Max. I may know who did it."

For what seems like minutes, Neumann continues to stare at Böhm, his expression unchanging. It's as though his thought processes are emerging from a frozen state, slowly thawing and beginning to make connections, draw conclusions, form opinions. Something stirs in his eyes, a glimmer of light escaping from black despair, a hope. He lifts his head sharply.

"You know who it was?" His voice is suddenly stronger, louder. "You *know*?"

"I think so, Max. I don't have hard evidence, but . . . Well, it's damn near hard evidence. It's enough to . . ."

"What? What do you know?" Neumann is transformed. He sits erect in his chair, hands thrust forward onto the edge of the desk. His face is enlivened, colour rising. He breathes rapidly, searches Böhm's face for something, insistent. "What?"

The transformation takes Böhm by surprise.

"It's someone in the SS. One of Himmler's men, one of his personal staff. It looks like . . ."

"How do you know?"

Neumann's eyes drill into Böhm's as if they're trying to drag the information out of his brain.

"A canary. One of mine. He came to me today after he heard about Kurt. He says the man who did this is the same one who killed the priest in Schöneberg, the one at Saint Norbert's church."

"Dassler? Father Dassler?"

"I don't remember his name, just that he was tortured. Like Kurt. His eyes . . . My man says he saw who did it."

"That was weeks ago. Why has your man waited until now to say anything? What's Kurt's connection anyway?"

Böhm hesitates, debates how much information to reveal, calculates what's in the Reichsmarschall's interests as well as in Neumann's. And his own.

"He was frightened, Max. This man, this creature of Himmler's, he's dangerous. Vicious, dangerous. We've seen what he can do. My canary was afraid he'd be in the man's sights if he said anything. But now, after . . . after what happened to Kurt, he realises nobody is safe. That's why he told me. He wants an end to it. He wants this swine brought down. As to the connection between the priest and Kurt – I don't know. It could be anything."

Neumann labours to take in what he's being told. He feels numb. The tortured unknown man in the Landwehr canal, Alois Neumann's death, Walther's likely culpability, Kurt Schneider's cruel murder – the weight of recent events is relentlessly crushing him beneath it, squeezing his life away in a series of sledgehammer blows. He's lost track of time, can't remember being happy, staggers from one level of despair to the next in an apparently endless downward procession. And yet, there's still a spark. Like the glow of a far-off match in a night forest, something stirs within the darkness, a part of Neumann that has life in it yet.

"Who is it, boss? A name. I need a name."

This is why Böhm's here. This is what needs to happen. He knows there will be inevitable consequences, foreseen and otherwise. He knows the situation might spiral out of control, turn on them all. The prospect of that eventuality, of open conflict between Himmler and Göring, makes him shudder. He thrusts the thought aside.

"The man you want is Stefan Schmidt, Max. Standartenführer Stefan Schmidt."

Neumann's head moves up and down, slowly, thoughtfully, and his eyes close as though he's committing something to memory. He's not. He's heard Schmidt's name before, whispered, hinted at, never anything more than rumour and suggestion, a bogeyman of the kind parents use to frighten children. But it's a name that makes everything fall into place.

"Max."

Neumann opens his eyes, meets Böhm's.

"If it *is* this Schmidt, then I hope someone tears his lungs out. But please, be careful. I like nothing I hear about Schmidt. He is as dangerous as anyone you've ever encountered. It would not be wise to underestimate him. Do not put yourself into his power. Remember, the Reichsführer stands behind everything he does."

"Of course," says Neumann solemnly, "I understand, boss. This one will be by the book."

Neumann sees Böhm believes him. But he's not sure he believes himself.

46

A rock pigeon alights on the sill of the Gothic-arched window overlooking Prinz Albrecht Strasse, peers intently into the warm room beyond the glass, fluffs its glossy grey-green-purple feathers against a raw chill day, . Whatever it sees in the room doesn't excite its interest, and it turns around to face the street far below. After a short stillness it flicks its tail up, shits on the window sill, then launches into the air and disappears.

Reichsführer Himmler turns his gaze from the departing pigeon back to his visitor sitting on the other side of the desk.

"Can we be certain the Kripos have it?"

Stefan Schmidt knows his boss, knows that he likes statements confirmed, facts verified, opinions corroborated. He knew in advance that the Reichsführer would want this assurance.

"As certain as we can be, sir. The Postmeister didn't see anything, but the girl he sent with the two men saw one of them take an envelope out of the box. It apparently held only one, or at least very few, documents. She says it was very thin, perhaps even empty. It is unlikely to have been empty, of course. Nobody secretes an empty envelope in a private post box."

"And the man you questioned, the Kripo? He would not confirm that they have the certificate?"

"He said nothing, sir, despite my best endeavours. He would not even acknowledge he and his superior had been to the Charlottenburg Post Office. It is difficult to explain, his resistance to my actions, but I would say he was almost contemptuous, despite his suffering."

Himmler studies his visitor in silence for a while, the thought running around his mind that this is the second time in recent weeks Schmidt has failed to extract information from a witness. First there was that Pole, the one who'd been following him. Now this police detective. Neither man succumbed to Schmidt's methods. Neither man gave up any information whatsoever. Himmler pushes the thought to the back of his mind for the moment. Time enough to ponder the issue later. He turns to a more pressing issue.

"It would seem, then, that the document is presently in the hands of the Kripo. Or at least in the hands of this Kriminalkommissar, this . . ."

"Neumann, sir. Max Neumann."

"Yes, this Neumann. If he has it, then presumably he's done nothing with it, shown it to nobody else. Had he done so, the consequences would by now be upon us."

Schmidt notes it is 'us'. Not 'me'. The word jars briefly, but a moment's thought tells him it is no more than hard fact – if the Reichsführer is brought low by this damned document, then he, Schmidt, will fall with him. Himmler is speaking again.

"We need the document without delay, Stefan. Without delay. What do you intend?"

"I will obtain it, sir. If it is in the hands of Neumann, I will obtain it from him."

A glance from Himmler signals doubt, uncertainty.

"By inflicting pain, Stefan? That did not persuade his colleague. Is the Kriminalkommissar cut from the same cloth?"

"Not by inflicting pain, Reichsführer, at least not physical pain. I intend to persuade the man through other means. He will die, of course, but not until after I have the document."

Himmler listens as Schmidt outlines his intended course of action, gives his blessing at the end, and the Standartenführer leaves the office to set about his business.

✠

Neumann sits staring at his desktop, as he has for nearly an hour, sometimes sitting forward on the edge of his chair, sometimes half-reclining to ease the intermittent ache in his side and back. As often as not his eyes are closed, but he's not asleep, or even tired. His brain is firing without pause as he tries to fit together the jigsaw of facts, possibilities, opinions and implications that crowd against each other and clamour for his attention. He needs to understand. He needs to know as accurately as he can what it all means before he can decide where to go from here. And through it all runs the name he's been given. Schmidt. Standartenführer Stefan Schmidt.

The bell on his desk telephone jangles, intrudes, wipes his mind clear in an instant. He leans forward, shakes his head to marshal his thoughts, picks up the earpiece.

"Kriminalkommissar Neumann."

He hears the educated Viennese tones of Lotte Braunwald, Reichskriminaldirektor Tanzinger's secretary.

"Max, it's Lotte. I . . . I have heard about Kurt. It's dreadful. I'm so sorry. I liked Kurt very much . . . You know . . ."

"Thank you, Lotte. Everybody liked him."

"Yes." A pause, as though she is trying to think what to say next. "The Reichskriminaldirektor wants to see you as soon as you are free. Can you come now?"

Neumann is momentarily surprised to get the summons, but realises the top man probably means only to offer his condolences, as befits a leader of men. But again? He's already done as much at the Charité, when they all gathered there to see Kurt's body. So, if it's not that, then what does he want? Perhaps he want to announce a full-dress funeral, honours for Kurt. Or perhaps he . . ."

"Max, are you there? Can you come now?"

"Sorry, Lotte. Yes. Yes, I'll come straight up. Right away."

He's about to replace the earpiece when he hears Lotte again. It's little more than a whisper.

"Max, please don't say anything, but I thought you should know. The Reichskriminaldirektor. He told me not to tell anybody about this call, told me it never happened. Please, don't say anything to him."

Neumann gives the girl his assurance before he hangs up. The significance of Tanzinger's actions baffles him. Why would he not want anyone to know he'd summoned one of his own officers? The thought rattles aimlessly around for several seconds before Neumann gets up and heads for the door. In less than a minute he's walking into Tanzinger's outer office. Lotte Braunwald is, as usual, sitting behind her typewriter. She lifts her head, gives Neumann a wan smile before she stands and moves with him towards the door of the inner office.

"He says you are to go straight in."

Braunwald knocks once on Tanzinger's door, opens it, and steps back to allow Neumann past. He moves through the doorway and starts to raise his arm in the obligatory Hitler salute, but lowers it again as Tanzinger rises to meet him, impatiently waving away the half-formed gesture. Tanzinger points towards one of the sofas in the office and sits on the one opposite. Neumann sits, hands on his knees, waits for the other man to speak.

Tanzinger's weathered face is wearing an odd expression, one Neumann can't decipher. Part concentration, part worry, part something else. Neumann continues to wait. Seconds pass. Tanzinger seems lost in thought before his eyes meet Neumann's.

"We live in strange times, Max. Difficult times. And dangerous ones, too." He lapses into thought before speaking again. "I have been told about Standartenführer Schmidt. No need for surprise," he goes on quickly in response to Neumann's reaction, "it is my business to know these things. What have you been told?"

Neumann outlines his understanding of the situation, omitting that he received his information from Franz Böhm, but aware that Tanzinger probably knows that already. Tanzinger listens without comment until Neumann has finished.

"And now. What do you propose?

"I have not yet formed a view, sir. There are many factors to be considered. Standartenführer Schmidt is a senior SS man. The investigation is no longer straightforward, as you know."

Tanzinger doesn't respond immediately, just stares at Neumann as though assessing, calculating, thinking.

"Only you and I know this discussion is taking place." He sees Neumann's eyes involuntarily flash towards the outer office. "She knows that nothing has happened, that you are not here. Both of us will deny any of this if we have to. Am I clear, Max? We have never had this discussion."

Neumann doesn't understand what is happening, doesn't see where it is leading, is confused and apprehensive. Nonetheless, Tanzinger is abundantly clear – this is a secret meeting, whatever it leads to. That much Neumann understands.

"Yes, sir. That is clear. I am not here."

"Good. Now, let me be clear about something else. If, as

seems likely, Standartenführer Schmidt is the one behind this, if he's responsible for what happened to your partner, he is a dead man. Understood?"

The Reichskriminaldirektor's view about Schmidt doesn't surprise Neumann – it echoes his own. One way or another, Schmidt needs to be brought to justice and punished, and the only penalty applicable in the circumstances is death.

"Understood, sir. It is guaranteed. A court would . . ."

"No," Tanzinger breaks in, "I'm not talking about a court."

Neumann doesn't move as Tanzinger speaks, doesn't display any reaction, just absorbs what he hears. A heavy silence comes down to envelop the room. The surroundings fade away. It's just the two men staring at each other. Neumann is aware of his own heartbeat, the blood pumping through his veins. It's as though he's observing himself from a distance, in slow motion, in silence. He knows that this situation, this single moment in time, is a tipping point. That what happens next will determine his future, or the lack of one.

"No court. Understood, sir."

"I hope it is, Max. This Schmidt is known to me. He is a creation of Reichsführer Himmler, has been for many years. His loyalty and obedience is unquestioned. Where he comes from, why he behaves as he does, I don't know. But until recently he was in France on some kind of assignment from the Reichsführer, something to do with stamping out the Resistance there. The reports I have heard from there are consistent with what he's done here. He is an abomination, Max, an evil and perverted beast that needs to be put down. Killed. Finished."

Tanzinger pauses, seems to be gathering his thoughts, perhaps debating how far to go, what to say. Neumann waits. His own thoughts are running wild as the implications of the Reichskriminaldirektor's words take hold. Tanzinger leans forward on the sofa, grimaces before he speaks.

“This cannot be official. Any hint that it is, any suggestion I am involved, would be counter-productive. At the very least, I would lose my job. At worst, my head. As would you, Max, and God knows how many others. Himmler only has to snap his fingers and we’re all in hell. In hell, while Schmidt continues to walk free. I would have difficulty calling myself an officer and a man of honour if that happened.” Tanzinger sits back, lifts his hands and drops them again. “So, what are we to do? What you do, I will leave to you. For my part, officially I will do nothing. I will not be aware of your activities, will not sanction them, will play no part whatever. We must be perfectly clear about that, Max, understood?”

Neumann nods, doesn’t trust himself to speak until he’s heard it all. Again, he waits.

“What I *will* do is provide to you every resource I have at my disposal. Men, equipment, money if you need it. But it will all be off the books, unofficial. I will sign nothing, do nothing in front of witnesses, leave no trace of any action I might take. As I have said, both Lotte and I will deny this meeting took place, should that be necessary. You will be alone, Max, alone on a tightrope. With no safety net. There must be no misunderstanding.” Tanzinger pauses expectantly, doesn’t take his eyes off Neumann.

“There is no misunderstanding, sir,” Neumann replies without hesitation. “Thank you for your offer of additional assistance, but I will not require any.”

47

The drive from the Alexanderplatz Police Praesidium to Charité Hospital, not much over three kilometres, takes a little less than ten minutes. Neumann's car skirts Hackescher Markt in Mitte, heads on down Oranienburger Strasse past the crumbling rococo Monbijou Palace and the English Church of St. George, then brushes the tip of a bend in the Spree before turning southwards to his destination. Buildings beautiful and drab, old and new slide like a filmed panorama along the side windows of the BMW 303 and disappear behind it, but they don't register on Neumann's consciousness. As he pulls into the car park in front of the hospital he realizes with a start that he can't remember a thing about the journey there. And, as he gets out of the parked car, his mind is jolted again when he sees he's next to the same huge beech that marked the end of his and Karl Becker's journey yesterday to see Kurt Schneider's body.

Yesterday. Only a day has passed. It seems like a year. In any other circumstance, any normal circumstance, Neumann would examine his own state of mind, try to account for the lapses in memory and concentration. But not now. This circumstance is far from normal, and he spends less than a fleeting second analysing his psychological wellbeing before his mind fills once again with the subject which dominates his thoughts – Stefan Schmidt. More precisely, how to rid the earth of such a man.

Thoughts of Schmidt start to fall away the nearer Neumann gets to Professor Dürer's office, are gradually overtaken by mild curiosity about what the doctor is going to prescribe. Aspirin only barely subdues the back pain becoming more frequent these days, more intense. Surely there is something stronger, a medication preferably not addictive. Or perhaps surgery is the answer – something needing to be adjusted or repaired or removed. Perhaps that's why the professor was reluctant to go into details over the telephone, planning instead to persuade Neumann in the flesh. Perhaps there's an exercise regime that needs to be undertaken, or an expensive course of treatment he'll need to pay for.

The professor's office door looms in the corridor and Neumann lifts his left wrist to check his watch. Less than two minutes to go until three thirty – on time with time to spare. He knocks twice on the closed door, hears the sound of a chair being moved on a wooden floor, a few footfalls, and then the door is opened to reveal Professor Dürer in his usual immaculate attire. He flashes a welcoming look. Not so much a smile as an open-faced acknowledgement of friendship.

"Hello, Max. Come in, please." Dürer steps back, gestures towards the uninviting wooden chair for visitors. Neumann smiles in response, mutters 'Thank you', takes a seat as the professor walks around to the other side of his desk. Dürer sits erect, his hands in his lap, looks directly at Neumann for several seconds. His face is held in stiff neutrality. Neumann frowns, unsure of where the situation is heading.

"Thank you for coming, Max. As I indicated when we

spoke, I have discussed with Doctor Telemann the results of his examination, and the x-rays he ordered." Dürer pauses for a few seconds, drops his eyes to the desk, seems to be thinking. He lifts his gaze again.

"I have been a doctor all my adult life. One of the things I have learned along the way is that truth is the best policy."

Neumann's stomach drops. He doesn't know exactly what he was expecting, but it wasn't this. Dürer goes on.

"Johann has confirmed what I suspected from my initial examination. I am truly sorry, Max. You have an advanced cancer. Of the pancreas. It is a most serious situation."

Neumann stares at the professor, his mouth agape, incapable of words. The word 'cancer' hammers in his head, shoves aside normal thought processes. Cancer. A death sentence. He can think of nothing other than death, his death. Slowly, his mind adjusts, accommodates a new reality, lets in other thoughts. Neumann becomes aware he's stopped breathing, sucks in air and inflates his lungs. He blinks rapidly, as though clearing his head.

"Is there no cure, no drugs . . . ?"

"I wish I could tell you there is." Dürer shakes his head slowly, half-closes his eyes. "I'm afraid there is nothing we can do. As advanced as medicine is these days, some things are still beyond our control."

Bizarrely, a large advent calendar hanging on the wall behind Professor Dürer draws Neumann's attention. He sees tonight is Krampusnacht, the 5th of December, and the calendar's page for today luridly illustrates the half-goat, half-demon Krampus, the unlikely companion of St Nicholas who will turn up tomorrow. Neumann wonders if he will see Christmas this year, greet the arrival of 1942. The calendar focuses his mind.

"How long do I have?"

Otto Dürer has been here many times. He knows there is no

'normal' reaction to the revelation that your life is soon to end, no standard set of questions and answers. Some people erupt in anger, others deny, yet others offer up a witticism or off-colour remark. And some, like Neumann, want to know how much time they have left on earth.

Dürer spreads his hands, a gesture of vague generality.

"It is impossible to be definitive. Johann suggests perhaps a few months. I am of the view . . . I really am sorry, but . . . it may be somewhat less. The tumour is quite advanced, so big it can clearly be seen on the x-ray. I don't know what to say, Max. It is a terrible thing for you. And your wife."

Neumann closes his eyes for a few seconds, lowers his head. When he raises it and opens his eyes again, they display a hard focus. It's mirrored in his voice.

"What happens now? How long will it be before I can't function normally?"

Dürer once more spreads his hands. "Again, it is difficult to say. Perhaps within a month or so you will need to be hospitalised. Unfortunately, the pain will get worse. Far worse. We can control it to some degree, but for that you will need to be under constant care – in a hospital."

"Morphine? Is that what I'll get?"

"Yes, morphine, probably. It is quite effective in reducing pain, but . . . it has drawbacks. Nausea, vomiting, constipation, breathing difficulties, other difficulties. One or more of these things may affect you, but each patient is different." He stops, looks hesitant. "I might be able to get hold of something the Merck people produce, Eukodal. Twice as effective as morphine, but it is highly addictive. However, that does not . . ." Dürer's voice falls away. There is no need to spell out the irrelevance of addiction here.

Neumann nods a few times during the professor's exposition, as though reconciling himself to the prospect of a premature death preceded by unappealing pain relief. There's silence for several seconds when Dürer finishes. Abruptly, Neumann gets up and reaches across the professor's desk, his hand outstretched.

"Thank you, Professor, I am grateful for your help. For the moment, I need to spend some time alone, then with my wife. Perhaps after that we might talk again about how to proceed."

Dürer stands too, shakes the proffered hand, then moves around his desk to see Neumann out. He opens the door, places one hand on Neumann's shoulder.

"I am always available to you, Max. If there is anything you need, I hope you will let me know without hesitation."

Neumann gives a thin smile, nods his understanding, and walks away down the corridor.

✠

It's less than twenty-four hours after Neumann learned he'll soon be dead, a prolonged death attended by unimaginable pain or the debilitating effects of massive amounts of morphine. If morphine is available after the Wehrmacht's needs are met.

He sits forward at his desk in the Alex, stares at the case notes for the three dead priests, for the unidentified man fished out of the Landwehr Canal, for Kurt Schneider. He is drained, exhausted, tired beyond description, engulfed by an avalanche of events removed from his control – the death of his partner at the hands of Standartenführer Schmidt, the near certainty that Walther murdered their father, and now the knowledge that his own time in this world is almost at an end.

He feels as though he's arrived at a crossroads, one with multiple routes branching from it, none of them signposted, each one as uninviting as the other, none of them leading to salvation. And yet he has to keep going, has to choose one of the roads.

But which one? The question hangs over everything, must be answered, but the pull of lethargy and hopelessness is dragging him down. He can't decide what to do, doesn't want to. Wants instead to lie down and let it all roll over him, be like Hamlet and let 'that sleep of death' take him painlessly away. He knows he'll have to tell Irmgard, and soon, but can't bring himself to do it. Not yet. It will take all his courage, all his willpower to break the news. The pain Irmgard will feel when she finds out will only add to the weight already crushing him. If he could just go to sleep . . .

The phone on his desk shrills, startles him, and he knocks it over in his half-awake attempt to lift up the earpiece. He fumbles to pick up the two parts, earpiece in his left hand, speaking column in his right.

"Kriminalkommissar Neumann."

A switchboard voice he doesn't recognise. Someone agitated. Nervous.

"Sir, it's your wife! She must speak with you."

"Yes, put her through."

Now he's fully alert, apprehensive. He hears clicks and a short low burst of noise.

"Max! Max!" Irmgard's words struggle out through terror, tears, near-hysteria. "A man . . . He was here. He said he will hurt me, Max! Help . . . I . . ." She chokes back a wail of fear, coughs wetly, then there is only sobbing, whimpering.

"Did he hurt you? Are you hurt?" Neumann's exhaustion, his lethargy, now thrown aside, is replaced by naked fear and concern. "Are you alright?"

"I . . . I'm not . . . hurt. I'm . . . frightened, Max." Irmgard's words are hesitant, ragged, spat out between irregular gulping breaths. "He said he . . . he would come back."

Neumann is on his feet.

"Where is he now?"

"He's . . . gone. I've locked the door. He . . . Max, he might come back. He said he would."

"What did he want? Why did he threaten you?"

"I don't know. He . . . he just said . . . tell you he wants it."

"Wants what?"

"I don't know. He said you have . . . something. I don't know what it is. He was horrible. Please, come home."

A wave of fear courses through Neumann's body, chills him to the bone. A dread realisation. His words have to be forced out.

"A name. Did he give you a name?"

"He said that you . . . you know him. He's SS. A Standartenführer. Standartenführer Schmidt. Please, Max, he frightened me."

Neumann is transfixed by fear. And by anger. The emotions threaten to overwhelm him. He fights to keep his voice level, reassuring, in control.

"Irmgard, listen to me, please. Listen carefully. Stay inside, keep the door locked. Pull the curtains. I will send someone there to take you to a safe place. Open the door to nobody else, no matter what they say. The man I send will say 'Böhm sent me' and he will put his warrant disc against the window. Do you understand? 'Böhm sent me,' then the disc. Open the door only to him. Only to him."

"I want you to come. Please, come . . ."

"My way will be quicker. There are things I have to do here. Things to stop this man ever hurting you. Please, Irmgard, it's just for a while. Just until I can get rid of the man. Remember, 'Böhm sent me' and a disc. Tell me you understand."

"Yes." Hesitant, hurt, frightened. "Yes, I understand."

"Good. Now, make sure you are locked in. I will send someone immediately. You will be alright. Just follow them and you'll be safe. I will join you as soon as I can. You will be alright. I promise."

He ends the call still reassuring a frightened Irmgard, stands for a moment thinking, then bursts out of the office looking for Franz Böhm.

48

Neumann is back in his office. Böhm didn't need persuading when he heard about Schmidt's visit. He immediately despatched two men to collect Irmgard, each of them with their service pistol and a MP 40 sub-machine gun, instructed to convey her to a safe house in Wedding and stay there with her.

The immediate danger is averted, but Neumann knows it's not a solution, only a reprieve. Schmidt isn't going to simply give up, go away. No, he is still the problem, and he will still have to be dealt with. At the same time as he thinks the thought, Neumann realises that someone as relentless as Schmidt will eventually find the Himmler marriage certificate, however much carnage it takes along the way. The hiding place Neumann and Schneider originally thought secure, the hanging file marked 'Discipline' in his office, is secure no longer. Not now that Schmidt knows Neumann has the document. He paces his office floor, ponders the problem. The certificate needs to be moved, moved to somewhere outside the reach of Schmidt. But to where? What hiding place is safely beyond Schmidt's grasp?

Neumann continues to concentrate, walks back and forth like a caged beast. After less than a minute he comes to an abrupt halt, stands with arms hanging loose at his sides, stares vacantly at nothing for several seconds. He has the solution. The document will be safe. More importantly, it will be used to bring down Himmler, the man directly responsible for Schmidt's actions, for Schneider's death. As to Schmidt himself, that's a problem yet to be dealt with.

Neumann takes out his wallet, extracts a card from it, then picks up the telephone on his desk. He's about to contact the switchboard and ask to be put through to the number on the card when he stops, slowly puts the telephone down again. Too risky. A call like this one will be noticed. It's unlikely the girl on the switchboard would say anything to him directly, unlikely too that she would even think to report it, at least not immediately. But she might mention it later, even if casually on a break, and someone else might seize on it, take the matter further. Neumann isn't worried about recriminations from his superiors, but he realises the call would be a flag to someone like Schmidt, a signpost the man could follow. He replaces the card in his wallet, goes to the rack in the corner of the room for his hat and coat. He's about to put them on when the telephone rings. Neumann hesitates, decides to take the call, picks up.

"Kriminalkommissar Neumann."

It's that new switchboard girl again.

"There's a call for you, sir. A Standartenführer Schmidt."

The announcement paralyses Neumann. For long seconds he stands mute, astonished, his mind churning through possibilities. The switchboard operator speaks again.

"Are you there, sir? Shall I put him through?"

It breaks the spell. Neumann breathes in sharply, forces his voice into something approaching normal.

"Yes. Put him through."

The earpiece makes its usual noises. Then silence. Seconds tick by slowly as Neumann tries to ignore his racing heart, his fear, his growing fury. This is the man who has been to his home, has threatened his wife. Neumann steels himself against whatever is to come as he speaks into the silence.

"What do you want?"

He's not expecting the voice he hears in response. A vicious psychopath shouldn't sound cultured, shouldn't enunciate clearly and softly. Neumann tries and fails to envisage the man.

"For the moment, Kriminalkommissar, I require only a little of your time. There is a proposition I wish to put to you. I suggest it would be in your interests to hear it. May I continue?"

A loaded pause, then, "Yes," as with effort Neumann keeps his voice level, noncommittal, "Continue."

"Very good. My proposition is simple. You have something I want, a certain marriage certificate. I wish you to deliver the document to me. That is all."

"All?" Despite his raging emotions, Neumann can't keep a note of incredulity out of his voice. "What will happen then?"

"Nothing will happen then. You will give me the document, and that will be the end of the matter."

Neumann almost snorts with derision. The moment he gives up the certificate, he's a dead man. Schmidt must think he's a fool. He asks himself why the man doesn't simply torture him, force the document's location out of him, then remembers what happened with Father Rochlitz – someone who could have revealed the certificate's hiding place but accidentally died before he did. Neumann reasons Schmidt doesn't want to risk a recurrence. The internal debate takes only a fraction of a second, a minor dialogue in a whirlpool of competing thoughts, strategies and possibilities as Neumann listens to the other man, searches for an opening, a weakness, a failure on Schmidt's part. He tries to tease the man out.

“And if I decide not to surrender the certificate? If I decide to bring it to the attention of your superiors? Perhaps to the attention of the Führer himself.”

“Let me counsel you against such a course of action. First, you would be stopped at the very first hurdle. No senior officer in the Kripo, the Wehrmacht, even the SS, would convey the document further up the chain of command. Once they saw what it was they would realise failure to immediately arrest you would be tantamount to signing their own death warrant. Second, if you were so foolish as to even attempt such a course of action, your lovely wife would suffer beyond your imagination. She is, as you must be aware, a beautiful lady.” Schmidt pauses just long enough to give weight to his next words. “Such big brown eyes.”

The words hang in charged silence. Neumann feels something wrap cold fingers around his heart and squeeze. He can barely speak. There is no reason to think Schmidt is making an idle threat. None. Neumann sees the knuckles of his right hand, holding the telephone upright, are white.

“Do I need to go further, Kriminalkommissar? I think not. Very well. I will telephone again at nine tomorrow morning, when you will inform me of your decision. Think carefully before you decide. Good day to you.”

✠

The stripped Walther P 38 pistol lies on a square of felt on the bench in front of Emil Vogel, its finely-machined surfaces glinting dully beneath strip lighting. Despite Vogel’s coarse-featured overweight bulk, his sausage fingers manipulate the weapon’s components with delicacy and exactitude as inspects it. The P 38 is routine work for Vogel. It’s the standard service issue pistol for Kripo detectives. As Kripo armourer, he’s seen hundreds of the weapons before, but each one is still a joy to behold – not merely a death-dealing device but a beautiful concurrence of practicality, precision engineering and design. Even Vogel wouldn't argue the pistols have personalities, but he knows they are each as individual as any living thing. The one in front of him now is here because the detective it's been issued to complains it has twice jammed. A jammed weapon to many is an inconvenience, an annoyance. To a Kripo detective it could be the difference between life and death. Vogel knows this, is reminded of it every time what remains of his shattered right knee gives him grief. He'd still be a detective out on the streets if his pistol hadn't jammed more than a decade ago.

He's identified the problem – the extractor tension is too great, tipping the cartridges in the feed ramp just enough to hit the ramp at slightly the wrong angle. The cartridge then stops the slide from moving forward, the pistol jams, and someone's in trouble. A straightforward job. Vogel sets to work. He's only just started when the workshop telephone rings. Annoyed, he downs tools, walks across the room and grabs the earpiece off the wall.

"Armoury." His tone conveys his level of annoyance. Vogel is habitually blunt, brusque, but this time the opening word is spat out.

"Emil? It's Max Neumann . . ."

Vogel unconsciously stiffens, lifts his chin as though Neumann is standing there in front of him. The two have history. As a young Kriminalassistant, Neumann was there when Vogel's pistol jammed and his partner was killed only a metre away from him. Objectively, there was nothing Neumann or anyone else could have done to prevent the death, but Vogel was convinced otherwise at the time and hasn't changed his mind since. All these thoughts are stampeding through Vogel's mind for the thousandth time as he hears Neumann continue.

". . . I need a favour."

In different circumstances, Vogel would tell Neumann to fuck himself and hang up. Not this time. Vogel is sharply aware, like every other Kripo in Berlin, of what happened to Kurt Schneider. He knows first-hand the pain that accompanies the loss of a partner. And he always got on well with Schneider, who simply ignored the armourer's customary irascibility, treated him like he would any other colleague. Vogel reins in his long-standing resentment.

"What favour?"

"I need some equipment. Without paperwork. Unofficial."

"Why?"

"I won't go into details. It's to deal with the bastard who killed Kurt. I can't make it official. That's why there can't be any paperwork. It's for you, not for me – it's to protect your involvement."

Despite himself, Vogel is drawn in. Partly because he might be able to help get back at Schneider's killer, partly because he's curious about the secrecy Neumann's attaching to the situation.

"What do you need?"

Neumann tells him. Vogel's eyes widen as he listens. There's a long silence after Neumann finishes explaining his needs. Eventually, Vogel breaks it.

"Fuck. It won't be easy. Come and see me."

49

Harry Forbes swivels his head around, takes in the uninviting exterior of the little Prenzlauer Berg establishment on the corner of Belforter Strasse and Kolmarer Strasse. It's hard to reconcile the bar's cheerless frontage with the imposing Wasserturm building less than a hundred metres away. The circular seven-story water tower with its pierced octagonal rotunda looks like it's been transplanted straight from Florence, one of Brunelleschi's masterpieces looted by the Nazis and brought here to glorify the centre of the Third Reich. Neumann sees him staring.

"It didn't look so impressive when the KZ was in operation."

The comment lifts Forbes' eyebrows. He stares questioningly at Neumann.

"Concentration camp." Neumann points to a spot halfway between them and the tower. "There was a big machinery hall, over there. Had a lot of people in it for a couple of years. Tore it down about five or six years ago. No idea what happened to the poor bastards in there."

Forbes nods slowly, absorbs the information, can't decide what to do with it. The two men continue on to the bar.

Inside, the pervasive odour of smoke, sweat, stale beer and fried onions greets them. One short side of the premises is taken up by a counter of carved dark wood, brass rails along its length, a line of beer taps down one end. Glasses and bottles line the wire shelves behind. Feeble light from the single working bulb above does its best to coax reluctant reflections from the polished surfaces.

Neumann and Forbes order two beers and a plate each of the day's only offering, then head for a table and settle themselves. The barman brings the beers then returns to his post behind the bar, where he slouches against its edge. Incongruously, he's studying something in the *Berliner Börsen Zeitung*, the stock exchange's morning newspaper famed for its long and semi-comprehensible sentences. He's got plenty of time – besides Neumann and Forbes, there are only three other customers, shift workers from the nearby Dr. Oetker pudding factory by the look of them. They're drinking beer and playing skat for a few pfennigs.

"It's not what I was expecting. Not after Die Letze Instanz. That was a real restaurant. This looks like a hangout for loose women and small-time hoods."

Neumann flicks his eyes around the room. He's already familiar with the worn small tables and mismatched chairs, the faded curtains over windows facing the street. Whatever once covered the floorboards has long since departed, and now their unpolished rawness is discoloured by accumulating street grime from patrons' shoes. Neumann feels no need to tell Forbes the landlord has an impressively full Orpo charge sheet.

"That's because it is, Harry. And cops too. We're in good company. Drink your beer."

Forbes lifts his Bock, sips, lowers the glass again, just as a frail-looking old woman wearing a long apron and heavy boots appears from the kitchen with two plates. She wordlessly puts them on the table and leaves. Forbes leans forward, strains to see in the poor light.

"Bacon and broad beans," offers Neumann. "Eat."

"Bacon? How does the . . ."

"Don't ask," interjects Neumann, "not in a place like this."

Forbes shrugs, pulls his plate closer, picks up his knife and fork. He's dubious, but takes a mouthful, looks pleasantly surprised. He makes appreciative grunts. For a few minutes the two men eat in silence, sip their beers. Neumann forks in a few mouthfuls of the meal, but mostly pushes the food around on his plate. Forbes puts his cutlery down, takes a few sips of his beer before focusing on Neumann.

"Okay, what gives? Why am I here?"

As Neumann opens his mouth to speak, Forbes breaks in. "And don't give me any hogwash about wanting the pleasure of my company. You call me from a public phone booth, say it's urgent, want me to come out for a meal at a moment's notice, all mysterious and secret. So I come, sit here with you pretending to be all normal when you're not. I know you better than that. Something's up, something's wrong. So, come on, let's have it."

Neumann just stares, burrowing his gaze into Forbes as though he can see through the skin, into the heart, the soul. He looks drained, exhausted, old. Feels it, too.

"There's something I want you to have," he says slowly. "Something important. It's a document that needs to be made public, published, and I can't do it myself. And it can't be done here. It has to be got out of Germany. To the United States. You can do that."

Forbes has stopped eating, drinking, sits staring, a combination of puzzlement and incredulity.

"A document? What sort of document?" His voice rises in

tone and volume.

Neumann leans in closer, drops his voice.

"Something explosive. It won't bring down the government, but it will get rid of one of its biggest bastards. I can't get it published here. Nobody can. Just being found with it on me would mean a firing squad."

Forbes is momentarily stunned, stares at Neumann. "Jesus, Max, what have you got into?" His eyes are wide.

Neumann suddenly feels a great tiredness. All he wants to do is sleep, close his eyes, shut out the world that's collapsing on top of him. He wills himself to go on.

"I can't explain, Harry. It's too complicated, and . . . and I just don't have enough energy left to do it. I'm worn out. Seriously. Can you do it? Can you get the document to America, get it published there? It's very important to me."

"Sure, if it means that much to you. Depending on what it is, I could probably get it into the *New York Times*, or perhaps the *Washington Post*. I've still got contacts in the business, friends of Dad. I'm sure they'd help me."

"Good, good." Neumann's relief is obvious. He half-closes his eyes, lets his head tilt forward. Abruptly, he sits up again.

"There's something for you in this. Money, I mean. Any newspaper would pay to have the document. A lot of . . ."

Forbes waves a dismissive hand, starts to protest.

"No, I mean it," says Neumann quickly. "This could help you, get you back on your feet. I want you to take whatever you can get." Neumann reaches into his inside coat pocket, flicks his eyes around the room, then pulls out an unsealed brown envelope. "Here. See for yourself." He slides the envelope across the table.

Forbes picks up the envelope, takes out the marriage certificate, unfolds it on the table in front of him and bends closer to make out the words. For nearly a minute he's silent, bent over, once lifting his eyes to shoot a puzzled glance at Neumann. Then his body stiffens, his jaw drops. He bends closer to the document, moving his head left and right, apparently re-reading to confirm what he thinks he's seen.

"Oh, fuck. This is . . . this can't be what I think it is. Is it Himmler? The Reichsführer?"

Neumann nods.

"Jesus H Christ! This is the end of him. Once this is made public . . ." The implications hang unspoken, obvious, dramatic.

"You see why I want you to get it out of the country. You could do it in a diplomatic bag. You'd be protected, safe. Nobody would suspect anything. Will you do it?"

Forbes still looks shell-shocked. He carefully folds the certificate, puts it back in the brown envelope, then puts the envelope into his coat pocket. As he goes through the motions his expression is transformed. Now he looks thoughtful, serious, confident.

"I will, of course I will. Leave it with me."

The wall clock thunks its dead march of seconds as it edges its inexorable way towards nine. Neumann sits slumped in his office chair, his gaze fixed on the clock, watches the minute hand intermittently lurch forward. Outside, snow is falling. The sky is granite flecked with spit. For all the light that penetrates the window, it might as well be night. Neumann grimaces, shifts his position in the chair. The pains shooting across his abdomen and back are getting worse, not completely masked by the pills Professor Dürer has given him. The morphine will be better, Dürer says, but better to keep it in reserve if other medicine can keep the pain bearable. Neumann didn't argue. It seemed unimportant.

The telephone jangles. Neumann stares at it for a few seconds before slowly reaching out and picking up.

"Kriminalkommissar Neumann."

The coarse-voiced switchboard girl doesn't waste words.

"Standartenführer Schmidt for you," she snaps, makes the connection without waiting for a response.

"This is Neumann."

"Have you reached a decision, Kriminalkommissar?"

In other circumstances Schmidt's refined, cultured voice would sound reassuring, dependable, decent. Now it just sounds ominous, evil.

"Yes. You can have the certificate."

"I commend you on reaching a sensible decision. One which will spare your lovely wife a most distressing experience. Now, you will bring the document to . . ."

"No."

"No?" Schmidt's voice overlays incredulity with amusement.

"You can come and get it. I have to retrieve it, and that can't be done until later today. I should be able to give it to you by five o'clock. I'll make sure I have it by then."

A long pause. Neumann waits.

"Very well. I will not quibble about details. Where will you be at five o'clock?"

"At Father Rochlitz's apartment. I'll hand it over there."

Another long pause. Longer. When he speaks, Schmidt's voice holds overtones of menace.

"I hope for your sake, Kriminalkommissar, that you are not playing games with me. That would be unwise. Why do you wish to deliver the document in the late Father Rochlitz's apartment?"

"Because it's very near to where the document is being held for the moment. It will avoid a delay in the event my retrieval of the certificate is more difficult that I anticipate, that's all. The apartment is still empty. I have the key. I will be alone when you arrive."

Schmidt takes a few seconds to consider this.

"Very well. Make sure you are alone. If you are thinking of avoiding . . ."

"I'm not thinking anything. I will retrieve the document from where it is being held, then hand it over to you when you arrive. After you have it, we can all get on with our lives. The only thing I ask in return is that you leave my wife alone. Do I have your word on that?"

"Of course. Once the certificate is in my possession, I will have no further interest in you or your wife. You have my word as a German officer."

"All right. Then there's nothing more to say."

"Correct. I look forward to our meeting at five."

50

Max Neumann sits and smokes in silence amid the wreckage of Father Rochlitz's apartment, the rooms untouched since the old priest's body was removed. The landlord has never asked for the key to be returned, presumably because there's no prospect of any new tenant wanting to move in. Or because the landlord is dead, or in a concentration camp. Neumann's smoked more than a dozen cigarettes in the nearly seven hours he's been here. Within minutes of getting the 9am call from Standartenführer Schmidt, he was on his way, stopping only to post his letter to Irmgard at the safe house.

He thinks of her now, envisages her tomorrow when she gets the letter. Imagines her reaction, her emotions, her devastation. It has to be this way. He can't tell her face-to-face, can't risk being talked out of his intentions. In time, perhaps, she will understand. And given enough time, perhaps she will not think badly of him. What matters most is that she will be safe, and for that he's prepared to pay the price.

His preparations took less time than he anticipated, so he's had more than two hours of sitting and waiting, smoking and thinking, reconciling himself. A wry smile briefly wrinkles his lips as he reflects on how well he's feeling – for a dead man, that is. And he contemplates the nature of the man who will be here soon, concludes there's no redeeming feature he can detect. From everything he's seen, Schmidt is an abomination of a human being. Neumann nearly snorts with contempt as he considers the logic of such a man belonging to an organisation like the Schutzstaffel, an organisation itself part of the larger Party organisation. Vicious and corrupt from top to bottom. They are all perfect bedfellows.

Two loud knocks jerk Neumann back to nightmarish reality. He leaves his cigarette in his mouth as he gets up and walks to the door. He unlocks and opens it. Outside, against the far wall of the corridor, two uniformed SS troopers holding sub-machine guns have their weapons levelled at him. For a few seconds the three men stand motionless, then the older of the two troopers speaks without taking his eyes off Neumann.

"All clear, Standartenführer."

The sound of slow steps fills the silence. Then, from his right, Neumann sees Schmidt approach, pistol in his hand. Schmidt raises the weapon, points it at Neumann's face.

"You will please slowly walk backwards for three paces, Kriminalkommissar. If my men perceive any threatening movement, they will kill you instantly. Is that clear?"

Neumann's response is slow in coming. He can't take his eyes off Schmidt, can't help but think how ordinary the man looks, how this personification of evil seems no different from anyone else in the street. Yet in other circumstances, ones where the option was available to him, he would kill this man without blinking. In other circumstances . . .

"Is that clear?" The repeated question jolts Neumann.

"Yes."

"Good. Move now, please."

Neumann keeps his hands by his side as he walks backwards and stops. The two troopers follow him into the apartment, their guns trained on him. They take up positions on either side, about three metres away, before Schmidt moves into the apartment and closes the door behind him.

"Remove your cigarette and extinguish it."

Neumann drops the cigarette to the floor, grinds it out.

"Both hands on your head, please." Then, to the troopers, "Search him."

Neumann stands motionless while the younger of the pair slings his weapon and does a top-to-toe pat down before resuming his position.

"He is unarmed, Standartenführer."

"Very well. Please sit there, Kriminalkommissar," says Schmidt, pointing to the chair Neumann has just vacated. "You may lower your hands. If you attempt to rise from the chair I will shoot you. You are alone?"

Neumann nods. Schmidt turns to the older trooper. "Search the other rooms."

Neumann keeps his eyes on Schmidt and the pistol still aimed at his face. He hears thumps and scrapings by the troopers as they examine any potential hiding places in the kitchen or bedroom. They return within a minute.

"There is nobody else here, Standartenführer."

"Good. Go outside. Wait by the door. I will call out if I require you. Otherwise, do not enter."

The troopers come to attention, give a crisp 'Sir!', and leave the room, shutting the door behind them. Schmidt looks around, picks up an overturned dining chair and sits on it. He's about three metres away, his pistol still aimed at Neumann's face.

"So, here we are. You have something for me?"

"Yes, the certificate is here."

"Good. I was confident it would be. Although you are a

stupid man, Kriminalkommissar, you are not *that* stupid. Anything less than production of the document would mean unimaginable torment for you and for your delightful wife. Your loyalty towards her, your love for her, would not allow you to play games with me. And therein lies the crux of your stupidity. Your emotions, you see. It is a common enough failing – you are hardly unique in that respect. Still, that failing has brought you undone, as you see." Schmidt flicks up the barrel of his pistol as if to give emphasis to Neumann's predicament. He sighs, lowers the pistol to sit on his knee. "But enough of this idle talk. Where is the certificate?"

The question tightens Neumann's chest, sets his heart racing. It's what he has been waiting for. Everything has come to this, the world reduced to a brief exchange of words. The next few seconds will determine his fate, Irmgard's fate, will be the difference between success and failure. He keeps his voice level as he utters the words on which everything hinges.

"I'll get it for you," he says, starts to rise to his feet.

"No!" Schmidt raises his pistol in a blur, holds it at arm's length. "You will stay seated. Where is it?"

Neumann eases back down on his chair. His shoulders fall. He's a beaten man, a failure, a victim. He wearily waves his left arm in the direction of the old sideboard against the wall.

"There. Middle drawer."

Schmidt slowly gets off his chair and moves to the sideboard, never letting his pistol waver as he covers Neumann. He grasps the middle drawer's handle with his free hand, standing well off to one side, then slowly eases it open a couple of centimetres. It's enough for him to see the envelope lying in the drawer. He moves his head around, examines the drawer's interior, sees nothing else. He turns his attention back to Neumann, still sitting motionless in the chair.

"You are expecting to leave, Kommissar, yes? Now that the

document has changed hands." There's the hint of a smile on Schmidt's face.

"I am. You have no need of me now. Without the document in my possession, I'm just another cop. There's nothing I can do to harm you or the Reichsführer."

"You think so, do you? I refer you to my earlier remarks about your stupidity, which you demonstrate again. A man possessed of the knowledge you hold is a man who threatens the Reichsführer. And, indeed, the government itself. Such a man can hardly be allowed to walk free." Schmidt shakes his head in mock sorrow. "I must inform you that you will not leave here alive. It has to be so. I'm sure you understand."

Neumann slumps, lowers his gaze as he nods his understanding.

"What you may not understand is that your wife is also lost. Again, it has to be so. I assume you have told her . . ."

Schmidt's pistol jerks up to cover Neumann's sudden movement in the chair as he half-rises before sinking back.

"You gave your word! You said she would not be . . ."

"And you believed me. Fool. I am astounded a man so devoid of intelligence should have been permitted to be a detective. Of course she will die. Her fate and yours are determined now. It will scarcely be an onerous task, of course. Such a beautiful woman, as you know. It will be interesting to see how she is affected by pain of a kind you can scarcely imagine . . . No!" The pistol rises again. "Stay where you are!"

Neumann is a man enraged, desperate, provoked beyond tolerance. Fists balled, face contorted with anger, he glares at Schmidt, his jaw working.

Schmidt waves his free hand dismissively before he grasps the handle of the sideboard drawer and pulls it fully open. The movement is accompanied by a metallic scraping sound from inside as a cord attached to the back of the drawer drags with it the pullchain from a Model 39 ‘egg’ hand grenade tied to the sideboard’s frame. The fragmentation grenade is one of six, all tightly secured together. Each one is fitted with a red 1-second delay fuze cap.

Time slows beyond all recognition. Neumann registers the surprise, the shock, the terror on Schmidt’s face as he swivels away from the sideboard towards the door of the apartment. And he registers, for the briefest instant imaginable, the hail of metal and wood which shreds the Standartenführer from back to front, spraying Schmidt’s blood forward in a great halo of red. Then the hail reaches him.

Epilogue

"Lemme get this straight. You want me to ride shotgun for you while you meet some guy. A few hours work, you say, most of it sitting on my butt." A thought intrudes, demands a pause. "So why me? Why not one of the others? You got a corporal and four privates to choose from – they'd all be cheaper than me."

"You're the boss," explains Harry Forbes. "Nobody's going to question where you go or why. You can leave, take a weapon with you, come and go as you please. Nobody will suspect anything."

"And for this, for a few hours work, you're gonna hand over more than Uncle Sam pays me in a year. Have I got it right?"

In nearly fifteen years of Army service, the last six guarding US embassies in London, Rome and now Berlin, Sergeant Mike Barley has never come across anything like this. In each of his postings, diplomatic staff have occasionally asked him for a favour – deliver flowers to a mistress, pick up a parcel from a tailor, play chauffeur to some visiting relative. But never anything like this. Never anything involving a weapon. Or the possibility of danger. He's intrigued, but he's also sceptical, cautious. If something like this goes wrong, he could get hurt. Even at best, he'd be out of the Army on his ear if people at the top heard what he'd done. He runs an agitated hand backwards over his short-cut ginger hair.

"You've got it right, Mike. It's easy money. All you have to do is watch, make sure the guy I meet doesn't try anything. If he pulls out a gun or a knife, you stop him. That's all."

"You say 'stop him'. You mean shoot him, don't you?"

Harry Forbes expects the sergeant's hesitancy, his reluctance, tries to allay it.

"A last resort. Definitely a last resort. This other guy and me, we'll each have something the other one wants. Once we exchange, that's the end of it. He'll have no reason to get cute. All I'm saying is that if, *if* something goes wrong and he pulls a gun, you'll be there to save my life. If you saw someone, anyone, about to get shot and you could stop it, you would, wouldn't you? Well, that's all it is. Chances are we'll do our exchange and both walk away, and then you can come back to your quarters a thousand bucks better off than you were when you left."

Barley's lips wrinkle as he considers the proposition. His eyes drop. Combined with his sprinkling of freckles, the effect is to make him look younger than his years – he's almost the same age as Forbes. For several seconds he mulls over the situation. Then he comes to a decision.

"Yeah, okay. But I don't shoot anyone unless they've got the drop on you."

✠

The office is warm, dry and comfortable. Outside, through the big mullioned windows overlooking Prinz Albrecht Strasse, it is cold, wet and uncomfortable. The snow that drifted down for most of the day has stopped falling, now lies on the streets in increasingly dirty piles and pools of mush. He can't see it from his desk, but Heinrich Himmler knows the Strasse will be clogged with workers going home, slogging and squelching through the muck, standing shivering, waiting for a bus or tram to take them out of the city centre. He glances at his watch. Nearly five. Another hour or so, and he'll be on his way home too. At least he won't have to endure the sweaty damp miasma of packed public transport, or suffer the cold, for that matter. He briefly reminds himself of his good fortune in having a driver, a heated Mercedes-Benz W150, an armed escort everywhere he goes. Just rewards for his contribution to the Party. Life could be worse. He turns away from the windows, brings his attention back to the pile of papers on the desk in front of him.

The side door to the office opens without a knock.

"Reichsführer. Something of which you need to be aware."

Hauptsturmführer Knoechlein is respectful without being deferential. He's been the Reichsführer's adjutant-cum-bodyguard for nearly five years and the two men have settled into a trusting working relationship. Knoechlein always knows what his boss wants, is always ready to do it. He stands now, waiting on the response to his announcement.

"Yes, Ernst. What is it?" Himmler takes off his spectacles, looks up at the tall younger man with only mild curiosity. These situations are not uncommon. When you're effectively in charge of half the nation, there are always issues, urgencies, problems to be resolved. This will be yet another one.

"There is a man on the telephone who wishes to speak with you. Only with you, he says. He says he has something for you. He is very insistent."

"His name?"

"He will not give it, sir. He claims that when you hear what he possesses, you will want to speak with him. He says he has a certificate you will want to see."

The revelation electrifies Himmler. He whips his glasses back on, stares unblinking at Knoechlein for several seconds. Abruptly, he turns back to his desk.

"Put him through, please, Ernst. Close the door."

"Immediately, Reichsführer."

Knoechlein strides out of the side door, shuts it. Himmler stares at the telephone in front of him, waits. A few seconds later it rings. He slowly picks up the earpiece.

"Yes? Yes, yes, put him through."

A short pause.

"Yes, I am." The Reichsführer listens for several seconds before speaking again.

"Who are you?"

Now there is a long silence in the office. Himmler knots his brow in concentration as he listens to the caller's voice. At last, it's his turn to speak.

"I see," he says softly. "What you propose is acceptable. It will take some while to put things in order, you understand. I suggest we meet later this evening. Let us say at twelve. That will allow me time to make the necessary arrangements."

Again, Himmler listens, his concentration absolute, his eyes half-closed as he grapples with the unexpected.

"I understand. It is best I am not seen in a public place. But I can not come alone. My personal bodyguard will be with me. For protection, you understand. Berlin at night can be dangerous. No doubt you will have your own protection."

Again, he listens. It doesn't take long.

"Yes. At midnight."

The caller disconnects. Himmler slowly replaces the telephone's earpiece on its upright holder, sits motionless, his forearms resting on the desk, abandons himself to thinking. His lips are pursed, his eyes closed. A minute goes by – two, three, before he leaps to his feet and strides to the side door. Flinging it open, he confronts a startled Knoechlein at his desk.

"Ernst! Is Schmidt here?"

"No, Reichsführer. He left about an hour ago, just after four. With two men, two troopers. He has not returned yet."

Himmler takes a few seconds to re-assess the situation before issuing his orders.

"Have the Reichsbank President brought here. If he can't be located, get his deputy. At once, please. At once. Then report back to me immediately."

✠

Harry Forbes is chilled to the bone, extremity-numbingly cold. It's at least a couple of degrees below freezing, an early December foretaste of winter's ferocity. In the man's distinctive Texan drawl, Leland B Morris, the Charge d'Affaires at the Embassy, warned him the very day he arrived – 'Ain't a hill between us and Moscow, son, so rug up'. Forbes has come as prepared as he can, thick socks in winter boots, layers of clothing beneath his overcoat, knitted woollen skier's hat pulled over his ears, and still he's cold.

He's been in the abandoned factory office since sunset. A quick glance at his watch tells him there's less than seven minutes to go before December 7 ticks over to December 8. The gold Girard-Perregaux, with its little date window, was his father's, one of the few possessions Forbes still has from those better times, those times of wealth and the respect it brings. And those times will come again if this gamble succeeds.

The derelict office is part of a huge and decaying former meatworks on the south-eastern fringe of Friedrichshain, not far from where the River Spree turns into the Osthafen. Even in daylight, almost nobody comes here. Near midnight, in weather like this, the prospect of anybody appearing by chance is as low as the temperature.

Forbes slaps his arms together and stamps his feet before moving to the shattered glass of the window next to the door and yet again peering into the darkness. There's enough of a gibbous moon to dimly see the big paved courtyard and its surrounding buildings, everything still, ghostly indistinct, deathly quiet. He retreats back into the building, away from the window and its draughts, suspects the feeling of extra warmth inside is illusory. As he has done repeatedly for hours, he tells himself it will be worth it. Better this freezing vigil than to walk into some kind of trap, he tells himself, reassures himself that everything is as it should be.

Since Forbes parked the Embassy car under what is left of a half-collapsed packing hall on the other side of the complex, he's seen nothing else moving in the area, heard no sounds of any kind. If they were going to set him up, lay an ambush, they would have done it by now – he would have seen movement, heard noises. He can't see Sergeant Mike Barley, but that's as it's supposed to be. The man is somewhere on the second floor of the wing opposite the derelict office, positioned so he has a clear line of sight on the courtyard. That line will be clearer than the one Harry Forbes has, enhanced by the night-vision attachment on Barley's rifle.

He starts towards the window again but stops. There's a sound. A steadily-growing low hum, a rumble, something mechanical coming. Forbes moves to the side of the window, stares at a glow slowly brightening beyond the building line at the far end of the courtyard. He moves back a little, out of sight of whoever it might be.

As he watches, the mechanical noises grow louder, fill the night. He feels the office structure vibrate in resonant sympathy. Then the light turns into two piercing pinpoints and a large black Mercedes-Benz glides into the paved area and comes to a halt.

Someone switches the lights off, and all Forbes can hear now is the steady thrumming rumble of the idling engine. That sound ceases. Again, everything is silent. Forbes doesn't move, keeps watching. He's prepared. The stolen Embassy pistol tucked into his overcoat pocket will keep him safe. By now, it will be missed. As will he. It's a sacking offence, of course, but if his plan succeeds that will hardly be an issue. If his plan fails . . . Well, that's another story. The cold forgotten, he stares at the silent and stationary dark vehicle, waits.

As one, both front doors of the Mercedes-Benz open, and Forbes can make out two figures emerging. The men are in long black leather overcoats, peaked caps on their heads. They move to the front of the car and stand still. Forbes' heart is thumping against his chest, his breathing fast and shallow. He swallows hard against the fear welling inside, braces himself. It's time. He opens the door of the building and steps outside.

✠

Sergeant Mike Barley sees the Mercedes-Benz too, watches it move slowly into the middle of the paved courtyard and stop. Before it does, he's lifted his rifle and readied it on top of an old table he earlier dragged up to the open window. Now he half-lays across the table cradling his weapon, peering into the night-scope. He can easily make out details of the vehicle, can see two dark shapes sitting in the front seats. Two! Forbes said he was meeting one guy. This complicates things. Perhaps one of them will stay in the car, he reasons, just backup for whoever gets out. He maintains his position at the window, adjusts the rifle's sights. Hardly necessary, given he's less than thirty metres from his potential target. No need for a soldier's skills – any dumb hick could hit a man from this distance.

Barley sees the car doors open. Both doors. Two men!

Jesus, I wasn't ready for this. He concentrates on the night-scope, adjusts its focus as the two dark shapes move to the front of the car and stand still. They come into focus, and Barley's heart freezes. They're SS, and officers to boot. Both of them. Fear clamps his chest tight, grips his stomach with painful fingers. This wasn't what he bargained for. The prospect of shooting an SS officer sends his brain into overdrive as he weighs up the chances of success, the consequences of failure. It's all he can do to control his breathing. He wrestles desperately with his options as he sees Forbes emerge from the office building on the other side of the courtyard.

✠

The two figures in front of the car turn to face Forbes. As he gets closer he can just make out their faces. He knows one, at least by sight. Forbes struggles to keep his fear down. He's come this far, and there's no turning back. The biggest gamble of his life is about to pay off.

When he's about two metres from the men he stops. For several seconds the three say nothing, just exchange hard and non-committal looks. Heart thumping, Forbes breaks the tense silence.

"You have it?" He's looking at Himmler.

The Reichsführer has already thrust his hands deep into his overcoat pockets, as has his companion. Neither man moves as Himmler responds.

"My adjutant has it. And the document?"

"It's here." Forbes has it in his coat pocket, but doesn't want Himmler to know that yet. "The money first."

Himmler nods towards the other man.

"Hauptsturmführer. If you please."

Ernst Knoechlein removes his gloved left hand from his

overcoat pocket. He's holding a green cloth bag, tied with a drawstring, straining against its contents. He takes a step forward, hands it to Forbes, steps back again, replaces his hand in his pocket. Himmler and Knoechlein watch impassively as Forbes opens the bag, holds it up to his face as he peers inside. He lowers it, takes out a thick bundle of banknotes, holds it up to his face again.

"Hauptsturmführer Knoechlein has a torch if you wish to confirm there is one hundred thousand American dollars."

Forbes stuffs the bundle back in the bag before he replies.

"No need. I can see enough."

"In that case, my mysterious American friend, you will give me the document I have purchased."

Holding the cloth bag in one hand, Forbes reaches inside his coat and comes out with an envelope. Knoechlein slowly steps forward, holds out his left hand, receives the envelope, and turns to Himmler. He gives the Reichsführer the envelope, then again uses his left hand to reach into his coat and produce a small torch, which he passes to Himmler. He steps back, both hands again stuffed into his overcoat pockets.

Forbes and Knoechlein stand motionless and watch as Himmler takes the marriage certificate out of the envelope and examines it in the light of the borrowed torch.

✠

Mike Barley has settled, his fear still raging, but held in check by the decision to stand his ground and see this thing through. He watches Forbes walk up to the two black-clad men, watches but doesn't hear a short conversation, sees one of the men hand over a package. Forbes examines what's in it very closely, takes a while before he's satisfied. Then he takes something small out of his coat pocket and passes it to the man who handed over the package. That man gives the thing to his companion. Then he gives him something else, something from his own pocket.

The man who received the two items bends forward slightly. There's a sudden explosion of light, fierce and dazzling in the night-scope. Barley jerks his head away from the instrument, blinks rapidly, fumbles with the brightness adjustment, realises his target has operated a cigarette lighter, or perhaps a small flashlight. Still blinking, he again peers into the night-scope.

And freezes, terrified. The fear he felt earlier when he saw two SS officers was only a foretaste of the panic now filling his veins. Everyone in Germany, natives and foreigners alike, know what Heinrich Himmler looks like. Barley is in no doubt that the man illuminated in his night-scope vision now, his rimless spectacles glinting in the torchlight, is the Reichsführer himself.

✠

For over a minute Himmler peers intently, moving his eyes left and right, turning the document over, examining its seals. At last he is satisfied.

"Yes. It appears genuine."

"It *is* genuine," replies Forbes sharply. "This isn't a hustle."

Himmler seems amused at the American's indignation. He smiles indulgently.

"Of course. I would not have dragged the President of the Reichsbank away from his evening meal were I not convinced your offer was genuine. And he would not have spent a great deal of energy gathering together one hundred thousand American dollars." Himmler shrugs. "It is no matter, however. Events have somewhat overtaken both of us, it seems."

"Events?" The comment makes little sense to Forbes. He

lifts his chin. "What events?"

Forbes' puzzlement reinforces Himmler's amusement. The Reichsführer seems almost light-hearted.

"Distant events. You have heard of Pearl Harbour, perhaps?"

"Pearl Harbour?" Forbes repeats, mystified. The conversation is becoming surreal, meaningless. "What is it?"

"It is the base for your Pacific Fleet. The American fleet. It is in Hawaii. A little over four hours ago the Japanese Navy and its Air Service destroyed the fleet. Japan is now at war with your country."

The revelation stuns Forbes. Like every diplomat in every American outpost, he's been aware of rising tensions in the Asian region. But this! An attack on America! War. If he'd been at the Embassy instead of here, he'd have known by now. Everybody must know now. His brain races through possibilities and implications, labours to process the information and how it affects his situation. He's still desperately churning through what it all means when Himmler speaks again.

"Japan is an ally of Germany. If Japan is at war with America, then so is Germany. That fact suggests you are an enemy agent. An enemy in civilian clothes. A spy."

Forbes stares open-mouthed, overwhelmed by the suddenness and magnitude of events. Nothing could have prepared him for this. His nervousness, his apprehension, is roiling into naked fear. Until now, he was the citizen of a neutral country and, if pressed, a member of that country's embassy in Germany. Now, if what Himmler is saying is true, he's somebody else, somebody without any protection. Without conscious thinking guiding it, Forbes' right hand starts to move towards the pistol in his overcoat inside pocket.

"I advise you to keep your hands in sight."

Himmler's voice abandons the amusement it held earlier,

becomes the voice of authority. Forbes still can't speak. The ground has shifted beneath him, left him unsteady on his feet, rattled his mind. He feels like he's watching a movie, that this happening to another person. He slowly becomes aware Himmler is still talking.

". . . like all enemy agents, you are a threat to the security of the German people. In wartime, actions in defence of the Fatherland must be quick and decisive. For that reason . . ."

"But this can't be right. America isn't at war with Germany. America is a neutral country." Forbes is unaware his voice is rising as disbelief and desperation wrestle for supremacy. "You can't just decide someone is an enemy . . . only the German government can make a decision like . . ."

"I *am* the German government, you fool," says Himmler. "And I have decided." He turns slightly towards Hauptsturmführer Knoechlein. "Ernst?"

In a blur of motion, Knoechlein's right hand whips out of his overcoat pocket holding a pistol. He raises it at arm's length, points it at Forbes. The movement literally staggers Forbes, and he takes a half-step sideways. He regains his feet, stares open-mouthed at the pistol. Racing through his mind is the overwhelming thought that Sergeant Barley will fire now, save him. The need becomes a prayer as the micro-moments pass. There is absolute quiet, stillness.

✠

Mike Barley is moving as fast as he can without making a sound. Step by step, carefully in the dark, he descends the external fire escape at the rear of the derelict building, his rifle slung on its strap over one shoulder. He knows a tell-tale noise might be his death knell. He reaches ground level, starts to cautiously pick his way over the littered ground as he starts a looping journey back to where they left the Embassy car. If he can make it to the car, he'll be okay. Nobody else knows where he's been tonight. He can just go back . . .

A shot cracks open the night's silence, echoes around the empty buildings. Barley jumps in fear, stops. Listens to the silence. Seconds pass, then another shot. He's rooted to the spot, unable to do anything but wait and listen. He waits, waits. A minute goes by, perhaps two, and still the silence presses down. Then comes a sudden dull roar which settles to a thrum before rising and falling as a vehicle moves away, disappearing into the distance. Barley breathes out, continues heading towards the Embassy car.

✠

Forbes' mind is still full of the fevered prayer that Barley will fire as Knoechlein's bullet strikes him high in the chest, near his right shoulder, spinning him around as he collapses onto the snow-covered ground. He thrashes in the slush, his legs jerking back and forth. Pressing his left hand against the bloody hole in his chest, he manages to turn onto his back, half-groaning, half-crying as he does. He stares wildly at Knoechlein, who has taken two steps forward, pistol still raised. Then he turns his eyes towards Himmler, a look of entreaty, perhaps an appeal for sympathy or leniency. Knoechlein holds his pistol steady, fires again, and the second bullet smashes into Forbes' forehead.

Knoechlein replaces the pistol in his overcoat pocket and turns to face Himmler. The Reichsführer hands back the torch he borrowed earlier.

"A little light, please Ernst."

Himmler is still holding the marriage certificate and its envelope in his right hand. He drops the envelope to the ground and transfers the certificate to his left hand. Then, in the light of the torch held by Knoechlein, he reaches into his inside coat pocket and takes out an IMCO lighter emblazoned with the SS double sig runes. He flicks the flint-wheel, sparking a steady tall flame. Into it, he feeds a corner of the certificate in his left hand. The old dry paper catches immediately. Flame races up one side. Himmler twists his wrist to direct the fire across the certificate's width. Within seconds the document is fully aflame. Himmler continues holding one corner in his fingertips until even the glove he is wearing can no longer shield him from the heat. He drops the burning charred burden into the wet slush. It hisses and steams for a second or two.

Knoechlein directs the torchlight onto the incinerated certificate as it falls. For a short time both men stand silently staring at the black remnants. Then Himmler moves his left foot forward and presses them into the wetness of the ground. He puts his lighter back into his pocket and nods to Knoechlein, who steps over to Forbes' body and picks up the cloth bag of money. The two men return to their car and get in. As they do, a pair of black-clad figures silently rise from the floor behind the front bench seat of the Mercedes and sit down in the rear, the muzzles of their broom-handle Mausers pointed at the roof.

Knoechlein starts the car. Its engine fires, catches, settles down to an idle. Then the headlights flare into life and the big Mercedes-Benz turns around on snow-wet paving and slowly disappears back the way it came. Heinrich Himmler checks his wristwatch by the dashboard lights. Two minutes after midnight. It's another new day in the thousand-year Third Reich.

GLOSSARY

Allee – Avenue, a street.

Alex – Slang term used by Kripo (below) detectives for the organisation's headquarters, the Imperial Police Praesidium in Alexanderplatz, the functional centre of Germany's government.

Bund Deutscher Mädel – The League of German Girls, BDM, the girls' wing of the Nazi's Hitler Youth organisation.

Carinhall – Named after his first wife, Carinhall was the ostentatious country hunting lodge built by Hermann Göring in the Schorfheide Forest about 70km north-east of Berlin.

Der Angriff – ('The Attack'). Nazi Party daily newspaper started by Goebbels in 1927, full of propaganda and anti-Semitism.

Der Stürmer – ('The Stormer') Weekly tabloid published privately by Julius Streicher, the Gauleiter (below) of Franconia. Notorious for its vicious anti-Semitism and drawings of lustful Jewish men seeking to ravish pure Aryan maidens. The bottom of the title page carried the motto: 'The Jews are our misfortune.'

Dirndl – A traditional female folk costume in southern German rural areas. Consists of a tight, low-cut bodice, blouse underneath, high-waisted skirt and apron. Appropriated by the Nazis as part of the Party's push to establish a pan-German identity across Europe.

Einsatzgrüppen – death squads (sing. *Einsatzgrüp*) of SS, Security Police, Intelligence Service operatives and others who identified and executed potential threats after the Wehrmacht (below) had established control of a conquered territory. 'Potential threats' included, but were not limited to, Jews, collaborators, Roma, communists, intellectuals.

Eukodal – The opioid oxycodone, produced in Germany by the Merck pharmaceutical company. Reputedly, Hitler's personal doctor repeatedly administered small doses to him.

Gauleiter – a Nazi political appointee, responsible for governing a district (Gau). Joseph Goebbels was Gauleiter of Berlin from 1926.

Goebbels – Minister for Public Enlightenment and Propaganda, Joseph Goebbels was subject to widespread mockery for both his diminutive stature and a limp arising from a deformed foot.

Göring – Reichsmarschall Hermann Göring, long-time member of the Nazi party, President of the Reichstag (German parliament), head of the German air force (Luftwaffe). He was at the peak of his power in 1941.

Gruppenführer – SS rank equivalent to General.

Hauptsturmführer – SS rank equivalent to Captain.

Haus Vaterland – ('Fatherland House') A huge pleasure house after the style of Coney Island in the USA, with numerous restaurants, bars, cinemas and dance halls, all styled to gaudy effect.

Himmler – Reichsführer Heinrich Himmler, long-time Nazi party member, by 1941 head of the Schutzstaffel (below), the Gestapo, and every law enforcement organisation in Germany. The second most powerful person in the nation after Adolf Hitler.

Hindenburg – Paul von Hindenburg, WW1 general, President from 1925 until his death in 1934. Notable for his soldierly appearance and huge handlebar moustache.

Horst Wessel Lied – Militaristic song written by Horst Wessel, a district SA (below) commander 'martyred' by communists in 1930. It became the Nazi Party's official anthem thereafter.

Junker – A member of the German landed nobility, highly influential in politics and the military until well into the Nazi era.

Kriminalkommissar – Kripo (below) rank broadly equivalent to a police Detective-Inspector, or to an SS Hauptsturmführer.

Kriminalrat – Kripo rank broadly equivalent to a police Detective Chief-Inspector, or to a Sturmbannführer in the SS.

Kriminalassistant – lowest rank of Kripo investigator. Detective.

Kripo – The criminal police (*Kriminalpolizei*), as opposed to the Orpo (*Ordnungspolizei*, below), the latter dealing mainly with civil order and home defence.

Kristallnacht – ('Night of the Broken Glass'). Nazi paramilitary forces and some civilians on 9-10 November 1938 initiated an anti-Jewish pogrom, destroying property and killing Jews. There was no intervention by government authorities.

Kurfürstendamm – An elegant three-kilometre boulevard in Berlin's fashionable west, notable for its cosmopolitan prosperity, entertainment and shopping venues.

Oberleutnant – Wehrmacht rank equivalent to First Lieutenant.

Orpo – Uniformed 'Order Police' (*Ordnungspolizei*), responsible for civil law enforcement and emergency response including civil defence and coastguard. Also called 'Green Police' (*Grüne Polizei*), after the colour of their uniforms.

Pervitin – High quality methamphetamine tablets sold without a prescription until 1939, even available infused in chocolates. After 1939 use was still widespread, and in 1941 over 7,000,000 tablets were sold. The Wehrmacht bought millions for its fighting men.

Papiermark – 'Paper Mark' issued under the Weimar Republic (below), particularly notes issued during the era of hyperinflation in 1922/23. Replaced in 1924 by first the Rentenmark and then the Reichsmark, at the exchange rate of 1 new for 1 trillion old.

Pickelhaube – spiked military helmet used by German and Prussian armies until the middle of WW1.

Rathaus – The town hall, where the mayor's office is located.

Reichsluftahrtministerium – A gigantic office building with over 2,000 rooms, located on Wilhelmstrasse, the headquarters of the Ministry of Aviation under Hermann Göring.

Reichssicherheitshauptant – Reich Central Security Office (RSHA), established by Heinrich Himmler, incorporating oversight of the SS, Intelligence Service and the Security Police, the latter comprised of the Gestapo and the Kripo.

SA – (*Sturmabteilung*, 'Assault Division') Paramilitary group under the Nazis, notorious for its strongarm methods and intimidation of opponents. By 1934 it had swelled to over a million members. In the 'Night of the Long Knives' that year, Hitler executed its leaders and enfeebled the organisation, fearing it had become too powerful a threat to his leadership.

S-Bahn – Extensive above-ground railway system within Berlin.

Schliemann – Heinrich Schliemann, German archaeologist, who in the 1870s discovered at Hissarlik in Turkey the ruins of what was believed to have been the ancient city of Troy.

Schwanenwerder – ('Swan Island'). Located in southwest Berlin overlooking the Havel River and the Wannsee lake. Populated by wealthy businessmen and some of the Nazi hierarchy.

Schutzstaffel – ('Protection Squad'). The SS. Established in 1925 as Hitler's personal bodyguard. By 1941 it had expanded under Heinrich Himmler to hundreds of thousands of men and a fierce emphasis on Aryan heritage and German 'blood purity'. The SS was a feared and powerful organisation engaged in everything from combat (Waffen SS, below) to running concentration camps.

Skat – Popular German card game vaguely akin to contract bridge, with 'bids' and 'tricks', although for three players instead of four.

Standartenführer – SS rank equivalent to colonel.

Strasse – Street, road.

Tiergarten – Huge (210 hectares) and hugely popular park with recreational facilities near central Berlin.

U-Bahn – Extensive underground rapid train service in Berlin.

Unterfeldwebel – Wehrmacht rank, 'Under Field Sergeant'.

Untermensch – 'Inferior person'. (Pl. *Untermenschen*). Term used by the Nazis for a wide range of people including Jews, Poles, Roma, Russians and Serbs.

Untersturmführer – SS rank equivalent to Second Lieutenant.

Unterwachtmeister – Orpo rank equivalent to Constable.

Völkischer Beobachter – ('People's Observer'). The official daily national newspaper of the Nazi Party. By 1941, circulation was well over one million.

Wachtmeister – Orpo rank equivalent to Sergeant.

Waffen SS – The military wing of the Schutzstaffel, by 1941 numbering over 100,000 men. Responsible for some of the most savage military actions and atrocities of the war.

Wannsee – A premier swimming and recreational location on Berlin's western edge. Senior Nazi officers would meet there in early 1942 to map out implementation of the 'Final Solution'.

Weimar Republic – The name given to the German state in the wake of WW1. It lasted until the Nazi ascension to power in 1933.

Weg – Lane, path, 'way'.

Weihnachtsstollen – Traditional cake-like fruit bread eaten during the Christmas period, full of dried fruit, nuts and spices.

Wer ist's? – ('Who is it?'). German equivalent of *Who's Who*?

Wille und Macht – ('Will to Power'). A fortnightly 'educational' magazine for Hitler Youth. Lavishly illustrated, it was just one of many Party vehicles for inculcating Nazi aims and beliefs.

www.ingramcontent.com/pod-product-compliance
Lightning Source LLC
Chambersburg PA
CBHW020943310726
48980CB00001B/38
* 9 7 8 0 6 4 6 8 2 6 9 8 1 *